Dream Forever

also by kit alloway

Dreamfire
Dreamfever

Dream Forever

kit alloway

st. martin's griffin ⚜ new york

DREAM FOREVER. Copyright © 2017 by Kit Alloway. All rights reserved. Printed in the United States of America. For information, address St. Martin's Press, 175 Fifth Avenue, New York, N.Y. 10010.

www.stmartins.com

Designed by Anna Gorovoy

The Library of Congress Cataloging-in-Publication Data is available upon request.

ISBN 978-1-250-00125-2 (hardcover)
ISBN 978-1-250-11662-8 (e-book)

Our books may be purchased in bulk for promotional, educational, or business use. Please contact your local bookseller or the Macmillan Corporate and Premium Sales Department at 1-800-221-7945, extension 5442, or by e-mail at MacmillanSpecial Markets@macmillan.com

First Edition: March 2017

10 9 8 7 6 5 4 3 2 1

For Sara,

of course

List of Characters

Family

Josh Weaver
Will Kansas: Josh's former apprentice
Deloise Weaver: Josh's younger sister
Lauren (Laurentius) Weaver: Josh and Deloise's father
Kerstel Weaver: Lauren's wife, Josh and Deloise's stepmother
Dustine Borgenicht: Josh and Deloise's grandmother, Peregrine's
late wife (deceased)
Peregrine Borgenicht: Josh and Deloise's grandfather, and former
leader of the Lodestone Party

Dream Walkers

Winsor Avish: Josh's best friend
Whim Avish: Winsor's older brother
Saidy and Alex Avish: Whim and Winsor's parents
Haley McKarr: Ian's twin brother
Ian McKarr: Haley's twin brother (deceased)
Mirren Rousellario: heir to the deposed Rousellario monarchy
Katia: Mirren's cousin
Fel and Collena: Mirren's aunt and uncle
Young Ben Sounclouse: the local seer
Davita Bach: the local government representative
Aurek Trembuline: a dream-walker philosopher

list of characters

Zorie Abernaughton: head of the southwest Veil tear repair team
Geoff "Snitch" Simbar: a man with no soul
Feodor Kajażkołski: Dream theorist

Dream Forever

One

A corpse lay slumped on the floor in the center of the coffee shop, right in front of the holiday mug display. Customers stepped lightly around it as they passed from the counter to the cream and sugar station, their wet boots squeaking on the floor. The Christmas-caroled air smelled of ginger and cloves, and trays of frosted snowmen grinned from the display cases. Beyond the open doorway, shoppers thronged the mall hallway.

"Christmas nightmares," Josh said. "They come earlier every year." She glanced behind herself at Will—

But it wasn't Will standing behind her. It was Feodor.

He wore his usual expression—a mishmash of contempt and amusement—and his usual outfit, a white button-down shirt and high-waisted, pleated slacks, the creases ironed as crisp as the lines of his lips. Arms crossed over his chest, he waited patiently as Josh assessed the nightmare around them, as patiently as he had once collected souls in canisters, his congregation growing slowly, year by year.

Finally, though, he made a little fluttering gesture with his hand, as if to say, *Get on with it.*

Josh sighed and turned back to the corpse. Two months and she still expected Will to be at her side.

Stop thinking about Will, she ordered herself. *There's work to be done.*

The dead man wore blue jeans so dirty they looked black, broken-down shoes, and no shirt. Burst blood vessels stretched across his nose like networks of roots, suggesting years of hard drinking, but Josh doubted it was the bottle that had killed him. His entire chest had exploded, revealing a mashed cobbler of internal organs.

Josh knelt and touched his cold, stiff hand. This close up, he stank like a two-week-old steak. She closed her eyes and imagined the stone walls that protected her from the dreamer's fear.

Her mother had been the one who taught Josh to imagine herself surrounded by stone walls. They had begun working on the visualization when Josh was only eight—a year before she was even allowed to accompany Jona into the Dream. Now the image of white rock and gray mortar and the sense of security it provided felt as familiar as the weight of the plumeria charm she wore around her neck.

In her mind, she imagined using her fingertips to pick a well-worn cork from between two stones in the wall. When it popped loose, a waft of blue smoke slipped through, and Josh breathed it in, inhaling a taste of the dreamer's fear as she did so.

She will reclaim me, the fear whispered. *What has been promised must be paid. Tlazolteotl is hungry.*

Josh opened her eyes.

"What did you sense?" Feodor asked.

"This dead guy isn't the dreamer." Josh stood up and wiped imagined death germs from her hand. "She's over there."

Josh nodded toward a caramel-skinned woman in her fifties whose arms were strung with so many shopping bags that she was having difficulty pouring sugar into her coffee.

"And?" Feodor asked.

"And Tlazolteotl is coming to get her."

Feodor considered. "The name sounds Aztec. Try again. Try to see the shape of the nightmare."

Josh closed her eyes again, imagined those stone walls, pulled the cork from the hole, and breathed deep. Technically, she was breaking Stellanor's First Rule of dream walking: *Never let the dreamer's fear become your own.* There was a good reason it was the *first* rule: getting caught up in a dreamer's fear could render her helpless to the nightmare. But Josh had been breaking the rule almost since the day she'd learned it, and Feodor had a theory that her ability to do so was the key to accessing her abilities as the True Dream Walker.

She breathed in a big ole dose of fear.

That which you have lost you must give up. Tlazolteotl is hungry.

Tlazolteotl was somewhere in the mall, and she was coming closer. Josh tried to imagine what would happen when she found the dreamer.

She'll . . . what? Kill her? Eat her?

Strangely, what came to mind were the woman's packages.

But what does the corpse have to do with it?

Josh pictured the dead man, but he didn't fit with the images in her head. She just kept coming back to the packages.

Opening her eyes again, she saw that the woman was pouring creamer into her drink. One of her bags had knocked over a squeeze bottle of honey.

Tlazolteotl's going to steal her Christmas shopping?

Frustrated, Josh tried again. This time she thrust a fist through the imaginary wall, the stone crumbling around her knuckles. Blue smoke rushed through and billowed around her.

You have to follow it, Josh reminded herself.

She still didn't fully understand what that meant, any more than she understood why Tlazolteotl wanted the dreamer's Christmas shopping. But she'd first heard the words during a moment of wisdom, and she repeated them to herself when she was hoping for insight.

Now she waited, allowing her mind to show her whatever it wanted. From the darkness behind her eyelids, an image emerged, stepping out from the shadows and into the light of Josh's understanding. She saw Tlazolteotl—a huge, primal figure dressed in animal skins—coming into the coffee shop, grabbing the woman, opening the shopping bags, and thrusting her muzzlelike face inside, devouring the contents. Whatever was in those packages, it was more precious to the dreamer than her life, and Josh felt the chill of the woman's fear like a gulp of ice water.

Tlazolteotl is here. Tlazolteotl is hungry.

Josh moved before her eyes were open and managed to trip over the corpse at her feet. After jostling a table of ornaments, she found her footing and rushed through the coffee shop to where the woman was struggling to get the plastic lid back onto her drink. Her hands were shaking.

"Tlazolteotl is here," Josh said. "What's in the bags?"

"No," the woman begged. "Please. I can't."

"I need to know—"

"No!"

But Josh had already yanked one of the bags off the woman's wrist. She pulled the twine handles apart and looked into the pale pink paper bag.

At the bottom of the bag sat the woman's innocence.

Later, Josh wouldn't be able to recall exactly what she had seen. Perhaps innocence had no physical form. All she would remember was starlight the color of rose quartz and a sense of hope so grand it left no possibility for anything other than joy. Josh was still blinking when the woman grabbed the bag back.

"I can't lose it!" she shouted at Josh.

She ran out of the coffee shop, and Josh and Feodor ran after her. But Josh needed to close her eyes—*Someday, I'm going to figure out how to do this with my eyes open,* she swore to herself—so she took hold of Feodor's arm and said, "Lead me. Don't lose her!"

Trying to ignore her own motion and Feodor's voice calling, "Pardon! Make way for this young blind woman!" Josh went back to the stone walls. They stood close around her, like the walls of a well, and they were so real to her that when she began yanking stones out, they scraped her palms.

The blue smoke poured in around her, clouding her vision with the woman's terror. Josh felt the familiar burn of dreamfire. But she needed to see past the smoke, and she imagined herself crawling through the hole she'd made and out past the walls entirely.

On the other side, where the blue smoke had cleared, she saw the woman as a little girl in a pale green bathing suit, cowering behind the flimsy plastic curtain of a locker room shower. The outline of a man darkened the curtain, and thick fingers curled around its edge—

"No!"

Josh's own horrified scream snapped her back into her body. The shoppers who surrounded her stopped walking to stare, even the dreamer.

Josh ran to her, pushing startled shoppers aside. "You already lost it," she told the dreamer. "You lost it years ago."

"No," the woman said, beginning to push through the crowd again. "No!"

"Your innocence is already gone," Josh insisted. "Give it to her! Tlazolteotl can't steal what you offer freely."

"It's mine!"

"Don't make her take it!" Josh grabbed the woman by the shoulders and turned her so that they were face-to-face. "Listen to me! You have to accept what happened and let it go! She won't hurt you if—"

"I *can't!*" the woman wailed, and she tore herself away.

Behind them, something roared.

In the center of the mall food court, her head brushing the third-story ceiling, walked a giant copper-skinned woman. A curled gold bar pierced the septum of her nose, and enormous turquoise earrings hung to her shoulders. She wore an elaborate horned headdress and a red and green skirt, but her breasts were bare except for a multitude of beaded necklaces. Instead of a lower jaw, she had a muzzle, and when she opened it, she revealed a mouth full of dirt, blood, and very sharp teeth.

Tlazolteotl—the eater of sins.

"Oh, shit," Josh said.

The shoppers began to stampede away from Tlazolteotl, their screams drowned out by the goddess's furious roar.

"I believe this would be an appropriate time to abort," Feodor said.

Each of Tlazolteotl's steps shook the floor. With a growl, she knocked a forty-foot-high Christmas tree onto a jewelry kiosk.

"I can still resolve it," Josh insisted, even though her first instinct was to run like hell. "Come on."

She dashed after the dreamer, shoving people left and right. They were only figments of the dreamer's imagination, after all. It didn't really matter if they got trampled or eaten. The only person who mattered was the dreamer.

Josh found her cowering under the escalator.

"You have to give Tlazolteotl the bags," Josh said. "It's the only way to satisfy her."

The woman shook her head and clutched the bags to her chest. "No, I can't. I'm not ready."

"You are," Josh insisted. "If you weren't, you wouldn't be having this nightmare."

For the last two months, Josh had been entering the Dream and diving into dreamers' fears. It hadn't been easy and it sure hadn't been fun, and if Feodor hadn't been there to keep an eye on her, she would have lost herself entirely on more than one occasion. But in witnessing so much fear, she had noticed a pattern: nightmares had purpose. They were almost designed like tests intended to force the dreamer to grow or evolve in some way.

You have to follow it, Josh thought again.

"Nightmare?" the woman repeated.

"Yes. And if you just let your innocence go—"

But she'd said too much. The woman must have realized she was dreaming and woken up, because the Dream shifted, sending Josh and Feodor spinning through space.

They landed hard on an evergreen forest floor covered in pine-cones, and the corpse from the coffee shop landed right between them, hitting the ground so hard it sent pinecones bouncing.

"Gross," Josh said. A hundred yards away, she noticed a pair of black bears climbing a tree. Squinting, she was able to make out two people clinging to the tree's upper branches.

This nightmare could wait—at least for a few minutes.

"There is only one explanation for how this body passed from one nightmare to another," Feodor said.

"It's a real corpse," Josh said, like a good student. It disturbed her that she sounded like Will used to, when talking to her. What was she becoming—Feodor's apprentice?

The body seemed grosser now that she knew it was real, and the fall hadn't done it any favors. The man appeared to be in his sixties, but he'd obviously lived a hard life: his hair was long and greasy, and his open mouth exposed missing and rotting teeth. Black tattoos that had faded to blurry ashen smudges covered his arms.

"I haven't heard about any dream walkers being lost in the Dream recently," Josh said.

"This man does not strike me as a dream walker," Feodor said, a note of elitism in his voice. "He stinks."

"Dream walkers can be alcoholics, too," Josh told him, thinking of Will again. But she was more than certain that Will wasn't drinking these days.

The man's chest appeared to have exploded from within. Ragged, torn flesh revealed the jagged ends of broken ribs and a meaningless mass of shredded organs that Josh couldn't identify. The cavity ran from the man's breastbone down nearly to his belly button.

"This is an unusual wound," Feodor admitted. With a fallen stick, he poked around between the ribs.

"Let's drag him out of the Dream."

Feodor made a *hmm* sound, but he seemed intrigued rather than irritated. Focusing her mind, Josh flung her arm out from her body and felt power soar through her palm and into the midst of the forest, where a shimmering archway formed.

She grabbed the corpse's legs and Feodor caught him under the shoulders, and together they carried him out of the Dream.

Josh tried to set him down gently, but the dead man made a *thud* when he landed on the archroom's white tile floor. *Kerstel's going to make me bleach this floor,* Josh thought regretfully, wishing she'd put a towel down first. But her irritation was overcome by the excitement of realizing she had been right: the dead man was real.

"Do you have a scalpel?" Feodor asked, getting to his knees beside the corpse.

"Why would I have a scalpel?" Josh asked. "Never mind—don't answer that." She sat back on her heels. "This wound is too ragged for a knife, and too big for a bullet. Maybe if he was shot from behind with a hollow-point . . ."

They were rolling the man over to check for a bullet entry point when Whim Avish walked in.

"Oh, sweet Mother Mary!" he cried, jumping back so fast his shoulder slammed into the door frame. "What am I walking in on?"

Josh was on her butt, pulling on the dead man's hips so that she could roll him. "Do you see a bullet wound in his back?"

"I don't know! Who is that guy?"

"We found him in the Dream."

Feodor, wedging his foot under the corpse's hips so he could get down on the floor and see beneath the man's torso, said, "I don't believe he's been shot, but it's difficult to tell. There's been considerable seepage of fluids."

"Stop talking!" Whim shouted. "And stop *parbuckling* him! Dear God—my eyes!"

Josh and Feodor let the corpse fall back onto the floor.

"Parbuckling?" she asked.

"It's a word!" Whim insisted.

Will Kansas stuck his head into the archroom.

Will met Josh's eyes without hesitation. He always did. Over the last two months, he had been unfailingly polite and unreasonably friendly. He had acknowledged Josh's presence, asked her to pass the salt, picked up her gloves when she dropped them once. Sometimes he even smiled at her, in a genuine, forgiving way.

It was awful.

"Whoa," Will said at the sight of the dead man.

Could anyone else tell how wrong his voice was? It sounded so natural, so casual, with just a hint of acknowledgment that they used to be more to each other than they were now. Josh had never thought she'd miss Ian's cold shoulder, but this was worse. Will wanted them to be friendly—to be *friends.* Josh just didn't know how to do that.

Work to be done, she reminded herself.

She tried to focus on the corpse in front of her. "All I can think is that someone stuck a bomb down his throat. But that would have messed up his back, too."

"If I'm not mistaken," Feodor told Josh, "I believe this is the heart. Do you see how it has ruptured? Both chambers of each lung seem to have burst."

Whim started gagging.

"Whim, can you please go call the Gendarmerie and tell them that we just pulled a corpse out of the Dream?"

"Yeah." Whim coughed. "I'm going. Gladly. Come on, Will."

Josh glanced at Will as he left the room. He gave her another one of those honest, kindly, understanding smiles.

Does he not miss me? Josh thought. *Is that what he's trying to tell me? Is that why he looks so good?*

He looked better than he had since they'd first met, now that he was in counseling and on anxiety medication. The circles under his cornflower-blue eyes were gone, and his previous pallor had been replaced by a healthy, ruddy color.

Breaking up with me was the best thing he ever did for himself, Josh thought.

That was her real fear—that his equilibrium and contentment weren't an act, that he was legitimately fine without her. Was he hiding his pain, or did he just not feel any?

Feodor made a little *ahem* sound, which was his way of laughing at her. "The corpse?" he said.

"I'm thinking," Josh told him.

"Perhaps you would like to think of something more relevant," he suggested.

After giving him her best glare, Josh returned to examining the body, and only moments later, she found something that drove all thoughts of Will from her head.

"Feodor," she said tightly. "Look."

At the base of the man's throat, near where the skin began to split, were numerous small cuts. They didn't appear to be part of the fatal wound—they were straight and clean. Several cuts intersected to form a triangle at the end of a long, straight line.

Feodor cursed softly in Polish.

"Is it . . . ?" Josh asked, even though she knew it was.

He sighed heavily. "Yes. Someone carved the symbol we used on Peregrine into this man's chest."

Two months earlier, Josh had been faced with the choice of either killing her grandfather or risking letting him live. She'd compromised and carved an ancient symbol into his chest, one that would prevent him from entering the Dream universe. The only people who currently had access to the symbol were Mirren Rousellario and Peregrine himself.

"But I thought the symbol would stop the wearer from entering the Dream," Josh said.

Feodor gestured to the dead man's ravaged torso. "Obviously, it did."

Josh sent Feodor upstairs to hide in the library—only a dozen people knew he was back from the dead—and then rolled the dead man up in a sheet. It was a good sheet, too, and she'd probably catch hell for using it, but she thought he deserved something nice. It seemed like the least she could do, after dragging him out of the Dream and landing him like a trout on the archroom floor.

A gendarme named Burnette arrived at the house to collect the body. The Gendarmerie were the approximate equivalent of dream-walker police, but they only dealt with issues that couldn't be taken to the real police. Josh was pretty sure pulling a corpse out of an alternate universe counted.

"You don't look surprised," she noted when she'd finished explaining how she'd found the dead man.

Burnette sighed. "Look, I wouldn't tell this to anyone else, and I'm trusting you to keep it to yourself."

Josh nodded.

"This is the fifth corpse we've pulled out of the Dream in the last six weeks."

"The *fifth*?" Josh asked, aghast.

Burnette nodded, blond curls falling into her eyes. "Looks like we have a serial killer. We still can't figure out how they're being killed. Our best guess is one of those shark knives that blows things apart with a burst of air."

Josh said nothing. She'd always wanted to use one of those knives—but not on a person.

"We've only managed to identify one of the bodies. Homeless guy."

Josh wouldn't have been surprised to learn that this man was also homeless, and suddenly the entire scheme clarified itself in her mind.

Peregrine is going to homeless men, offering them a meal or a place to stay, and then using them as guinea pigs to try to find a way around the symbol.

A sickening rush of guilt hit her so hard she reached out for the wall.

"You okay?" Burnette asked. "Why don't you sit down?"

Peregrine had done some despicable things in his life, but this ranked near the top.

How is it so easy for Peregrine to kill people and still so hard for anyone to kill Peregrine?

Josh's grandfather had been missing for six weeks. After staying in the hospital for two weeks, having the stump where his hand should have been treated and the cuts in his chest stitched, he'd snuck out and disappeared. No one had heard from him since. He'd been supposed to take the reins of the new dream-walker democracy, but since he hadn't showed up, the junta was still in charge while they tried to figure out what to do.

Josh didn't know where Peregrine could have gone. She'd hoped that his disappearance meant he'd died, but she'd never kidded herself. Now she had proof that not only was he alive, he was actively trying to reenter the Dream.

"Do you have any leads on my grandfather?"

Burnette's pen paused in its travels across her notepad. "Do you think he's connected to this?"

There was no way Josh could explain what she knew without admitting to the fact that she'd mutilated her grandfather, or without exposing her friend Mirren.

"I wouldn't put anything past him."

After helping Burnette carry the dead man to her vehicle, Josh went to find Feodor in the library, where he was browsing the family diaries. She told him what Burnette had said, and her own conclusions about Peregrine's activities.

"One cannot fault the man's tenacity," Feodor said when Josh was finished.

"Let's try to avoid complimenting him," Josh said.

Feodor shrugged. He had the most graceful, elegant shrug Josh had ever seen, a little ballet-movement of a shrug.

"He has overcomplicated the testing process," Feodor replied. "I would have experimented on animals in his position." He considered, tapping his lip with one finger. "Cats would have been of sufficient size."

Trying to ignore that thought, Josh said, "Glad to hear it."

"However, we may be able to use his thoughtlessness to our advantage. If we map out where each body was found, we might be able to pinpoint the archway from which he's operating."

Clever, Josh admitted to herself. "I'll ask Burnette if she'll send me the case file."

"Do you think she will?" Feodor asked skeptically.

"Sometimes people give me special access because I'm Peregrine's granddaughter."

That was only part of the truth. Josh had a reputation among dream walkers as a prodigy, and they were usually more than happy to bend over backward for her.

"Ironic," Feodor said, but he smiled at her in a way that made her feel like he saw right through her. "Unfortunately, triangulating the bodies will give us, at best, a rough idea of where Peregrine might be."

Not to discount the lives of the five men Peregrine had killed, but Josh had a larger concern. If he found a way back into the Dream, he was likely to hurt a lot more people. "What are the chances he'll figure out how to deactivate the symbol?"

Feodor considered. "I could do it. But then, Peregrine is not me."

"Well, that's reassuring," Josh said.

"However . . . the power of obsession to propel a man to acts of which he might not otherwise be capable should not be underestimated. I believe Peregrine will continue until he finds a way."

That was not reassuring.

Two

"I really think I'm over it," Will Kansas told his counselor.

Malina wasn't technically a therapist, but as a pastor, she'd been trained in counseling, and because she was a dream walker, Will could tell her the truth about what had happened to him. They were sitting in her office, which smelled pleasantly of herbal tea and was cluttered with little statues of angels.

Malina lifted her eyebrows at his words. "That's pretty quick," she said. "How long has it been? Six weeks?"

"Eight," Will corrected. Eight weeks since they'd gone into the Hidden Kingdom. Eight weeks since Will had killed Bayla. Eight weeks since he'd failed to kill Peregrine.

Eight weeks since he and Josh had broken up.

"How do you know you're over it?" Malina asked.

"I've stopped having flashbacks and nightmares. I've stopped thinking about it all the time. I feel—mostly—at peace with what I had to do to save everyone. I took down my stalker wall."

"Okay," Malina said, but the way she broke the syllable told Will she wasn't crazy about his answer. "That's all good evidence that your post-traumatic stress is under control, but I'm not sure how that indicates you're moving on."

Isn't holding it together enough? Will wondered. It felt like it should count for something.

"Did you try out for track like we talked about?"

"No."

"Did you join the Amnesty International Club?"

"No." Before she could ask what other activities he had avoided, Will said, "I just keep thinking that Peregrine's still out there. What's the point of starting something new when I know he's going to come back and screw it all up?"

"You're certain he'll come back."

"As long as Josh has power he doesn't have, he'll be back to try to take it. I doubt he's done with Mirren, either."

"How's Josh doing?"

In the two months since they'd broken up, Josh had tested out of her senior year and graduated early. She spent ten hours a day in the Dream, most of them with Feodor. She'd stopping eating meals with her family, and Will was pretty sure she was living on protein bars and candy. She'd also quit brushing her hair and was getting dressed in the dark, apparently, but her bizarre appearance was only part of the wiry, disheveled look she'd developed. Every time Will saw her, she seemed distracted, hassled, confused by the presence of other people, and more than once he'd caught her muttering to herself in Polish. Whatever was going on with her had ruined her already tenuous grip on the margins of normal behavior.

"Same as usual, I guess," Will said.

Malina didn't let him get away with the deflection. "Do you miss her?"

"Yeah," he admitted. "I . . . still miss her. I wish things had gone differently."

"What do you wish had gone differently?"

Everything, he thought.

"I wish we hadn't lied to each other. I wish I'd asked for support when I needed it. I wish she had confided in me. But mostly I wish Feodor and Peregrine were gone. I think we could have worked things out if not for them."

"Have you talked to Josh about what happened?"

"No."

That was an understatement. Josh barely spoke two words to him. Then again, he barely saw her. She spent all her time with Feodor.

At least, Will *thought* she was spending all of her time with Feodor. Except for when she was dream walking, she wasn't at home very much.

"Do you want to talk to her about it?" Malina asked.

"I don't know. Sometimes. Sometimes I want to explain why I had to break up with her."

"What would you say?"

"That I did it to protect myself emotionally. That it had less to do with her than it had to do with Feodor and Peregrine and all that chaos. I want to tell her . . . that it wasn't because I didn't care about her."

"Do you think she knows that?"

Josh, with her monstrous capacity for guilt and self-blame?

"Nope."

"Would you feel better if you told her?"

"Nope," he said again, because he'd told Josh more than once. Even before they'd broken up, he'd warned her about the path she was leading them down. She couldn't hear it, or she couldn't hear it from him. He knew that if he told her again, she'd just add it to the list of things she blamed herself for.

"I don't know what the point of talking to her would be. Nothing has changed. Peregrine is still out there. Besides, if I try to talk to her, I'll just get sucked back into that codependent cycle where she does something reckless and I help her so she won't get hurt."

"Yeah, let's talk about that for a minute," Malina said, shifting in her chair. "You know that we all create narratives in our minds about things that have happened to us. We create a story around the events so they make sense to us."

Will nodded.

"The narrative you've created is that as long as you're around Josh, you'll be in heightened danger and at risk for getting hurt—not just emotionally, but physically as well."

"Right."

That *was* what he thought.

"Let's try challenging that narrative for a minute. We don't have to decide that your narrative is wrong, let's just play with it for a while. When Feodor was torturing Josh in his memory chamber, who came up with the idea to kill Feodor's body?"

"I did."

"And when the three of you were dying, who convinced Josh that she had the ability to save you?"

"I did," Will said uneasily.

"When you were trapped in the Hidden Kingdom and Josh was, again, near death, who pressed the activator to disable Bayla and Peregrine?"

Will pursed his lips and then said, "I see what you're getting at. But it isn't that simple. We never would have been there if not for Josh."

"You never would have been there if not for Peregrine, either.

Or Feodor. Or Whim, for that matter. What if the story isn't Josh getting into trouble and you enabling her, but you and Josh saving everyone?"

Will could feel himself getting defensive—an antsy, itchy, argumentative feeling.

"But why is that narrative more true than the one I've been telling myself?" he asked.

"It isn't. One isn't truer than the other. You get to pick which one to keep telling yourself, and I'm suggesting that the one you've *been* telling yourself isn't making you happy."

"But I just told you how well things are going."

"No, you said that if you weren't so afraid of Peregrine and Feodor, you'd be joining school activities and getting back together with your girlfriend."

Will ground his teeth. He *needed* a narrative that would protect him. He *needed* to feel safe. And if he had to sacrifice his relationship with Josh to feel safe . . .

The scary truth was, he didn't know if giving her up had been worth it.

"You're assuming Peregrine will go after Josh again. That may or may not be true, but either way, you have no control over it. Why not look back on what happened before as evidence that *if* Peregrine comes back, you'll be able to handle whatever he throws at you?"

"But I couldn't handle anything last time," Will protested. "I completely freaked out when Josh brought Feodor back."

Malina shrugged. "And then you and Feodor helped save everyone. I'd call that a win. Look, one of the things post-traumatic stress disorder does is perpetuate a sense of impending danger. It makes you believe that whatever trauma you've experienced is likely to occur again. I think you would be happier if you pushed back against that feeling."

Will wasn't sure he liked the idea of letting his guard down—but then, that's exactly what Malina was saying was the problem. PTSD made it hard to relax. "What if I start telling myself not to worry about Peregrine, and then he shows up again and everything goes to hell?"

"Then you'll deal with it, just like you have before. But spending the time between now and then worrying about him and withdrawing from life won't make you better prepared to meet him. It will just make you anxious."

Will remembered how his anxiety had made him insist that Josh and Feodor not build stronger devices with which to face Peregrine two months before. He'd demanded that they come up with a different plan, and that plan had backfired, exactly as Feodor had predicted it would. Malina was right that his anxiety hadn't helped him before and probably wouldn't help him again.

"I'll think about it," he said.

Malina smiled. "That's all I ask."

Afterward, Will's adoptive mother let him drive home, partly because he was practicing for his license, and partly because Kerstel was so pregnant that she could barely reach the steering wheel.

"Do you worry about Peregrine?" he asked her.

"Of course. Some mornings I still wake up thinking he's a god. I worry about that."

Kerstel—and nearly every other dream walker Will knew—had been brainwashed by Peregrine to believe that he was humanity's savior and that his political rival, Will's friend Mirren, was evil. It had taken weeks of deprogramming to get Kerstel to see that she had been influenced through her dreams.

"But I also worry about climate change, Putin, and how to raise my son to treat women as equals. I have a limited amount of energy I'm willing to give to worrying." Kerstel shifted beneath her seat belt. "Why? Are you still worrying a lot?"

"I guess. Malina seems to think so. I just wish I felt more prepared to deal with Peregrine, because I know he's going to come back."

"Maybe," Kerstel agreed. "You know, if you and Josh weren't refusing to speak to each other—"

"I speak to her all the time."

"—she would be the perfect person to help with that."

Josh had prepared him for a lot of things: knife fights, bear attacks, quicksand. But if she didn't know how to defeat Peregrine, how could she teach Will?

After helping Kerstel inside, Will found his friends in the living room. Deloise was sitting forward on the couch, her back straight and her hands clenching her skirt, but Whim was standing, as if he'd been so arrested by the television that he forgot to sit down. A few feet away, Whim's sister Winsor sat slumped in her wheelchair. They were all staring at the television with stiff, white faces, except for Winsor, who just looked confused.

"What's wrong?" Will asked, sitting down on the couch beside Deloise.

"Snitch escaped," she said hollowly.

Will's stomach dropped. Geoff Simbar had been a family friend, ages ago. Then he'd gotten caught in Feodor's private Dream universe and had his soul sucked out. Feodor had sent him back to the World as a zombie.

Snitch—which was the name Will had given Geoff before they found out who he was—and his partner had attacked the family, killing Josh's grandmother and nearly killing Winsor, Kerstel, and the baby.

"Who's Snitch?" Winsor asked.

"He's a bad guy," Whim told his sister. "Very mean to animals. But you don't have to worry about him."

Winsor frowned beneath her new cat-eye glasses. "Then why do you all look so scared?"

"You know how much Del loves animals," Whim said.

Winsor had spent five months in a coma while her soul was trapped in a gas canister. Josh, Whim, and Feodor had managed to put her soul back into her body, but tests revealed that she'd suffered a traumatic brain injury. While her body struggled to build muscle that had wasted away as she lay in bed for five months, her mind was struggling to relearn the interpretation of brain signals. She was irritable, confused, and—Will secretly thought—frightened.

Will wouldn't have tried to sell Winsor a lie in that situation, but she was Whim's sister, not his.

On television, a reporter was standing outside a three-story brick building, speaking to another woman in a blue business suit.

"—kind of security measures exist here, warden?"

"You have to understand," the warden said, "that almost the entire prisoner population is here for nonviolent crimes such as staging abuse, secrecy violations, and embezzlement. This facility was never intended to house offenders with the kind of violent tendencies Geoff Simbar displayed. We did our best—"

The reporter interrupted. "Are you saying that it's the prison's fault he escaped?"

"Geoff Simbar?" Winsor asked, as if the name rang a bell.

"I'm saying that we repeatedly informed the junta that this facility was insufficient to ensure that Mr. Simbar remained contained, and they provided no help."

"What do we do?" Deloise asked, twisting her hands together. "Do you think he'll come here?"

"He has no reason to come back here," Will said, although he didn't know if that was true. "Where's Josh?"

"Not here," Whim said.

"I'll try her at Feodor's," Deloise offered, pulling out her phone.

Will watched the television while Deloise called. DWTV played the same clips over and over—a hole torn in an apartment ceiling, shingles and insulation all over the floor, a shot over the edge of the building showing the three-story drop.

"How did he drop that far and not break his legs?" Whim asked.

Will remembered how strong Snitch had been. Without his human soul, he'd barely responded to physical pain.

Will watched clips of gendarmes with flashlights marching

through the woods around the brick building, scent hounds on leashes, a warning for dream walkers not to confront Snitch on their own.

Deloise hung up. "Josh wasn't there, but Feodor said Snitch wouldn't come here—"

The doorbell rang.

Deloise grabbed Will's arm, digging her French manicure into his skin. Whim released a little scream and spun to look at the hall-way door.

"Be quiet," Winsor told her brother. "Screaming hurts my head."

"Del, Will, with me," Whim said, and they followed him into the foyer just the way they would have followed him into a night-mare. Will and Deloise fell into fighting stances, and Whim counted with his fingers before yanking the door open.

The guy standing on the porch was not Snitch. In fact, Will didn't recognize him at all. College-age, he had sandy blond hair, and although he was frail and leaned heavily on a walker, his build suggested he could have been an athlete.

Or maybe had been, once.

A young woman accompanied him, obviously concerned about his ability to walk. In her, the athleticism was more pronounced, and she was dressed in a soccer jersey.

"You!" Whim said accusingly, at the same moment the stranger shouted, "Winsor!" His voice was rough and desperate. "Winsor!"

"I told you to leave her alone!" Whim said, and he tried to slam the door shut. The stranger attempted to slide through the door before it closed, but his knees buckled and he ended up on all fours, the front half of his body inside the foyer and the back half on the porch.

"You can't shut me out forever!" the stranger cried. "You have to talk to me!"

"Whim!" Deloise cried. "You're going to cut him in half!"

"This is the guy I told you about, the one we had to ban from the rehab center."

"Winsor!" the guy yelled. "Please, talk to me!"

Deloise pulled the door open, and the guy collapsed on the foyer floor.

"Oh my God," the young woman with him said, kneeling down. "I'm so sorry. I had no idea—"

"I can't go on like this!" the guy told her. "I can't!"

"I know," she said. She tried to help him up, but he only stumbled farther into the house, and Will had to catch him when he fell again.

"Winsor!" the guy gasped, and Will turned his head to see Winsor sitting in her chair in the living room doorway.

"Winsor, do you know this guy?" Will asked.

Winsor trembled for a moment, then shook her head.

"You're lying!" the guy shouted, flailing in Will's arms. "Why are you lying? I know you remember me! Why are you lying?"

"You two need to leave," Whim told the young woman.

"Winsor!" the guy screamed, as Winsor retreated back into the living room.

"I'm so sorry," the young woman said. "I didn't know he would—"

"She's lying!" the guy insisted. "Molly, she's lying!"

"I'm sorry," Molly repeated. "He suffered a head injury earlier this year, and he thinks he knows your friend. Sam, let's get back in the truck."

Sam? Will thought.

"She has to talk to me," Sam moaned. He was crying then, and his knees were shaking so badly that even his walker couldn't keep him upright.

"Are you Sam Applethwaite?" Will asked.

"Did Winsor tell you about me?" Sam begged, tears running down his cheeks.

"No," Whim said firmly. "We read about you in the paper. Now go."

Despite his bizarre harassment, Will felt for the guy. Taking out his phone, Will said, "Give me your number, and I'll make sure Winsor gets it, okay?"

Whim's eyes flashed, but he didn't protest.

"Thank you," Sam said, clutching Molly's arms. "Thank you."

He gave Will his number and they helped him back to his sister's truck, where he collapsed into the passenger seat.

"I'm so sorry," Molly repeated. "He hasn't stopped talking about her since he woke up from a coma a few months ago. I thought maybe they really did know each other."

Will glanced at Deloise, who was helping Sam with his seat belt and reassuring him that they'd give his number to Winsor.

"It's okay," Will told Molly. "We understand."

Whim was standing in the doorway glaring at them when they came back. "You shouldn't encourage that guy. He's a stalker."

"You didn't tell us he was *Sam*," Deloise said.

"What difference does that make?"

"Winsor woke up screaming for him!" Deloise hissed, keeping her voice down so Winsor wouldn't overhear them. "Their souls were locked in a canister together for five months! Maybe they . . . communicated or something."

"So what? She doesn't want to see him."

"That's true," Will admitted. "However they may or may not know each other, Winsor doesn't want to see him. I think we have to respect that."

"All right," Deloise said reluctantly. "But I *am* going to tell her that Will has Sam's number if she wants it."

"Fine," Whim said, throwing his hands up. "Whatever my princess wants."

"*Don't* call me that."

Deloise had dumped Whim for cheating on her. She was pretty serious about it, and Whim was pretty serious about getting back together with her. He'd even enrolled in culinary school to prove to her that he was getting his life together.

"So what did Feodor say?" Will asked, in part to prevent them from having the princess/don't-call-me-princess argument again.

"He said he doesn't think Snitch will come here," Deloise repeated. "He said he's more likely to go back to the cabin and try to reenter Feodor's pocket universe there, and we should make sure the Gendarmerie sends some people over so Snitch doesn't hurt the construction workers."

More than a year after it had burned, Deloise's father was rebuilding his late wife's cabin.

Deloise swallowed. "I asked him why Snitch isn't in a coma, like Winsor—and Sam—were. He said he put the soul of a killer bee in Snitch's body."

"What? How is that possible?" Whim asked.

It actually explains a few things, Will thought, remembering how tenaciously Snitch had fought. He put an arm around Deloise's shoulders, but he couldn't think of anything to say that was comforting. Whatever he said would have been the equivalent of watching storm clouds gather while promising her it wouldn't rain.

Malina was right, he admitted to himself. *I don't want to sit here like a fish in a barrel and wait for Peregrine or Snitch or whoever to come shoot me.*

I'd rather take the fight to them.

Three

Behind the temple where the Lords of Death held court, Haley McKarr huddled in a ball and dreaded the sunset.

"Hello, little brother," Ian said.

Haley didn't even feel himself moving until he was throwing his arms around his brother. Ian laughed and returned the hug, and suddenly Haley was six years old, hiding behind Ian while another kindergartener threw rocks at them.

Ian was still laughing when he pulled away. "I guess you missed me."

Even though they were identical twins, no one had ever had trouble telling Haley and Ian apart. They had the same green-hazel eyes, but Ian's look was bold where Haley's was shirking. Ian favored preppy polo shirts and khakis, and Haley preferred the protection of oversized cardigans and well-worn jeans. Ian's dark curls lay cropped close to his skull, while Haley's tumbled into his eyes like a waterfall.

Thanks to Haley's slouch, Ian was even—

"Are you taller than me?" Ian demanded. "What the hell?"

Haley shrugged and withdrew into his shoulders, but Ian pulled him up by the arm so he could compare. "How did you grow more than an inch in—wait, how long have I been dead? A month?"

"A year," Haley admitted—although the question was actually quite complicated—and he jumped when Ian burst out, "A *year*? I've been dead for a *year*?!"

Haley shrank back. Ian's soul had been separated from his body during the fire at Josh's mother's cabin. While Feodor had used Ian's body as an errand boy, his soul had haunted Haley, sometimes even possessing him, for seven months afterward. Haley had a hard time remembering everything from those months; Ian had lived large, partying, drinking, smoking. He'd even gotten a very embarrassing tattoo on Haley's left calf. When Ian's body died, his soul had gone on to Death, and that was the first time he and Haley had truly been apart.

"You've only been here for five months," Haley said.

"Still. I knew time moved slower here, but damn. I didn't think it had been a year—or five months." He snorted. "Now you get to be taller than me for the rest of eternity."

"Sorry," Haley muttered.

"Oh, stop it," Ian said. "I'm not really mad at you."

Haley knew that wasn't true, but he was grateful when Ian hugged him again.

He felt something, though, something like being poked with a screwdriver. It came not from Ian, but from his aura. Between the swirls of hot-rod red and cobalt blue, there were patches where Ian's energy field had become dark and brittle, the movement of the energy twisted. Pulling away to look, Haley saw that a cold, dark space stood—like cooled ash—in the center of Ian's heart chakra.

Something is wrong, Haley thought. *Something is terribly wrong.*

Haley had seen auras all his life. He could even see them with his eyes closed. When he looked at someone, he saw the energy fields in and around their bodies as clearly as he saw their clothing. When he touched them, he caught glimpses of their pasts, their futures. He'd learned to interpret the colors, the movement of the energy, the routes between chakras. But most of all, he just *felt* something when he was near them, some sense of the forces that were carrying them through life.

The first time he'd seen Josh's aura, he'd been so scared he peed himself. He had only been three at the time, but he still remembered it.

But he had never seen anything like what he was looking at now. It was like part of Ian's aura had *died.*

"So, what happened?" Ian asked.

That's what I was going to ask you, Haley thought, but something stopped him from saying the words.

When he didn't reply, Ian said, "You know—how did you pass away, bite the big one, kick the bucket? How did you *die?*" He leaned close and asked in a confidential whisper, "You offed yourself, didn't you?"

He thinks I killed myself?

Of course he did. Because Haley had always been the weak one.

"No," Haley said. "I didn't kill myself."

"Are you sure?" Ian nudged him with an elbow. "You can tell me—we're twins."

"I didn't kill myself," Haley repeated, cringing at how defensive and whiney his voice sounded. "I'm not even dead."

Ian laughed. He had a giant laugh, one Haley had always felt sucked up all the air in a room. "I've got bad news for you. This is a dead-folks-only party, little brother."

Was it strange that Ian couldn't tell he was alive? The other dead had stared at him with curiosity, some with confusion, a few with jealousy.

"I'm not dead," Haley repeated. "I'm here as a hostage."

"A hostage? What does that mean?"

"Josh and—" He'd almost mentioned Will, and he wasn't sure that was a good idea. "It's a long story," he said instead.

Ian snorted. "We've got time, little brother. We've got more time than we'll know what to do with." He clapped Haley on the back. "You can wait till later, if you want. I can tell you're freaked out. Come on, let's get away from here. I hate the temple."

He strode off toward the rolling hills that seemed to make up the Death universe, but Haley hesitated to follow, wondering if he needed to stay close to the temple so that he could be nearby when his friends came back for him.

They will come back for me, he told himself, remembering how Mirren had kissed him before she left. *They won't leave me here.*

"Hurry up, little brother," Ian called, and Haley forced his feet forward.

He had to scurry to catch up to Ian, but their strides fell into unison as they crossed a stone bridge. Ian noticed and grinned, and for a few yards they walked in deliberate synchronicity.

"Where are we going?" Haley asked as they fell into a more natural stride.

"Wherever we want. There are no rules here, nobody to answer to, nothing to do, really. It's actually like the most boring place ever."

The description seemed odd to Haley. Death was *the most boring place ever*?

"Sometimes I climb trees," Ian said. "There's a pond where I skip stones or go swimming. I've even chased a couple of squirrels."

Squirrels?

Something wasn't right. If there was one thing Haley had felt since he entered Death, it was that this was a place of transition. It wasn't an eternal recess where the dead just hung out.

"What are those people doing?" he asked.

He had noticed that, a few dozen yards away, the dead had gathered around a bonfire. They stood in solemn silence, and although Haley was too far away to see clearly, he caught glimpses of their energy fields moving, rising above them . . .

"They're weirdos," Ian said. "You don't want to get caught up with them, trust me."

Haley's eyes lingered on the bonfire. He thought he could make out visions in the energy above the flames, but Ian tugged him away.

"You still doing that?" he asked.

Doing that? Haley thought. *How would I have stopped?*

His mother had been willfully blind to his gifts. His father had refused to see them until he couldn't see anything else, and then he'd left. Mirren had accepted them, but of course she couldn't understand. Ian was the only one who had ever truly understood Haley. To hear him say that he'd thought perhaps Haley would have stopped seeing auras was not only unexpected, but disconcerting.

"I thought maybe it wouldn't work without me there," Ian added. "Like, a twin thing."

"Oh," Haley said.

Now that they were together again, Haley became aware of how much he had changed since Ian died. He had spent their childhood desperately grateful for Ian's acceptance, and would once have gladly agreed that Ian's presence was necessary for his abilities to function. Now he knew they were entirely his own.

"Come on," Ian said. "There's a tree with these awesome fruits— like grapefruit, but sweet. You look hungry."

Torn, Haley glanced back at the people around the bonfire. "Can I just see what they're doing?"

"I told you, they're idiots."

Haley had no desire to anger his brother, but he had a feeling that what was happening was important. "Please? Just for like two minutes?"

Ian crossed his arms over his chest and released a short, angry burst of air through his nose. "Fine. Two minutes."

Haley didn't wait for Ian to change his mind, just scurried toward the bonfire. The dead stood very still around it, but as he got close, he heard two of them speaking, their voices almost inaudible, their motions minute.

"Yes," a man told the person beside him. "I think it's quite all right."

"This was peaceful," the woman replied. She touched his arm, and they turned and walked away from the fire, passing Haley as they did so.

The woman smiled at him, and though there was curiosity in her expression, she didn't question Haley or pause. He turned back to the bonfire when she was gone.

This close, he could see that the auras of the people clustered around the bonfire were expanded. Their colors were rich and bright, and noticeably missing the streakiness of anxiety or muted shades of depression he was used to seeing in the auras of the living.

Something was flowing out of the dead and into the bonfire. He thought at first that it was their auras, but it was something else, some other form of energy he had never seen before. Or had never been *able* to see before. He watched as a tendril moved away from a woman standing nearby, and it was gauzy, vague, and oddly thick. Curious, Haley brushed his fingers through it.

Instantly, he felt a rush of pain and fear. He held his hand up before him, blinded by white light, and he heard the sound of flesh smacking flesh and then the wail of a baby. Flailing in the freezing air, he was thrust upon warm skin and felt huge arms wrap around him. He smelled something, some*one,* and when he breathed deep, he recognized the scent. This was his mother. This was home. He was safe.

Haley jerked his hand back and sucked in a great breath. When he opened his eyes, he saw the last of the woman's birth memory float into the intense blue flame. When he looked back at the woman, her aura was an even cleaner, sweeter shade of yellow.

They're releasing their lives, he realized. *Their memories, their personalities . . . they're releasing them. That's what this place is for.*

He understood then what Death was. When people died, they came here to make peace with the lives they had just lived. They were releasing their memories, not their true selves. The true self was indestructible—Haley had always known that. Beneath his thoughts, his personality, his character, was a higher self, a soul that had never been born and could never die. Each time the dead gave up the people they had been, they released the pain, the fear, the confusion of life. With each offering, their auras grew more exquisite and luminous, and when they walked away from the bonfire, they were far more peaceful than when they had arrived.

"Haley!" Ian called.

Haley turned to see him standing just as he had been, arms crossed, glaring. His aura was still laden with every memory, every injury, every pain he had carried when he died, and worse, a wealth of fear at the idea of losing himself. Ian had believed in what Haley saw, but he had never trusted in the existence of a soul.

"I should have known you'd be into that hippie-dippie crap," he said when Haley reached him. "You're going to leave me—just like Dustine did."

Haley started. "Dustine?"

Dustine is here, he thought. *If I could find her—I could ask her about Josh's abilities—maybe there's a reason I ended up here.*

Ian's eyes were brooding. "Crapped out all her memories and then took off through the gates."

"What gates?"

Ian pointed. A quarter mile or so along the path they were walking stood an enormous set of golden gates, spread open like wings.

"Where do they lead?" Haley asked.

"How should I know?"

"You've never been past them?"

He knew the question was a mistake the instant he asked it.

"Why should I?" Ian demanded.

"You shouldn't," Haley assured him. "You don't have to. I'm sorry. I just meant—maybe we could go together and find Dustine."

"No," Ian said flatly. He yanked a pear off a nearby tree and began walking again. "By the time you find her, she won't even remember you."

Haley recalled watching the woman release her memory of birth and wondered if Ian was right. Maybe finding Dustine was pointless.

They'd both grown up with Dustine; she was their grandmother in every way except biologically. And although she'd been a tough lady who wasn't always quick to show affection, Haley had felt safe with her. She'd never hesitated to call Ian out when he was being a jerk, and Haley craved that protection now. Besides, Haley was beginning to fear that if Haley didn't find a way to force Ian, he would remain in Death forever, refusing to let go of the person he had been and so never moving on. Haley couldn't bear the thought of his brother stuck in limbo forever.

There was one other reason to find her: "I need to talk to her about Josh."

"Why?"

"She's in trouble."

That got Ian's attention. "What's wrong with Josh?" he asked.

Haley swallowed. "I can't tell you while we're here."

Ian tossed the pear onto the ground and strode toward Haley so forcefully that Haley took a step back. "Cut the crap. What's wrong with Josh?"

The answer was on the tip of Haley's tongue, but he didn't let himself say it. He just shook his head.

Ian grabbed his shoulder. *"Haley. Now."*

With a trembling hand, Haley pointed to the golden gates. "I'll tell you once we're on the other side of those."

Ian's eyes—more gold than hazel—pounded at Haley's. In a low, dangerous voice, he said, "I should kick your ass."

Be brave, Haley told himself. *You have to be brave.*

He knew he wasn't brave. But all his life, he'd been doing something in place of bravery: he'd run.

Haley sprinted like a rabbit.

"Jerk!" Ian shouted after him. "You're going to leave your own brother here? Who *does* that?"

Since school had let out, Haley had been running in the mornings with Josh and Will. Josh pushed a brutal pace; sometimes she even made them run down the center of a nearby creek, a practice her mother had invented. Haley had been doing that Romanian circuit training video, too. He was in the best shape of his life, and he knew when he heard Ian's breathing recede that he had a significant lead.

He blew past the dead and through the golden gates. If something happened when he passed beneath their arches, he didn't feel it.

Twenty feet farther down the path, he stopped running and turned around. Ian was walking toward the gates, his arms crossed and his jaw clamped shut. Haley walked back toward him until they stood ten feet apart, the gates between them.

Haley panted as his heartbeat slowed down. He knew the look on Ian's face—he was both angry and hurt, and he wanted Haley to know it. His aura had darkened, and a grayish-green mist hovered around his gut.

Beyond Ian, Haley could see the rolling hills where his brother had spent the last five months. Such a pleasant, easy place, with the beauty of the temple rising up at the far side. Such a safe place. Haley understood why Ian had stayed there; for much of his life, Haley had longed for such a sanctuary of his own.

But souls, Haley knew, weren't meant to be static. They could slow down, rest, even hibernate for a time, but—like the fruit trees that dotted the landscape—they would always start growing again.

"What the hell are you doing?" Ian asked, and his tone was so mirthless and dangerous that it nearly pulled Haley right back through the gates. "Do you think this is funny?"

He gave Haley what Haley had long thought of as "the look." It was something he did with his eyes and his forehead and the set of his jaw that brokered no argument, allowed no dissent, and contained a warning that if Haley didn't do exactly what Ian wanted, there was going to be trouble.

"Do you think it's funny?" Ian repeated. "Answer me."

"No," Haley whispered.

"How long have you been here?"

Haley shrugged. "I don't know."

"Less than two hours. How long have I been here?"

When he waited for an answer, Haley whispered, "Five months."

"Five *months,*" Ian repeated. "Which one of us do you think knows more about this place?"

I'm not ten years old anymore, Haley told himself. *I don't have to let him talk to me like this.*

The problem was, he didn't know any other way to answer.

"You do."

"And if I tell you that going past the gates is dangerous, what does that mean?"

"Going past the gates is dangerous."

The dead passing by were watching them; some of them had even stopped to watch. Haley blushed, remembering all the times Ian had berated him in front of their friends. Josh had been the only one who ever stepped in and told Ian to stop.

Ian was still standing there, giving him the look, and when Haley glanced up, Ian widened his eyes, as if to say, *What are you still doing standing over there?*

Haley only knew one way to placate Ian.

"Please," Haley said. "I don't want to go alone."

Ian gave a disapproving frown, but some of the anger left his face. He walked through the gates, casting a glance upward as he did so. Haley hugged him tightly.

"The things I do for you," Ian muttered.

Four

Josh's father woke her up by flipping on the light in her room, thrusting a cordless phone into her face, and saying, "Please, for the love of God, get a cell phone like every other teenage girl in the country."

The clock read 2:18 a.m.

"Sorry," Josh said with a wince as she took the phone. "I'll tell her not to call this late."

Laurentius wandered, bleary-eyed, out of Josh's room.

"Zorie?" Josh said. There was only one person who called her at two in the morning.

"Hey. We've got a tear on a farm in Selmy."

Josh scribbled down the directions Zorie gave her, then pulled on a pair of running pants, a long-sleeved shirt, and a soft shell jacket, and snuck downstairs on her tiptoes. No sense in waking anyone else up.

This wasn't the first time her father had demanded she get a phone, Josh reflected as she pulled out of her driveway. It had become a minor household war, and one Josh knew she would eventually lose. But right now, it afforded her a freedom that she valued. If people were used to being unable to reach her, they were less likely to question where she was all the time.

As she got onto the deserted highway, she thought back to the corpse she'd found a few days before and the case file she'd received from Gendarme Burnette. All of the corpses had had damage to their lung tissue suggestive of chloroform inhalation, which Josh saw as more evidence that Peregrine was responsible for their deaths; with his left hand missing, he wouldn't be able to overpower anyone without the help of an easily obtainable drug, and chloroform could be cooked up at home.

Josh had known, even before she helped carve the symbol into

Peregrine's chest, that his inability to enter the Dream wouldn't stop his quest for power. But she'd never expected him to disappear— he had always loved being the center of attention—and now she had no idea where he was or what he was plotting. Because of that, she and Feodor had been forced to take a defensive position and wait for him to appear. They were working on various projects that might help them protect the Dream—one of which Josh was going to try out that night—but they had agreed that the single best way to prepare to face Peregrine was to help Josh access her abilities as the True Dream Walker.

And so far, they hadn't made much progress on that.

Nearly two hours later, Josh parked her car on the side of the road next to a field. Nothing was growing there yet, but the earth had been recently tilled. The edge of the road was crammed with cars and pickups, and a tanker truck had been driven right through the fence and across the dirt rows.

"Damn," Josh muttered as she climbed out of her car and got her first good look at the Veil tear. She estimated it was near sixty feet long, and it hung in the air a good twenty feet off the ground. The tear itself was a jagged line traced across the sky. It looked like a giant hose being shaken in midair, spewing a waterfall of white sparkles and light not just from its ends but all along its length. The tear was still thin, but it would widen—like an open- ing mouth—if given the chance.

Anyone driving down the road is going to see that, Josh thought. Luckily they were outside a small town.

The Veil separated the Dream from the World and from Death. Josh had been taught that it surrounded each universe like a bubble, but now that she had Feodor's memories to draw from, she under- stood that it was more like an energy vibration that separated one reality from the next. The best way to avoid tears was to keep the emotional turmoil level in the Dream as low as possible, but inevi- tably, a tear would still occur once in a while.

Normally, nightmares couldn't leave the Dream universe. They became insubstantial and dissolved, like a drop of food coloring in a bucket of water. However, if they interacted with enough Veil dust while exiting the Dream, they could remain intact for minutes, hours, even days. All archway edges were sealed in order to prevent Veil dust from leaking out of the place where the Veil had been cut, but of course no seal was perfect. All archways leaked a little, and Veil dust tended to cling to living things, which was why dream walkers emerged from the Dream covered in a faint shimmer. It was why, if Josh got wet in the Dream, her clothes were still wet when she entered the World. But the archway seals were tight enough to prevent anything large from coming through.

The problem with a Veil tear was that it wasn't sealed at all. Veil dust was pouring out of this one, and Zorie's people were preparing to spray additional, ionized Veil dust on it.

"Is it the aurora borealis?" a man standing nearby asked. He was wearing pants, an undershirt, and suspenders, and he was staring at the tear in a way that made Josh certain he wasn't a dream walker.

"It's actually gas," Josh told him, which was the usual party line.

"I just finished planting three days ago," the man said.

"Sorry," was all Josh could think to say. They were pretty much going to wreck his field.

She walked up to a small woman with a sharp face and short black hair, both of which were hidden behind a gas mask.

"Hey, Zorie."

Zorie's voice was muffled by the mask. "Hi, Josh—Sal, don't drag the generator!" She yanked her mask off to shout again. "Sal, get it off the ground!" She wiped the sweat from her face. "I'm going to kill him if he gets dirt in that thing."

"You're using the light spray method? Why not try to suture the tear?"

"We already did. Every stitch we made tore right out."

Teams like Zorie's used various methods for closing Veil tears, depending on the size and location of each tear. None of them worked every time. The method Zorie's team was about to attempt involved spraying the tear with Veil dust and then flashing lights of various colors over the dust—essentially the reverse process of opening an archway.

"You want us to wait until you've done your thing to start?" Zorie asked Josh.

"No, no. Don't wait on me. If I succeed, you'll know."

Josh went back to her car and sat on the trunk. One of the projects she and Feodor had been working on was a new method of Veil repair. It required only one piece of equipment: a bundle of wires connected to a control box the size of a pack of mints. At the end of each wire was a node that Josh attached to her scalp or chest with a drop of medical goop. The nodes vibrated in a certain sequence, the speed and strength of which Josh could change via the control box.

The idea was that the repetition of the vibration sequence would coax her own body's vibrations to match it, and that vibration would signal the soul that it was time to enter the Dream. Josh would remain conscious within the Dream, but since she'd also be a dreamer, she'd be able to change the Dream with her thoughts, and she could simply instruct the Dream to close the tear.

Feodor called it the Vibrational Harmonic Acclimation Guide— or VHAG. This would be the first time Josh tried it since they reprogrammed the pattern.

Once Josh got all the nodes attached, she turned on the VHAG and closed her eyes. The vibration of the nodes wasn't unpleasant, but the strange pattern they created—like twinkling Christmas lights all over her head and chest—disoriented her. That was their purpose, of course. The longer she wore the VHAG, increasing the speed and intensity of the vibrations every few minutes, the dizzier and woozier she felt. Her body slumped backward onto the rear window of her car, and she began to lose feeling entirely. All she could sense was her mind, and it was struggling to break free, trying to shrug off her mortal form, but something was holding her back.

This was as close as Josh had ever gotten to merging with the Dream, and it wasn't much closer than she'd been able to get two

months ago—or six months before that. She'd hoped the new vibration sequence would give her the last push she needed to escape her body, but so far, it didn't seem to be—

"*SHEEP!*" someone screamed, and Josh opened her eyes.

The scene before her was brilliant. Men and women in gas masks
were spraying iridescent rainbows of Veil dust from fire hoses.
The fine mist of delicate colors burst into the air and over the tear
like a magical healing shower. Behind them, a half-dozen indus-
trial lights fit with colored filters were flashing one after another,
running from one end of the color spectrum to the other and back.

Sheep began to leap out of the tear.

"Uh-oh," Josh said. She shut down the VHAG, climbed off the
trunk so she could open it, and pulled out her gas mask. Sheep
were pouring out of the tear, bounding over its lower edges as if
they were leaping fences. Some crashed to the tilled earth and
couldn't get up, their legs broken, creating a pile of agony on which
other sheep landed.

And the nightmares came marching out, two by two, Josh remembered her grandmother saying once, months and months ago.

As she buckled on her gas mask, Josh's eyes strayed from the
mound of scrambling sheep to the tear itself, and she saw what was
coming next.

She ran toward Zorie, vaulting the fence as she went. "Wolf!"
she shouted, but her voice was muffled behind the mask, and she
couldn't take it off because she was running through a literal rain
of Veil dust, which, if inhaled, could cause permanent insanity.

"Wolf!" Josh yelled, but no one was looking at her, they were all
transfixed by the mangled, bleating sheep. The injured animals had
formed a high enough pile that the sheep coming out of the tear
were landing on them without injury, rolling down the pile, and
then running scattershot across the field.

One of Zorie's guys was futilely trying to corral the sheep, and
he was directly in front of the Veil tear. Josh sprinted, dodging stray
sheep, and grabbed him by the cuff of his shirt, dragging him away
from the tear just as the wolf emerged.

Josh felt its shadow pass over her back as it leapt, and she turned to see it land on the ground beyond the sheep pile. The wolf was a giant, mangy thing with wiry black fur tinged with silver, its jaws dripping with strings of saliva. Its legs didn't break, or even falter, as it landed. Without an instant lost to disorientation, the wolf turned around and drove its muzzle into the sheep pile, snatching the animals up like appetizers. The gas mask Josh wore barely muted the sounds of the shrieking sheep and the *snap* of their bones as the wolf bit into them. Its muzzle flung ropes of blood across the white fur of the other sheep, and Josh was about to run toward it—to do what, she couldn't have said—when a shotgun blast filled the air.

The wolf fell to its side atop the sheep, and it whimpered in a way that was almost endearing, as if the pain had rendered it a puppy again. Blood gushed from its chest. Josh watched the farmer she'd spoken to when she arrived pump his shotgun, aim, and fire again. This time the wolf went limp.

Beside her, Zorie swore. She had finally turned off the Veil dust pump, but there was plenty left in the air. Josh went up to the farmer and took her mask off.

"Wear this," she said. "The gas isn't safe."

"Gas my ass," he retorted. "Gas doesn't—whatever the hell I just saw. I gotta put those sheep out of their misery."

"Wear the mask," Josh insisted. *If only to keep the blood off your face.*

The farmer accepted the mask, but he hesitated before putting it on. "You think anyone owns those sheep?"

"They're all yours," Josh assured him.

Five

The next morning, in the familiar chaos of the kitchen, Will ate a bowl of cereal and eavesdropped on his parents.

"We can't have people calling at all hours of the night," Kerstel told Lauren. "Not even Zorie. And especially not after the baby comes."

"Josh promised me she'd get a cell phone," Lauren said, ladling eggs onto his wife's plate.

Who is Zorie, and why is she calling Josh in the middle of the night? Will wondered, stirring his cereal with his spoon. Behind him, Deloise was trying to teach Whim's father, Alex, how to use the espresso maker. Again. Whim was examining the custard he'd made as homework for culinary school. Winsor was using a special, thick-handled spoon to eat her oatmeal, but most of it was ending up on the table.

Deloise's phone beeped, and she glanced at it, frowned, and then held it up for Whim to see. "Did you do this?" she demanded.

Whim smiled broadly. "It's awesome, right? I paid a guy in game credits to make an emoji of you."

"Whim! Why, why did you do that?"

His smile softened. "Because I love you. It's cute, right?"

"I want to see," Winsor said, and Deloise handed her the phone. "Why are there flames coming out of her head?"

"Oh, well, Carlos's English isn't that great, and I think he got confused when I said she was more beautiful than the sunrise—"

"Change it back!" Deloise demanded. "And don't ever hack into my account again."

"I didn't hack into it," Whim protested. "You had me set it up for you!"

"Well, now I'm telling you to stay out of it!"

"Boundaries," Will said to Whim. "Remember our whole talk about respecting her boundaries?"

Whim scrunched his face up. "What were we eating at the time?"

"Pizza," Winsor guessed.

Whim stared at her for a moment, and then said, "Can somebody take Winsor to PT this afternoon? I have to tutor this girl who doesn't know the difference between baking soda and baking powder."

"Just your type," Deloise snipped.

"Uh, she is *not* my type, and she's also the most irritating person I've ever met. She thinks cream of tartar goes in tartar sauce."

"I can take Winsor," Alex offered.

"Thanks, Dad. I've gotta go. Text me if you need anything, Winny."

Winsor scowled at him, then waited until he'd gone out the back door with the tray of custards to ask, "What's cream of tartar?"

None of them knew, and the back door had hardly closed before it was opening again. Josh walked into the kitchen and stopped short, as if confused by the sight of people. "Oh," she said.

"Have you been out all night?" Kerstel asked, and before Josh could answer, her father said, "Is that blood on your clothes?"

Josh *did* appear to have blood on her clothes, and her face, and her neck. Her North Face jacket and her running pants were covered in dirt the length of her left side. Not only that, but her hair was standing out in stiff clumps all over her head.

"What happened?" Deloise asked. "And what's going on with your hair?"

"I have medical glue in it, and this is sheep's blood," Josh said. "Maybe some wolf. I'm fine."

"You were wrestling animals?" Lauren asked.

"No, of course not. Who wrestles animals? I was out with Zorie."

Kerstel cast an exasperated glance at the ceiling. Will—who wanted to say something and knew he shouldn't—wondered what the hell Josh could have been doing all night. Experimenting on sheep? Carving mutton—and whatever wolf meat was called?

Josh opened the fridge and pulled out a roll of summer sausage. As she walked away, she ripped one end open and took a big bite. She'd made it almost to the hallway when Winsor said, "Josh, what's cream of tartar?"

Josh blinked at her. "It's a natural byproduct of winemaking used as a stabilizer in egg dishes."

And then she left.

After school, instead of driving home, Deloise and Will got on the highway. He knew Malina had suggested he spend less time worrying about Peregrine, but that had been before Snitch escaped, and Will couldn't help but think that Peregrine was somehow involved. That morning, Will had called the prison Snitch had escaped from and arranged to see his cell. He'd made sure to introduce himself as Josh Weaver's apprentice, and from there, all doors flew open to him.

This was the first time he'd done something dream walker related without Josh. He was taking Deloise with him instead, and he was nervous as hell, but he also felt like he was taking a positive step forward.

"Who's Zorie?" Will asked Deloise on the drive.

"Oh, Zorie Abernaughton. She's the director of the southeast Veil repair team. She runs around closing Veil tears."

"Is that dangerous?"

"Um . . . I'm gonna say yes? And Zorie's—she's a cowboy. Reckless. I guess Josh is helping her team." Deloise shook her blond hair back over her shoulders. "It's like Josh has gone back to being completely oblivious to everything but dream walking."

Will felt an irritating worry in the back of his mind. If Josh was running around all hours of the night with this Zorie person, how close an eye was she keeping on Feodor?

Then Deloise started ranting about Whim and the emoji. She and Will had promised to be one another's breakup buddies, meaning that they could search each other out and vent as often as necessary and trust that the other wouldn't repeat any of it.

"Because," Deloise reiterated, as she wound down, "I am a smart, kind, interesting person who doesn't have to lower herself to being with someone who puts their relationship woes out on the Internet and cheats on me with two-faced Bs."

"That is all true," Will agreed.

Warden Skotrez met them in the lobby and—despite her disappointment that Josh hadn't been able to come along—insisted on giving them a forty-five-minute tour of the facilities. Deloise had to keep manually closing her jaw as they walked from one luxurious room to another.

"After Versailles, this is the most beautiful place I've ever been," she whispered to Will.

The Pryliss Sanitarium was neither a prison nor a mental hospital. It was actually a dozen beautiful condos, each with a private bathroom, a kitchenette, and a unique decorating scheme. The prisoners ate in a dining room with linen napkins and real silverware and enjoyed a hot tub and steam room after working out in the state-of-the-art gymnasium. Unlike most prison inmates, they received weekly counseling, and their families and friends were encouraged to visit as often as they liked.

"So, I'm guessing not a lot of people get shanked here," Will said as they walked through the hall where weekly culture enrichment programs were hosted.

Warden Skotrez, a petite woman of Cuban descent with curly black hair, laughed. "We did have two guests quit speaking to each other for a month last year. But no, there's no violence here to speak of. We're truly an establishment that works to rehabilitate, not to punish."

Will couldn't help but wonder, as they spoke with the world-class chef, whether or not being treated in a place like this would have saved his mother from alcoholism. The weekend jail stays for drunk-and-disorderly and the revolving-door trips to rehab certainly hadn't.

"And it's very rare that our guests are sent here for violent offenses. Most have been referred for dream staging, secrecy violations, or Veil dust abuse. That's why the situation with Mr. Simbar was so far beyond our ability to handle."

Trying to butter up the warden, Will said, "You know, I'm one of the only people who has dealt with Geoff Simbar besides you and the Gendarmerie. I'm shocked that anyone thought this was the appropriate place for him."

Warden Skotrez nodded.

"Obviously, you're doing subtle, intensive rehabilitation work here. Geoff Simbar wasn't going to respond to that. He needed a cage."

The warden loosened up some then. "I told the captain of the Gendarmerie and Peregrine Borgenicht himself that this wasn't the place for Mr. Simbar. I told them both that he was causing problems with the staff and with the other guests. No one would listen. Here, I'll show you what he did to his room."

Although Will had exaggerated, he hadn't exaggerated much. He'd fought Snitch, watched him try to murder a dreamer, seen Kerstel in the hospital after Snitch and Gloves nearly killed her. The man fought like an animal—literally, if what Feodor had said about giving him the soul of a bee was true. A stay in a luxury hotel wasn't going to change him.

Warden Skotrez led them to the third floor and then to the very end of the hallway. "Most of this floor is empty. He was less disruptive here."

She opened the door to a room entirely different from the others they had seen. Instead of a Western or New Orleans decorative theme, this room had been stripped down to the bare walls. A partially shredded mattress lay amid a heap of ripped blankets. The carpet had been torn up to reveal steal plate beneath, and some of the wallboard had been removed to the same effect.

"You replaced the walls with sheet metal?" Deloise asked.

"We had no choice," the warden said. "He literally tried to dig his way out of his first room. He injured his hands horribly. The kitchenette, the bathroom—he destroyed everything. He even yanked the pipes from the wall. He was a danger to himself."

Will glanced up through the hole in the roof at the blue tarp used to cover it. "But you didn't reinforce the ceiling."

The warden sighed. "It never occurred to us that he could escape that way. The ceilings are twelve feet high. We don't even know how he reached them."

"It looks like he jumped up and bashed them with his head," Will said. Silently, he added, *Just like in* Super Mario Bros.

"Give me a boost," Deloise told him, and he got down on one knee so she could climb onto his shoulders. When he rose carefully, she grabbed the edges of the hole in the ceiling to steady herself.

"See anything?" he asked.

"The ceiling plaster is broken off, but . . . hold on." She removed a lighter from her pocket—every dream walker Will knew carried a lighter, just out of habit—and lit it. "I can't believe he had the hand strength to tear shingles, but I don't see any cut marks."

As she spoke, Will noticed that the flame of her lighter was reflecting off the steel plate revealed by the ravaged carpet. Just for an instant, he though he saw . . .

"Del, come down." She climbed—with impressive grace—back to the floor, and Will pulled his own compact and lighter from his pocket.

"What are you doing?" the warden asked.

"I thought I saw . . ." Will opened the compact and lit the lighter, bouncing its light against the compact's mirror and around the room. He spent a moment adjusting the beam and casting its light across the far wall, and then, just as he was beginning to think he'd imagined whatever he saw, the Veil shimmered into view.

Warden Skotrez gasped. "It's an archway!"

Although its boundaries hadn't been marked in stone as they

usually were, there was no mistaking the soap bubble–like sight of the Veil.

"How is this possible?" the warden asked.

"He built an archway in the middle of his cell?" Deloise asked.

"He couldn't have! We never gave him access to fire or mirrors."

"I don't think he built the archway," Will told her. "I think somebody else built it, and used it to break him out. All this business with the ceiling was just to make it look like he escaped on his own. Try putting your hand through it, Del."

Deloise reached out, but her hand passed through the Veil and out the other side as if the archway didn't exist. "I can't reach into the Dream. It must not open in this direction."

"Someone opened an archway from the Dream into this room," Will said. "Then they reached in and pulled Geoff out."

"This is outrageous!" the warden cried.

"Who would want to free him?" Deloise asked.

Will shook his head. "I don't know. Did he have any visitors?"

"His wife visited—once," Warden Skotrez said. "Poor woman. She ran out of the building sobbing."

Will remembered the expression on Josh's face the first time she'd seen Ian after she realized Gloves had been using his body. She had been so brave, and seen so clearly that he was not the boy who had loved her. But Will wouldn't have blamed her if she'd run screaming.

"After that," the warden was saying, "a man came to visit him. A number of times, in fact. He wanted to write an article about Mr. Simbar."

"A reporter?" Will asked.

"No, no, we kept all the reporters out. No, this man is a philosopher, a scholar. He's written quite a wealth of work on dreamwalker ethics. His name is Aurek Trembuline."

The name meant nothing to Will, nor to Deloise, judging by her shrug.

"He's a wonderful man, very warm. He was very patient with Mr. Simbar. My God, who do I call to have this archway removed?"

"Try Zorie Abernaughton," Will suggested.

Before they left, the warden begged Will and Deloise not to share what they had learned with anyone. "Especially not the press," she added, which made Will think she knew that Whim was behind the now infamous anti-junta dream-walker blog, *Through a Veil Darkly*.

"We won't say a word to anyone," Deloise promised her.

As soon as they were in the car, Will said, "We've got to tell Josh."

"But we don't know anything."

"Yeah, but . . ."

But Josh is the one we always go to with stuff like this.

"This has to be related to Peregrine somehow, right?"

"What would Peregrine want with a guy with no soul?" Deloise asked.

"I don't know. That's why we should tell Josh—she always figures out things like this."

"You saw her this morning," Deloise said. "She's a complete wreck. She can barely dress herself, and she's out all night killing sheep and closing Veil tears. She's already under enough stress. Besides, wasn't this about proving you don't need her?"

"What? No. It's about making myself more confident in my ability to face Peregrine. Or Snitch. Or whoever else might come along."

"Then shouldn't we figure it out ourselves instead of running to Josh at the first sign of trouble?"

Will thought about that. He *did* want to feel competent without Josh. And things between them were so awkward lately . . .

"Okay," he agreed. "We won't tell Josh. But I'm going to look up that guy the warden mentioned, Aurek Trembuline."

"Now *that* sounds like a plan."

Six

A week after Josh helped Zorie with the sheep nightmare, she drove to the west side of Tanith, where train tracks crossed the streets and bleak, ugly warehouses rose like square boulders on all sides. Outside of a building that still bore a faded sign reading RIVERA CHAIR FACTORY, she parked on the street. She walked up the overgrown, broken sidewalk to the front door, unlocked the door, and called out, "It's me!" in Polish as she let herself in and turned to type her code into the security system.

When Feodor had convinced the Lords of Death to let him remain temporarily alive, Josh's stepmother had—very reasonably, Josh thought—declared that there was no way he was going to live in her house. Although Mirren's grandparents had confiscated Feodor's money when they exiled him, Mirren had given it back to him, and Feodor had purchased the chair factory as his new home. But Josh hadn't been willing to let Feodor wander where he pleased, so she'd injected him with a microchip linked to the security system. If he took two steps off the porch without deactivating the system, every person in the Avish-Weaver household would get a call.

"Good morning," Feodor said without looking up from the book in his hand. He was sitting in one of the two battered leather armchairs that made up the sitting area.

The sight of Feodor always filled Josh with mixed emotions. On the one hand, she could never forget the deaths he had been responsible for, including her grandmother's, or that he was the reason that Winsor was suffering so, or that Haley was still trapped in the Death universe. On the other hand, she understood Feodor in a way she had never understood anyone. Because she had his memories, she could see the World through his eyes, and despite the wrong conclusions he had drawn from his life, she couldn't help having compassion for him. She bore him an uncomfortable sort of affection from knowing him so well.

Even worse, she was grateful to him for the knowledge he had given her. She loved what her mind could do now, how it could put together ideas and create new ones, and how the realization of those possibilities was no longer beyond her reach. She and Feodor could talk for hours about Dream theory, about physics and evolution and genetics, and sometimes she felt them sliding dangerously into the territory of being friends. For obvious reasons, that wouldn't do.

Luckily, Josh could see his faults most clearly when they talked science, the lack of boundaries in his thinking, the faulted morality that allowed him to contemplate doing things she never would. While she found some of his proposals repugnant, part of her longed to be as pure a scientist as he was, as willing to sacrifice all else to the search for knowledge.

Feodor's warehouse wasn't especially large, but it was still a warehouse. He had done little to change that aside from adding a stove to the break area and converting the loft—once the manager's office—into a bedroom. Morning light shone in through the glass windows that made up the walls, diminished by the years of filth on the glass, which was so thick it provided a measure of privacy from the street outside. The cement floor was clean swept, and metal desks sat in various places around the room. Feodor had only been alive again for two months, and somehow he had already managed to acquire over a hundred books, which were loaded onto the wooden shelves that partitioned the kitchen from the rest of the factory. Josh couldn't resist wandering over to look at the new titles.

"Would you care for coffee?" Feodor asked.

"Dziękuję," Josh said with a shake of her head, slipping into Polish as she always did with Feodor. "Any news?"

Ostensibly, Feodor was still around because he was collecting souls to return to the Death dimension. But he was doing it very slowly, and in the meantime, Josh had every intention of taking advantage of his intellect. In addition to the Dream-universe protections they were working on, he was also heading the real-World search for Peregrine—making flyers for Whim and Deloise to hang, putting notices in local newspapers, monitoring the e-mail tip line. He'd even gotten Peregrine's story featured on the *Unsolved Mysteries* website.

"A woman in California wrote to tell me that she believes Peregrine is working for a small circus as a trapeze artist."

"A one-armed trapeze artist?" Josh asked with a grin.

"Apparently. She referred to him as a 'carny,' which I gather is derogatory." Feodor glanced up from his book at Josh, then frowned. "What is this outfit you've assembled? I find it . . . disconcerting."

With no clean laundry, Josh had borrowed one of Deloise's tops: a pale lavender T-shirt with a heart outlined in lace. But Deloise was taller than Josh, so the shirt was too big, and she'd had to pair it with green running shorts. She knew she looked ridiculous, she just didn't care. She had more important things to spend energy on these days.

"This coming from the man who owns twelve copies of a single outfit," Josh told Feodor. "Any other tips?"

"Perhaps brushing your hair—"

"I meant the tip line."

"Oh," Feodor said, although Josh had no doubt he'd understood her perfectly. "I also received a report that Peregrine is living in a trailer in North Carolina, cooking and selling methamphetamine."

"That seems likely," Josh said.

"The forensic accountant you hired says there is evidence that Peregrine was diverting funds to an offshore account, but that she was unable to determine the destination."

"This is getting us nowhere," Josh said, and tossed herself into the other armchair, deflated. "You realize we screwed ourselves by preventing him from entering the Dream, right? If he were still able to dream, we might have been able to convince Will to use his crazy looking-glass skills to find Peregrine's soul in the Dream, which might have given us *something*. Instead, we're spinning our wheels and wasting time building . . ." She didn't know the word in Polish and had to settle for "*gizmos* that don't even work."

"Gizmos?" asked Feodor, who apparently didn't know the word in English.

"Small, crappy devices that say they'll do something awesome but usually break the second time you use them."

"Did the VHAG break?" Feodor asked with concern.

"No, it just didn't work. I don't know what we're doing wrong. It *should* work."

"Perhaps the sequence needs to be adjusted . . ."

"We've adjusted the sequence two dozen times." Josh shook her head, staring up at the ceiling. "What does it matter, anyway? The VHAG won't help us find Peregrine or help me access my abilities."

"Actually," Feodor said, rising, "I have found something interesting as relates to your abilities."

He fetched a worn hardback book covered in brown fabric. The title had been rubbed away, leaving only a smattering of gold dust on the cover, and the marbled endpaper in the front had torn, leaving the binding exposed.

Feodor turned to the title page. *Ptolemaic Prophesy*. The publisher listed was Dashiel Winters Press, which published nothing but limited editions written by dream walkers for dream walkers.

"Where did you get this?" Josh asked.

"EBay!" Feodor gave Josh a rare smile, one that was neither condescending nor mocking. "Truly, I am not surprised that the Internet began as an academic file sharing system. It has facilitated the exchange of information on a level that not even Gutenberg could have imagined."

"I wonder how this ended up online," Josh mused, turning a few pages.

Her eyes landed on a chapter titled "The Hilathic Dream Walker Prophesies."

"I was not previously aware of this volume," Feodor said. "I believe this may be the only extant copy. It contains a version of the primary dream-walker prophesies that conflicts with the better-known translations. I've written them out for comparison."

He pointed to his chalkboard; he thought dry-erase was a chemical abomination. Josh read the first translation, the one she had grown up hearing.

> In the age of excess, before expected,
> the True Dream Walker will arrive,
> whose every thought will be reflected.
> The Dream to please him will contrive.
> He'll strike down the unbelievers,
> return the Dream to its pure state
> put the archways to the cleaver
> and sentence us to rightful fates.

"It's Pellok's translation," Josh said. "1873."

"Yes. Unfortunately, Pellok's translation was based on Merwin's from 1515. Merwin was not only a seer, but a Catholic priest, and his translations were unduly influenced by his religious views. He insisted upon believing that the return of the True Dream Walker and the Second Coming of Jesus Christ were the same event. He was also overly concerned with making the prophesy rhyme. Every modern translation I have found is based on Merwin's work, Pellok's included—except for this one." He held up the book, then pointed to a second set of lines on the chalkboard.

> In the age of imbalance, unexpectedly
> the summoned Dream Walker will come into being
> who can control the Dream
> by opening Heaven.
> He whose heart is enveloped in flame
> He whose heart beats in time with the dreamer's
> He whose heart tears down separations.

He will be struck down
as the universes return to their original state.
The boundaries will be put to ruin.
The World will end in light.

A chill went through Josh as she read. "I'm going to be struck down?"

"Perhaps all life will be struck down, if the Dream returns to its original state. If you strip the Judeo-Christian nonsense from Pellok's version, the two translations are not so far apart. But the section that interests me is the three lines that discuss the Dream Walker's arrival."

"The section where I *die* doesn't interest you?" Josh asked, forgetting for a moment that he wasn't one of her friends, that he didn't care if she died or not.

Was it weird that she wanted him to care?

"You assume too much," Feodor said calmly. "'Struck down' does not necessarily mean you will die. You may merely be knocked unconscious or gravely injured."

"Skippy," Josh said in English.

"Skippy?"

"It means you've laid all my fears to rest," she told him.

Feodor smiled smugly; he had a keen ear for sarcasm.

"What do the lines about his heart mean?" she asked.

He whose heart is enveloped in flame
He whose heart beats in time with the dreamer's
He whose heart tears down separations.

"My suspicion is that it refers to breaking Stellanor's First Rule."

That made a sort of sense, Josh supposed. She had felt very close to the dreamers whose fear she had shared.

"Do you find it at all weird that these prophesies refer to a man?" she asked.

"No. Recall, Merwin believed he was writing about Christ."

"I guess he found it unthinkable that Jesus could come back as a woman," Josh said, remembering how Will had once told her that everybody in old writing is "he."

Maybe Merwin got confused in his vision when everybody called me Josh, she thought, and the idea actually made her smile.

Leaning against the edge of the table, Feodor said, "Tell me what you know about your birth."

"Nothing. I mean, everything was normal."

"And you are certain that your parents are your biological parents?"

Josh kind of wanted to hit him. "I'm completely sure."

"Hmm. May I read your mother's diary?"

"She didn't keep a diary, just a log where she tracked how many nightmares she resolved."

"And your father's?"

"My dad isn't going to let you read his diary."

"Perhaps you could . . . borrow it."

Josh ignored his suggestion. "I don't know what it is you think you're going to find. We should be figuring out how to keep me alive."

"Look at the descriptions in these prophesies. They contain one common theme—something happens that precipitates your appearance. You are summoned, or you arrive. Nowhere does it say you are *born*. Nowhere does it say you live and then are discovered. Both of these prophesies contain the suggestion that something happened to cause you to be here."

He wasn't wrong, Josh could admit—at least to herself.

"Maybe it's your fault," she said.

Feodor blinked. "Pardon?"

"You tried to destabilize the Dream so that the True Dream Walker would show up and save the World. Maybe you succeeded."

He laughed a little then. "You flatter me."

"Really? That was literally your plan, wasn't it?"

"At the time, yes. However, I no longer believe I would have succeeded in accomplishing anything besides the collapse of the three universes."

"You don't think the True Dream Walker would have appeared to save us?"

"Of course not."

"Of course not?" Josh repeated. "You've done kind of a one-eighty on that, haven't you?"

"A one-eighty?"

"You've completely reversed your opinion."

"Ah. Yes, I have."

The topic didn't seem to interest him, but it interested Josh. "What changed your mind?"

"It was not so much a change of mind as . . . a change of brain. It is my suspicion that, when the Lords of Death returned me, my reconstituted body was created in a state of perfect neurological health."

"Wait, you're admitting that you were mentally ill?"

He shrugged. "In the parlance of the modern age."

He obviously didn't want to admit he'd been psychotic when he tried to destroy the Veil. Josh supposed it was a matter of pride. Either that, or he was trying to convince her that he was sane now so that he could plot to do terrible things without her suspecting him.

That was the closest Feodor had ever come to admitting he had been ill during his first life. It was the closest he had even come to apologizing for what he had done.

Josh wished she could trust him. Unfortunately, being mentally ill and morally bankrupt weren't the same thing; he could be one and not the other.

Seven

"Hey, Whim, do you know a dream walker named Aurek? Like the vacuum cleaner, but not spelled the same?"

Will was sitting in the living room with the usual suspects: Deloise, who was doing Winsor's nails; Winsor, who had made Whim put a five-pound bag of flour on the back of her hand to keep it from trembling; and Whim, who was messing with his phone.

The only one missing is Haley, Will thought. Strange how much he could miss the presence of someone who had only ever hovered at the outskirts of such scenes.

"Aurek Trembuline?" Whim asked, with raised eyebrows.

"Yeah, that's it. Who is he?"

Whim shook his head ruefully. "He's like a hippie dream walker. Only he's also totally amoral. He used to be a minor dream theorist, now he writes pseudophilosophy. Everyone thinks he's a joke."

"Why would he be interested in Snitch?"

"Probably because he thinks Feodor is some kind of rebel folk hero. Trembuline was pretty popular until he wrote a book about how what Feodor did at Maplefax was an example of courage that all humans should follow."

"He thought that causing a huge tear in the Veil and destroying an entire town was courageous?" Deloise asked.

"Yeah."

"Our Feodor?" Winsor asked, who was used to seeing Feodor come around with Josh.

"He's not ours," Whim told her. "But it's the same guy."

"He destroyed a town?"

How bizarre that Winsor just thinks of Feodor as a friend of Josh's, maybe even as a friend of her own, Will thought. *She missed so much.*

While Deloise explained—briefly and without detail—how Feodor had destroyed a town long before they knew him, Will said to Whim, "You think Aurek would talk to us?"

"I'm sure he'd talk to *you*. But what would be the point?"

Will heard the back door open and close in the kitchen, and he was surprised to see Josh cross into the hallway without Feodor in tow. They trained together almost every day now, and Feodor's constant presence had been acting as a sort of exposure therapy to help Will get over his fear of the man.

"Hey, Josh!" Whim called as Josh passed the doorway. "Come say hi!"

Josh entered the room in a cloud of upset. She walked into the back of Deloise's chair before even noticing that her sister was in the room. The nail polish brush in Deloise's hand hit the bag of flour and left a dark pink streak across the paper.

"Shit, sorry," Josh said.

"This is my friend Josh," Whim said to no one in particular. "She's beautiful, she's brilliant, and she's blind."

"You aren't funny," Deloise told him.

"Sometimes I am." He held out a can of Pringles to Josh. "I apologize, friend. Please, break potatoes with us."

Distracted, Josh took the can, peered into it, and then handed it back as if she didn't know why she'd taken it in the first place. "What do you want?"

Deloise shook her head. *She's like one of those children raised by wild dogs,* Will thought.

"How's it going?" he asked.

Josh squinted at him. "What?"

"How are you?" Whim clarified. "How are your endeavors progressing? How are your affairs?"

"What he said," Will added.

He smiled at her.

Josh swallowed twice and then said, "Stop smiling. Don't smile at me anymore."

Winsor glanced up from her nails. Deloise's brush hovered in midair.

"I don't want to do this anymore," Josh said, "this weird, friendly, let's-play-nice thing. I hate it."

There was a long silence, and then Deloise said, "You know, there's better light in the kitchen. Let's go in there."

"I think I fancy a pedicure," Whim said.

"But I want to watch them fight," Winsor protested as Del wheeled her toward the kitchen.

In a matter of seconds, Josh and Will were alone in the living room.

Will didn't know what to say. He could tell from the rough way Josh was breathing that she was upset, and not just with him. She'd been upset when she walked in, and he didn't know if it was his place to work that through with her or not.

For once, she didn't make him dig.

"I don't want you to smile at me anymore," she said. "I've had enough of you punishing me."

"Punishing you?" Will repeated, getting up from the couch.

"Or whatever therapy thing you want to call it. I get it already: it's over, you're glad, you don't want me back. You can stop rubbing it in."

Will had never met anyone so good at misinterpreting other people.

"I'm sorry," he said. "I'm genuinely not trying to punish you. I was trying to make things easier between us."

"By shoving it in my face how great your life is without me?"

She wasn't just upset—she was actually angry at him. Will fought the urge to feel offended and angry himself.

"I just thought that, if I was kind of casual about everything, it would be easier for us to live in the same house," he told her. "I didn't mean to hurt your feelings, and I didn't mean to make you think that us breaking up meant nothing to me."

Josh had her arms crossed over her chest, but her eyes darted up for an instant to meet his. A little voice in Will's head was saying, *Careful, careful. Be careful with her.*

He told himself not to touch her, but his hands were just moving, unstoppable as waves. "I know this sucks," he said, resting his hands lightly on her upper arms. "It sucks for me, too."

She gritted her jaw—out of anger or against trembling, he didn't know which.

"Then what are we doing?" she whispered. "If you don't hate me, what are we *doing*?"

He didn't want to tell her that there was a difference between loving someone and being healthy for them. Besides, she wouldn't care. If she'd fallen in love with an atomic bomb, she would have held on until it obliterated her. That was just the kind of person she was.

She's not going to get over me, Will realized. *She never really got over Ian. She won't get over me.*

His heart beat hard, just once, at the thought that she felt that kind of loyalty toward him, and he remembered a promise he'd made to her once, to do what he could to lessen her pain. *I would do anything, if you'd only tell me what to do.*

He hugged her. There was nothing else to do. She kept her arms stalwartly crossed, let them dig into his chest like the edge of a fence, but after a moment, she hid her face in his shoulder and leaned into him. "I don't hate you," Will told her. "I've never hated you, not for a minute."

"Then what are we doing?" she repeated, her breath a warm misery against his skin.

He could have said so many things. *We're doing the best we can. We're taking care of ourselves. We're waiting to see if I can learn to be brave.*

That's the truth, isn't it? he thought. *Josh has no fears and no doubts. I'm the one who's still afraid.*

He couldn't say that, but he should have said something, because in a moment she was pulling away, shaking her head, and walking out of the living room without looking back.

Will rubbed his neck. *I know this sucks,* he thought again. *Believe me, I know.*

He was suddenly glad that he had a session with Malina the

next day. Maybe she'd be able to help him sort out what had just happened.

Will wandered into the kitchen and dropped into a chair beside Deloise.

"I take it that didn't go well," Whim said, not looking up from his phone.

"Apparently by trying to be nice to Josh, I've given her the impression that she never meant anything to me."

"Duh," Winsor said.

Will lifted his eyebrows.

"Ian self-destructed when they broke up. That's how she knew he cared."

Deloise capped the nail polish bottle. "That's very insightful, Winsor."

Winsor shrugged. "I had a front-row seat."

"Yeah, well, I'm not going to self-destruct to make Josh feel better," Will said. "If she wants to fault me for being nice to her, that's her problem." He rocked onto the back legs of his chair, the scene replaying in his mind, wishing he felt as easy with the decision as he pretended. "I am kind of blown away that she flat-out told me what was wrong, though. Josh used to hate confrontation."

"Maybe she's maturing," Deloise said.

"Maybe she has no idea what she wants," Whim countered. "Now, I, on the other hand, know exactly what and *whom* I want. I am currently trudging a path of self-improvement in order to make myself the man said *whom* needs and wants me to be—"

"Stuff it, Whim," Deloise said. "We aren't getting back together."

"Of course we are."

"I don't get back together with guys who cheat on me."

"Ah, but you see, that's why I'm reading *Fidelity: Teaching a Stray to Stay*. Will recommended it to me."

"Seriously?" Deloise asked Will.

"I thought it might give him some insight."

"And has it?" she asked Whim.

"Not really. It says that men who cheat are selfish, entitled man-children, which I'm quite certain doesn't apply to me."

"So much for insight," Winsor muttered.

"Speaking of man-children," her brother said, "what is the deal with this guy Sam who keeps trying to talk to you?"

Winsor was having a good day, as far as Will could tell, but not so good a day that she was able to hide her emotions. She shifted uncomfortably in her wheelchair, as if trying to escape its confines. After an ominously long pause, she said, "I don't know him."

"Winny, get real. A guy doesn't scream your name like Stanley Kowalski because he doesn't know you," Whim said.

Winsor wouldn't look at him.

"Whim," Deloise said.

"You can't seriously expect us to believe that you don't know him—"

"*Whim*," Deloise repeated. "Leave her alone. She'll talk about it when she wants to."

Whim snorted and got up from the table. "Girls," he muttered as his long legs carried him out of the kitchen. "Come on, Will. Let's go chew tobacco and talk trash about skirts."

Will made no motion to follow him. Deloise held up the nail polish bottle and pretended to hurl it at Whim.

"Was he upset?" Winsor asked.

"I don't think Whim ever really gets upset," Deloise said. "He just fakes it to manipulate us."

"I think she meant Sam," Will said. When Winsor didn't confirm or deny, Will said gently, "Yeah, he was upset. He was pretty desperate to talk to you."

Pain flickered across Winsor's face. "My head hurts. Del, could you . . ."

"Yeah, of course."

Deloise went down the hall to get Winsor's headache medicine, but she'd hardly left the room before Winsor was whispering to Will.

"Do you know? Does everyone know?"

He had to guess at her meaning. "Just me and Del."

Winsor nodded and released a shaky breath. "It's so strange . . . It can't be real."

Will chose his words carefully. "Do you know Sam from the canister?"

"I don't know how I know him."

"That's okay," he told her. "I mean, I know it's probably bizarre and confusing, but . . . your souls were hanging out together for months in there. It makes total sense that you feel like you know each other."

"No, you don't—" She rubbed her head then, and if she hadn't had a headache before, Will suspected she did now. "We were . . ."

When she didn't continue, Will put his hand over hers. "It's okay," he repeated. "Whatever happened is okay."

She didn't open her eyes. "No, it's not. It's really not." She blinked then. "Who are you to tell me it's okay? You don't know—"

Her voice had risen, and she began trying to push her wheelchair back from the table, but she just kept knocking into the trash can.

"What's wrong?" Deloise asked, returning with a pill bottle.

"I'm sorry, Winsor," Will said. "I didn't mean to upset you."

"You don't understand!" she shouted at him. "You weren't there! I shouldn't even be in this house, I don't live here anymore, I moved out!"

She began to shake violently then. "Winsor, calm down," Deloise said. "Take a deep breath—"

"It's not safe here!" Winsor yelled at her. "It's not—I can't— I have to . . ."

She grabbed her head with both hands, still shaking, her face flushed.

"Winny?" Whim asked, rushing back in the room.

"Whim," she cried, and held out her arms. Whim picked her up—she hardly weighed anything anymore—and sat down on a chair with Winsor in his lap.

"I don't want to talk about him anymore," she said, sobbing against her brother's neck.

"You don't have to talk about him ever again," Whim promised her. "Never again, all right?"

Over her shoulder, Whim lifted his eyebrows at Will, who shrugged helplessly. Whim raised his hand, as if to say, *I've got her*.

Deloise set Winsor's pills on the table, and she and Will walked into the hallway. He was almost to the stairs when he heard Winsor say, "I was already there for a thousand years."

Eight

Music throbbed in the darkened club. The dance floor was an inky black pond below. Josh couldn't see where it ended, saw no bar, no tables, just an endless sea of bodies. The ceiling was so high above them that the violet lights strung across it looked like purple constellations. The air smelled like amber incense and jasmine.

She had no idea who the dreamer might be. It could have been anyone. The lights were so low she couldn't even make out the faces of the people a few feet away. She and Feodor had jumped into this nightmare together, and she couldn't see any more of his face than the distasteful scowl on his lips.

A man—she thought he was a man—put his hands on her hips, trying to get her to dance, and Josh shoved him away. He said something; Josh couldn't tell if it was an apology or an accusation.

Josh closed her eyes and imagined the stone walls that protected her mind. When she removed the cork from the wall, though, a strain of music came through instead of a wisp of smoke. She heard the slow pound of drums, a synthesized throb, and a woman's voice—delicate, wispy.

Despair. What's the point in trying? It's easier to just dance.

Josh realized she was moving in time to the music. The beat seemed to have snuck into her bones.

"Focus," Feodor said sharply.

She imagined her walls again, but this time the music poured through them, wearing at the mortar and stone like a fast-moving current.

The music filled her with a seductive, irresistible sadness. The pain was inevitable, and so exquisite. There was a bittersweet pleasure in feeling so miserable.

She tore herself away from the feeling and opened her eyes. "It's too intense," she said. "I'll get lost."

"You're afraid," Feodor said, and he sounded so irritated that Josh wanted to prove herself to him.

"I'm not afraid. I'm being careful."

"Overly so. We have wasted weeks being careful."

Confused, Josh closed her eyes again. She imagined her walls, but they were half-crumbled, and the music swam around her on a current of air—no, a blast of air, a wind of ennui that swept her away.

You have to follow it, she told herself.

Eyes still closed, she let herself dance. She had never felt so in control of her body, of each tiny muscle in her neck as she rolled her head back and forth on her shoulders, of every vertebra bending and twisting, of the subtle rocking of her hips. Someone touched her; she didn't mind. She was uncatchable.

Indulgence. That was the word. Forget trying to be strong. Forget trying to prove herself—to Will, to Feodor, to her mother.

The dreamer came to her as if she had called, a man with thick black hair and eyes like dark moons. He put his hands on her hips, and she didn't have the strength to push him away, to refuse the meager comfort of being touched. For the first time, she realized that all those years of training had taught her to move her body in ways that could be sexy.

The nightmare, she thought distantly, through the cloud of music. *This is still a nightmare . . .*

Beneath the music, she heard the muffled sound of stone walls crumbling.

The hand on her throat had been replaced by a pair of lips. Josh had never felt so beautiful, so desperately sad. She wanted to throw everything to the wind, quit trying, sink into this paradise of unhappiness.

I just wish someone else understood, she thought.

The music understood. The dreamer with his hands around her waist and his mouth on her skin understood. The darkness understood.

Josh knew she had forgotten something. But she didn't care. All she could remember was the way Will had hugged her in the living room, and how hard it had been not to hug him back, not to give in to the comfort he had offered. Was it so wrong that she was tired of being the strong one?

I can't go on pretending I don't miss him.

She began crying. The tears rolled freely down her face, joining in the dance of heartbreak the rest of her body was acting out. She felt no shame, no fear at expressing herself so freely. Just the opposite; for the first time in her life, she held nothing back.

Her feet grew warm. She assumed the warmth was caused by the friction of her dancing feet, but it climbed up her ankles and then started up her shins. That's when she heard a sloshing sound.

The club was completely dark by then, so Josh saw nothing when she looked down. But she could feel the water creeping up her legs, and dancers around them began to push and shove toward exits. When the music shut off, it was replaced by shouting.

This, too, seemed fitting and right—to die in the dark, to literally drown in her misery. She and the dreamer wrapped their arms around each other and waited for the pain to end. They were resigned . . .

Except for one thing.

She wanted Deloise to get her lighter after she died.

Ian had given her that lighter, a rose-gold Zippo, with the words TO J.D., LOVE ALWAYS, IAN. She'd carried it through Feodor's universe, through the Hidden Kingdom, through a thousand nightmares.

I'm just going to toss it into the archroom and then I'll come back here and die, she told herself, and she threw open an archway to the basement with a flick of her hand.

The sight of the bright white room startled her.

Wait a sec . . . What the hell am I doing?

She'd been dancing, and thinking about how beautiful sadness could be, and how she wanted to die—

Die? she thought. *I don't want to die.*

She'd gotten caught up in the dreamer's fear. Now she was clutching him as the warm water sloshed around her knees, and people were screaming as they fought each other to reach exits Josh wasn't even certain existed. She'd completely lost Feodor.

"It's too late," the dreamer told her.

Josh let the archway to the basement close and then tightened her arms around the dreamer's neck. She hadn't gone this far to fail at connecting with this nightmare. Trying to hold on to her sense of self, she imagined inhaling the dreamer's fear.

I want to die. And no one's going to stop me from killing myself.

To the dreamer, his death felt inevitable, even though he wasn't completely convinced he wanted to die. Deep inside, he wanted someone to stop him. He just didn't think anyone would.

But we're surrounded by people, Josh thought, and suddenly she saw how the nightmare would play out.

The club would empty. The water would rise. The dreamer would call out for help, but it would be too late, and he'd slowly drown, the back of his head knocking against the club's ceiling.

"You have to ask for help," Josh told him.

"Everyone's tired of helping me. I'm always the needy one."

"That's not true. But you have to ask them now, before it's too late!" She squeezed his shoulders, hopefully hard enough to hurt him. "Ask now!"

The water had reached the tops of Josh's legs.

"Um, help?" the dreamer said, so softly that no one but Josh heard him.

"Louder!" she told him.

"Help!" he called.

"Louder! Tell them what you need!"

The dreamer's shouts were edged with hysteria. "I need help! Somebody help me! I gotta get out of here!"

Someone nearby called back, "Over here! Grab my hand."

A doorway of light began to grow, not too far away, and Josh saw a line of people holding hands and working their way outside. The last person in the line grabbed the dreamer's hand and pulled him after them, and he grabbed Josh's hand. Together, they sloshed through the growing water. By the time they reached the doorway, Josh was swimming, her feet not even touching the floor.

The water didn't pass through the doorway, but hung there, as if against an invisible barrier. Josh stumbled out into a parking lot lit with streetlamps and the flashers of police cars. Fifty or more people wearing soaking wet club clothes were lingering around, watching the doorway—including Feodor, who wore a pleased smile.

"That's all of them!" a nearby cop cried, and everyone began to cheer. "We did it!"

A firefighter rushed forward to wrap Josh and the dreamer in big gray blankets.

"Listen to me," Josh said to the dreamer. "You have to remember this dream, okay? You have to remember to ask for help."

"This is a dream?"

"Yes, and you're going to remember it when you wake—"

The nightmare resolved in an explosion of gratitude and relief. Not for the first time, Josh splashed onto the archroom floor.

"Brava!" Feodor cried, before they'd even gotten up. "A masterful performance!"

"Masterful?" Josh repeated as she climbed to her feet. "I could have died!"

Judging by the fact that Feodor's clothing was only wet up to his belt line, Josh was certain he'd left the nightclub while she was still contemplating killing herself.

Feodor shrugged. "What is reward without risk?"

"I completely lost myself in that nightmare, and you let me!" Josh insisted. "What kind of shitty partner are you?"

She realized how ridiculous the question was as the white walls of the archroom bounced the words back into her ears. Feodor wasn't her partner, and he never would be. He wasn't even her friend.

He made no reply, but his lips curled with disgust, as if the idea of being her partner, of some loyalty between them, was repulsive to him. All the niceties of his manners were gone, as though his mask of politeness had slipped, had been shaken off by her words, and she was looking at his true face.

The moment stretched uncomfortably between them until Josh said, "What I meant was, it's your job to make sure I don't lose myself in a dreamer's fear."

"I was working on a theory," he said, and then he was recognizable again, his expression of detached intellectual interest firmly back in place. "What if losing yourself in the nightmare is the only way to merge with the Dream?"

"That's crazy."

Feodor smiled, gleefully almost. "Nevertheless, it worked, no?"

Josh didn't have a response to that, and Feodor gloated all the way home.

Later, though, she wondered if he was right. What if she needed to be so in touch with a nightmare that she *had* to lose herself to the dreamer's fear? Was it really crazy, or was it the best way to help? If she had let herself get completely lost in the nightmare about Tlazolteotl, would she have been able to help that dreamer let go of her innocence?

Or had it just felt that good to grieve over Will?

She'd let herself mourn for exactly one night, sobbing in Deloise's arms and waking up the next morning with a stuffy head and sore eyes. While still sitting in Deloise's bed, she'd written out a list on her sister's lilac stationery:

Restore Winsor's soul.
Return souls/Save Haley.
Send Feodor back.
Find Peregrine.
Become the True Dream Walker.

Those were her priorities, in order. Ten weeks later, and she'd only crossed off one item. Granted, it was a pretty big one, but she'd thought after her early success that the others would come more quickly.

Those were the things she worked on, thought about, obsessed over, to keep from feeling Will's loss. And that had been a good plan, until tonight, until the heartbreak nightmare had brought all the heartache back.

Suddenly, she wanted quite desperately to talk to Will. Not even to beg him to take her back, just to tell him how hurt she was and how much she missed him and how alone she felt. He would understand, he would let her talk, he knew how to listen.

But she sensed that if she let herself pour her heart out to him, she'd walk away feeling his loss more than ever. She'd done such a good job of not moping over him, of focusing on the work. She didn't want to get sucked into sadness now.

So she turned the lamp on, and got dressed, and went out.

Nine

As with so many other doors, Josh's name unlocked Aurek Trembuline's with ease. As soon as Will mentioned her, Trembuline was delighted to set up an interview.

Will read a lot of Trembuline's writing before the meeting, and he tried to explain the man's philosophy to Whim as they drove toward Trembuline's office.

"Trembuline's big theory is that everyone should be following their hearts. He believes that each dream walker has an innate sense of purpose, and that nothing—no limitations, no government intervention, no moral qualms—should stop them from fulfilling their vision for their lives."

"Okay, we should all follow our dreams," Whim said.

"Yeah. Except, if your heart tells you to go murder a bunch of people, he thinks you should do it. That's why he called what Feodor did at Maplefax 'courageous.' He thinks Feodor was following his heart."

"I think Feodor was following the voices in his head."

"I agree. Trembuline's theory doesn't make any sense to me, especially not the part where he says that if we all follow our instincts, no matter how extreme, the three universes will naturally fall into balance."

"What? Just . . . why? Why would he think that?"

"I don't know. I'm hoping that if I ask him, it will open up some conversation."

Trembuline had an office; Will wasn't exactly sure why. The plate on the door read AUREK TREMBULINE, NATURAL PHILOSOPHER. He knocked.

The man who answered the door was not at all what Will had expected—no glasses, no sweater with elbow patches, no pipe. In fact, he looked nothing like an academic. He wore jeans and a faded

T-shirt for a band called Gangster Fun. He was balding, but wore the hair he had left in a long ponytail, and he was barefoot.

"Come in, come in," he said, smiling.

The walls of Trembuline's office were covered with framed photographs of smiling children. They varied in age and race, but Trembuline was at the center of every picture, his arms wrapped around the kids.

A leather sofa sat against one wall, a writing desk beside it, and on the other side of the room was a small wooden altar with a round meditation cushion in front of it. A goddess Will couldn't identify sat on the altar.

"Wow," Whim said, looking at the pictures. "Do you do some kind of charity work with kids?"

"Oh, no," Trembuline said as he plunked down in a papasan chair. "They're mine."

Whim did a double take. "All of them?"

"Yup. All twenty-two."

"You have *twenty-two* children?" Will repeated.

"I know, it's a lot. Eight different mothers. I guess I'm just afraid of being alone in my old age." Trembuline laughed.

Well, Will thought, *that's a whole new kind of crazy.*

"Don't worry," Trembuline said, "you don't have to pretend you find it normal. I'm not really into pretense. I'd rather you were just honest."

"Well, that's a relief," Whim said. "'Cause I can't even think of anything polite to say."

Trembuline grinned and opened a minifridge. "You guys like energy drinks?"

"Sure," Whim said. He and Will each accepted a can of something called Napalm Gorilla+Squirrel.

Trembuline cracked his open and chugged it. After a shrug, Whim did the same. Will took a swig—it tasted like Mountain Dew and gasoline—and then set the can down.

Afterward, Trembuline burped loudly and said, "What can I do for you gentlemen?"

Will was so scattered by the bizarre display that it took him a moment to find the words. "Well, like I said in my e-mail, I'm pretty new to dream walking—"

"Yeah, you're Josh Weaver's apprentice." Trembuline raised his hand. "Up top, man. That's quite a score."

Will, feeling decidedly uncomfortable, high-fived the man.

"What's she like?" Trembuline asked, wiggling his eyebrows.

"Um, she's great," Will said. "She's . . . an encyclopedia of dream-walking knowledge."

"I'm sure she is. I bet it's no chore sticking your nose in that book."

What the hell are we talking about here? Will wondered.

He cleared his throat. "So, I was just reading some of your articles, and I—"

"Which ones?"

"Oh, uh, 'Personal Dream Walker Ethics,' and 'The Agreement Framework.'"

"Huh. *The Daily Walker* called 'The Agreement Framework' a theory of Communist karmic bullshit."

"I thought it was okay," Will said weakly.

"They hate me over at the *Walker*."

Trembuline's pupils were huge, Will noticed. *This guy's high as a kite,* he realized, *and not just on energy drinks.*

Trying one more time, he said, "I'm curious about—"

"You know what? Instead of talking about it, let's do it! Right? Let's really get in up to our elbows. I've got some more zafus over here."

The next thing Will knew, Trembuline was pulling out circular meditation cushions, and they were all sitting on the floor in front of the altar. While Trembuline looked for his lighter, Whim leaned over to Will and whispered, "Dude, my heart's beating like three hundred times a minute."

This is going nowhere, Will thought.

Trembuline lit a small lamp with a piece of purple cloth thrown over the shade—Will was pretty sure that was a fire hazard—and turned off the overhead lights, then set fire to a stick of vanilla musk incense.

"Let's rock out," he said, taking a seat on his zafu. "This is what it's all about, boys. *The experience.* Rub your hands together. Fast! Faster!"

Will rubbed his palms together until he thought they would ignite.

"Hold your hands up."

Will followed Trembuline's lead and held his palms about two inches apart.

"Move your hands closer together. Now apart again. Now a little closer. What do you feel?"

"I feel it!" Whim said. "It's like . . . like a resistance."

Will hadn't noticed, but now that Whim pointed it out, he did feel something when he moved his hands together. Almost like something between them was bouncing them back.

"You've got it, buddy! Close your eyes."

Reluctantly, Will closed his eyes.

"Now, imagine something you love. Like, really love. Like, a lot. Imagine it right between your hands, and feel how much you love it."

Will tried to imagine Josh, but he had too many conflicting emotions. It felt simpler to imagine Kerstel instead, how comforting it was to go home knowing she would be there; that no matter how good the book, she'd put it down if he needed to talk; the way he could count on her to notice if he was upset.

"Open your eyes."

Will opened his eyes. His hands were a foot apart.

"Whoa," he said.

"Holy crap," Whim said. His hands, too, had moved farther apart.

"See how the energy grows when you tap into love?"

Will wouldn't have believed it if he hadn't experienced it for himself. When he pressed his hands in closer, he felt the same resistance as before, only more intense now, as if whatever hung between his palms had grown denser, thicker.

"Close your eyes again," Trembuline said. His voice was less animated than before, drowsy, hypnotic. "Take that ball of energy between your hands, that ball of love, and pull it into your own heart."

It's just the power of suggestion, Will thought, even as he felt a warmth he couldn't explain suffuse his chest. He realized he was smiling and he didn't know why. He just felt happy.

"Think of a question. Any question. Even the hardest question in your whole life, the one you're afraid to ask."

The question wasn't hard for Will to find.

Can Josh and I ever be together?

"Feel all the good energy in your heart. Stop listening to your thoughts. You don't have to stop thinking, just stop paying so much *attention* to your thoughts. Just wait. Make a space for your heart to give you the answer."

Will had always known he thought too much, got too wrapped up in his head. He felt relieved that he didn't have to stop thinking—he doubted he'd pull that off. But it felt nice to detach from the thoughts and just watch them pass by like boats on a river.

He let out a deep breath. That, too, felt good.

Suddenly he saw Josh in his mind. Not the way she'd looked lately, distracted and disheveled, but the way she'd looked after their first encounter with Feodor, during those weeks of recovery when they had done nothing but hang out in the living room, watching movies and talking, both too loaded with pain meds to have nightmares or foreign memories. He'd never seen her look so light, before or since.

And then he knew the answer.

Keeping her at arm's length won't keep you safe. It won't make you happy, either.

He felt a rush of relief at admitting a truth he'd already known.

But how do I start trusting her again? he asked.

The only way to learn to trust her is to trust her.

The answer was so obvious. There was no way around jumping back into the pool.

But it isn't trusting Josh that's holding you back. You don't trust yourself.

I don't? Will thought, stunned.

You don't trust yourself to make the right choices.

Yeah, well, I've made almost as many bad choices as Josh. I didn't tell her when I saw her dreaming about Feodor, I did Veil dust and drank, I got us all caught by Bash and nearly killed.

And you learned from all of it, his heart said.

"Dude," Whim burst out beside him, "I don't think I deserve Deloise. I'm not good enough for her. I think I blew things up between us so she wouldn't figure that out!"

Will opened his eyes and saw Trembuline nodding like he knew what Whim was talking about. "Yeah, man. Totally."

"I'm such a jackass," Whim marveled. "Maybe I'm not mature enough yet to be with a girl like her."

"I want to have another baby," Trembuline said, still nodding. He took Will's abandoned energy drink and chugged it. "I'm gonna get Ginger pregnant with, like, quadruplets."

The idea of Trembuline having more babies snapped Will out of his pleasant, hazy revelation. "Yeah," he said uneasily, "maybe think on that some more."

But Trembuline and Whim were still nodding at each other. "This was amazing," Whim said. "I'm gonna read all your books. I think you're onto something."

"Awesome. Whatever I can do, buddy. Anytime."

Then they were standing up and doing some kind of complicated handshake that they must have worked out telepathically beforehand, and Will was saying desperately, "Wait, wait."

"Gotta go, friend. Gotta get my kids from day care."

Do you have a tour bus? Will wondered. Aloud, he said, "There's just one question I have to ask."

Trembuline shrugged acceptance, even as he nudged them toward the door.

"Did Peregrine Borgenicht ask you to interview Geoff Simbar?"

Suddenly Trembuline appeared a lot less high and a lot less friendly.

"That's a weird question," he said. "You said you were here to talk about my work."

"We did talk about your work. Now I want to talk about Geoff."

Trembuline shook his head, and this time his nudge toward the door felt more like a bulldozing.

"At least tell me this," Will begged. "What did you and Geoff talk about?"

Trembuline smiled. "Oh, you know . . . *life*."

Then he shut his office door in Will's face.

Whim was standing with his mouth hanging open, his eyes wide. In the hollow of his throat, Will could see his hummingbird pulse flicking beneath his skin.

"Let's go," Will said.

Whim couldn't shut up the whole drive home. "That was mind-blowing. I totally understand why I screwed things up with Deloise now. My debonair charm, my glittering wit—it's all just to make up for my own deep-seated feelings of inadequacy. I cheated on Del so she would break up with me before she found out how pathetic I am underneath my unfathomable exterior. That guy is a genius."

"That guy," Will said, "thinks Feodor is a genius. And he's probably in league with Peregrine."

"No way. He's just interested in altered states of consciousness. He's got, like, *wisdom*. I mean, who would have guessed that my being a terrible boyfriend was actually the result of being such a sensitive, complex person?"

"Oh, brother," Will said.

"Didn't you get anything out of it?"

"Yeah," Will admitted. "I did." He realized he was smiling again.

"Haaaa!" Whim said, pointing a finger at him. "You thought it was amazing, too!"

"Watch the road." Will put a steadying hand on the wheel. He felt himself blushing.

"You're gonna get back with Josh, aren't you?"

"Yeah, probably," Will admitted, and Whim let out a *whoop!*

"See? The guy *is* a genius!"

"No, that's what I'm trying to tell you. You and I got real insight from whatever it was we did back there, but what if my instinct told me that the best way to get over Josh was to strangle her in her sleep? Trembuline would say that's what I should do."

"But see, I don't think your heart would ever tell you to do that. How can filling your heart with a big ball of love energy lead to it telling you to strangle someone?"

"Apparently it's led Trembuline to father two dozen children! Don't you find that weird?"

"Yeah, it's weird, but it's not evil. I mean, maybe that's his destiny."

Will shook his head. "You're starting to sound like him."

"I can't wait to tell Del everything I saw. She's gonna be blown away when she sees how much I've changed."

"Changed? What are you talking about?"

Whim laughed. "You were sitting right next to me, Will. I'm a changed man. Del will get it. We'll be the power couple of the century."

"What are you talking about?" Will nearly shouted. "Is it the energy drink, or do you actually think that meditating for five minutes fixed all your relationship problems?"

"Let's hit that Starbucks up ahead."

"*No.* You've had enough caffeine to last the next two months."

They stopped for coffee anyway.

Ten

"There's no way Josh is the True Dream Walker," Ian said. "I would have known."

Haley and Ian walked side by side down a wide dirt road. They'd left the meadows and low hills behind and were now deep in a forest, and only the width of the road allowed enough of a break in the canopy to let sunlight reach them.

Sour green pride rippled through Ian's aura as he spoke. Haley wondered if Ian was upset because he hadn't noticed Josh's gifts, or because he didn't have them himself.

"Is that why she got an apprentice?" Ian asked. "Because people think she's the True Dream Walker? She's not as talented as people think she is, you know."

"Her scroll predicted—"

"Her scroll," Ian scoffed. "You'd think after what happened to me, she'd be smart enough not to open her scroll." He kicked a stone off the road and sent it flying into the forest. "What's that guy Will's deal? He's trying to get with her, isn't he?"

That wasn't exactly how Haley would have characterized Josh and Will's relationship, but he was afraid of angering Ian by arguing, and Ian took his silence as an agreement.

"Jesus. Was she just, like, desperate after I died? She looked awful when I saw her. Her hair was way too long."

I think I forgot how bad Ian and Josh were for each other, Haley realized.

"*Will* probably likes long hair. He probably wants to turn her into a sports model or something." Ian's shoulders twitched, as if he had an itch or a sore muscle. Little starbursts of red and green peppered his aura. "How's Winsor?"

Ian was the last person in the three universes that Haley wanted to talk to about Winsor. She had been Haley's girlfriend, and she'd cheated on him with Ian, sparking the fight that led to Ian's soul getting ripped out. Haley didn't like the way Ian had jumped from complaining that Josh was with someone else to asking about Winsor, like he still thought of Winsor only as someone he could use to hurt Josh. As if the fact that Haley had loved her didn't matter.

"She's in a coma," Haley said. His voice shook.

"A coma?" Ian stopped walking to stare at him, and for a moment, a genuine purple concern broke through the dark spots in his aura.

Haley told him about Winsor, who had been in a coma the last time he saw her. Remembering how still she had been, how her aura had collapsed around her to a faint, still green cloud, he felt a deep sadness, but Ian's face split into a grin.

"So she'll probably die soon," he said. "I mean, it sounds like she doesn't have much time left." He nodded. "That'll be good. Things will be a lot better with her around here."

Astonished, Haley said nothing. He stared at Ian, at the terrible, ashen patches in his energy field, and thought, *This is not my brother.*

Years before, Whim had said something about Ian that had stuck in Haley's mind. "Ian is equal parts asshole and hero," Whim had said. "And on any given day, one part wins out over the other."

Haley had always thought that because he was Ian's brother, he ended up seeing more of the asshole part, but he couldn't count the number of times Ian had stood up for other people. He'd once confronted a man in a coffee shop who said something cruel to his girlfriend. The guy must have weighed twice what Ian did. When his English teacher got breast cancer, Ian had secretly organized the student body to cook dinner for her family three times a week.

Ian had been a study in contradictions. He'd confronted bullies while bullying his own twin. He'd defended a stranger's girlfriend while dismissing his own girlfriend's tireless efforts to balance the three universes. He'd worried about his English teacher's family while completely ignoring his own mother. But Haley had never stopped believing that Ian had the hero half inside him, waiting to be embraced.

Now he felt like he couldn't find that part at all.

"Winsor's not going to die," Haley said desperately. "I'm sure Josh made Feodor put her soul back in her body."

"Yeah, but you said her brain was dying. Even if she wakes up, she'll be a vegetable."

Haley rarely felt offended; he'd always thought that somehow he had no right. But he was offended on Winsor's behalf then. Yes, the coma would change her. No, her brain might never be the magnificent intellectual machine it had been before. But her life would still be worth living. One day, years away, she would be grateful— not for what she had suffered, but for what she had learned from suffering.

"She's better off here with me," Ian said. When Haley didn't agree, he said, "Oh, what, you still want her for yourself? She's out of your league, Haley. She always was."

The words stung. *Family poison stings the worst,* Dustine had always said, and Haley believed it. In his life, no one had hurt him more than his brother.

The sting made him do something stupid. "I have a girlfriend," he said.

"Yeah, right." Ian laughed. "Have you actually managed to talk to her?"

Haley blushed. "Yes."

"Who is she? Do I know her?"

"No. She's . . . She's the lost dream-walker princess."

Letting out a *whoop* of laughter, Ian said, "Yeah, right." He punched Haley in the arm, hard enough to hurt. "You're a terrible liar, Haley."

"I'm not lying. She's the last Rousellario."

"You're so full of crap."

"I mean it."

Ian stopped walking again so that he could give Haley the look, the one that said he was appalled by Haley's immaturity. "Stop it. You're talking about a real person, who's dead. It's disrespectful."

Haley wrapped his arms around himself, longing for a cardigan. "I'm not lying."

"Haley, *stop it*. You and I both know you're lying. You made her up. Admit it." Then he said, "*Haley*," in a sharp tone that was a warning he was about to lose his temper.

Staring at his feet but seeing Mirren's face, Haley said, "I made her up."

"Don't do that again. It isn't cute. It just makes you look more pathetic."

"Sorry," Haley whispered.

They started walking again. Haley's face was hot. Part of him was furious, part of him wanted to hit Ian in the face, and part of him was just relieved that he didn't have to hold Mirren up to Ian's inevitable scorn. He could keep her memory to himself, beautiful and intact, like an apple with no brown spots.

They rounded the top of a hill, and in the valley below sat what appeared to be a medieval village. A stone wall enclosed the village, but there were no gates to bar the entrance, just a wooden bridge to carry them over the moat.

The building at the heart of the village wasn't large or grand enough to be called a castle, but it was too large and too grand to be anything else. Wooden doors hung wide open to allow them inside, and sweet-smelling hay covered the stone floors. A hallway led them into an open, airy hall where the dead were dressing and undressing.

"What the hell's going on here?" Ian asked.

In the center of the hall, another bonfire burned. The dead would enter, undress, and throw their clothing in the fire. A part of their sense of "self," their idea of themselves as a particular, singular person, burned up with the clothing. Haley watched the burdens of that personhood leave them, and afterward they seemed lighter, the colors of their auras purer and brighter than ever.

When their clothes and their sense of self burned away, they would turn and put on one of the garments hanging on the walls. Haley saw robes, kimonos, saris, and numerous other pieces of clothing he couldn't name, many of them in white or black, but some in gray or purple or even pink.

"This is the gayest thing ever," Ian said.

Haley saw the poppy red burst into Ian's aura before he saw the anger in his brother's face. Alongside the red, streaks of neon yellow tore through his base chakra.

He knows what's going on here, Haley thought. *And he's terrified.*

"Let's get out of here," Ian said and began stomping across the hall. Haley followed, smiling apologetically at the dead who turned to watch.

Before they reached the door on the far side of the hall, a woman in a white kimono stepped in front of Ian. Her aura was sky blue with edges of gold, as beautiful an aura as Haley had ever seen.

She reached out to touch Ian's cheek.

"Let go," she told him.

Ian began to tremble visibly. Black tentacles of rage burst from his gut, but they couldn't touch the woman's aura, the golden edges of which protected her.

"She's just trying to help," Haley told his brother. "The purpose of Death is—"

"You think I don't know what the purpose is?" Ian barked at him. "I know why you brought me here." Furious, Ian grabbed a rack of robes and knocked it over.

"I know what you're trying to do!" Ian shouted. "You're trying to turn me into one of them! You're trying to make me disappear!"

"No," Haley said weakly. "I'm not . . ."

"You're jealous of me, just like you always were!" Ian ranted. "You want to destroy me! Why, so that you can have my life? So you can be the cool, smart brother with the perfect girl and the perfect life?"

The charred places in his aura had become dark, swirling eddies of gray with red centers, like live coals, and they were burning away larger and larger areas.

This is what happens when you fight letting go, Haley thought. *He's going to destroy himself.*

Ian had always been volatile, but not like this. He hit Haley in the chest with both hands, knocking him back a step. "You want to be me?" He hit Haley again, energetic sparks flying from his hands, stinging Haley's skin. "You want my life? Try to take it!"

"No," Haley tried to say, but the final shove sent him sprawling onto the floor. He rolled into a ball, pinched his eyes shut, and covered his hands with his ears.

Help, help, help, he thought.

He heard Ian's footsteps slamming against stone as he ran out of the castle. Then a gentle touch on his arm, and when he opened his eyes, the woman with the sky-blue aura was kneeling beside him. She gave him a luminous smile, and the love that radiated from her extended to surround Haley, the golden edges of her aura encompassing his own, like a cloak she had thrown over him.

Haley released a deep breath. Neither he nor the woman spoke, but they communicated in a silent, energetic exchange.

Thank you, Haley told her.

I love you beyond measure, the woman told him.

Returning her love felt effortless. Haley trusted her completely.

Your brother is unwell, she warned Haley. *He could hurt you.*

Can he be healed? Haley asked as the woman helped him up.

Only by the one who set him on this path.

Haley wasn't certain who that was. Feodor? Gloves? Ian himself?

Again, he wondered if Dustine could help. Holding an image of her in his mind, he asked the woman if she'd seen her.

She came this way long ago. Keep going and you will find her.

Eventually, they said farewell, both grateful for the love that had passed between them, and the woman moved away, her aura more beautiful than ever.

Haley left the castle and followed the road on the other side of it. A quarter mile farther, and he found Ian, sitting on a fallen tree and hurling stones at a tree trunk. His aura had retreated to its usual reds and blue.

Haley sat down on a log, leaving a few feet between himself and Ian. He knew better than to say anything.

Ian threw another stone. He'd hit the tree trunk in the same place so many times that the bark had crumbled away.

"I used to be somebody," he said. "I mattered. The World was a better place with me in it. I wasn't ready to die."

He got up from the log to hunt around for another rock, finally finding one at the edge of the road. Clenching his jaw, he lobbed it at the tree trunk hard enough to rattle the branches above.

"And no offense," he said to Haley, "but what did you ever do with your life that was so important?"

Haley didn't reply. Ian didn't really want him to, and besides, he had no argument. He hadn't done anything important with his life. He hadn't even graduated from high school. He'd let Winsor use him to manipulate his brother. Sure, he'd fallen in love with Mirren, but she was probably better off without him, truth be told. No politician needed a partner so shy that people thought he was a deaf mute.

"I mean, people probably don't even notice you're gone," Ian said.

"Probably not," Haley echoed. What would they have noticed? That there was one less body in the room with them? That Whim's bad jokes fell against a little less silence? That there was more pizza to go around?

"Don't take this the wrong way, but they were more my friends than yours."

"I know," Haley whispered.

Ian was the one they had invited places; Haley had always been an afterthought. Not to Deloise, but her kindness had been closer to pity. He'd always wanted to be close to Josh, but between his awkwardness and hers, they had a hard time having a conversation.

"Remember that time they forgot you at the amusement park?"

"Yeah."

He'd been too embarrassed to call and tell them, had taken a cab home instead and hoped no one would realize he hadn't been in either car. But he'd admitted it to Ian, and Ian had told everyone. He felt his cheeks flush just remembering it.

Ian dropped back onto the log. "I just think . . . if one of us had to die, I don't know why it should have been me."

Haley turned his head so Ian wouldn't see the tears in his eyes. He felt ashamed of how pathetic he was, what a waste he'd made of his life, and maybe Ian was right and it should have been him—

"I'd be really surprised if they actually come back for you."

Ian was probably right about that, too.

I love you, Mirren said in his mind.

He remembered standing within the branches of the willow tree on the front lawn, holding her while the rain came down around them. She'd never seen a thunderstorm before, and she'd been so excited and so sad at once.

Don't let me lose myself, she'd said, and the memory of how soft and real she had been, how tightly she had hugged him, weakened Ian's arguments. Haley believed she had loved him, truly he did, because he had watched, amazed, as the love grew in her aura, like a seed blossoming.

He sent the prayer back to her. *Don't let me lose myself, Mirren. And please, please, please, come back for me.*

Ian had fallen into a depressed silence, and he seemed startled when Haley stood up and said, "Let's keep going."

"No," Ian said. "I'm done."

Haley began walking. "Then I'll go alone."

"No you won't."

He walked for half a mile before Ian caught up with him.

Eleven

A few days later, Kerstel asked Josh to help Whim and Alex cook Sunday dinner. "I've got work—" Josh tried to say, but her father was shaking his head.

"We barely see you. You're coming to Sunday dinner. And you're going to help cook."

Cooking was not on Josh's priority list. Neither was pleasing her father. But she didn't feel like arguing, and—if she was truthful with herself—she was tired of living off snack cakes and beef jerky. When she went down to the kitchen on Sunday afternoon, she offered her services to Whim and his father.

"Wonderful," Whim said. "I need someone who can chop."

"That would be me."

Josh was very good with knives, and she sat down at the table beside Winsor, who was slowly but diligently slicing cheese into cubes with a fairly dull blade. Even though she'd been partly responsible for restoring Winsor's soul, Josh was ashamed of how little time she'd spent with her former best friend. She just didn't know how to avoid being painfully awkward, and Winsor barely resembled the smart, witty, angry girl Josh had grown up with.

"How's it going, Winsor?" Josh asked.

Winsor shrugged. "I can't get these right. They all come out lop-eared." She frowned. "Lop-eared?"

"Lopsided," Whim told her.

"Right. Or . . . No, I think it's lop-eared."

"That's bunnies."

"And cheese!" Winsor insisted, and her face darkened.

"Okay, okay," Whim said, his tone light. "Bunnies and cheese." He leaned down to kiss the top of Winsor's head.

"Sorry," Winsor said. She pushed her new glasses up her nose with frustration. "I'm always embarrassing myself," she told Josh. "I can't stop . . . I get so upset and I know it's over nothing, but . . ."

Josh was deeply grateful then that Whim had passed out copies of articles about traumatic brain injuries. "That's normal with TBI."

"Who cares?" Winsor replied tartly. "It sucks."

Josh didn't have an answer to that. Or to Winsor's next question.

The dark-haired girl leaned close to Josh and, after casting a glance at Whim and her father, whispered, "Where's Haley? Where's he really?"

Josh looked down at the carrots she was chopping. They'd all agreed not to tell Winsor that Haley was trapped in the Death universe until she was stronger, but Josh didn't know when she would be strong enough, and Winsor had started pushing the issue.

"He went away," Josh said finally. "He's traveling again, like he did before. But he'll come back."

For a moment, Winsor's gaze was as sharp and perceptive as it used to be. "I don't believe you," she said.

Josh wanted to blurt everything out then, but she bit her tongue. "He's all right," she said instead. "You don't have to worry about him."

Winsor threw her knife down on the table and said, "Everyone's lying to me! Why is everyone lying to me? Is he dead? Is that it? Do you think I can't handle knowing he's dead? I can handle it!"

"He's not dead," Josh insisted. "He isn't."

"Winsor, sweetie, you're shouting," her father said, and came over to hug her. She pushed him away.

"Tell me the truth."

The house phone rang. Alex answered it and held it out to Josh, who put a hand over her other ear to block out Winsor's continued protests.

"It's Zorie. We've got another tear. It isn't a big one, but it's in your neck of the woods, so I thought I'd call."

Josh, who was happy to bail on the situation, said, "Great. Where is it?"

"You're not going to believe this—it's in the Greenville Opera House. Right onstage."

The Greenville Opera House was less than twenty minutes' drive from Josh's home. It was a run-down 1920s-style opera palace full of threadbare red velvet and ornate carvings covered in chipped gold paint. In addition to the occasional opera, it provided a home for numerous mediocre theater troupes, the spring and fall Tanith High School plays, and a men's barbershop quartet called the Pony Boys. Half its income came from an annual summer showing of *Ghostbusters*.

Nine police cars sat in the parking lot, all parked at crooked angles and with their lights on. Nearby was Zorie's truck and a van marked FBI. Josh pulled up between them and hopped out, her VHAG and gas mask in a backpack. The cop at the door started to shoo her away before she even reached the steps to the entrance, and he looked skeptical when she said she was with Agent Abernaughton, but Zorie shouted to let Josh in, and the cop stepped aside.

"You're awfully young to be FBI," he said.

"I'm a consultant," Josh replied.

She passed through the lobby and into the theater itself, where she got a good look at the tear. Vertical, it began onstage, then cut through the floor and down into the orchestra pit. Josh couldn't see where it ended, but she bet it wasn't more than twenty feet long, and it was only a foot wide. Veil dust spurted into the room like a special effect, coating everything in glitter.

Josh knew that Zorie's team was going to have a hard time closing the tear because it passed through two rooms. They'd either have to coordinate the lights from the stage and the orchestra pit, or they'd have to try to stitch it. Zorie's people were already setting up the stitches—giant magnets attached to freestanding frames. The Veil dust on their gas masks made them look like sparkly aliens.

Josh waved to Zorie, then took a seat near the back of the theater. This far away, she didn't need her gas mask, but it was better
not to waste time in a room slowly filling with hallucinogenic dust,
so she worked quickly to attach all the electrodes to her head and
chest, and then carefully put the mask over the electrodes. She felt
more machine than human.

She closed her eyes and turned on the VHAG by memory. The
pattern of pulsations against her skin felt hypnotic, and despite the
discomfort of the mask and the sound of Zorie's team members
shouting to each other, she relaxed against the velvet-upholstered
chair.

She adjusted the VHAG, then again, then again. The pattern
grew faster and more intense, but Josh seemed to have reached a
plateau. She could barely feel her body, and yet she couldn't escape it.

It's like there's nowhere to go, she thought.

Something crashed onstage—probably one of the frames. One
of Zorie's guys cursed. Instinctively, Josh opened her eyes.

Both frames onstage had crashed. Far worse, the tear had widened dramatically in the time Josh had her eyes closed. It was at
least seven feet wide now, and a blizzard of Veil dust gushed from it.

That's where I need to go, Josh thought.

With a shout that was half laugh, half shocked exclamation, she
sprang out of her seat and dashed down the center aisle. She vaulted
onto the stage before any of Zorie's people noticed, and they barely
had time to shout before she leapt through the tear into the Dream.

The moment she crossed between universes was glorious. For
just an instant, she was surrounded by silver light, as though she
were inside a firework or a star. She had to close her eyes against
the intensity of the light, but she could feel the Veil dust through
her clothes, a cool twinkling on her skin.

She landed on her feet in a pharmacy, and the mundane calm
of the place startled her. A Muzak version of "MacArthur Park"
was playing over the intercom. At the pharmacy counter, a man in

a white coat was saying emphatically, "I need your insurance card. This is a library card. I can't use this."

"But it's a government-issued ID," a little old lady was saying. "Doesn't that prove who I am?"

"I know who you are," the pharmacist told her. "I need to see your *insurance* card."

"What about this one?"

"No! This entitles you to a free muffin after you've bought twelve!"

Smiling, Josh sat down at the blood pressure monitoring machine. This was a perfect nightmare in which to try the VHAG. Closing her eyes, she started the machine again, and this time she'd barely gone through the sequence twice when she burst out of her body as though her soul had been shot from a cannon.

Despite her newfound insubstantiality, Josh slammed into the pharmacy ceiling and bounced back into midair. The pharmacist and the old lady both looked up at her, and Josh held a hand in front of her face. It was gossamer, but it was there.

She began to laugh. "I did it!" she called to the pharmacist.

"That's nice," he muttered, and took the old woman's wallet out of her hands.

How does this work? Josh wondered, exhilaration making her shiver. She could see her body slumped over the blood pressure machine. It looked all right.

I bet my thoughts determine everything.

She tried swimming through the air, and she moved just like she would have in water. Then she held her arms out in front of her like Superman and shot through the pharmacy at breakneck speed, before deciding that swimming felt safer. A few strokes carried her back to the pharmacy, where the pharmacist was now going through the old woman's wallet for himself.

A few yards behind him, amid the shelves of medication bottles, hung the tear. It had already swallowed the back of the store, and it was wide enough that Josh could see a couple of people in gas masks on the other side.

Seal, she thought.

And the tear sealed.

Her success felt anticlimactic. She thought a thought, and the Veil tear closed. It was so simple, and so quick, and only the knowledge that she had just permanently changed Veil repair forever filled Josh with excitement.

Then she realized something else. She could control everything in the Dream, just like she'd been trying to do for so many months.

She turned her attention to the pharmacist—the dreamer. Closing her astral eyes, she imagined her stone walls—

They were gone. No more struggling to connect to the dreamer, no more risk of losing herself in the dreamer's fear. The shape—the *meaning*—of the nightmare was obvious to Josh. That pharmacist felt like no one in his life worked at anything as hard as he worked at everything. This nightmare was a reflection of that frustration.

Let's give him what he needs, Josh thought.

With Josh instructing her mentally, the old woman put her hand on the pharmacist's arm and said, "I want you to know how grateful I am to you for being so patient with me. You make my life easier."

The pharmacist's scowl softened. "Thank you, ma'am. I do my best." He held up a piece of white paper. "I think this is your insurance card."

The nightmare resolved and Josh, buzzing with happiness, jumped back into her body. As the blood pressure station dissolved, she opened her eyes to find them wet with tears, and she thrust her hand out and opened an archway halfway between nightmares.

She opened the archway to her own basement. She'd have to get Deloise to drive her to her car later, but this way she avoided Zorie questioning how she made it out of the Dream.

Josh landed on her feet, as softly as she ever had. The deafening silence in the archroom was anticlimactic, too, but Josh knew what she had just done, what she had accomplished, and that she had changed dream walking forever. She yanked off her gas mask, sat down on the floor, and cried.

Twelve

Will had been down this hallway more times than he could count. Once, as a small child, and then a hundred times in his nightmares. This long, white hallway with the steel doors running along either side, where the slit windows were crisscrossed with embedded wires, where the doors were always locked, was Detox.

The calm silence of the hallway contrasted with the chaos he saw through the windows into each room. In one, a tornado blew through his childhood bedroom, tossing stuffed animals and train pajamas and bottles of booze through the air. In another, Winsor lay still in her coma, a shriveled husk of a moon-white body, her new glasses still perched on her mummified face.

Will tried the door, but it was locked. He didn't know what he could have done to help Winsor anyway.

The next door, too, was locked, but he saw a familiar face inside: Josh.

She sat in the far corner of the room, turned so that only one side of her face was visible. A strange darkness clung to her, obscuring most of her body, but Will could see that her hair was clean and brushed, and she was wearing a maroon sweater that he'd always thought flattered her. He could only see one side of her face, but her cheek was flushed and full, the shadows banished from beneath her eyes, and there was an ease in her expression that told him he'd have no trouble making her laugh. He'd never seen her so happy.

"You look beautiful," he said, and she met his eyes with her one visible eye, such a soft, gentle green.

The doorknob turned beneath his hand.

Josh smiled as he entered the room, but she didn't move from her peculiar half-visible position. A line seemed to run down the center of her face, hiding half of it in darkness.

She held out a hand to him, and he took it. "I thought you were mad at me," he said.

Her hands were softer than they'd been the last time he touched them—the calluses were gone, but the strength remained.

"I was just scared," she said. "You know that when I'm angry, it's because I'm secretly scared."

"Yeah," he said, "I know that."

He tried to recall the reasons they'd broken up, but all the memories flittered away from him. All that remained was how much he cared about her.

"I love you," he said, and he reached into the darkness to touch her cheek, turn her face so he could kiss her.

"I love you back," Josh said, but her voice was mixed with another voice, deeper, softly accented.

As her face entered the light, Will screamed.

The right half of her face was Josh's, the right half of her body was Josh's, but the left . . .

The left was Feodor's.

The cheek Will had touched was Feodor's. Beside Josh's gentle green eye, Feodor's gray one—as chilly as a winter drizzle—stared back at Will. His thin, crisp lips—attached to Josh's softer ones. His flat chest sat beside the small curve of Josh's right breast.

"What's wrong?" Josh/Feodor asked, speaking in two voices.

Will scrambled backward across the floor, but the door blew shut behind him.

"Don't you love me anymore?"

Josh/Feodor stood up and stalked toward Will, and the Feodor half was wearing an inky black cape that swirled around him like darkness. From the canine tooth on his side of the mouth, a fang extended.

"Don't touch me!" Will shrieked, because they were both reaching for him. As they bent forward, Josh's plumeria pendant dangled from their neck.

"Will," said a voice behind him.

Will spun on his knees, holding out his fists against this new threat, but it was Josh he saw standing in the doorway, real Josh in a pair of stained gray yoga pants and a blue T-shirt with a wrung-out neckline, looking hassled and confused.

"You're asleep," she told him.

"I am?"

"He is?" asked the amalgamous monster behind him.

The nightmare began to dissolve, and Will reflexively stopped it. *Steady,* he thought. *Steady, steady, steady.*

"Sit," he told the nightmare.

The Josh/Feodor monster sat back down on its stool, quietly, like an obedient child.

The real Josh stared at it as Will got to his feet.

"Thank you for coming in to get me," he said.

As if she hadn't heard him, she said, "Is that how you see me?"

"No," Will said reflexively. "I mean . . . no."

Josh gave him a look that made it clear she didn't believe him.

"Well, apparently that's how your subconscious sees me."

The Feodor-half smirked.

"No," Will said helplessly. He didn't know what to say to make her feel better, and he was afraid that his nightmare depiction of her had already said too much.

"You think I'm a monster," she said, and her voice was tight.

"No, I don't," Will told her. He took her hand, trying to distract her from the freak in front of them, but she tugged it away. "I'm just afraid that you're losing who you are because of him."

"But this isn't who I am." Josh lifted Feodor's cape and used it to cover his half of the face, leaving only hers visible. "This doesn't even look like me."

The disparity was even more obvious now that she and Will's dream version of her were side by side. The real Josh was wiry and hard, muscles constantly coiled in readiness, pale from too many hours spent in the Dream, her eyes perpetually narrowed. The dream-Josh was beautiful—relaxed, enthusiastic, comfortable in her own skin.

"That's how I see you," Will said. "When you're at your best, that's how I see you."

Josh didn't say anything for such a long time that Will turned to look at her, and he was shocked to see tears in her eyes.

"Josh," he said, and he grabbed her arm as she tried to leave.

"If that's who you want me to be," she said, and then started over, rubbing furiously at her eyes. "I will never be that person!"

"Josh," he said again. "You already are."

She shook her head but stopped pulling away. "I'm nothing like that."

"You are. When you aren't running yourself ragged and blaming yourself for everything and too busy saving the World to take care of yourself, that's exactly who you are."

She kept shaking her head, but she couldn't seem to look away from the vision of herself in the corner.

"I can't do anything differently," she said.

"You don't have to. You aren't the problem."

"Then what is?" Josh asked, perplexed.

This wasn't how Will had imagined having this conversation—if, in fact, they ever had it. "When we broke up, it wasn't you I was trying to get away from. I know that now. It was them."

Then he said something ridiculous, something that—later—he would be almost unable to believe he had said. Maybe he had been thinking about the distant future, or maybe his judgment was off because he was asleep, but he said, "When Peregrine and Feodor are dead, we can be together."

Josh's lips parted with astonishment. "What?"

"That came out wrong," Will said, immediately realizing how insane his words sounded.

There was no softness left in Josh's green eyes, no tears, just outrage.

"You want me to kill two people so you'll get back together with me?"

"No, that's—that's not how I meant it."

She pulled away from him. With a thrust of her palm, she created an archway where the door to the hallway stood.

"Josh, please, listen to me—"

"One thing I learned from Feodor," she told Will. "If you start killing your problems, you'll never stop."

She jumped through the archway. Will followed, but he woke up alone in his bed.

"Dammit," he said, and punched the pillow beside his head. "I really screwed that up."

He lay in the dark and imagined Josh, two stories below, flying out of the basement archway.

And jumping right back in.

Thirteen

"hat was pretty much the most awkward nightmare she could have dream walked in on," Deloise agreed the next day.

"No," Whim said. "The *most* awkward would have been a nightmare where you were getting it on with Deloise."

"Whim!" Deloise cried.

"Or maybe that would be the most awkward nightmare for *me* to walk in on," Whim mused. "Maybe Josh and I should walk in on it together."

"Please shut up," Will said.

Winsor giggled.

Despite it being a Monday morning, Will and Deloise weren't in school because of an in-service day. Whim had decided to pretend to be sick when he heard no one else was going to classes.

And Josh was gone—where, no one knew. She was probably in a garden with Feodor feeding jelly beans to puppies.

Winsor wasn't feeling well, but she didn't like being alone, so she was tucked beneath the covers and Whim was kicked out beside her, happily pawing at his tablet and finding funny videos to play for her.

The bedroom they were in had belonged to Dustine when Will first moved into the house. Now Winsor used it, since her own bedroom was on the second floor and she didn't have the strength to go up the stairs yet. The room's furnishings hadn't changed, though: Dustine's double bed with the blue-and-white Ohio Star quilt, Dustine's antique dresser with the big mirror hanging over it, Dustine's imitation-ivory crucifix on the wall.

"Anyway, we started talking," Will said, "and then somehow I ended up saying that if she'd just kill Peregrine and Feodor, we could get back together."

Deloise wrinkled her nose.

"Why did you say *that*?" Whim demanded, laughing.

"Why do you want her to kill Feodor?" Winsor asked.

"It came out wrong. I just meant . . . that I still want to be with her, but I can't live with constant danger."

"You probably should have said *that*," Winsor told Will, her eyelids drooping.

"Is there anyone I could kill to convince you to get back together with me?" Whim asked Deloise.

"I'm not going to answer that."

"I hate sitting here, trying to live a normal life, and waiting for Peregrine to show up," Will said. "I want to take the fight to him."

"That might be hard," Deloise pointed out, "since we have no idea where he is."

Whim said, "Let's break into Peregrine's house."

"Why would we do that?" Deloise asked, outraged.

"So we can find a clue about where he went. And also so we can get some exclusive photos of the inside of his house for my blog. Because readership is *way* down."

The idea appealed to Will; it was a means by which to engage with Peregrine without actually being in danger from him.

"But you have to come, Del," Whim added.

"Why?"

"Because I don't want to be eaten by Peregrine's Dobermans. And I don't want to be arrested when the security system goes off. *And* I don't want to get shot by one of the armed guards. So we're going to need Deloise to play the distraught granddaughter and sweet-talk us in."

Deloise groaned. "Why are you always dragging me into stuff like this?"

"Um, when have I *ever* dragged you into something like this?"

Before they could start arguing, Winsor said, "I want to go."

Everyone looked at her—slumped against the mountain of pillows, hair a crow's nest, eyes only half-open.

"And we want you to come," Whim assured her. "But I think you need to stay home and rest today."

"But I always have to stay home and rest," Winsor complained, struggling to sit up. Her head rolled dangerously on her neck. "I'm tired of resting."

None of them had the heart to tell her no.

Peregrine's house was a monstrosity of modern art. Gray concrete boxes attached to each other in strange ways; the place resembled a compound more than a home, except that its third floor was significantly larger than its first, as though a toddler had decided to see how precariously he could stack his blocks. Tinted windows without shutters looked out onto gravel instead of a lawn.

"Wait, is that it?" Will asked as he got out of Whim's Lincoln Town Car.

"Oh, that's it," Whim assured him. "Peregrine had it custom-designed by a famous Brutalist architect after Dustine left him. I'm sure there's some sort of psychological significance to that . . ."

If there was, Will didn't get it. The place was just *ugly*.

"I don't hear the dogs," Deloise said, helping Winsor into her wheelchair.

"Maybe they starved to death," Whim said. He walked up to the gray steel door and tried the cold metal handle. "Too much to hope for, I suppose. Where's the guard?"

Will took a quick walk around the house, but he found no one. The lights were off inside. When he peered through one window, he noticed that the oven and microwave clocks weren't on.

"Somebody turned the power off at the breaker box," he told his friends when he reached the front door. "And there's no guard."

"If the power is off, will the alarm still work?" Deloise asked.

"After three months?" Whim said. "I doubt it. But if the cops show up, you can just say you're his granddaughter."

"I don't want to get arrested," Will told him.

"We won't. Who commits a robbery with a girl in a wheelchair?"

Whim was already getting a toolbox out of the back of his Lincoln. Will crossed his fingers and hoped the alarm didn't go off.

They ended up having to break a window in a first-floor powder room. Deloise wriggled through and unlocked the front door.

The exterior had been ugly, but at least it had been simple; the interior was a psychotic wash of colors and objects. So much stuff had been crammed into the entryway that Will immediately drove Winsor's chair into a sculpture stand. Luckily the pointy iron sculpture—a cactus, maybe? Or a turkey?—didn't fall.

On one wall hung a painting of three soldiers kicking a fallen refrigerator. On the opposite wall hung a print of a partially autopsied horse. Above them dangled a chandelier made from baby doll arms holding lightbulbs in their hands.

"What is all this?" Will asked as they passed a living room furnished with only suede-covered dental chairs. On what Will thought was supposed to be a coffee table—it was made of bundles of newspapers wrapped in chicken wire—sat a half-dozen pornographic Etch A Sketches.

"Peregrine thinks he's a modern art connoisseur," Deloise said. "But his taste is . . . questionable."

"You just don't understand the avant-garde," Whim said sarcastically, and he gestured to a teddy bear with sad eyes sitting on a black box. On the front of the box was a red button above a label that read DO NOT PUSH BUTTON.

Whim pushed the button.

"You're fat!" the bear told him. "You're ugly! I hate you!"

"Nice," Deloise said. Winsor cracked up.

"Josh must loathe this place," Will said.

"You have no idea," Whim told him.

They decided to search room by room. Deloise and Will took the second floor and left Whim and Winsor to explore downstairs. The first room off the staircase—the steps of which were all welded street signs—was Peregrine's office. Aside from more terrible art, the room was relatively bare. The desk was just a grand piano lid on six legs.

"He must not work at home much," Will said. "He doesn't even have a computer."

"He doesn't even have a pen," Deloise pointed out. "I think this whole room is for show."

"I think the whole house is for show," Will said.

In the bedroom, they found a perfectly made bed on a plastic pedestal, above which hung a near life-sized oil painting of Peregrine, surrounded by his dogs. Six brightly colored, formal dreamwalker robes attired headless mannequins. Like the office, the bedroom felt like no one called it home.

"In here, Will," Deloise said from the walk-in closet.

Here they found the first real evidence that someone lived in the house. Several shirts had been knocked off their hangers, a pair of shoes had fallen to the floor, and a sock drawer sat open.

"Someone went through here," Will said. "Maybe the gendarmes."

"The gendarmes wouldn't have done this. Probably Peregrine stopped here before he went wherever he went, and he packed in a hurry." Almost by habit, she reached out to close the sock drawer, then frowned. "This drawer is really shallow."

Will examined the closet, but didn't find anything out of the ordinary. It was hard to tell in the dim light coming from the bedroom window.

"The ceiling light in here isn't centered," Deloise pointed out. "Neither is the island."

"Maybe it's avant-garde," Will said.

"Maybe." Deloise stepped outside the closet, then back inside. "Are disproportionally thick walls postmodern?"

Will stood beside her so that he could see what she saw.

"Someone moved this closet wall in. You don't think . . ."

Deloise smiled. "I do think."

They started searching for a mechanism. Will opened drawers, yanked on hanging bars, flicked the light switch up and down. Deloise pulled the clothes off the racks so she could see the wall clearly, but nothing happened, and nothing that looked like a trigger appeared.

"Wait," she said. "Let's think this through. The wall can't move left because it would go into the bedroom. Right, it goes into the bathroom. Maybe it pushes back."

Together, they braced their shoulders against the wall and shoved. Nothing happened except that Will's shoulder hurt.

"Maybe it pulls out," he suggested.

They each grabbed hold of a shirt bar and pulled. The wall didn't budge.

"Maybe it's just a stupid-thick wall," Will said. "Or maybe it is a fake wall, but it won't move with the power off."

Deloise blew out a puff of air, making her bangs lift as if with a breeze. "Maybe," she admitted, but her affectation gave Will an idea.

"It goes up!" he said. "We have to lift it up!"

Taking hold of the edges of the shelves, they each heaved up. Will was expecting the wall to weigh more than it did, and the force of their lift caused the entire wall of shelving to fly up from the floor. It disappeared into the ceiling, revealing a narrow staircase behind it.

"Good gracious," Deloise said.

Flicking their lighters, they followed the stairs down into a deep basement.

"This is spooky," Will admitted in a whisper.

The flame of his lighter illuminated two more mannequins, one wearing a ball gown and another in a tux. Will jumped before realizing they weren't alive.

"What am I looking at?" he asked, touching his chest as if that might slow his heart.

The basement looked like the backstage of a Broadway theater. Costumes hung from clothes racks. A makeup table with a lighted mirror sat beside a wall of wigs and prosthetic noses. Trunks full of props sat open along one wall, and Deloise found a pair of candles to light.

The most striking feature, though, was the painted iron garden archway in the middle of the room. When Will used his lighter to reflect the candlelight at it, the space within the arch filled with shimmering Veil.

"This must be where Peregrine staged nightmares," Deloise said. "What else would he have been doing with all this stuff? Look." She pulled a golden crown from one of the prop boxes. "Didn't the people who had nightmares about Mirren say she was always wearing a crown?"

Among the costumes were numerous dresses, some of them very royal. Among the wigs was one that closely resembled Mirren's long red hair.

But the longer Will looked, the older the objects he found appeared. One of the trunks had a layer of dust as thick as snow on the top, and inside were old-fashioned suits and furs that smelled strangely sweet.

"Del," Will said. "This isn't just stuff he used to stage nightmares about Mirren. He must have been staging nightmares for *decades*."

Deloise sniffed a bottle of foundation and wrinkled her nose. "I don't even think they still make this brand." She gazed around. "You know what we have here? Proof. We can prove he rigged the

Accordance Conclave, prove he made people hate Mirren for no reason."

"Yeah," Will said, but he was distracted by a shimmer at the far end of the basement. Moving toward it, he flicked his lighter, and he realized he was standing in front of a metal door. It hung open far enough that Will could see it was as thick as the bank vault door that protected the archway at home.

"Hey, Del, over here."

He pushed the door open with his shoulder and stepped inside, holding his lighter out before him.

It was a bedroom. With the vault door lock on the inside.

Unlike the bedroom upstairs, this one contained an unmade twin bed heaped with comforters and down pillows. A worn flannel robe hung from a hook on the wall, and slippers had been kicked off beneath it. A bookshelf was stuffed with fantasy and romance paperbacks, their spines broken and peeling. An enormous television took up most of one wall, complete with every game console Will had ever heard of, and in front of it was a tricked-out gaming chair.

"Oh, heavens," Deloise said. "What is this? Was he holding somebody prisoner down here?"

Sadness like a weighted vest settled over Will. "No," he said, and reached out to touch the bedsheets. They, too, were flannel. "This is his real bedroom."

"What do you mean?" Deloise asked.

Will sat down on the bed and sank into it up to his hips; he'd never sat on such a soft mattress. "I think the bedroom upstairs, like the rest of the house, is just for show. I think this is where he came to be by himself."

"But he always ranted about the evils of television and video games," Deloise pointed out. "There must be a hundred games down here."

"Yeah. He was a hypocrite. And he was ashamed of that."

The walls were painted a light blue, the carpet was almost as soft as the bed, and a night-light stuck out from one of the electrical outlets. It wasn't so much a bedroom as a secret retreat where everything was cozy and comfortable and safe.

Safety, Will thought. *That's what he wanted here. To be safe from the world, from judgments, from pretense. He came down here to be himself.*

"This is Grandma Dustine," Deloise said, picking up a framed photograph from the nightstand. She sat down on the bed next to Will, atop one of the comforters, then shifted around so she could pull something from beneath the blanket.

It was a stuffed rabbit, the fur threadbare, the paint worn away from its eyes, its ears so thin they flopped over its face.

Deloise released a little cry. "This is the saddest place I've ever seen."

"Yeah," Will echoed.

"What do you think is wrong with him?" she asked.

Will sighed. He touched the rabbit in Deloise's hands, found the fur still soft. Through the open door, he could see the racks of costumes and rows of wigs.

"I think he wants to be someone else. I think he wants people to see him as brilliant and sophisticated and debonair. And I think he desperately wants control over his life, even if that requires control over other people."

Will had been afraid of Peregrine for months. But what he had forgotten—and what he had only remembered when he entered this strange sanctuary—was that people who committed acts of great cruelty were those who had experienced great cruelty. He'd witnessed it in Feodor, and he was witnessing it again, here, with Peregrine. Beneath the angry, controlling, manipulative monster he had become was just a man who wanted to feel safe.

Truth be told, Will wanted the same thing. He had come here to find something he could use against Peregrine, but he knew he would never confront Peregrine about this place.

Despite everything Peregrine had done to him, Will wasn't willing to let his pain make him cruel.

Fourteen

Mirren Rousellario lived an hour outside of Tanith in an old farmhouse on a hill. She lived with her aunt, uncle, and cousin, and when Josh drove up, Mirren's family was planting bulbs in the flower beds in front of the house.

Katia tossed her silvery hair back and wiped her dirty palms on her jeans when Josh walked up. "Hi. How are you?"

She offered Josh her hand; Katia wasn't quite as good as Mirren was at adapting to social conventions. They shook. "I'm fine. How're you?"

Casting a confused eye at Josh's too-large jeans, she said, "We're putting in tulips. Would you like to help?"

"No," Josh admitted. "I kind of hate gardening."

Katia laughed. "So do I, but that's never stopped Mom from making me do it."

Katia's mother didn't look too excited at Josh's visit; she never did. Josh suspected she'd made Collena's shit-list for helping Mirren try to restore the monarchy. Then again, Mirren would almost certainly have died if Josh and Will hadn't pulled her out of the Dream, so Josh didn't feel too badly about it.

"Is Mirren around?" she asked.

"She's in the trimidion." As Josh walked toward the side of the house, Katia called, "Don't let her make you help with the tiling!"

Mirren had only been to Josh's house a couple of times since they'd gotten back from the Death universe with Feodor in tow, but Josh saw her at least once a week. Sometimes she came out to help Mirren build.

Sometimes they worked on the other thing.

About a hundred yards behind the old farmhouse sat a stone structure. It had nine sides, each of them containing an arched, open doorway, and within each of the doorways hung an ornate iron lantern. The structure was huge and stood close to three stories. Josh found Mirren inside. She had carved a pool into the floor, the bottom of which was nine or ten feet belowground. In the center of the pool was a circular island that could be reached by nine narrow stone walkways that extended from each of the doorways.

Hanging above the concrete island was a red granite pyramid twelve feet tall. Doorways had been carved into each side, so that there was an empty space in the middle; essentially, the doorways led nowhere. But the carvings at the bottom corners indicated that the granite pyramid was actually a trimidion.

Mirren, her red hair coiled up in a messy bun, was sitting on the floor of the empty pool, grouting tiles. She lifted her face when Josh said her name, and a faint smile crossed her face.

"Hello, Josh. I was hoping you'd get here in time to help with the tiling."

Josh climbed carefully down into the pool. "How could I resist?"

Having been born a year after the Rousellarios were deposed, Josh had never seen a royal trimidion, but she had Feodor's memories of the one Mirren's grandparents had built. Most trimidions measured the emotional turmoil in a fairly limited geographical range. Supposedly a royal trimidion could measure emotional turmoil in the entirety of the three universes, but as far as Mirren knew, the secret of making them do so had died with her parents. Then again, royal trimidions were also rumored to be able to heal people who entered them, grant wishes, and function as time travel devices, so Josh wasn't sure how much to hope for.

This building was going to be Mirren's royal trimidion.

Josh joined her on the half-finished floor. The granite trimidion swung above them on its monstrous chain, making her a little anxious. She hated to imagine that thing coming down on them.

Mirren offered her a water bottle, and Josh took a sip. "I was actually trying to avoid the tiling."

Mirren smiled, though her gray eyes were—as usual—serious. Josh was always surprised by how beautiful Mirren was, even sweaty and tired and with grout on her smooth cheek. "I can't blame you. It's incredibly monotonous."

"Have you got the trimidion working?" Josh asked, noticing that one corner hung lower than the others.

"No, not yet. I was hoping I'd figure out how to activate it once I had the major pieces in place, but nothing's coming to me." She wiped her forehead on her sleeve. "Can you imagine doing all this for nothing?"

"You didn't do it for nothing," Josh told her.

Mirren had showed her the note Haley had left for her before he went into Death. *Build the royal trimidion,* it read. Mirren kept it in a little glass vial that hung around her neck.

She picked up her trowel again. "How's Feodor?"

"He's good," Josh said, and then thought it was the wrong thing to say. "He's . . . fine, or, whatever Feodor is."

"I'm not going to hold his being fine against you, Josh. You know that."

"I didn't mean it that way. I meant . . . He always pretends to be in the same mood, you know? He's always got this front up. So who knows how he's really feeling."

"If anyone could, it would be you."

"Everybody seems to think so," Josh said tartly, recalling Will's nightmare.

Mirren lifted an eyebrow.

"Never mind," Josh said.

"No, now you have to tell me."

"I didn't come out here to complain about Will. And you're busy—"

"I'm more than capable of smearing grout and listening at the same time."

Josh sighed. "All right. Last night I was dream walking . . ."

She told Mirren about Will's nightmare that she had been half-possessed by Feodor. One thing Josh had discovered about Mirren— she was ridiculously poised and dignified and had perfect manners, but she was surprisingly easy to talk to.

"I don't know what to make of any of it. For two months I thought Will was trying to make me feel bad, and now suddenly he says, 'No, no, I actually want you back.' Did he mean he was working on it in counseling? 'Cause I thought he went to therapy to be less anxious, not to get back together with me. And why was I so pretty in the nightmare? He can't really see me that way. I just literally don't look like that." Josh fell back against the central pillar, exhausted. "Sometimes I wish he'd just yell at me and sleep with my best friend like Ian did. At least I'd know what that meant."

She was only half kidding.

"Oh, Josh," Mirren said, and then she chuckled. "Do you have any idea whether or not you *want* Will back?"

Yes. Josh almost spoke the word before she had fully thought it, and then a rush of longing filled her like a full-body flush. She had been trying so hard not to think about him that she hadn't realized how much she wanted him back.

"I wasn't the one who wanted to call it quits," she said. "That was all him. But it's not like I've changed since we broke up, not in the ways he'd like me to."

Mirren was shaking her head. "What?" Josh asked.

"May I give you a piece of advice?"

"Sure."

"You have to stop letting Will's opinion define your self-worth."

Josh stared at her. "What?"

"*You have to stop letting Will's opinion define your self-worth. What does it matter if Will thinks you're prettier than you are, or if he thinks you're half Feodor? What does it matter if he smiles at you or not? You know who you are, and hopefully you know you're a generous, loyal, incredible person.*"

Josh brushed the compliments aside. "Yeah, but I built those devices—"

Mirren put her hand on Josh's arm. "I would have done the same thing."

Josh shook her head, afraid she had something in her ears. "You would have?"

Leaning toward her, Mirren said, *"Of course.* We would have had to be stupid to pass up that opportunity. The chance to bring balance to the three universes? It's only what our people have been working to do since before recorded history. Yes, the situation turned out badly. That's your grandfather's fault, and Bash's, and Bayla's. Only a small part of it is yours."

"But Will said—"

"Will may not be cut out for this work, Josh. I know that's inconceivable to you, but it's the truth. He's going to be a great psychiatrist, sitting in his office and helping people sort through their feelings. He understands people, and he understands how they think. He's good at what he does. But you and I, we're good at what we do, and what we do is keep the balance." Mirren frowned. "The biggest mistake I've made was letting him talk you out of building more powerful devices. I should have stopped him."

"He was afraid I wouldn't—"

"You already said it: He was *afraid.* He was acting out of fear. That's what gets dream walkers killed. Will is a good person, and I hope he calms down and realizes how lucky he is to have you, but you don't have to answer to him."

I don't? Josh thought.

The idea felt like a bucket of cold water tossed in her face. Shocking, and yet . . . somehow refreshing. Still, Josh was afraid to hope; the relief felt too good.

"Maybe," she said. "I've made so many mistakes . . ."

"Oh, and you're the first one? Should everyone who's made a mistake avoid ever making another decision? No. You just try to make a better decision next time."

That's dedication, Josh thought. *You try again. You jump back into the Dream.*

"I'm sorry," Mirren said. "I shouldn't be telling you how to live your life any more than Will should. I just . . . You know, all anyone talks about today is Feodor the madman, but before Maplefax, people thought he was a genius. He was a visionary, and he did great things. He could have done more great things if he hadn't let his emotions tear him up inside. I don't want to see the same thing happen to you. Maybe it's better to be without Will if it gives you a chance to learn to trust yourself. Del says you've only been single for a year out of your entire life, and that you believed everything Ian told you about yourself, too."

"That's true," Josh admitted. She and Ian had been together before they were old enough to understand what being together meant, and he'd told her a lot of things about herself that, after he died, she realized weren't true. "I still can't quite believe Will broke up with me. I thought . . . that he understood dedication."

"Well, maybe he needs some time away to find clarity, too."

Josh remembered the nightmare, how he had said, *I'm trying to learn to trust you again.* Maybe he needed time away from her to do that.

Tired of thinking about him, she said, "Thanks, Mirren."

"I would hug you if I weren't all grouty."

Josh hugged her anyway. She wanted to say something, felt afraid of offending Mirren, and then decided to risk it. "You know, I don't make friends that easily. That first time we met with Davita in the kitchen, and you said Will and Haley and I were your friends, I was kind of shocked. We'd only known you a couple of days."

"I remember," Mirren said with a smile. "I felt rather bold saying it."

"Well, I just want you to know that I'm really grateful you did."

Mirren hugged her again. "Oh, Josh. I wish you could see how much you've changed."

Changed? Josh wondered. *Maybe . . .*

"Your fashion sense notwithstanding," Mirren added.

"I know, I need to buy new jeans. And new sneakers."

"Your shirt is inside out. And you have something in your hair . . ." Mirren picked it out and pursed her lips. "It's floss."

Josh winced. "After we get Haley back, I'll start dressing like a human being again. I promise."

"I'll believe it when I see it."

A phone rang. Mirren crawled on her knees to a toolbox nearby and dug a phone out. "Hello? . . . Oh? . . . Actually, Josh is here." She held out the phone. "It's Will."

Josh took the phone reluctantly. "Hello?"

"Hey," Will said. "I didn't know you were at Mirren's."

Josh didn't know what that meant. Was she supposed to tell him where she went? *You don't have to answer to him.* "Well, I am. What's up?"

"Del and I are at your grandfather's. You need to come over here right away. Bring Mirren."

Fifteen

"Are you crazy?!" Whim shouted at Mirren. "This is your moment! This is your chance! You have to stand up and take it! Call a press conference!"

Will watched Mirren sit down at the makeup table in Peregrine's basement. He could still see her face in the lighted mirror over the table—they'd turned the power back on—but Mirren was carefully controlling her expression. Even in her muddy jeans and flannel shirt, she was a diplomat.

"For once," Davita Bach said, "I agree with Whim."

"Thank you," Whim said.

Davita was a local representative of the junta—the government the dream walkers had just voted to abandon in favor of a democracy. Before the coup twenty years prior, she had been a staunch supporter of the monarchy, and her political career had been

somewhat stunted by her continued loyalty. Will had never entirely trusted Davita, but he believed she wanted to see Mirren in
power.

"People are already calling for a new election since Peregrine
disappeared," Whim said. "If we prove he rigged the last one, the
junta will hold another election for sure."

"And what will that accomplish?" Mirren asked. "Just because
there's a crown in his prop box doesn't prove that the nightmares
Peregrine staged are the reason everyone hates me—not to those
same people. And it certainly doesn't mean that the people who
voted against me will suddenly change their minds."

"We might be able to stall and put off the election for a few
months," Davita said. "The junta is considering a six-month extension of their leadership in order to sort out what to do with the
Lodestone Party now that Peregrine's missing. We could push to
hold a new election close to the end of that term, to give you time
to campaign."

"So that Peregrine can stage more nightmares to turn people
against me?" Mirren asked.

"He's probably dead in a ditch somewhere," Whim told her.

Mirren laughed grimly. "That's wishful thinking if I ever heard
any."

"At least let me call the Gendarmerie and have this place docu-
mented," Davita said. "Let Whim put the photos on his blog. That
way when you're ready to run again, we'll have proof of what Peregrine did."

Mirren sighed and then nodded. "All right. But keep my name
out of it." She touched the top of the makeup table with her fingertips before letting her hand come to rest there. "Do you think I
could have a few minutes alone down here?"

Josh, who had been leaning against the wall in silence during
the entire conversation, pushed herself onto her feet. "Sure."

She'd barely said a word since she arrived, and Will wanted to
know what she made of this place—which Whim had already nick-

named Peregrine's staging dungeon—but the tension from the nightmare still hung between them.

Instead of heading for the stairs, Josh went over to Mirren and hugged her. Mirren touched Josh's arms around her chest, and she smiled when Josh whispered in her ear.

"Thank you," Mirren said.

Startled, Will followed Josh up the stairs. He had *never* seen her reach out like that, not to someone outside her household family, and rarely with them. She hadn't even looked uncomfortable.

When she paused to examine the teddy bear that had insulted Whim earlier, Will said, "That was nice of you."

Her finger hovered over the button beneath the teddy bear, then abandoned it. "What was?"

"With Mirren, just now."

She frowned as if confused. "All right. Thanks."

As she started to walk away, Will blurted out, "I want to apologize for last night."

She shrugged. "I wasn't sure you remembered it."

"Thank you for waking me up. And . . . I'm sorry for what I said. I didn't mean to imply that you should kill Peregrine and Feodor."

She considered him for a moment before asking, "What *did* you mean?"

"That it's my anxiety about them I can't handle, not you."

"Huh," was all she said.

Passing the teddy bear, she walked over to a display of postcards from Nazi concentration camps. Will wasn't sure if they were meant to be sarcastic or ironic or just offensive, but each included a photograph of one of the camps with a slogan like CAMP DACHAU—WISH YOU WERE HERE!

"What do you see when you look at these?" Josh asked.

"The postcards? I don't know. Bad taste?"

She nodded. "What I see is that this postcard is mislabeled." With one fingertip, she tapped a black-and-white photo of a sign that read DUST SPREADS TYPHUS 5 MPH. "This was taken at Belsen, not Auschwitz."

Will didn't ask how she knew; he didn't have to. Josh turned away from the display, as if she didn't want to look at it any longer, and leaned against the wall with her arms crossed.

"You want Feodor and Peregrine out of your life so that you can feel safe. I get that. But that means you need to get as far away from me as possible, because *I am Feodor*. His memories are never going to go away. He told me he couldn't remove them if I asked him to, and frankly, I'm not sure I would ask. You might not like me like this, but *I* do." She glanced back at the postcards and shook her head. "All I've ever wanted to do is balance the three universes. Now I have the intelligence to actually do it. But to you, Feodor's memories have corrupted me."

Will wanted to argue with her, but he was afraid she was right. His nightmare had already proven as much.

"I made a mistake," she said. "Granted, it was a big mistake, and you were right that I went a little power-crazy. But if you can't trust that I learned my lesson, if you don't believe that my intentions were always to help people, then it's probably best we keep our distance."

She didn't sound angry, or even defensive. She didn't sound like Feodor. She sounded like someone who knew she had no power over the situation, and was okay with that.

Will envied her that acceptance.

"I never doubted your intentions," he told her. "Maybe your judgment, but . . . if I could—if I were able to trust you again . . ." He swallowed. He was so afraid to ask. "Would you want to—"

"Yes," she said without hesitation, before he'd even finished asking. Then a smile broke through her seriousness, a sheepish half smile he remembered from all the times he had managed to coax her into vulnerability. She slipped her fingers through the belt loops in his jeans and tugged him close to her. He wasn't expecting that, and he had to brace his arms against the wall on either side of her.

She whispered, her breath brushing his ear. *"Hell yes."*

And before he could reply, she had ducked under his arm and was gone.

Davita called the captain of the Gendarmerie and convinced her that Will, Whim, Deloise, and Winsor shouldn't get in trouble for breaking in, given the evidence they were about to hand over. Within the hour, gendarmes swarmed the house and taped off the basement, but not before Whim took about a hundred photos of the staging dungeon. Will didn't let him take photos of Peregrine's private bedroom. That felt like a secret none of them had the right to share.

By the time the Gendarmerie arrived, Winsor couldn't even hold her head up, and her eyes kept closing and her jaw falling slack halfway through a sentence.

"I need to go home," she said.

"We will, soon, I promise," Whim assured her. "I just want to talk to whoever's heading the hunt for Peregrine."

"Please," Winsor begged, tears in her eyes. "My head hurts."

Whim blinked, and then shook himself. "I'm sorry," he told his sister. "I'm being selfish. Of course we can go home."

As soon as Deloise climbed into the backseat, Winsor lay down on her side to rest her head on Deloise's leg. Deloise stroked her hair, but they'd already pushed Winsor too far, and she cried the whole way home. Whim had to carry her to bed.

"That was depressing," he told Will afterward, while opening a can of tuna in the kitchen. "I knew we shouldn't have let her come."

"If she'd stayed here, she would have felt left out. We didn't really have a good option."

"I hate seeing her like this," Whim admitted. "I keep trying to assure myself that she's going to get better, but I'm starting to think this is as good as she'll get."

"It's barely been three months. The brain heals slowly."

"She just used to be so smart. Much smarter than me. Now she forgets words. Her head hurts all the time. She cries for no reason.

This morning she yelled at me for moving her shoes out of the hallway."

Will nodded. In one of Winsor's worse moods, she'd accused Will of stealing her lip balm.

"I think she'll improve," Will told Whim. "She's getting stronger physically, and she'll probably feel better when she can do more for herself. But even if this is as good as it gets . . ." He thought of Haley's awkwardness then, and Josh with her shirt inside out, and his own misfit past. "I have a feeling everybody will still love her."

"Well, obviously." Whim stared morosely into a bowl of tuna and mayo, then straightened up and said resolutely, "Okay. From now on, Project Support Winsor is priority number one. Project Get Deloise Back is officially being downgraded to priority number two."

Will smiled at that. Whim obviously hadn't realized that being kind to other people *was* the way to win Deloise back.

"So, do you feel less afraid of Peregrine, now that we've uncovered his dirty secret?" Whim asked.

"I don't know. I pity him—that's new."

The doorbell rang. Will didn't know who else was around, so he got up and went to the foyer.

A man was standing on the doorstep with a pet crate covered in airline stickers. "I have a delivery for Whim Avish," he said. A cab sat parked behind him in the driveway.

"Whim!" Will shouted, peering into the crate. He had a bad feeling about this. "Did you order a live animal?"

Whim cursed cheerfully and came running to the door. "Yes, yes, yes! Thank you so much!"

"Sign here," the cab driver said.

Whim tipped him twenty dollars and carried the crate into the living room. He called Deloise on his phone and said only, "Darling, please come downstairs. I have a surprise for you."

Will watched in horror as Whim opened the crate and removed a tiny, adorable bundle of white fur with two black eyes shining out of it. "You didn't . . ."

Whim grinned. "I did. It took me three months, but I found one."

Ever since Will had met her, Deloise had been talking about how, when she had her own apartment, she was going to get a Bolognese puppy. They were expensive, and hard to find, and made rather nice pets, but Will couldn't believe Whim had been stupid enough to buy her one.

Whim had tossed a throw blanket over the crate and hidden the puppy behind his back by the time Deloise walked in. "Del," he said, dropping to one knee, "I know I've hurt you and treated you disrespectfully, and I'm truly sorry. I love you, and I think you're the sweetest, kindest, most beautiful girl in the three universes, and I hope you'll accept this gift as a token of my regret for the way I've treated you."

Will almost couldn't watch as Whim held out the trembling puppy. Deloise screamed, clapping her hands over her mouth, and her knees dipped dangerously.

When she could speak again, she said, "If I weren't a hard-core pacifist, I would slap you across the face right now."

"Really?" Whim said, and his smile began to fade at the ends.

"What the *bleep* is the matter with you?" Deloise cried, unwilling to swear even in these circumstances. "You bought me a puppy without asking me? Without asking any of our parents?"

"You've always said you wanted a Bolognese puppy—"

"Yes, in the future, when I don't live in a third-floor apartment! I'm going to have to run up and down the stairs twelve times a day taking it out!"

"So you'll keep her?" Whim asked. He held the puppy up beside his face and made an expression that Will suspected was meant to be cute.

"No, I'm not keeping her," Deloise said, but the words were obviously an effort.

"But she already loves you," Whim said. "I've been telling her all about you." He held up one of the puppy's paws in a tiny wave and spoke in a squeaky voice. "Please, Deloise, I've been waiting so long to meet you. I know we're going to be best friends."

"Oh my God, stop!" Deloise cried. "No, no! Is she even a rescue?"

"Dude, nobody abandons these things. They're too cute."

"Send it back!" Del told him.

Whim sighed. "All right. I'll send her back." He shook his head. "You don't know how much I went through to get this one. They said she's the runt of the litter."

Deloise bit her lip.

"I'll call the airline and see if I can get her on a flight back to New York. If the pet store will even take her back."

"The *pet store*?" Deloise asked with a gasp. "Do you know where those puppies come from?"

Whim cast an uncertain glance at the puppy. "Bigger puppies?"

"You bought a puppy mill puppy!"

Will was pretty sure Whim's confusion was genuine. "What's a puppy mill?"

Deloise took the puppy out of Whim's hands and snuggled it close. "We won't send you back to that bad pet store," she told it, rubbing her face against it as she walked out of the room. "We'll find a nice family for you. Even though you're the cutest thing I've ever seen and you smell like milk and baby powder . . ."

Whim smirked. "No way that puppy's going back to New York," he told Will.

"You really didn't get anything out of that boundaries talk we had, did you?" Will asked.

"Was it something about geography?"

Will shook his head, then followed Deloise upstairs.

He wanted to play with the puppy, too.

Sixteen

"We should go back," Ian said for the hundredth time.

After the incident at the castle the day before, Haley and Ian had both been out of sorts, and they'd only walked a few more miles before stopping at a cabin on the side of the road that appeared to be available to anyone who wished to use it. They stayed the night in twin beds beneath hand-stitched quilts, but neither had slept well. Ian tossed and turned, while Haley lay motionless in the dark, kept awake by both Ian's restlessness and his own fear of going to sleep in his brother's presence.

Is Ian right? Haley wondered as the night dragged on. Had he made so little use of his life that he no longer deserved it? Maybe Ian did deserve a second chance more than Haley; maybe he would do more for the World than Haley would ever dream of.

In the morning, they started out on the road again, finding it wider and in better repair than the part they had traveled the day before. Despite that, Ian complained about everything: his head hurt, he was tired, he was hungry, he was thirsty, his shoes were giving him blisters, the sun was too hot, they were wasting time, Haley was being annoying.

"What do you want to talk to Dustine for anyway?" he asked midmorning, just after the dirt road turned to gravel.

Unlike most of Ian's comments and questions, Haley answered this one.

"Josh is having a hard time being the True Dream Walker. Maybe Dustine knows something that could help."

"She doesn't know anything. She probably doesn't even remember who Josh is."

That is possible, Haley had to admit to himself. But he was keeping his fingers crossed that Dustine would know how to help Josh access her abilities.

The road turned, and beyond the bend, a city appeared. Rows of Victorian mansions gave way to run-down tenement buildings and four-story factories coughing gluts of sooty smoke. The dead, wearing pristine robes and contented smiles, seemed entirely out of place.

"What a dump," Ian said as they followed the dead down a paved street.

The transition between the rich and poor sections of town was embodied in a single large building. The front half was a beautiful Victorian building with ornate decoration on the window arches and roof edges, painted purple with blue and white accents. The back half was a factory with walls made of dirty windows and numerous smokestacks from which plumes of black smoke emerged.

Ian reluctantly followed Haley inside.

A spectacular library filled the front half of the building. Bookshelves were built into the walls, their cases elaborately carved wood polished to a gleam. Wingback chairs were clustered around marble fireplaces, and the dead sat in them, reading enormous leather-bound books with gilt-edged pages. Sometimes they spoke to one another in soft voices, but mostly they focused on the volumes in their laps.

"I don't like this place," Ian muttered, walking close behind Haley. "It smells like smoke."

"That's probably just from a fireplace," Haley assured him.

"Who wants to spend eternity reading, anyway?"

Stepping close to one of the bookcases, Haley noticed that each handsomely bound edition included a name in gold lettering on the spine. CAITLYN CALDWELL. MEGAN CAMPBELL. LUNEITA COTTON.

They're alphabetical, Haley realized. He followed the cases backward toward the door, traversing thick floral carpets, until he found the Bs. *Border, Borkin, Borst.*

Dustine's volume wasn't there.

What did that mean? Had she already been here and taken the book with her? Had her book been removed?

Haley didn't know how much farther he could convince Ian to go with him. Then again, he needed more time to convince Ian to let go of his old life. He hadn't even really started.

Maybe now was the moment to do that.

"Let's look over here," he said, following the cases toward where he suspected the M section would be.

They walked toward the back of the library, where they encountered a glass wall that separated the two halves of the building. On the other side of the glass was the interior of a factory. A huge furnace sat directly beyond the door, and within it burned a fire so hot the flames were tinged with blue. The dead were throwing their books into the furnace and watching the pages burst into sparks. The details of their lives were burning up, too, and the dead, ever lighter, passed beyond the furnace to a rear door.

"Jesus," Ian said, his voice breathy. "Like cows to the slaughter."

Haley bit his lip. He knew Ian was terrified of this letting-go process, but it wasn't something he could put off forever. At least, not without damage to his soul. To Haley, the process was beautiful and freeing.

He tugged Ian away by the arm and led him through the stacks until they reached the M section. Ian's volume was right there, waiting for him, a thick red book with a stylized M on the cover.

Haley pulled it out. He began to open the cover and then stopped, not sure it was his right. Instead, he held it out. "This is your book," he told his brother. "The story of your life is inside. But it isn't all you are. What you truly are is unkillable. Putting this book in the furnace won't hurt you—it will free you."

Ian's aura darkened as though the light within it had dimmed. "Yeah?" he asked. He grabbed another book from the shelf. "What if I throw this one in the furnace?"

He held the book so that Haley could read the spine.

HAELIPTO MICHARAINOSA.

When Haley looked back at Ian, his twin was smiling, but it

wasn't a smile Haley had ever worn. The corners of Ian's mouth were tucked too deeply, his teeth clenched, his lips pulled so tight they lost their color.

"Ian—" Haley said, but Ian was already running.

Stunned, Haley lost a moment before following him back through the stacks. He ran through the doorway to the factory as Ian reached the side of the potbellied furnace. With another sick, gleeful smile, he held the book of Haley's life just within the furnace door.

"One more step," he warned.

The dead who had been standing in line to visit the furnace looked between Haley and Ian, but their faces were serene. *Please*, Haley thought. *Help me. Help him.*

"Please," he said to Ian. "Please don't."

He didn't know exactly what would happen to him if Ian threw the book in the furnace, but he knew it would ruin his chances of ever returning to the World.

"You thought you could trick me," Ian said. "You want me to forget who I am."

"No," Haley said. "It isn't forgetting. It's letting go."

"Letting go of what? Myself? You want me to forget that I was on the lacrosse team, that I had a girlfriend who was crazy about me, that everybody at school thought I was awesome, that I had awesome friends—"

"That's not who you are!" Haley cried, before realizing he'd raised his voice. "That's just ego stuff! It's an illusion! The real you is indestructible. It's your soul, Ian. You have to let go of all that stuff from your life so that your soul can enter the Dream to be reincarnated."

"You think I'm gonna fall for that?"

"I'm serious. Death isn't heaven. You can't stay here forever." Haley pointed to the lofty dead, at the sweetness in their faces. "Look at them. They're letting go. See how peaceful they are? You don't have to be scared."

"I'm not scared!" Ian hollered, and he stretched his arm so far into the furnace that Haley lost sight of the book. If the heat hurt Ian, he didn't show it. "All I see is a bunch of retarded hippies with amnesia!"

Haley trembled. The charred spots in Ian's aura were surrounded by rims of fire, and they were growing, eating away at his energy field. The sight of them made Haley feel hopeless.

"What's wrong with you?" he asked miserably.

"What's wrong with *me*? What's wrong is I'm not supposed to be here! Why can't you see *that*?"

Haley stared at his brother.

"I'm not supposed to be dead!" Ian stalked toward Haley, the book forgotten in his hand. "I had a life, Haley. I was going to get a scholarship to college and get my MBA and run my own business. I had a whole life planned out." By then, wicked orange rage had filled his aura to its edges. "*I* wasn't the one who was supposed to die!"

He stalked closer and closer, and even though Haley knew he was taller, Ian seemed to tower over him.

"What did *you* ever do? Nothing, that's what. You wasted your life hiding under the bed."

Ian's aura fractured at its edges, losing its spherical shape and becoming a spiked mace. Haley tried to shield himself energetically, but Ian's rage tore right though, piercing Haley with arrows of fury. He actually felt the pain, in his chest, in his throat, but he didn't feel his knees weaken until he'd already hit the floor.

"Look at you," Ian said. "You're balled up like a baby, because you *are* a baby. You'll always be a baby."

And that, Haley knew, was true.

"What have you got to go back to?" Ian asked. "Nothing! You dropped out of high school. You're so terrible with girls that you have an *imaginary* girlfriend. Your friends barely tolerate you."

Ian's fury cut through him, tearing Haley apart like a sheet of paper. He began to nod convulsively, and he felt his own aura breaking down, fracturing.

"Your own father walked out on you. You're stupid, you're bad at sports, you look like a homeless person. I mean, what's the point of your life?"

"I don't know," Haley whispered.

"You don't deserve life."

I don't deserve life. Haley heard himself sob.

"You're the one who should be letting go."

I'm the one who should be letting go.

"Say it!" Ian grabbed Haley's hair and jerked his head up. Through his tears, Haley saw a horrible, blotted mask that vaguely resembled his brother's face. Flushed red cheeks made him look like a demon.

An arm snaked out and a hand wrapped around Ian's wrist. "Ow!" he shouted, and released Haley. "Let go of me!"

Haley wiped his eyes just in time to see a man with a pulsating, plum-colored aura pull the book from Ian's fingers. He held it out to Haley, his other hand firmly clamped around Ian's wrist, and said simply, "Run."

Sobbing, Haley took the book and ran.

Seventeen

When Josh and Mirren arrived for coffee, Feodor was in a ridiculously good mood.

"Your Highness," he said, bowing as he opened his door. "I'm honored. Please, please, come in."

Josh followed Mirren into the chair factory. Mirren hadn't been there before, and she wore an amused smile as she glanced around at the books and dirty windows. Feodor appeared to have made some effort to tidy up; the papers were mostly in stacks, and he'd thrown a white sheet over the coffee table.

"I made *makowiec,*" Feodor said. "I so rarely entertain. Please, make yourself comfortable. Coffee?"

"Please," Mirren said as she sat down in one of the battered leather armchairs.

Feodor bustled into the kitchen area—which was separated from the sitting area only by a bookshelf. "You never make me *makowiec,*" Josh accused him through the books.

"Is it customary to serve refreshments to one's parole officer?" he asked, returning with a coffee service on a silver tray. "I had no idea."

Josh rolled her eyes, but secretly, she didn't appreciate his comparison. Hadn't she let him buy this crazy factory and fill it with books and computers and whatever else the Internet could offer him?

"Where did you get that?" she asked, gesturing to the coffee service, and then said, "No, don't tell me—eBay."

Feodor nodded briefly, but if he understood her implication, he didn't show it. "Shall I be mother?"

Josh knew he'd picked up the expression from his lover, Alice, during the two years after the war when they'd lived together in England, but she was surprised Mirren recognized it. "Please," Mirren said, and Feodor poured them each a cup of coffee, prepared Turkish style with the grounds in the bottom of the cup.

Josh normally hated coffee, but the way Feodor made it gave her a rush of comforting déjà vu. He'd grown up drinking tea, and only when he reached America had he really discovered coffee. After that he'd drunk little else, eventually graduating to the Turkish style.

He served the *makowiec,* a poppy seed cake with nuts, on gold-edged china plates. "What are the chances I have the recipe for this in my head somewhere?" Josh asked, digging into her slice. That, too, brought back happy memories of home—Feodor's home, and Feodor's mother, and their apartment in Warsaw.

"If you don't, I'll write it down for you," Feodor offered magnanimously. He pulled up a chair and sat down near the coffee service, ready to wait on them.

"This cake is delicious," Mirren told him. "And congratulations, to both of you, on your VHAG invention. You've made a huge contribution to dream walking."

"I don't suppose my name will appear on the announcement," Feodor said dryly.

"I'm sure Josh will find some way to credit you," Mirren assured him.

He shrugged. Josh knew he didn't really care one way or the other. He was far more interested in making sure Mirren's coffee had enough cream.

They talked about the VHAG and its possible applications—which, ostensibly, was why Feodor was throwing this little tea party—and debated whether or not to distribute it. "It's dangerous," Josh pointed out, "giving people the power to control the Dream."

"We could limit distribution to Veil repair teams like Zorie's," Mirren suggested. "But that's still a lot of VHAGs out there. One is bound to fall into the wrong hands."

Josh wanted so badly to see the universes balanced. "But if we distributed them, it's possible that we could bring the three universes into perfect balance, at least temporarily."

"Inevitably, that balance would be broken by people using the VHAGs to stage nightmares," Feodor said. "Temptation makes slaves of all men."

Mirren set her cup and saucer down on the coffee table. "I'm afraid I agree with Feodor. It's too risky."

Josh stared glumly at the crumbs on her plate. She knew Mirren and Feodor were right, that the risks didn't outweigh the benefits, but that didn't stop her from feeling deeply disappointed.

Strangely, some part of her was also proud of herself. She'd made a smart decision this time. She'd told others what she was doing; she'd taken their advice. If she had acted like this with the circlet and vambrace six months before, her life would be very different.

"One True Dream Walker is enough," Feodor added. "Billions of them would be problematic."

Josh gathered the crumbs with a fingertip. "That's the thing, though. Without the VHAG, I'm not the True Dream Walker. I can't do anything useful. We can either have a World full of True Dream Walkers or none at all."

"You have made excellent progress—"

"At losing myself in dreamers' fears? Yeah, I'm great at that. But how is me getting killed going to bring balance to the universes?"

Mirren frowned as Feodor poured her another cup of coffee. "How certain are you that Josh is getting closer to controlling the Dream, Feodor?"

"Quite certain. She must merge with the Dream before she can control it. The dreamer's fear is a bridge she can walk to that merger."

"I just don't know if that's going to work," Josh said. Feodor offered her more cake, and she waved him off. "I mean, what if we're going in completely the wrong direction? The prophesies about the True Dream Walker are old, they've been translated over and over, and they're *prophesies*. What if I'm not supposed to be able to control the Dream? What if there is no True Dream Walker?"

"Haley told you that you were the True Dream Walker, didn't he?" Mirren asked.

"Yeah. He said it's in my scroll."

"Haley wouldn't lie."

"Of course not. I'm just saying maybe he's wrong. Maybe Young Ben is wrong. Maybe the prophesies are wrong."

"Then how do you explain what happened in the Hidden Kingdom?"

Mirren was referring to the way Josh had miraculously healed herself and several other people. A lot more than that had happened, but Josh hadn't talked to anyone about it. She wondered if now was the time to tell Mirren and Feodor.

Feodor was fussing with a napkin, wiping up a drop of coffee that had spilled on the serving tray. Josh waited until he was finished to say to him, "In the Hidden Kingdom, you knew I was dying when you asked me for the activator."

Suddenly she had all his interest. "Yes," he admitted without hesitation.

The memory still frightened Josh, the sense of being slowly forced out of her body as if she were being shut down one nerve, one cell at a time.

"How did you know?"

He thought. "There is an expression on the face of someone dying, not so much in the eyes as . . . the tilt of the head, I suppose. As though they are already looking away toward another place, as though they can see things the living cannot. They are . . . distracted, by whatever comes next."

Josh repressed a shiver. *That is creepy as hell,* she thought.

"After you left," she said, "I passed out. I knew I was dying. But instead . . . I went somewhere else."

Feodor tilted his own head.

"I went to a white place. It didn't have walls really, everything was just white and misty. There was a black stone pillar with water pouring out of the top, like a fountain, but the water didn't seem to be coming *from* anywhere. And on top of the pillar was, like, a white stone egg."

Mirren sat up very straight then, her eyes wide. To Feodor, she said, "The Cradle?"

"Possibly," he said, although he seemed less excited and more skeptical than Mirren did.

"The Cradle?" Josh repeated, and then Feodor's memories came back. They had always been there in her mind—just like the recipes for *makowiec* and Turkish coffee and pierogies—waiting to be woken with a word or image, and now they blossomed like ink stains behind her eyes.

Many months before, Josh had drawn a Venn diagram for Will, to explain the three universes. "What about this place where all three universes overlap?" he had asked.

"That's where the diagram breaks down," Josh had said. "Because there's no place where the three universes really overlap. Or, I guess I should say that dream theorists think there *might* be such a place, but no one has proven it."

She hadn't given the idea another thought. Until now, when everything Feodor had ever read or thought about such a space came splashing back through her mind.

The place where the three universes overlapped had no official name—just dozens of nicknames. The Cradle. Simtumu. The Dream Forge. No one knew for certain that it existed, but every dream-walking culture seemed to have a legend or a myth about it. The details differed—it was heaven, it was hell, it was where the True Dream Walker lived. The egg Josh had held had a name, too—the Omphalos. The Greeks had called it the Belly Button of the World.

Josh became aware that Feodor was watching her hungrily. "What?" she asked.

He shook his head. "I can almost see the memories coming back to you."

Josh realized for the first time that he was jealous of her. He'd worked to educate himself for decades; to see such a wealth of knowledge simply handed to Josh must have made him envious.

"You think I went to the Cradle?"

"Did you touch the Omphalos?" Mirren asked.

"Yeah, I held it." Josh fiddled with her napkin, uncertain how to go on.

"And?" Feodor asked finally.

"I saw all these souls, moving from the World to Death to the Dream, like they were part of a giant, choreographed dance. I could see the path each soul was taking, where they were supposed to go next, and it all fit together, everyone fit together in this sort of— it was like a moving constellation of souls."

"You are describing the cycle of reincarnation," Feodor observed dryly.

He was giving her a look he usually reserved for Whim. Mirren, on the other hand, wore a soft, amazed expression.

"That's beautiful," she said, and Feodor cast her a withering glance.

His disparagement bothered Josh very little. He had been too cynical for such things since long before she was born.

"You don't have to believe me," she told him. "But even you can't deny the fact that I healed you."

Feodor had been dying of a gunshot wound to the gut when Josh had her vision.

"I looked at your path, and it didn't end with you dying at that moment. So I healed you. And I healed Katia's leg, and I fixed the Hidden Kingdom when it was about to collapse."

Feodor gave one of his acquiescing shrugs, as if her point meant nothing.

"But you didn't heal your grandfather?" Mirren asked.

"I was too anxious to see his path. I started to panic, and that snapped me out of that place, or that mind-set, whatever it was. I couldn't hold on to that feeling."

Feodor was frowning then, not with irritation but with perplexity. "You entered what seems to have been the Cradle, but you did so without an archway."

"Death can be entered without an archway," Mirren pointed out.

"But it requires a ritual, which creates a temporary archway." He thought. "The first time you accessed your powers as the True Dream Walker, were you not at Death's doorstep also?"

Josh had been lying in the Dream with a broken skull and a shattered elbow, watching Will bleed out. She didn't know if she had been dying, but she had certainly been desperate.

"I didn't go anywhere that time. I felt like I merged with the Dream."

"What are you thinking?" Mirren asked Feodor.

"I wonder if the two experiences are not different sides of the same coin. This egg you touched—was it the egg that allowed you to heal us?"

"Yes," Josh said. "But—I felt like I could have done *anything* while I was holding it. Like I had . . ."

She didn't want to say it in front of Feodor, but he finished her thought.

"Unlimited power."

She lowered her head. "Yeah."

Feodor had been given unlimited power once, in his own pocket universe. He could have made that place anything he wanted it to be, peopled it with everyone he loved, created his own vision of paradise. Instead, he had recreated Warsaw during World War II. He hadn't done it on purpose. No matter how many times he attempted to rebuild the city of his childhood, the war always returned to destroy it, because deep inside, Feodor believed the loss was inevitable.

If Josh had managed to keep on holding the egg, what would she have done with that power? What subconscious beliefs would have begun manifesting?

"You didn't happen to look at your own soul's path, did you?" Mirren asked.

"I did," Josh admitted. "But it didn't pass through the three universes like the others. It just showed up out of nowhere, and I couldn't see where it led."

Feodor murmured something under his breath that she didn't catch, but she didn't ask him to repeat himself. "Did you deliberately heal yourself?"

"No."

"And yet you awoke healed."

"Not just healed—healed completely. The elbow Gloves shattered hasn't bothered me once since then. I haven't had a headache, my eyesight is better, even my hair seems thicker."

"That's amazing," Mirren said.

"Yeah, but I don't know how to do it again. I don't know how to do any of it."

"Perhaps," Feodor said, "you don't need to. Perhaps this ability to enter the Cradle and return healed is part of your abilities as the True Dream Walker. You've expressed concern over losing yourself in a dreamer's fear, but if you do so, and you are killed, it appears that this ability will heal you."

"Wait a sec," Josh said, and she felt relieved when she saw her uncertainty echoed on Mirren's face. "That's kind of a stretch, isn't it?"

"I don't know," Mirren admitted, "but it certainly isn't a theory I'd want you to test."

"I mean, I didn't actually die either time. I was just in really rough shape. Maybe the key to entering the Cradle is desperation."

Feodor smiled at her, the same way he would have laughed at her, like he knew something she didn't. "Perhaps I am wrong."

That's the problem, Josh thought.

You never are.

Eighteen

Will spent several days debating what his next move should be. He was certain that Trembuline knew more than he was admitting, but Will didn't have any way to force him to talk. He still had no clue where Peregrine was. And word around the house was that Josh and Feodor had invented a way to seal Veil tears that was faster and safer than any current method, so he doubted he needed to worry about what Feodor was up to.

I guess he and Josh are off saving the World without me, Will thought, sitting on the couch next to Whim in the guys' apartment. The bitterness in his mental voice surprised him. Since when did he want to be included in such adventures? Hadn't he broken up with Josh in order to *avoid* having to save the World?

He didn't know anymore, but he liked this feeling that he was doing something proactive to prepare to meet Peregrine. Unfortunately, he only had one idea left to try. It was a long shot, but he'd convinced Deloise to go with him. "You want to go poke around in Mirren's archives with me and Del?" he asked Whim.

"No. I'm working on an exposé of Amish puppy mills for my blog."

Will clapped him on the back. "Well, at least you're using your powers for good this time."

Deloise drove them over to Mirren's farmhouse, where they rang the bell.

Katia answered, her silvery-blond hair pulled up in a high ponytail. She didn't look like she was in a very good mood: her brows were drawn together and the corners of her mouth angled down sharply. She softened a little when she saw her guests, though.

"Hi," she said.

"Hey. Is Mirren home?" Will asked.

"No, she and Josh went to tea at Feodor's place."

Will and Deloise looked at each other, their faces mirror images of surprise.

"Feodor's having a tea party?" Deloise asked.

"Josh is drinking *tea*?" Will asked.

"Who is it?" Collena called from deeper within the house.

"I've *got it*, Mom!" Katia hollered. "It's just Will and Deloise." She rolled her eyes. "Are you guys doing something?" she asked hopefully.

"Well, we were going to ask Mirren if she'd mind letting us look for some information in the archives in the Hidden Kingdom, but if she's not here—"

"I'll take you!" Katia grabbed a jacket off a coat stand and yelled, "I'm going out, Mom!"

"What?" Collena called back. "Where?"

"It doesn't matter! I'm sixteen! I can go out with my friends! I'll be home by ten!"

She slammed the door before her mother could respond.

Katia was so busy complaining about her overbearing mother that she got them lost on their way to the secret entrance to the Hidden Kingdom, which had been moved after Davita showed Peregrine the original entrance. Will finally had to look up directions on his phone.

"Um, I've never been to this part of town," Deloise said as she turned in to the Unlock and Load storage facility. "And I really wish we'd come here before dark."

"Isn't it gross?" Katia said. "I mean, who would keep their stuff here?"

As they drove between two banks of shuttered storage units, Will said, "My mom and I lived in one of these for three months when I was nine."

"Oh, Will, really?" Deloise said.

"Where did you pee?" Katia asked.

"Gas stations. We'd shower at Mom's friends' houses. It wasn't that bad," he added, although what he was remembering was how incredibly dark the storage unit had been once the door went down, and how there was no way to lock it from the inside.

They pulled up at unit 115 and Katia keyed the code into a heavy-duty lock. "Hey," she said, "Mom will kill me if she finds out I brought you here. So if she asks, just say we went to Waffle House."

"Sure," Will said, but he was starting to wish he'd gone to tea at Feodor's.

The entrance to the Hidden Kingdom was through a Hula-Hoop that had been tossed into the unit, along with various pieces of secondhand furniture and a lot of garage sale candles. "This way it's easy to move," Katia explained, tossing the hoop onto a clear spot on the floor.

The other side of the archway dropped them into a windowless room. A light automatically came on when they arrived, illuminating concrete walls, a steel door, and a touch-screen panel.

"Is this a vault?" Will asked.

"Yeah," Katia said. "Mom went completely crazy and had it put in right after the thing with Peregrine. This will take a minute. The security system is ridiculous."

It took her a solid five minutes with the touch screen before the vault door opened. Finally, though, they stepped through a coat closet into the foyer of the castle where Mirren and Katia had grown up.

When Will thought of the castle in the Hidden Kingdom, he always thought of marble. There were more than a hundred varieties that made up floors, walls, end tables, statue stands, sinks, bathtubs, even toilets, and Will never got tired of looking at the different colors and patterns.

"Mom comes here once a week to dust and vacuum," Katia said, as she started down the stairs toward the basement. "Can you believe it? That woman needs a hobby."

Behind her, Will and Deloise laughed silently. Even Will, whose mother had abandoned him to the state when he was twelve, had never referred to his mom as "that woman."

"Wait," Will said as they reached the record room. "Do you know how to open the files?"

"Oh, yeah. Mirren taught me. She wasn't supposed to, but she was worried that if something happened to her, no one would ever figure out the system. What did you guys want to look up, anyway?"

"We aren't completely sure," Will admitted. "But I was thinking that there might be something about Peregrine in the prophesies about the True Dream Walker. Maybe something about her having an archenemy."

"Well, there are plenty of prophesied enemies for her to fight," Katia agreed.

Katia and her parents also knew that Josh was the True Dream Walker. It had been kind of hard to hide after Josh magically destroyed the chains that bound Fel and Collena and healed the bullet wound in Katia's leg.

Collena must have replaced the carpet in here, Will thought as he walked into the low, red record room. *All the bloodstains are gone.*

He wondered what she'd done with Peregrine's hand.

"So do you want, like, stories about the True Dream Walker?" Katia asked. "Or art? Or theories about the first True Dream Walker? Or do you want to read the prophesies about the new True Dream Walker?"

"Definitely the prophesies," Will said.

"I don't know anything about the first one," Deloise admitted. "Only that he had an assistant named Hazel, who Josh is named after."

Josh's second middle name—chosen after a role model—was Hazel.

"It's actually pronounced Ha'azelle in Hilathic," Katia said, already jamming keys from the three enormous key rings into a file cabinet. Each cabinet required three keys and a spin code to open. "The Hilaths were super into saying the same vowel twice in a row. Also, there's a popular theory now that Ha'azelle *was* the True Dream Walker, but the story was recast for misogynistic reasons."

She chattered on as she opened drawers and pulled out files, occasionally pausing to ask if something interested them. When she'd run out of things to show them, they carried the pile over to a library table.

The fact that they had no idea what they were looking for made the work long and—if Will was being honest—tiresome. Most of the information about the first True Dream Walker was recorded in the form of improbable, somewhat bizarre legends, and most of the information about the return of the True Dream Walker was in the form of esoteric poetry—*translated* esoteric poetry.

"I think this says that Josh will be able to communicate telepathically with cows," Deloise said after an hour. "But the story is really specific that it's only this one kind of cow—*im'meme* cows?"

"They mean aurochs, which are extinct," Katia said.

Despite being almost nothing like her cousin, Katia had one thing in common with Mirren: a very thorough education.

"I can read this," Will said, "but I have no idea what I'm supposed to get from it. It's a prophesy written by this German woman—Kyferin?"

"Oh, yeah. She was definitely smoking something. Is that the story about the pie?"

Will read the story aloud. It involved a vision Kyferin had had, that three witches dragged the moon from the sky and baked it into a cake. When they cut the cake, the True Dream Walker popped out.

"Only it doesn't say True Dream Walker, it says Beguiling Dream Walker."

"Beguiling?" Katia asked. "That's wrong. Where's the original German?"

While she got up to retrieve a pair of books, Will finished the story. "'Then the True Dream Walker took a dancing stick and tore down the sky and put it in a cauldron. He tore down the sleeping sky and the waking sky and put them in the cauldron, and he cooked them for seven days and seven nights. He said to the Beguiling Dream Walker, "Help me stir the skies," but the Beguiling Dream Walker tried to empty the cauldron, and the True Dream Walker pushed him in.' Wait, what?"

"There are two different dream walkers?" Deloise asked.

"I've got it," Katia said, slamming a giant dictionary down on the table. "So, 'cake' here should definitely mean 'pie,' 'beguiling' means 'false,' just like I thought, and 'dancing stick' should probably be 'walking stick.'"

Will blinked. Everything was moving too fast suddenly. "Did you say that Beguiling Dream Walker should be *False* Dream Walker?"

Katia glanced back at the dictionary. "Yeah."

"There's a False Dream Walker? Could he be Peregrine?"

"Maybe. There are a few prophesies about him. Not much. They're all about him fighting with the True Dream Walker, because the True Dream Walker wants to merge the three universes."

Deloise's jaw dropped. "That can't be right."

"It is," Katia insisted. "This part about mixing all the skies in a cauldron? That's what that means."

"But . . ." Will had trouble forming the thought. "But that means that, instead of balancing the three universes, Josh will combine them, right?"

"Yeah," Katia said again, seemingly oblivious to the implications of what she was saying. "There's a good Sumerian prophesy about it, hold on."

She climbed onto her knees on her chair so she could reach across the table and hunt through the files spread across the table. "Is that even possible?" Will asked Deloise.

"I don't know," she said. Her face was pale. "I don't know anything about dream theory. But I know it's not something Josh would ever want to do. All her life, she's been obsessed with balancing the three universes."

Katia held out another piece of paper. "This one is my favorite. The translation's really good, too." She read it aloud.

The child shaped her mouth and spoke.
"Mother, tell me of the world's end.
Mother, tell me of the close of time.
Mother, tell me of the city's fall."
The mother shaped her mouth and spoke.
"Child, I will tell you of the world's end.
Child, I will tell you of the close of time.
Child, I will tell you of the city's fall.
When the sky is full of fire,
when the mothers fear for the children,
when the grandmothers fear for the grandchildren,
the door will be opened for the Dream Walker,
the entrance march will be played for the Dream Walker,
the rituals will be performed for the Dream Walker.
Then the choice will be made.
The water below will rise up.
The water above will fall down.
The water will swell over the city's white walls.
Like the flood of old, the water will swell over the city's white walls.
The Anzu bird will not know the sky from the sea.

The temple priests will not know the sea from the land.
The sheep will not know the land from the sky.
When the dam breaks, the fields will be flooded.
The spirits of the living will forget the World.
The spirits of the dreaming will forget the Dream.
The spirits of the dead will forget the Death.
That which is separate will be combined.
The honey will mix with the milk.
The milk will mix with the ashes.
The ashes will mix with the bread dough.
That which should be separate will be combined."

"You sort of have to like Sumerian poetry to appreciate it," Katia finished. "They were super into repetition."

"Wait," Will said. He was having a hard time with Katia's ADD. "How many of the prophesies about the True Dream Walker say he'll combine the three universes?"

"Umm . . . half? Maybe? It's definitely the most common theme. The other prophesies are all sort of random, like the telepathic cow thing."

"But that means the end of the World, right?" Deloise asked.

"No, it just means it would all go back to the way it was before."

"Before what?" Deloise insisted.

"Before the first True Dream Walker."

Will could tell Katia was getting annoyed by their anxiety. "Katia," he said, "I know we must seem ridiculously stupid to you—"

"Not stupid," she muttered. "Uneducated, maybe."

"—but please remember that Del didn't get your education, and I've been a dream walker for less than a year. Please, explain what you mean about the way it was before the True Dream Walker."

She sighed and sat back in her chair. "Some people believe that before the first True Dream Walker came, the three universes were all one big universe, and that it was the True Dream Walker who separated them, and that one day he'll return to make them one again."

"Why would he do that?" Will asked.

"I don't know. Why did he make one universe into three in the first place?"

"But not everyone believes that, right?"

"No, not everyone. Some people think he'll create heaven on earth, some people think he's Jesus, and some people think he'll show up and have a giant showdown with the False Dream Walker, like at the end of *Pacific Rim.*"

Will stared at her and then covered his eyes with one hand. "Del, I can't . . ."

"What Will's trying to ask," Deloise said, "is who wins?"

"The True Dream Walker. Of course. Otherwise what's the point of the story? It's extremely archetypal—good versus evil and all that."

"What happens to everyone if the three universes merge?"

Katia shrugged. "There are a million different theories. I think we won't sleep or die anymore. We'll live forever, and when we imagine something, it will just happen."

"A World without Death," Will said. He felt like he was sinking through his chair and into the floor. "Wouldn't Feodor love that?"

Deloise's eyes widened. "You don't think—"

"Katia, what are the chances that Feodor knows all of this?"

"Um, like one hundred percent. He literally wrote the book on medieval prophesy, remember? Also, I think he coauthored a paper that tried to mathematically prove the three universes were once one."

What are the chances Feodor told Josh all of this? Will wondered, but he didn't ask aloud because he didn't want Katia to answer.

Any answer besides zero was wrong.

After they dropped Katia off—her mother was waiting for her on the porch, wrapped in a comforter—they actually did go to Waffle House.

They sat without speaking for a long time, Del's hands wrapped around a mug of tea, Will shifting uneasily in the hard booth.

You wanted to be prepared to face Peregrine, he told himself. *You wanted to arm yourself with knowledge. You wanted to feel like you could protect yourself. How do you protect yourself from the end of the world?*

"We have to tell Josh," he said, just like he had after they'd visited the prison.

This time, Deloise nodded. "Yeah." She bit her lip and then said, "Just because something's written in a prophesy doesn't mean it will happen."

"It's written in a lot of prophesies."

"Maybe one guy made it up, and then other people built on it. Maybe we're interpreting them wrong. Maybe Josh gets a choice."

What if she makes the wrong choice?

She had before. And Will was trying so hard to trust her—to trust that she knew what she was doing with Feodor, that she wasn't letting him pull the wool over her eyes—but this was a big place to start.

"Josh would never merge the universes," Deloise said. "Not unless it was what's best for everyone."

Will nodded like he believed her. He wanted to. He was just so afraid that Josh wouldn't have all the information she needed to choose correctly.

"I'll tell her," he said.

"Are you sure?"

"Yeah."

He didn't want to be the one to tell her. He just wanted to watch her when she got the news.

Hopefully she wouldn't be surprised.

Nineteen

When Josh came out of the archway, Will was sitting on a folding chair in front of it. His unexpected appearance startled her, and she slid across the floor on her wet shoes.

She caught herself before she fell. "Is that . . ." Will tried to ask, craning his head forward to get a better look at her.

"It's pudding," Josh told him. "And lasagna. And stewed green beans."

"High school food fight?" he guessed.

"Retirement home riot."

"Ah."

He didn't say anything else, just held out a towel. Josh wiped her face and, as best she could, her arms. Then she took her shoes off and wiped up the floor, and when she was finished, Will still hadn't spoken.

"What's up?" she said finally.

She didn't know how to read him then. He looked more than serious, almost a little sick.

"We need to talk."

"Is something wrong?"

He wet his lips, but they weren't dry. Josh felt like he was stalling. "I don't know. But we need to talk about it."

Dread filled Josh. *This can't be about us,* she thought. *But what else could it be about?*

"Come upstairs so I can change."

He said nothing as they went up to the third floor, but every step, Josh felt the stairway closing in around her. A memory of Feodor's came back to her then, of the last time he had been alone with his lover, Alice. They'd met at the end of the war and moved to America together, and she'd stuck by him as he slowly went mad. Finally, though, it had become too much. He'd been running experiments in their basement, and the memory that came back to Josh was of how Alice had taken him firmly by the hand and led him up the stairs to the living room. He'd known she was going to say she was leaving, but he'd been so immersed in his own madness that he hadn't cared.

Josh, though, could look back at the memory without the shadow of Feodor's lunacy upon it and appreciate how tightly Alice had held his hand as she dragged him from his laboratory, how determined she had been to treat him like he could understand her.

I miss her, Josh thought, though of course she had never met Alice. It didn't matter; the woman was a part of Josh now, the way she was a part of Feodor.

In her room, Josh pulled clean clothes from the basket Kerstel had left on the floor and went into the bathroom. After a moment's hesitation, she left the door open a few inches. What did she care if Will saw her naked at this point?

Besides, she knew he wouldn't look.

"What do you want to talk about?" she asked, rubbing a wet washcloth over her face.

"Well . . . This is sort of awkward, talking like this." She heard the springs in her recliner whine as he sat down. "You know I've been in counseling, working on my PTSD. One of the things Malina suggested was that I should try to build confidence that I can face whatever Peregrine throws at us next. I thought that maybe I could . . . sort of arm myself with knowledge. So Del and I went to the Pryliss Sanitarium."

Josh's washcloth stopped moving up her legs. "Where?"

"It's the prison Snitch escaped from."

Oh, Josh thought. She started washing again. As Will described his trip to the prison and his subsequent meeting with Aurek Trembuline, she slowly got dressed, but she was distracted from both his story and her clothing by a single question.

"Why?" she asked, opening the bathroom door. "Why didn't you tell me you were doing any of this?"

She understood that he didn't trust her. She understood that he thought Feodor's memories had in some way corrupted her judgment. But not sharing potentially important information related to Geoff's escape and—quite possibly—Peregrine's latest scheme made no sense.

Will was sitting in her recliner with his elbows on his knees and a braced expression on his face.

"I wasn't sure it was worth your time. I'm not even sure what any of it means." He rubbed the back of his neck. "I guess I knew I should have told you, but . . . You said you didn't want to be friends."

Josh couldn't quite believe that was his reasoning. She went back into the bathroom, and he followed her.

"You've barely been speaking to me," he said.

"*That's* your excuse?" she asked. She yanked a brush through her hair, cursing the length of the strands. She wanted to cut it all off.

"I didn't mean to go behind your back," Will told her.

"Of course you did. If you hadn't, you would have just come out and told me what you'd found." She threw the brush down on the counter. "I don't even care that you went behind my back. I don't care that you don't trust me. But like it or not, I am the point person on this Peregrine thing. Whatever my stupid destiny might be, there's no doubt that he's tied up in it." Suddenly she thought of something. "Or were you going to track him down yourself and kill him before I could stop you?"

"No," Will said breathlessly. "Of course not."

She knew from the way he said it that he was telling the truth, and she knew that should have dampened her anger, but she *wanted* to be angry. It felt good to talk carelessly.

She went into the bedroom and put on a pair of sneakers.

"Josh, wait. I'm trying to—this isn't how I wanted this to go."

"I don't know what that means, and I don't have time to figure it out. I need to go."

"Please, just stay for a minute."

Then he was taking her hand and Josh was remembering Alice

on the stairs and Mirren saying, "Will isn't cut out for this work," and the time he had kissed the inside of her wrist to make her stop freaking out—the first time he'd kissed her.

"I don't want you to do this alone," he said. "Whatever you're doing, I want to come with you."

"Why?"

"Because the truth is, regardless of the rest of the emotional stuff, I love you. And I want to be part of your life. Even when it's dangerous and scary."

Three months ago, three weeks ago, maybe even three days ago Josh would have thrown her arms around him. But today, all she could think was that their relationship problems were far less important than finding her grandfather.

Also, she didn't believe him.

"You're wrong," she said. "You're lying to yourself."

The look on his face hurt her, quite unexpectedly. She would have thought she was angry enough now not to care, or that she had given up on him enough to accept the inevitability of their hurting each other. But no. He looked like she'd stabbed him in the gut, and she clenched her hands as if around imaginary hilts.

Then his face hardened. "How would you know how I feel when we barely talk? You're mad that I didn't tell you what I was doing—what are *you* doing, Josh? Where do you go all the time? Nobody even knows where you are."

"I don't have to answer to you."

Will crossed his arms and nodded. "Because I'm just the apprentice, right?"

Now she was angry. "No!" she snapped. "Because you *quit* being my apprentice, and my partner! You quit showing up to train just like you quit showing up for me! You want to be an apprentice? Go ask Del to train you!"

She was across the living room before Will could even take a step. He followed her, though; she could hear his steps like echoes of her own in a dark alleyway.

"We need to talk about this," he insisted. "Where are you going?"

She didn't answer. Maybe she would never answer another question he asked.

Will grabbed her arm as she entered the stairwell. "I'm not giving up," he said. "I'm not giving up this time."

Again, the pain in his expression hurt her. He was afraid, she realized. Afraid that if she walked out this time, she might not walk back. At least, not back to him.

Maybe that was why she told him.

"I'm going to get Feodor, and we're going to find Aurek Trembuline, and we're going to find out what he knows about Peregrine."

Will set his jaw. "I'm coming with you."

Josh sighed. The anger had already worn her out. "Fine."

Twenty

Will waited in the car while Josh went into the chair factory to get Feodor. Will had never been inside it, and he was kind of curious, but Josh didn't seem to be in the mood to give a tour. By the time she had disarmed the security system, Feodor was already walking out the door, pulling on a brown wool trench coat as he did.

He looked surprised to see Will when he climbed into the car, and he said something in Polish that Will gathered was probably a wry remark.

"No, we aren't," Josh said. "And speak English when we're around other people."

Will couldn't figure out whether or not Josh was still angry at him. Probably. She hid a lot of emotions under the safe tarp of anger, emotions she didn't know what to do with. He hadn't done a great job making her feel safe to explore those feelings, he knew that. And he'd been so caught up in their argument that it wasn't until he saw Feodor that he realized he had forgotten to tell her the most important thing.

It would have to wait.

Josh was right that Will had quit on her. And on dream walking. He hadn't set foot in the Dream since they'd left Mirren's universe. He'd destroyed the one tie between them that Josh had considered sacred, and he knew it was something she never would have done. Even after they'd broken up, if he had showed up for their usual morning run, she would have run with him.

How broken is too broken? he wondered.

The funny thing was, when he thought back to the meditation with Trembuline, or when he sat in the dark car and watched the passing streetlamps cast Josh's face in light and then shadow, light and then shadow, he still felt the happiness he'd experienced when listening to his heart, like a little coal burning in his chest.

She'd put on the same sweater she had worn the night of the Valentine's Day dance, when she'd confronted him in the school library. Will wondered if she'd done it subconsciously.

The drive to Trembuline's house was an hour and a half long. Will pulled one of Trembuline's papers up on his cell phone and gave it to Feodor to read. Halfway through the drive, after they'd stopped for coffee—and in Josh's case, a twenty-four-ounce hot chocolate—he asked Feodor, "What do you think?"

"Of Trembuline?" Feodor asked. "I think he has attempted to use philosophy to justify doing whatever he wants. He advocates anarchy in order to rationalize his prepubescent sense of alienation and his thoroughly American desire to be *special*." Feodor handed the phone back to Will. "I also think he should be castrated."

Josh choked on her hot chocolate.

"But didn't you believe basically the same thing?" Will asked. "I mean, you tried to end the World because you were in so much pain. You put your needs before everyone else's."

"My actions came from a place of deep despair and a belief

that ending the World would prevent people from continuing to suffer," Feodor said, "a concept which, in the strictest sense, was not incorrect. I acted out of compassion, albeit in a destructive way."

"So if that's what you believe, why aren't you still trying to end the World?"

Will held his breath after the question, afraid he had given himself away, but Feodor only stared out the window. "I am no longer in a place of deep despair."

Will honestly didn't know what to make of that.

They reached Trembuline's house shortly before ten at night. He lived in a fairly large house, a recent construction, and children's bikes and pogo sticks were scattered across the front lawn. The lights were on inside.

"All right," Josh said, "this is it."

"Do we have a plan?" Will asked.

"Not really."

"Please," Feodor said, "allow me to take the lead."

"Why would I do that?" Josh asked.

"He may take someone older more seriously."

Josh considered. "All right," she said. "But no funny business."

They knocked on the door. A moment later, a little girl in a pirate costume opened it. "Hi," she said.

"Ellie," a woman said, following her into the entryway. "You're not supposed to open the door unless you know who's there." She smiled at her visitors while putting her hands on the little girl's shoulders and pulling her close. "How can I help you?"

Will heard the sound of other children in another room. Not surprisingly, it sounded like *a lot* of children.

"May we speak to Mr. Trembuline?" Feodor asked.

"Are you selling something?"

"No, no. We are fans of his work and wish to discuss his philosophies."

"You probably should have called his office," the woman said, but she shouted, "Aurek!" over her shoulder.

"Hey," Trembuline said when he walked in and saw Will. This time he was wearing board shorts and an airbrushed tank top that read MINDY'S DIVORCE SATURNALIA! "You came back. Cool."

"Mr. Trembuline?" Feodor asked. He held out his hand. "It is an honor to meet you."

They shook.

"What can I do you for?" Trembuline asked.

"We are hoping to speak with you about your work."

"I'm hanging out with my kids tonight."

"Please, we have driven several hours. We will not take too much of your time."

Trembuline shrugged. "Okay, just for a few minutes. Come on up to my study."

Trembuline's study had a lot of posters and photos on the walls. The posters were for ska bands, and the photos were of his multitudinous children.

The three of them sat down on the couch, and Trembuline straddled the desk chair.

"What do you want to talk to me about?" Trembuline asked.

"Let me begin," Feodor said, "by telling you what an appreciator of your work I am. There has been so much talk of government spy agencies and drones that can kill us from out of the blue; your philosophy of decentralized power and complete transparency is refreshing."

"Thanks. I've been thrilled with the events since the dreamwalker election. I think we're heading toward a really exciting collapse."

"You were not pleased with the results of the election?" Feodor asked.

"I'm not pleased with any election that increases governmental control of private actions."

"But I am curious—you say that you disapprove of government, yet you endorsed Peregrine Borgenicht during the election."

"Peregrine is a great man," Trembuline said. "I rarely meet anyone so willing to go after what they want."

"Did you know that he staged dreams in order to convince his wife to marry him?"

Will hadn't known that, and apparently Josh hadn't either. "What?" she said sharply.

Feodor held up a hand to quiet her, his gaze never straying from Trembuline's.

"I didn't know that," Trembuline admitted, "but I'm not surprised. The heart wants what the heart wants, right?"

"Yes, of course, but what did his wife want? They were quite unhappy together."

"Every marriage is unhappy in one way or another. Maybe marrying her was what his heart wanted at the time, but later his heart wanted something else. If that's true, he should have divorced her."

"That seems to imply that following one's inner wisdom does not always lead to happiness."

"Happiness isn't the goal. Union with the inner wisdom is the goal. The ability to hear that wisdom clearly and act on it without hesitation, without limiting oneself to behaviors that society find acceptable, that's the goal."

Delicately, Feodor said, "What if other people's wisdom tells them to hurt your children?"

Trembuline smiled. "I don't make exceptions for myself," he said. "I'm not a hypocrite."

Feodor let the statement hang in the air before asking, "Why did Peregrine Borgenicht send you to interview Geoff Simbar?"

Will noted the hardness that entered Feodor's expression as he asked the question, and the anxiety that entered Trembuline's expression at hearing it.

"I interviewed Geoff for my own research," Trembuline said.

"And then you reported back to Peregrine," Feodor insisted.

"I might have mentioned the interviews to him. Hey, you guys want some energy drinks?"

"No," Will said firmly.

"What did Geoff tell you? What was his mental state?" Feodor asked.

"What did you say your name is?"

"I didn't," Feodor told him. "How much of what happened to Geoff did he remember?"

"A lot," Trembuline admitted. "More than I would expect a normal person to remember."

"More in what sense?"

"He remembered an astonishing number of details, but he had no sense of context. He would tell me the same thing three times. I'm not sure he even realized I was the same person from one interview to the next."

"How much of the experiments Feodor Kajażkołski performed on him did he remember?"

"All of them, I suspect. But he couldn't connect the dots. The details of one experiment were jumbled up with another, they were all out of order."

"And where is Peregrine?"

Trembuline smiled uneasily. "I'm not sure. You know, speaking of Kajażkołski, you kind of resemble—"

Feodor's voice grew softer but somehow more dangerous. "Where is Peregrine?"

"I don't know, honestly. We've been communicating through e-mail."

"Before or after you broke Geoff Simbar out of prison for him?"

Will watched Trembuline's robust color fade.

"I didn't—that's not—I think he might be hiding out in his basement—"

"You *think*?" Feodor repeated.

"Yeah, I think—maybe . . ."

The pleasant little smile Feodor had worn throughout the interview vanished. "Would you like to know what *I* think? I think you are a self-centered fool who has co-opted others' lives to bolster a theory that a first-year philosophy student could knock over with a sigh. I think you are so in love with yourself that you have lost all perspective and all empathy. And I think that you interviewed Geoff Simbar at the behest of Peregrine Borgenicht, and that you are continuing to help Peregrine because of the mistaken belief that breaking rules will make others admire your independence and nerve." He stood up, and Josh and Will scrambled to do the same. "I think that you will tell us where Peregrine is, or we will quietly beat you to death."

Uh-oh, Will thought.

"You aren't going to beat me to death in my own home," Trembuline said, but his voice shook. "My kids are downstairs."

Feodor smiled again. "Perhaps the discovery of your body will bind them together as a family."

Will flashed Josh a frantic look behind Feodor's back. Feodor's own gaze was a steady drill boring into Trembuline's eyes.

"Feodor," Josh said.

Trembuline inhaled deeply, and Will knew he was about to scream. Feodor must have seen it, too, because he moved like a tiger. Before even Josh could react, he had Trembuline's chair flipped backward and his foot on the man's throat.

"Feodor," Will said. "Feodor, stop!"

Trembuline made a gargling sound and scratched at Feodor's boot. To Will's horror, Feodor removed a small, thin knife from his jacket pocket. He began tossing it from hand to hand, directly above Trembuline's face.

"As to your treatment of me," he said conversationally, "I thought it was sloppy."

"Feodor, stop it," Josh said, but Feodor's only response was to begin letting the knife flip a time or two in the air before he caught it.

Do something, Will begged her silently. His own limbs were stiff with panic and uncertainty. *Please, do something.*

He could see the tension in Josh's body, the readiness to attack, but she held back. Will didn't know what she was waiting for, if she trusted that Feodor wouldn't actually hurt the man, or if she was just hoping his interrogation technique would work.

"Had you bothered to so much as read *one* of the articles I published on dream ethics," Feodor said, "you would have found that I abhor people like you, who act only in their own interests with no concern for the welfare of others. They remind me of someone . . . who could it be?"

Now the knife was flipping too many times for Will to count, flying so high up in the air that it neared the ceiling.

Luckily, Trembuline chose that moment to confess. "Yes, okay, I broke Geoff out of Pryliss."

"What does Peregrine want with him?"

"He wants his body. He wants to put his own soul in Geoff's body."

That was the worst news Will had ever heard.

"Clever," Feodor said. "And where is he?"

"I swear I don't know where he is, but I know someone who might. Please don't drop that knife on me."

Feodor tossed and caught the knife one last time and held it tight.

"Oh, Jesus, please don't kill me. I'm sorry. He said he was going to go see someone named Alice Connelly."

Josh gasped, but Feodor grew as still as a hunting cat. "Who's—" Will started to ask, and halfway through his sentence Josh and Feodor smashed into each other as Feodor tried to pounce on Aurek and Josh tried to stop him. Aurek screamed, and Will stumbled back against the couch as he scrambled to get away from them.

Josh got her hand around Feodor's, but not until the knife was inches from Aurek's throat. "Drop it, or I'll break your thumb," she warned.

Feodor's face was red with blood. His lips snarled and smiled at the same time, and suddenly he was the Feodor that Will had been afraid of for so many months, the fiend who would not only kill Trembuline, but enjoy it.

"I'm warning you," Josh said. She said something in Polish then, but Feodor didn't move.

The study office door opened, and a little boy in pajamas said, "Daddy?"

Josh snapped Feodor's thumb.

Feodor cursed. He did so in Polish, but Will didn't need a

translation to know he was cursing. The little boy screamed. When Feodor dropped the knife, it landed on Aurek's throat but bounced harmlessly to the side.

Feodor looked at Josh then with an expression Will remembered from the first time they'd met in Feodor's universe, an expression to shrivel flowers. A dangerous black hatred strobed out of his eyes. Will began to tremble.

But Josh appeared to be immune to it. She stared back just as hard, and then she said, "You looking for round two?"

Feodor muttered something in Polish and stormed into the hallway.

"You can sit up front," Will told Feodor when they got back in Josh's car. He was afraid of having Feodor at his back.

"Where did you get the knife?" Josh demanded, tearing out of the Trembulines' driveway.

"EBay," Feodor said.

"I told you no weapons. I made that very, very clear."

"I live in a bad neighborhood."

Although Will figured that was probably true, Josh brought the car to a screeching halt—only three doors down from where they'd started—and grabbed Feodor by the chin, forcing him to look at her.

"You listen to me, *Fedya*. If you think I would hesitate to kill you, think again. It'll be cathartic."

"I have no fear of Death."

Josh put the car in park. "Do you have a fear of prison? Because I have no doubt that Trembuline's wife is calling the cops, and we can just sit here until they arrive."

Will was glad he couldn't see Feodor's face.

"You wouldn't," Feodor hissed.

Josh crossed her arms over her chest and leaned back in her seat.

"Without me, you'll never get your friend back," Feodor said.

She laughed. "You have an astonishing ability to underestimate

people, Feodor. Do you really think I've been sitting around, letting you return your measly three souls a month? I figured out how
the collection device works. I built a second one, a much more
powerful one. I've already used it to return more than forty souls
to Death."

The explosion of happiness in his chest stunned Will.

Haley, he thought.

"I've kept you around because you've been helpful with prophesies and figuring out my abilities, but don't think for a moment
that I *need* you. I'll have Haley home by the end of the month."
She grinned. "I'm not the stupid little girl you take me for."

Will was so proud of her in that moment. He'd been so terrified that Feodor was playing her, but she was the one playing him.
Whatever else was distracting her, she hadn't lost sight of the most
important thing: bringing Haley home.

"You cannot perform the ritual to enter Death without assistance—"

"You mean somebody to play the singing bowls?" Josh asked, a
laugh in her throat. "I built a machine to do all that. Designing a
recliner would have been harder."

Even though he couldn't see Feodor, Will could feel the waves
of fury wafting off of him.

"You aren't here at the pleasure of the Lords of Death," Josh said.
"You're here at *my* pleasure. It's time you figured that out."

The car windows were steaming up. Feodor's resembled frosted
glass.

Sirens broke the silence.

"Please start the car," Feodor said, his words clipped.

"Are we clear?" Josh asked.

A long silence. The sirens grew louder.

"We are clear," Feodor said.

Josh smiled and started the car.

Twenty-one

Feodor wanted to drive to Alice's house immediately, but Josh insisted they have his broken thumb treated first.

"Peregrine could be there at this moment," Feodor said.

"If Peregrine went to see her, he's long gone by now."

Feodor finally convinced her to buy a disposable cell phone and use it to call Alice's house. One of her grandchildren answered, and Will pretended to be the police and gave a phony story about having received a tip that something was wrong there. The grandson said everything was fine.

"Satisfied?" Josh asked.

Feodor said nothing.

Because he had no ID and no insurance, Josh had no choice but to drive him back to Tanith and take him to a dream-walker vet who sometimes helped other dream walkers with injuries. Especially when they didn't want to risk police involvement.

The vet's name was Philo, and he didn't seem surprised when they showed up on his doorstep at midnight.

"Hi, Philo," Josh said.

Feodor held up his hand, from which his thumb dangled grotesquely.

"Looks like a pretty bad sprain," Philo said, and laughed.

An hour later, they were back on the road.

Feodor continued to insist that they go immediately to Alice's, and Josh was more than certain that if she left him at the chair factory, he would find a way to get there on his own—chip on his shoulder be damned.

"You want us to drop you off at home first?" she asked Will.

"In for a penny," he said.

He hadn't stopped smiling since she'd revealed how much progress she'd made toward getting Haley back. Will hadn't smiled at Josh like that in a very long time, and it made her happy and confused at the same time. Did she want his approval? Did she need it? And was it worth having damaged her working relationship with Feodor?

Josh didn't know.

Alice lived eight hours away by car. They decided to drive as far as they could before finding a hotel. Feodor, of course, wanted to drive all night, but Josh refused to make any promises.

"It never occurred to me that Alice was even still alive," she admitted as they got onto the highway. "She must be close to a hundred years old."

"Ninety-eight," Feodor corrected sourly.

Turning to look into the backseat, Will said, "How do you know where she lives?"

Feodor had his hand, complete with cast, cradled in his lap. He wasn't in a great mood. "I Googled her."

Will laughed, and Feodor's eyes narrowed.

"Sorry," Will said. "I didn't realize you knew how to Google things."

"I never should have let you get the Internet," Josh said, shaking her head. "So tell me, what did you find out?"

"After I was exiled, she married a man, a *plumber*." Feodor pronounced the word laden with distain. "They moved to Springfield and had four children. She worked as an emergency room doctor for thirty years. Now she lives with her daughter and grandchildren."

Feodor hated that, all of it, Josh knew. He largely despised domestic life, and he abhorred the thought that someone as intelligent as Alice had married a blue-collar worker. But Josh secretly felt happy for Alice, happy that after a decade with Feodor, she had been able to walk away and find real happiness.

"Not to change the subject, but what Trembuline said about Peregrine switching bodies with Snitch, that isn't possible, is it?" Will asked.

Yes, Josh thought, but she didn't say it because she could tell by the speed of his speech that Will was anxious.

"No," Feodor said. "I'm the only one who knows how to do so. Besides Miss Joshlyn, I suppose."

Josh *did* remember Feodor's protocols for transferring souls between bodies, which was why she was concerned that Peregrine might just pull it off. "If Snitch can tell Peregrine exactly what you did to him, he might be able to put the pieces together."

"Unlikely," Feodor pronounced. "I treated the magnets and crystals out of Kapu—er, Snitch's sight. Peregrine has no way of knowing how I treated them."

"Josh?" Will asked hopefully.

"That's true," she said, even though to her, the treatment of the magnets and crystals seemed so obvious that she couldn't imagine Peregrine struggling to figure it out. She hoped that the protocol only seemed obvious to her and Feodor. "Feodor's right that it would probably be impossible for Peregrine to sort it out on his own."

"That's good," Will said, and he sank back into the passenger seat.

Not long after, Feodor fell asleep. Philo had given him some pain meds to take. Josh had never seen Feodor sleep, and seeing him so vulnerable felt strange.

"I keep thinking he's faking," Will whispered to her.

"He probably is," Josh whispered back.

She could feel Will staring at her. "Can we talk?" he asked, his voice still low.

"Um, yeah." She shifted uncomfortably against her seat belt, which suddenly felt like the straps of an electric chair.

"Why didn't you tell me you were returning souls?" Will asked.

"Like you said, we haven't been talking much lately."

"Yeah, but . . . That's where you've been all the time? You could have told me that."

"Yeah," Josh said, "but I don't have to. I told Mirren and Dad. That was enough."

Will fell quiet. When he spoke again, his voice was sad. "I guess you didn't have to tell me. And I'd like to say that I would have helped, but we both know that's not true."

After they'd gotten back from the Hidden Kingdom, Will had refused to help bring Haley back from Death. He'd correctly pointed out that they didn't need him, but it had still stung Josh, the feeling that he couldn't stand to be around her even when she was doing something good.

He picked at a spot on his jeans. "You're right that I bailed on you. I did. I even tried to go back to the county home."

"You did?" Josh looked away from the road to see the rueful smile on his face. "What happened?"

"Your dad beat me to it. He called them and said I was going through some emotional stuff and not to listen to me if I called. Then he sat me down and told me that he didn't care if I ever set foot in the Dream again, that I was his son now and that was the end of it."

Josh wished her father was there so she could hug him.

"He also said it would be helpful if you and I could get along, but that he'd understand if we couldn't. And I guess that was when I decided to be as nice to you as I could—not to hurt you, but because, if your dad could be that good to me when I was being so ungrateful, I wanted to live up to his example. It never occurred to me that you'd think I was doing it to hurt you."

Josh felt vaguely embarrassed that she'd made such an assumption. "I thought you hated me."

"Josh, I've told you before, I never hated you."

She hadn't said much until then, but she felt all the thoughts and questions and things she'd wanted to say to him since they broke up pushing to get out. Releasing them felt dangerous, though, the same way tapping into a dreamer's fear felt dangerous. She could lose herself.

"You might not hate me," she said, "but I'm not the girl you want anymore. I'm not . . . the girl you fell in love with."

Will fussed with the hole he'd torn in his jeans, and Josh re-settled her hands uneasily on the wheel.

"You know," he said, "you've changed so much since we met. Finding out you're the True Dream Walker, inheriting Feodor's memories, trying to save Winsor . . . You're always surprising me. Sometimes I feel like I can't keep up. When we met you had no confidence in anything except your dream walking. Then you inherited Feodor's memories and—honestly—a little of his arrogance with it. And now I have no idea what's going on with you. You're friends with people I've never even heard of. You're working on secret projects. I barely see you." He held up a hand when Josh started to speak. "No, wait. Let me finish. It's as much my fault as it is yours. Like you said—I bailed on you. I freaked out, and I ran, and I kept telling myself that I didn't miss you because I thought it would keep me safe from getting hurt again. And it wasn't until I didn't know anything about you anymore that I realized how much I hated not having you in my life."

The words loosened something in Josh's chest, like the cork in her stone walls, and a wordless pain flooded through her.

Will continued. "I'm not saying I should have done it differently, because I don't think I could have. I was in a really bad place. But I know that I hurt you, and I'm sorry for that. I'm truly sorry."

Josh watched the speedometer fall. She couldn't keep driving. She couldn't watch the road. She pulled the car onto the shoulder, turned off the engine, and just sat there.

She was going to tell him how she felt, but she only wanted to do it once. Once—and right. She wanted to be an adult about it.

"I should have told you about the nightmares from the start. And the devices, and all of it. Partly I didn't tell you because I knew you'd want me to stop, but mostly I was just afraid you wouldn't love me anymore."

Will put his hand over hers. "And then when you did tell me, I broke up with you."

"Yeah. And I didn't—I still don't get it. I thought you understood what it meant to commit to something, to someone, and I thought you knew how hard it was for me to let you in—"

"I knew. I'm sorry."

"I was an idiot. But I need to know that I can be an idiot and you'll still love me, because I've spent so many years trying to be a perfect dream walker and I've never pulled it off. If you're another person who needs me to be perfect, I just can't do it."

"I don't need you to be perfect," Will said, unbuckling his seat belt. "If you can forgive me for not being perfect."

"Yeah, of course," she said, and then they were hugging, the center console wedged between them. Josh didn't think she'd ever felt anything as comforting as Will's arms around her; she didn't realize how much she had missed his touch.

If Feodor was watching them from the backseat Josh didn't care—let it be a lesson to him about how normal people handled their pain.

"I want to get to know you again," Will told her, but the idea made her freeze up.

"What if you don't like this me? What if I'm too Feodor for you?"

"Josh, you've spent the last three months working around the clock to save Haley. You've wrangled Feodor, you've made new friends, you've revolutionized Veil tear repair, and you just let yourself be vulnerable with a guy who broke your heart. Whoever you turn out to be, I'm pretty sure I'm going to love her."

Josh was afraid of believing that, and despite all the longing that hug had awoken, she wasn't ready to rush back to him. That surprised her, and at the same time relieved her.

"I'll think about it," she said. When Will winced, she started to apologize, but he stopped her.

"It's okay. I want you to be sure. I know I'm asking a lot." He gave her a smile that was both forced and sad, but still a smile. "Take your time. I'll be right here, waiting."

She nodded, although suddenly asking for time seemed like a

stupid decision. What was she going to do—consider the matter carefully and then tell him he wasn't worth the risk?

No. Josh had always been a risk-taking kind of girl.

She restarted the car. "Do you want to stop somewhere for food? I'm starving."

Will peeked into the backseat. "Feodor is snoring."

"It's probably for our benefit."

"Probably." He reached out to twist a strand of her hair around his finger. "You know you're the only girl I've ever loved."

She caught his hand and held it. "Well, don't stop now."

After they had stopped for fried chicken—"Chicken in a box?" Feodor had asked with dismay—and milkshakes and biscuits yellow with fake butter, and Will had taken over the driving, they debated how to approach Alice and her family.

"We could always try the school project angle," Will said. "We could claim we want to ask her about World War II."

"Simply tell her you're Dustine's granddaughter," Feodor said from the backseat.

"What good would that do?" Josh asked.

Feodor snorted. "Don't you recall? Dustine was Alice's dearest friend."

"She was?" Josh said, and then the memories hit her like a head-on collision.

Alice and Dustine, lounging on the beach. Alice and Dustine, laughing on the screened-in porch. Alice bringing Dustine home late one night, Dustine's eye blackened. And Feodor getting in the car and driving over to Dustine and Peregrine's place and—

"Josh?" The alarm in Will's voice broke through the memories.

"Sorry," Josh said. "Sorry."

"You okay?" Will asked.

"Yeah." She rubbed her head. "I just . . . the memories came back all at once. I don't know how I could have forgotten. Dustine—I mean Grandma, and Alice were so close for so long . . . Of course she'll be willing to talk to me."

"I want to speak to Alice," Feodor said from the backseat.

"She might not even recognize you," Josh said. "She might have Alzheimer's or dementia or something."

"And if she does recognize you," Will added, "the shock might kill her."

"I want to see her," Feodor repeated.

"There's no rationale for that," Will said.

They went back and forth, but Josh already knew that she'd let Feodor see Alice. It would shock the old woman, but Josh knew too well that Alice had been the only person Feodor had loved after the war. In his saner moments, trapped in his own universe, he had missed her. And though Josh couldn't read his mind today, she had no doubt that he regretted how he had left things between them. That was one regret she didn't want to carry any longer.

Alice lived in a picturesque ranch house, set off the road on a few acres of land. They rang the doorbell just after nine in the morning.

A buff teenage boy answered, wearing blindingly tight bike shorts and a bodybuilder-style tank top. "Hey," he said.

"Hi," Josh said. "Does Alice Connelly live here?"

"Yeah, she's my grandma. Can I help you?"

"Um, I'm actually the granddaughter of a friend of hers. I was hoping to talk to her."

"What friend?" the guy asked suspiciously.

"Dustine Borgen—"

"Dustine!" he cried. He flung the door open. "Come in. I'm Alex."

Josh stepped into a messy living room crammed full of free weights and half-dead potted plants. Will and Feodor followed her. "So, she mentioned Dustine?"

"They used to talk on the phone every Sunday morning." He shook his head. "Honestly, Nanna's been going downhill ever since she heard Dustine died."

"Is she unwell?" Feodor asked.

"No, but nobody lives forever, you know?" Alex said, leading them down a hallway. "She just had breakfast. She's gonna be so psyched to see you. In here."

Turning to Will and Feodor, Josh said, "Give me a couple of minutes alone, all right?"

"Of course," Feodor replied politely. They'd agreed on this before. Josh was going to let Feodor see Alice, but not until she'd warned the woman, and not if Alice was too old and hazy to understand.

"Nanna," Alex said, "there's somebody here to see you. This is Dustine's granddaughter."

Alice's bedroom looked like it might have been a rec room in a past life, and somebody had stuck a wall and a door on it when Alice moved in. The fake wood paneling on the walls was interrupted by a brick fireplace and a sliding glass door that led to the backyard. An impressive flat-screen TV hung above the mantel, tuned to a news network. The bed was partially hidden beneath a yellow and lavender quilt, and the old woman sitting up in it wore a chenille bed jacket over her nightgown. Her thin white hair had been combed off her face.

"Dustine . . ." she said in a creaky voice.

"This is her granddaughter," Alex repeated.

"Oh? How delightful."

"I'll give you guys some time," Alex said, closing the door when he went.

"Let me turn this off," Alice said, reaching for the TV remote.

"Oh, that's all right," Josh said.

"Nothing but heartbreak on anyway," Alice insisted, and turned off the TV.

Josh swallowed. She didn't realize until then that she had been imagining Alice as she last saw her—young and fashionable and fearless. Now she looked so small and so old, her face hardly recognizable beneath soft and wrinkled skin. Her once proud shoulders were hunched forward, and her gums had retreated, making her teeth look huge.

But when she smiled, Josh knew her again instantly. Her bright brown eyes hadn't changed at all.

"Alice," Josh said, her voice rough with tears.

Alice held out a cool, bony hand, and Josh took it.

"Dustine told me so much about you," Alice said. After all these years, her English accent was as crisp as ever.

Feodor's told me so much about you, Josh almost said. She clasped Alice's hand between her own, wanting to warm the old woman's cool skin.

"Did Josh come as well?" Alice asked.

"Josh?" She realized then that Alice thought she was Deloise. "No, you mean Deloise. *I'm* Josh."

Alice's smile faltered, and her eyes narrowed.

"Joshlyn," she said, and Josh didn't understand Alice's strange tone of voice.

She leaned forward as if to get a better look, and then she pulled her hand out of Josh's so she could touch Josh's cheek, her hair, her shoulder. She had a doctor's touch—firm, mechanical.

"I haven't seen you since you were three years old," she said. She fell back against her pillows. "Dustine . . . I'd like to offer my condolences about Dustine. She was my best friend. I would have done anything for her."

"I think she felt the same way about you," Josh said, although she didn't know that for certain. Only now that Dustine was gone did Josh realize just how tight-lipped her grandmother had been.

"We used to joke that one of us should have been born a man so we could get married. Would have saved us both a lot of trouble. She made this quilt, did you know that?"

"No," Josh said. "It's beautiful. Grandma Dustine gave my friend a quilt, too, one that—demonstrates the three universes."

She'd hesitated for a moment, not sure if she should bring up dream walking or not. But Alice just nodded and said, "She made that quilt."

"Really? She told me that Great-Aunt Lasia gave it to her."

"No, no. I remember her making it. Lasia hated sewing."

Josh began to worry that Alice's mind was less clear than it had initially appeared. "Alice—"

"Mrs. Connelly, dear."

"Mrs. Connelly, I came to talk to you about someone you used to know. His name is—was, Feodor Kajażkołski."

Alice looked at Josh with surprising sharpness, then at the closed bedroom door, as if she could sense him there. "Who told you about Feodor? It wasn't Dustine."

Actually, Dustine *had* told Josh about Feodor, but not until she had no choice, and even then, she'd lied about knowing him. "This will sound strange. But some friends and I—we went to see him. In his universe."

"No, no." Alice frowned. "That can't be. Too many years . . . He never could have survived."

"But he did survive," Josh insisted. "And he . . . he came back."

As if she hadn't heard, Alice said, "Your eyes . . . they remind me of his."

Josh froze.

"Not the color. Something in the way you watch me." She abruptly turned her face toward the window. "Feodor never recovered from the war. Even when he was happy, there was a shadow over him. I couldn't lift it, and finally it . . . took him."

"Alice," Josh forced herself to say, "Feodor isn't dead. He came back from his universe. He's waiting in the hallway to see you."

She decided to skip the part about retrieving Feodor from Death. She was confusing the old woman enough.

"You must be mistaken. Feodor died a long time ago."

"I'm going to bring him in now, all right? He looks younger than you remember. Try not to be shocked."

That was the best Josh could do. In retrospect, she probably should have brought Will in and let him explain. But it was too late now, and all she could do was open the door and beckon Feodor inside.

Josh had never seen him hesitant before, but the steps he took were small, and he swallowed as he entered the room.

"Hello, Alice," he said.

Alice gasped. What little color her pale face had vanished, and she gripped the edges of the quilt in both fists as if she were about to pull it over her head.

"It can't be," she said.

Feodor gave her one of his polite little smiles. "Begging your pardon, I must insist that it is."

Alice stopped shaking her head and leaned forward, as if to see him better. "Feodor?" Then she began to laugh. "Feodor. Feodor. It is you."

"*Słoneczko,*" Feodor said, and then he was standing at her bedside, holding her hands in his, just as Josh had done, and they were both crying.

As much as Josh wanted to stay and be part of the reunion, as much as she felt like she *was* part of it, she forced herself to back out of the room. As she gently closed the door, Feodor turned and caught her eye, and he mouthed the word *dziękuję.*

Thank you.

Josh nodded and left him alone with Alice. Will was wearing the same sappy smile she felt on her own face.

"What did he call her?" Will asked.

"*Słoneczko?*" Josh smiled deeper. "It means 'sunshine.'"

They stood in the hallway, smiling at each other. Will didn't ask if it was safe to leave Feodor and Alice alone; they both knew it was.

Twenty-two

"So," Will said as Josh pulled back onto the road an hour later. "What did Alice say?"

In the backseat, Feodor was staring out the window with a small smile on his lips.

"Pardon?" he asked when Will spoke to him.

Will had never seen Feodor look happy before. He hadn't really been sure the man *could* be happy. Not before today. Now, Feodor's gray eyes were light, and though he kept wiping his smile off his mouth and straightening his expression like he was shaking out a bedsheet, the smile always crept back.

For the first time, Will wondered if Feodor was capable of love.

"You remembered to ask Alice about Peregrine, didn't you?" Will asked.

"Yes, of course. She said she hasn't spoken to him in half a century. However, she did have a visitor about six months ago: Bash Mirrettiso."

"Dammit," Josh muttered. "That long ago?"

"He introduced himself as a young dream theorist at Willis-Audretch, no doubt compared himself to me. Unfortunately, Alice's thinking is not entirely clear, and she told him where to find my papers."

"What?" Josh cried. "Why? We told her—*you* told her to burn them!"

Will tried to ignored Josh's creepy use of the word "we."

"She felt unable to do so for . . . sentimental reasons," Feodor admitted.

"What's in those papers?" Will asked Josh.

"Everything he was working on up until a year before Maple-fax. Light harmonics, spatial barrier theory, the subtle body . . ."

Josh trailed off, and Will put his hand on the steering wheel, worried by the faraway look in her eye.

"Do the papers explain how to treat the magnets and crystals he'd need to switch bodies?" Will asked.

Josh clenched her jaw. "Yes."

Will's pulse began to thrum quickly through his temples, and he took a series of slow breaths to calm himself.

"Everything's written in Polish," Josh pointed out.

"He could get a translator," Will said. The slow breaths weren't working for him. His doctor had given him a medication to take when the anxiety got too bad, but he'd left it at the house.

"If Peregrine can decipher my work," Feodor said, "which is, as you Americans say, 'a big if,' and combine it with the details Geoff can provide, it is possible that he could recreate some of my experiments. However, I don't believe that is likely."

Will ground his palms on the knees of his jeans. *Mirren said Feodor's last manuscript barely made sense,* he reminded himself. *If someone as well educated in dream theory as Mirren couldn't follow it, there's no way Peregrine could. He isn't even patient enough to read through it.*

"What happens if Peregrine pulls it off?" Will asked. "Once he's in Snitch's body, he can control the Dream, right?"

"Probably."

"So he'll start staging nightmares."

Josh gave a grudging nod.

"This is really bad," Will said. "I'm . . . I'm very concerned about how bad this is."

He unbuckled his seat belt and put his head between his knees. At least when Peregrine had been staging nightmares from his basement there had been practical limitations. Not only had he needed to dress up and work with the dreamer's existing nightmare, but he'd had no control over whose nightmare he walked into. With complete control of the Dream, Will was pretty sure he'd be able to call any sleeping soul to him, and he could create elaborate dreams for them—dreams that changed the way they felt or thought.

"Will," Josh said, and he felt her put her hand, small and hot, on his back. "Do you want me to pull over?"

"No," he said, but he stayed with his face hidden in the cave of his body and repeated a mantra he'd worked on in counseling.

In this moment, I am safe.

He repeated it mentally about a dozen times before he was able to sit up and put his seat belt back on. Afterward, Josh reached for his hand, and he gave it to her. She flashed an apologetic smile too.

"I'm okay," he said.

"I know."

From the backseat, Feodor said, "Alice expressed an unusual interest in you, Josh."

"I know," Josh said. "She got really weird when she realized who I was."

"You're her best friend's granddaughter," Will pointed out, trying not to worry about Peregrine. "I'm sure she saw a lot of Dustine in you."

"No," Josh said. "It was something else. At first she thought I was Del, and she wasn't freaked out at all."

"She asked a number of questions about you," Feodor said.

"What kind of questions?" Will asked.

"Whether or not Josh has unusual skill in dream walking. If she has unusual skills in other areas. If she is wise."

Will saw Josh jump in her seat at the word "wise."

"Alice's questions," Feodor continued, "suggest that Dustine observed something unusual about you."

"Everybody observes it," Will said. "The whole dream-walking world knows how good Josh is."

"I don't believe that's what she meant," Feodor said. "Josh, all of this continues to point to the idea that something extraordinary happened before you were born."

"Continues?" Will asked.

Josh told him about the prophesies, which made him feel guilty on top of his anxiety.

I left her to deal with all of this alone. Or with Feodor, which is as good as alone.

At the same time, he felt the heaviness of these new problems pressing down on him. More to deal with, more to try to survive with love intact.

He squeezed her shoulder.

"I talked to Dad," Josh said. "He doesn't remember anything unusual about my birth or the year before it. He said Mom was a nervous mother, but I was her first baby."

"Did you ask Alice about Josh's birth?" Will asked Feodor.

"Yes. She refused to answer, although indirectly. She did, however, imply that we should ask Ben Sounclouse."

"Young Ben?" Josh repeated. "Because he's a seer?"

"No," Feodor said, "because he was your grandmother's lover for decades."

Josh nearly swerved off the road again.

"Young Ben and my grandma?!" she shouted.

In the backseat, Feodor wore an amused smile.

"They were engaged before he deployed for World War II and was incorrectly reported dead. Dustine developed a severe depression, and Peregrine staged nightmares for her to convince her to marry him. Only later did they learn that Ben was alive."

"Why didn't she leave Peregrine?" Josh asked.

"She spoke of it many times, but she was afraid he would kill her if she left. I suspect that each time their relationship became tumultuous, Peregrine resumed staging nightmares for her, nightmares that made her afraid to leave."

"That's terrible," Will said. "That takes domestic violence to a whole new level."

"So she just stayed with Peregrine and had an affair with Young Ben?" Josh asked.

"That was the situation when I was exiled," Feodor said. "Dustine and Ben were . . . quite devoted to each other."

"You know," Will said, "Ben has aged really fast since Dustine died. And he's put on a lot of weight."

"All those times he came over for tea with Grandma," Josh marveled. "It never occurred to me that they were dating."

She was interrupted by Will's phone ringing.

"Hey, Whim," Will said, glancing at the ID as he answered. "What's up?"

"Where the hell are you, man?"

Whim's voice was even higher than usual. He sounded like he'd chugged one of Trembuline's energy drinks.

"I'm with Josh and Feodor. I texted Kerstel about it. What's going on there?"

"Kerstel's having the baby!"

Will's adrenaline jumped to life. "Right now?"

"I mean, if not now, pretty soon. You've got to get back here!"

"We're about eight hours away. We'll probably miss it. Can you tell her we love her?"

"Yeah, and guess what else happened? That weirdo from Winsor's party showed up again."

"The guy with the walker? Sam?" Will couldn't figure out how these two things were on par with each other in Whim's mind.

"Yeah. He took a taxi here. Winsor was already having a rough day. She went completely hysterical, took her bedtime meds, and went back to sleep. What's this guy trying to do? Torture her?"

I think it's her that's torturing him, Will thought to himself.

"Josh and I'll track him down and have a talk with him. Maybe we'll take Feodor."

"Jesus, hasn't Feodor done enough to him already?"

"I was actually thinking that Feodor could help him put what happened in context, but I take your point."

When he hung up, Josh said, "What's going on?"

"Kerstel's in labor." Despite his anxiety over Peregrine, Will couldn't help smiling. "We're gonna have a baby brother, probably by the time we get home."

"Skippy," Josh said, although she sounded overwhelmed by the idea.

In the backseat, Feodor lay his head against the window.

"Isn't that lovely," he murmured.

They dropped Feodor off at the chair factory and drove home. Although it was only dinnertime, Will was exhausted. He hadn't slept in more than twenty-four hours, and the emotional toll of seeing Trembuline and Alice had drained him. But just as Josh turned the car toward home, Will got a text from Deloise.

"Josh, we have to go to the hospital," he said. "Your little brother was just born."

"That's awesome. Did they name him Ziggy?"

Will wasn't certain how serious his parents were about naming their baby Zigoshinoc—or rather, how serious they *had* been.

"No," he told Josh. "They named him Keri. Because he's a girl."

Josh laughed all the way to the hospital.

Twenty-three

Haley ran farther than he ever had. He couldn't even guess how far he'd gone—eight, ten miles? He just kept running, the book of his life tucked under one arm, until his knees began to weaken and black spots flickered in his vision.

Stumbling to a walk, he staggered into the forest. He didn't want to risk being visible from the road in case Ian was following him.

Beyond a little hill, he found a small stream and sat down on its edge. He had his hand in the water before he remembered the warning Mirren had given him before they entered Death. *Don't eat anything, drink anything, accept any gifts, walk barefoot, or tell anyone your name.*

Reluctantly, Haley withdrew his hand from the water. He wasn't actually thirsty, he realized; he just wanted to cool down.

He guessed it was a few hours past noon, but it was hard to tell in the forest. Shafts of golden sunlight broke in between the branches, illuminating floating pollen and small, harmless bugs. The stream was nearly silent. But despite the peace of the place, Haley couldn't relax.

Ian wanted Haley's body.

He still felt sick. When he held out his arm, he saw that the usual shy, nervous violet color he displayed was spotted with ugly gray vortexes. He couldn't repress a little cry at the sight of them.

Ian poisoned me.

Overwhelmed by hopelessness, he curled up beside the creek and cried.

I'm never going home. Mirren and Josh aren't coming back for me. Ian is going to destroy my soul so he can have my body.

He cried because he was tired, and afraid, and because there was no one there to watch him. He cried because his brother had turned against him, had lost the ability to love, had lost *himself*—

Don't lose yourself, Mirren said. *Don't lose yourself.*

Haley didn't know if saving himself from Ian was possible. He was almost afraid to hope it was, because he didn't think he had enough energy to fight. And maybe that was for the best. Maybe Ian *did* deserve a second chance. Maybe that's why God had sent Haley here.

The book, still clutched to his chest, grew warm. Haley sat up to look at it and saw that it had its own aura, a rainbow of different shades. The colors twinkled as if beckoning him.

Gently, he opened the cover. On the first page, his name was written in a dramatic hand in black ink. Haley turned that page, and he couldn't hold back a smile when he realized that his life was written in the book . . . as a graphic novel.

Haley had always loved graphic novels. He'd read all the good ones, from *Blankets* to *Violent Cases* to *Maus,* fascinated by stories of people stronger than he was. Now he saw his own life, every frame in full color, every aura meticulously shaded, every glimpse of the future illustrated.

He saw himself and Ian as infants, indistinguishable in matching blue onesies. He watched himself meet Josh, watched his father leave, watched his mother's anxiety worsen. He read along as Ian opened his scroll and destroyed his own life, then took over Haley's body and ran from country to country abusing it. Finally he reached the pages where Mirren appeared, her hair a voluminous red cloud on the page, and then the transition to Death, where this new, twisted Ian appeared like all comic villains, enormous, hulking, bathed in shadows.

What he read in those pages wasn't how he had wasted his life; it was how hard he had worked to do no harm.

With his expanded perception, he could have manipulated people, taken advantage of people, shared their secrets, exposed their most private dreams, forced them to change. But he never, ever had. Instead he had watched them and learned who they really were and who they wanted to be, and by the time he met Mirren, he was ready to start helping nudge people to grow into themselves. She had given him that opportunity.

I haven't wasted my life, he realized. *I've just been getting ready to help people.*

The last frame showed Haley, sitting by the stream and reading the book of his life. But the rest of the pages were blank.

I haven't seen the future since I've been here, he realized, gently closing the book, which felt more precious than ever. *Maybe the future doesn't exist here.*

He wasn't disappointed that the book couldn't tell him what would happen next.

It meant he still had a chance to survive.

He hiked back to the road and began to walk. The road—now dirt again—wound up and down mountains, each one taller and steeper than the last. Haley huffed and puffed and stopped to stretch, but the dead he passed by moved effortlessly. Some of them floated several inches off the ground.

Haley didn't know how he could ever have been afraid of them. Their auras were luminous and trimmed with gold, and their faces radiated profound joy and peace. Once, when Haley twisted his ankle on a loose rock, a little boy with a spring-green aura healed it for him. Haley felt happy every time he saw one of the dead now.

People are so afraid of Death, he thought, working his way across a rope bridge. *If they could see this, they'd never be afraid again.*

Midafternoon, he ascended a mountain and found a long, flat plateau on top. Mist swirled around the plateau, suffused with the sweet colors of the auras of the dead.

In the middle of the plateau, a two-story bonfire burned. Haley couldn't see a source of fuel; the flames came out of the very rock. The longer he gazed at the fire, the more he thought that the flames seemed to bend near their orange tips, into a shape almost like a doorway.

He watched as, one by one, the dead walked into the flames and through the doorway. They didn't come out the other side.

It's an archway, Haley realized. *It's the archway between Death and the Dream.*

Many of the dead weren't going through the archway, though. Or at least, they weren't going through the archway immediately. Instead they sat or stood with another dead person, their hands clasped, looking at one another, their energy fields entwined, communicating in some way Haley couldn't name.

He was loath to interrupt them, but he waited until a teenage girl with a pumpkin-orange aura began to walk away from her partner, and he said, "Excuse me. Is Dustine still here?"

She smiled at him and pointed. Haley couldn't have explained how she knew who he was talking about, or how he'd known she would, but he sensed that information was less restricted here, less personal. Everyone became omniscient as they gave away their personalities; souls had access to all knowledge.

Haley thanked her, and she gave him a kiss on the cheek that left him awed by her joyfulness. Then she walked into the archway of flames.

He went in the direction she had pointed, working his way around the people standing in pairs. A woman with an aura the color of sapphires drew his attention, and he couldn't resist stepping closer to her.

She released the hands of the man who had been standing with her, and he smiled at her before walking away. Then she turned to Haley and offered her hands.

Haley tucked the book between his elbow and his side, and put his hands in hers. When he did, her rich blue aura enveloped him, and—with a start—he recognized the aura he had seen in a less pure state so many times before.

Dustine? he thought.

She sent him a burst of absolute love, so intense it made his breath catch. He tried to tell her how much he loved her, how she had been his grandmother as much as Josh and Deloise's, but she knew.

She knew everything.

Haley, you are so worthy of life. Don't let anyone tell you otherwise. Never doubt it. Never doubt that the Universe loves you.

I'll try to remember.

We all forget. We remember and forget, remember and forget. But over time, remembering becomes easier.

She was Dustine, and yet she wasn't. She was Dustine without the baggage of life, the fears and desires that made everyone human. All that was left was her heart.

Haley's fears, though, were still mostly intact, and his mind blurted out all the questions he had.

Will Josh and Mirren come back for me? Will Feodor help them? Will Ian finally let go?

Dustine's heart smiled at him.

Ian is coming.

What? Haley gripped her hands more tightly. *How?*

Time moves more slowly the closer you come to the archway. Ian has been following you for many hours. He is not far away. If he catches you, he will take your body.

What do I do?

On the other side of the flames is a tunnel. Go through the flames and into the tunnel. Follow it.

Follow it where?

That is for you to decide. But remember, no one can pass through Death without being transformed. Go. Time is short.

Wait! I have to ask you about Josh—

Tell her that she will find the answers where the three universes overlap. Go. I love you.

Then Dustine released him, and when Haley opened his eyes, he couldn't see her.

What he did see was Ian, climbing the last few steps up to the plateau.

Catching sight of Haley, Ian grinned, then bent down and picked up a big rock.

Haley bolted across the plateau, darting around people holding hands, even vaulting over one couple who were sitting on the ground. Pushing past a man walking up to the bonfire, Haley jumped off with both feet and sailed headfirst into the flames.

The heat was tremendous. For an instant he felt it lifting him up like an elevator, and he smelled burning hair. He waited as long as he could before tucking his head between his elbows and diving down.

He landed in an awkward forward roll with the book crammed into his stomach. His right hand landed on a coal, and he rolled over a burning brand as he came out of the dive. Pain bloomed in his palm and in a line connecting his shoulder blades, reminding him how human he still was, how physical his body was, and he was grateful for that.

He knew that Ian would run around the bonfire, and that doing so would cost him time. Haley needed to be gone before his brother arrived. The far side of the bonfire was curiously dark, and as he started to run again, he stepped in a hole in the ground he hadn't realized was there.

On the other side of the flames is a tunnel.

Feeling with his hands, Haley climbed into the tunnel. It was too low for him to stand, he had to crawl, and the darkness there was as complete as he had ever imagined.

His heart began to pound. Maybe Ian was right and he was a coward. He didn't want to be here, crawling into a sightless abyss on his hands and knees, his burned palm protesting as he clutched the book of his life to his chest.

Be brave, he told himself. *You have to be brave.*

But he wasn't brave, was he? He never had been.

You were brave to stay in Death, Mirren's voice said. *Don't lose yourself now.*

He kept crawling.

Was that a light up ahead? Or were his eyes playing tricks on him in the darkness?

From somewhere behind him, a voice echoed down the tunnel. *"Haley!"*

Haley scrambled faster. Loose rocks cut into his knees. The tunnel went deeper, the air growing colder. He switched the book from one hand to the other; laying his palm against the ground felt good now that the stone was freezing. In the silence, his frantic breaths sounded like flapping wings.

Be brave.

The echo of his breathing changed, and he rose up on his knees to feel above him. The ceiling was too high for him to reach, so he gingerly stood up, knowing he would make faster time on his feet. Waving his arms ahead of him so he wouldn't run into anything, he stumbled forward.

"Haley!"

Was Ian's voice closer this time? Haley's name bounced around too much for him to know.

The air kept getting colder, and once he slipped on loose gravel and slid a dozen feet down an incline. He had to be near the heart of the mountain.

He began to see light again, but this time it grew stronger instead of vanishing. The light was orange, and it glowed against the red granite walls on either side of Haley.

The light illuminated his feet first and then climbed up his legs as he descended into a low chamber. A woman stood before an archway carved into the stone wall, and although she was not a large woman, Haley couldn't see past her to where the archway led. On either side of her, a torch hung from a sconce in the wall.

The woman's aura was as black as the tunnel had been. So were her eyes.

"HALEY!" Ian screamed.

Haley skidded to a stop before the woman. She was beautiful, with thick black hair that hung to her knees and copper-brown skin that glowed in the torchlight. She wore a purple linen dress that covered her from neck to ankles, leaving just her bare toes peeking out from beneath the many fringed tiers of her skirt. Hanging from her neck were a dozen or more beaded necklaces made from blue stone flecked with gold.

Haley had never seen an aura so completely, utterly black, and for a moment he wasn't sure what to make of it. But when she held out her hand to Haley and he took it, he felt instantly that she was like the fire: an agent of transformation.

She smiled at him, and her smile was benevolent despite her black teeth and her black eyes that stretched forever into darkness.

Choose, she whispered.

What had Dustine said? That it was Haley's choice where the tunnel led?

"I want to go to Mirren, wherever she is," Haley told the woman. She let go of his hand.

"Please," Haley said. "Please let me past. Send me to Mirren."

She said nothing, did nothing. Her smile was gone.

"Haley," Ian said.

His limbs stiff with dread, Haley turned around. Ian was standing at the other end of the chamber, breathing heavily.

"Well, little brother," Ian said with a smile. "Looks like this is the end of the road."

"If you kill me, you won't get my body," Haley pointed out.

"I don't need to *kill* you. I just need to make you give up." He pulled the rock from his pocket. "I need to *convince* you."

He's going to torture me, Haley realized, *just like Feodor tortured Josh.*

"Yeah," Ian said, as if reading Haley's mind. "I definitely learned a few things from Feodor. Did I mention that we hung out, before Josh came to get him? Smart guy. Really smart guy."

Haley wanted so much to live. He looked away from Ian, back to the woman standing before the archway. Her black eyes were unreadable, but Haley thought he heard her voice in his head.

Transformation.

He realized what he had to do at the same moment Ian bashed his head with the rock. The burn on his back pained him when he landed, but not as much as his head, which bounced off the stone floor with a sickening *thwack*.

The chamber went black, but Ian's laughter reached Haley through the darkness.

"God, Haley, you're making this too easy. What the hell were you thinking when you offered to stay here? That you'd impress everyone with how brave you were? That you'd be the big hero?"

Haley opened his eyes. The light felt like it went right through his eyeballs and pierced his brain, and his stomach swam.

"Well, don't worry," Ian said, crouching down beside Haley. "I'll make good use of your life."

He picked up his rock again.

Haley forced himself to sit up. He had the book pressed to his chest, both arms strapped over it.

Don't lose yourself, Mirren said, but Haley understood now that the statement had a second meaning, one he hadn't contemplated before.

The story of his life had been beautiful, but it wasn't who he was. Just like he'd told Ian, his soul was indestructible. Even if Ian's poison ate away his energy, his soul would remain. He didn't have to cling to the book because it wasn't who he truly was, it was just the story of this incarnation.

He offered the book to the woman with the black eyes.

"What are you doing?" Ian asked, but when he tried to grab the book, an invisible force seemed to push him back.

The woman accepted the book reverently from Haley. Then she offered a fine-boned hand and helped him to his feet.

"Stop it!" Ian shouted. "What are you doing? Let me go!"

The woman stepped away from the archway, and where there had been only darkness before, now there was a red granite door with a handle made of gold. Haley barely had to touch it before the door swung open, surprisingly light. It opened into some sort of building lit with lanterns and full of stone bridges over calm waters.

Haley turned back only once, to see his brother fighting the invisible barrier, scratching and flailing like an angry cat.

"This life isn't me," Haley said. "You could take my body, and the true me, my soul, would be fine."

"You're crazy!" Ian shouted at him.

"I hope you find the courage to let go."

The woman smiled at Haley.

No one can pass through Death without being transformed, Haley thought, and he stepped through the doorway.

Mirren woke from a strange dream. She could only remember bits and pieces of it, but she recalled Haley running and the flash of golden light on water. Had she been holding him, stroking his hair? Or had that been a fantasy?

Unable to sleep, she wrapped the cardigan Haley had given her over her nightgown and went out the farmhouse's back door. The lawn was silvery with moonlight and dew, and the grass felt cool and prickly beneath her bare feet.

She had finished the royal trimidion two days before, and yesterday she had filled it with water. Retrieving a box of long matches from a box near one of the entrances, she went around to each of the nine doorways and lit the colored lanterns hanging there. Stone walkways connected each doorway to the platform in the center of the structure, over which the red granite trimidion hung. Instead of having three solid sides, the pyramid was hollow, and an archway had been carved in each side.

Mirren didn't know why she had built it that way. That had been the design in her head, so that was how she had built it. Sitting on one of the walkways, she thought about how pointless the design was. So far, it didn't even work as a trimidion, and the granite weighed more than a thousand pounds. Every time she looked at it, she was afraid it would fall.

Suddenly the lanterns flared—all of them at once. Mirren looked at them, alarmed, and she almost missed the movement in the red granite pyramid. Just as she looked back, silver light burst from the three doorways, and against it, a figure grew so fast that Mirren didn't realize it was a person until it exploded out of the doorway marked Death.

Haley stumbled down the walkway, tripped, and landed on Mirren.

His weight pinned her to the stone. He was covered in fairy dust and there was blood matted in his hair and he was grinning like she'd never seen him grin before.

"Haley," she tried to say, but his name caught in her throat.

He made no move to climb off of her, and she was glad for his weight, so glad to feel him pressed against her. With trembling hands she touched his face, making sure he was real, and she laughed when he smiled again, and then he laughed, and then he kissed her.

"Thank you," he whispered. "Thank you, thank you, thank you."

He was home.

Twenty-four

The next evening, Young Ben Sounclouse came over to bless the baby. In a month or two, when Keri was stronger, the Weavers would throw a big party to introduce her to dream-walker society, but a seer traditionally blessed a baby as soon as she was born.

Will was right, Josh thought, watching Young Ben come through the back door. *He looks ten years older than he did at my birthday party.*

Young Ben had been old for as long as Josh could remember, but now he appeared ancient. His hair was nearly gone, and his eyes had grown rheumy. He couldn't control a spasm in his left hand, so instead of holding the baby, he sat beside Kerstel on the couch to look at her.

"Well, aren't you a beauty?" he said, and his voice had lost some of the boom and authority Josh had always associated with it. "Just like your mama."

"Her name's Cashew," Winsor said, and then, "God dammit! It's—I mean, her name is Cashew—I mean—God *dammit!*"

Looking confused, Young Ben fiddled with his hearing aid.

"Don't worry about it," Kerstel told Winsor, whose brain wouldn't stop insisting that the baby's name was Cashew. "Her name's Karowena Irenia Kisamponi Weavaros. We're going to call her Keri."

Winsor beat her knee with a fist, something she did when she was frustrated.

"I think Cashew is a cute nickname," Deloise offered, putting a gentle hand on Winsor's fist to calm her.

"I don't mind it," Kerstel agreed.

There was lots of oooing and ahhhing over Keri, who had her father's brown eyes and just a dusting of her mother's strawberry-blond hair. As far as Josh could tell, she didn't do much. Josh was already tired of watching her eat and sleep, and she didn't know how many months would have to pass before the baby became interesting.

"You aren't breast-feeding?" Young Ben asked as Keri finished off yet another bottle.

"Breast-feeding is a form of female slavery," Kerstel told him.

Young Ben looked horrified, which only made Kerstel laugh.

The blessing was brief. Everyone present—the entire Avish-Weaver household—gathered around the baby, lit their lighters, and reflected the flame light onto Keri. Young Ben traced the five petals of the plumeria flower on her forehead, and said, "May you be blessed with compassion, commitment, courage, modesty, and might." He traced a spiral, the symbol of the Dream, over her heart. "May the True Dream Walker watch over you, that you always walk safely."

"Walk safely," everyone echoed.

Josh wasn't too attached to Keri yet, but she found the ritual beautiful. *Another little dream walker is born,* she thought. *Another little link in the chain going back to the beginning of time.*

She couldn't imagine breaking that chain by merging the three universes.

Before Young Ben had arrived, she and Will had had a long talk. Not about their relationship—Josh wasn't ready for another one of those—but about information they needed to share now that they were finally speaking to each other again.

She'd told Will about her vision of the Cradle and the Omphalos, and Will had told her about the prophesies suggesting that the True Dream Walker would merge the three universes and the possibility that Peregrine was the False Dream Walker. Although Josh wasn't surprised that Feodor had withheld the information from her—she remembered it, of course, as soon as Will reminded her—she was surprised by the idea itself. Why would the True Dream Walker set up the three universes and a system to keep them in balance, and then return thousands of years later to destroy that balance and all the work dream walkers had done? Josh just couldn't fathom it, especially not while she watched another little dream walker being welcomed into the fold.

"Are you crying?" Deloise asked her.

"No," Josh said, and wiped her eyes.

Everyone laughed, and Deloise hugged her. "You softie."

The gathering broke up when Keri began to cry. Lauren and Kerstel took her upstairs, and Saidy and Alex went up to their apartment, probably to watch game shows and argue, which was how they spent most of their evenings. Soon Young Ben was alone with the younger members of the household.

Josh was sitting on the love seat next to Will, and they were both pretending that it didn't mean anything, that they weren't aware of the places where their bodies touched.

But secretly, Josh was very aware.

She was also aware—for the first time—that there was a small white puppy in her sister's lap.

"Where did that puppy come from?" Josh asked.

For some reason, Deloise blushed. "A bigger puppy," she said innocently and buried her blush in the dog's white fur. Whim began to laugh.

"What am I missing?" Josh asked Will.

"I'll tell you later," he said. "Ask Young Ben about your birth."

"Oh, right," she said, "Ben, I was talking to Feodor about Grandma yesterday. And, uh, well, he told me that you and Grandma had an affair."

Suddenly the room went quiet. Ben started to smile, then caught himself.

"What?" Whim said.

"Who?" Winsor asked.

"What?" Deloise repeated. She stopped lifting the puppy for a kiss and just let it hang in midair.

"Dustine was the love of my life," Young Ben admitted. "We were supposed to be married, before the war."

"You and Grandma?" Deloise asked.

"She was the most amazing woman," he continued. "So smart,

and clever, and funny. I was . . . enthralled, from the moment I met her."

Deloise gave her head a hard shake, as if to clear it. Whim took the dangling puppy out of her hands.

"Enthralled," Winsor repeated.

"I wanted to tell you girls," Young Ben said, "but Dustine was afraid of Peregrine. He'd have killed us both if he ever found out."

"Why didn't she leave him?" Deloise asked.

"For the same reason. And then when she did finally leave . . . well, he'd gotten into her head once, we both knew he'd be happy to do it again."

"What do you mean, he'd gotten into her head?" Whim asked.

"Staging!" Suddenly Young Ben's voice was echoing off the walls. "He staged nightmares for her while I was overseas. Made her think she was in love with him! By the time I got back, they were already married."

Josh had heard Feodor say as much the day before, but it still horrified her. Wasn't there anyone Peregrine had truly loved?

"That's messed up," Winsor said.

"Are you serious?" Whim asked Ben, suddenly interested. "Can I put that on my website?"

"No, you can't," Deloise scolded him. She sat down beside Young Ben. "I'm so sorry. That's just horrible."

"It took us years to find our way back to each other. Never could have done it without . . ."

"Without Alice," Josh finished.

"Who?" Winsor asked again.

"She was Grandma's best friend," Josh told her.

Young Ben just nodded. "Never could have found her again without Alice. Alice gave your grandmother the cabin. It was our place, where we went to . . . to get away from Peregrine."

"Oh my God," Whim said. "This is sliding rapidly into the too-much-information category."

"I thought I'd take that to my grave," Young Ben said. He smiled a wet, loopy smile. "I'm so glad I got to tell you girls before I died!"

"Tell us about the cabin?" Winsor asked.

"No, he means Grandma," Deloise said.

"No—I mean, yes. But also . . ." He smiled again, tears in his eyes. "Girls, I'm your real grandfather."

All Josh could think was that if Whim's eyes got any bigger, they were going to burst out of his head.

Deloise started to speak, then stopped. She looked at Will as if for help.

"Oh," Will said.

"Um," Josh added, just before her brain went blank.

"*You're* our grandfather?" Deloise managed to ask.

"Yes." Ben held her hands and beamed at her.

Whim buried his face in a pillow, but his shoulders shook with silent laughter.

"Did Mom know?" Deloise asked.

"Oh, yes. Figured it out all on her own. Such a smart girl."

He's senile, Josh thought. *He's . . . confused.*

"Wait," Winsor said. She pointed at Young Ben. "You're her"— she pointed at Deloise—"grandpa?"

Young Ben nodded.

I can't even remember what I wanted to ask him about, Josh thought. *I have no idea why I came downstairs.*

"That's amazing," Deloise said. "I mean, I would much rather be related to you than to Peregrine." Then she laughed and hugged the old man. "Hi, Grandpa!"

Young Ben began crying. Whim was crying, too, for an entirely different reason.

"Are you laughing at my new grandpa?" Deloise asked Whim indignantly.

"No," he said. "I'm laughing at your sister."

Only then did Josh realize that her protracted shock might be hurting Young Ben's feelings. She stumbled over to pat Ben's shoulder. "It's . . . I'm glad you're my grandfather instead of Peregrine," she managed, feeling awkward.

"Oh, Josh," he said, and pulled her into his lap to hug. "You know, your grandmother was so proud of you. Both of you."

"She was more proud of Josh," Deloise said. "We all know it."

"No, you should have heard the way she talked about you. Called you her little Mother Teresa."

Josh didn't know if Ben was making that up or not, but as she watched Deloise smile, she didn't really care. Peregrine had never had time for Deloise.

For the next half hour, Josh listened to Young Ben talk about Dustine, about their torrid love affair, about how much he had loved Josh and Deloise's mother, Jona. That finally reminded Josh of what she'd wanted to ask.

"Young—er, Grandpa Ben," she said, and was rewarded by a big smile. "I wanted to ask you if anything weird happened around the time I was born, or before I was conceived."

Young Ben kept one arm around her and the other around Deloise. "You'd have to ask your father about that," he said and winked. Whim began laughing again.

"No, not like—um—as long as we're confessing things, I might as well tell you that I know I'm the True Dream Walker."

It was Young Ben's turn to look shocked. Then he shook his head slowly. "Just as smart as your mother."

"Not really. Haley told me."

"Haley," Ben said with a nod. "He's going to be the next great seer."

That didn't surprise Josh a bit. "No kidding. Anyway, I'm just trying to make sense of these prophesies about the True Dream Walker, and they keep talking about important things happening right around when I was born. And they never use the word 'born,' it's always 'summoned,' or 'arrived.'"

"You think you weren't born?" Whim asked.

"No, I'm just wondering if anything weird happened."

"Well," Young Ben said, and then lapsed into thought. "The only thing I remember was that crazy woman-power retreat your mother went on with Dustine and Alice. They drove out to the cabin for three days to skinny-dip and invoke fertility goddesses or some such thing. Lauren and I laughed at them, but a month later your mother was pregnant, so maybe it worked."

Josh had a hard time imagining her grandmother involved in such a scene. She had always been so practical. And Alice hadn't believed in God, let alone goddesses.

"But, you know," Young Ben continued, seeming to think aloud, "Dustine changed a couple of years before you were born. When Peregrine overthrew the monarchy and killed Mirren's parents— that's what gave her the courage to finally leave. That was the final straw. It sent her into a depression, though. For a couple of years she was . . . in a dark place. All that changed when you were born."

"Me?" Josh asked, surprised.

"She said she felt hope again when you were born."

"That's so sweet," Deloise said.

"She was a beautiful person." Ben tightened his arms around Deloise and Josh. "Well, girls, your father should probably hear this from me. Why don't I go talk to him for a bit?"

"I'll go with you," Deloise offered, and she and Ben headed down the hall holding hands.

"Just think," Whim mused. "None of us will ever forget where we were when we heard that Young Ben was Josh and Del's real grandpa."

Twenty-five

"Would it be just terrible of us not to tell your family that you're back until tomorrow?" Mirren asked Haley that morning.

They'd talked all night, sitting in the royal trimidion until the lanterns burned out and then sneaking into the house and up to her bedroom. Haley had told her everything about Death—about its purpose, about Ian, even about the transformation he had experienced and her part in it. He felt like a profound fear he'd been running from all his life—the fear of Death—had been relieved. Once he'd started talking, he couldn't stop, as if years of unspoken words were gushing out of him.

"I know it's selfish," Mirren said, leaning against him on the bed. "I know everyone is so worried about you. I just don't want to share you yet."

"One day," Haley agreed. He was already a little overwhelmed by having been plunged back into the World so unexpectedly. Plus, he hadn't yet figured out how he was going to tell Josh what had happened to Ian. "Just one."

Mirren turned her face up for a kiss.

They snuck out before her relations woke up, leaving a note and stealing the family car. First they had breakfast at a local diner, and Mirren showed Haley her favorite spots around the little town where she lived. Then they wandered into a gift shop and stumbled upon a beautiful wicker picnic basket, and decided to buy it, fill it up, and drive to the beach.

Haley took her to the spot where Josh's grandmother's cabin had once stood. It had burned more than a year before, and now a crew was excavating the spot in preparation for rebuilding. Haley and Mirren stood nearby, watching a crane pull pieces of smoke-stained cement out of the old basement.

"This is where Ian's soul got separated from his body," Haley said.

Mirren, standing beside him, let her head come to rest on his shoulder.

"I think that's what went wrong with him. Most souls go straight to Death; they accept that change. But Ian's soul hung around for so long, he got confused. He started thinking that maybe he didn't have to go."

"What will happen to him?"

Haley repressed a shiver. "I honestly don't know."

They watched the construction for a while, and then Haley said, "I'm glad they're rebuilding. Maybe we'll spend the Fourth of July out here again next year, like we used to."

"I would love that," Mirren said.

They walked the half mile to the beach and sat down on a new plaid blanket. It was too cold to swim, but Mirren insisted on taking her shoes off and stepping in up to her ankles. She'd never seen the ocean before.

"It's so cold!" she cried. "The sand—I'm sinking!"

She looked so beautiful to Haley, her long red hair blowing around her face, her skirt bunched in one fist, a luminous smile on her face. He didn't think he had ever seen her so carefree.

But there was a sadness lingering in her aura, a deep red wound, and as he watched her dry her feet on the blanket, he asked her about it. "Tell me about the election."

She sighed and told him about Peregrine's landslide victory, followed by his sudden disappearance. "I don't care that I'm not a queen, but I wish I could do *something* to help the dream walkers. Peregrine didn't just defeat me, he managed to hobble me." She dug in the sand beside the blanket, looking for seashells. "I waited so many years to be part of that community, and now I'm here in the World and I'm as isolated from it as I ever was."

Haley understood. He had spent most of his life feeling isolated, too. Sure, he'd had friends, but he'd always been on the outskirts of their group, the one somebody—usually Deloise—had to remember to invite along. He'd been a pariah in school—the weird kid, the homo, the deaf-mute. In fifth grade, the principal had actually told Haley's mother to consider teaching him at home. "He'll never survive middle school," the woman had warned.

Haley had survived—mostly thanks to Ian. Ian had beaten back the bullies, and when he turned his anger on Haley, Josh had beaten Ian back.

What Haley had wanted, though, wasn't to be protected; it was to be wanted, and he imagined that Mirren needed the same thing now. Feeling inspired, he grabbed her under the knees and behind her shoulder blades and scooped her into his lap.

"Haley!" she cried, but she was laughing. "What are you doing?"

He kissed the tip of her nose. "I'm reminding you that you aren't alone."

She touched his face with her long, cool fingers. "You are so dear to me," she said softly.

"I love you," he told her. "Don't worry. You'll find a way to help. I know you will."

She nodded, just a little. "I believe you."

Mirren's aunt and uncle were bewildered by Haley's appearance in their yard and alarmed by their niece's obvious affection for him. Katia was welcoming, but her constant chatter made Haley nervous. After an awkward dinner together, Haley decided it was time to go home.

They all drove over together. Haley could barely wait until the car stopped to jump out.

I made it, he thought as he ran up the back steps.

The kitchen smelled like dish detergent and coffee grounds. Haley's favorite water bottle sat upside down in the drying rack by the sink, as if Kerstel had refused to put it away, certain Haley would be home soon to use it. He ran past the chugging dishwasher and into the living room, where he found Lauren and Kerstel watching the television with the volume on low. Within arm's reach was a bassinet that contained not only a baby with a blue-green aura, but a small white puppy with a hazel aura.

"Haley!" Kerstel cried, and she jumped off the couch to fold him into her arms.

Lauren hugged them both, and they were full of questions about how Haley had made it home. But he felt a throb of energy from behind him, and he knew whose it was before he saw her, sitting in the hallway in a wheelchair.

Winsor.

She looked terrible. Her aura had always been a glorious combination of blue and yellow, but now it looked as if it had been broken and rearranged incorrectly, like a badly made stained-glass window, with strange grayish-purple shapes thrown in. But Haley felt a great burst of joy inside him at the sight of her soul back in her body.

"Haley?" she asked.

He let go of Kerstel to kneel down in front of Winsor. "Hi."

She reached out a shaking hand to touch his hair. "They wouldn't tell me where you went. They always lied to me."

She was trembling, and Haley wished his family had just told Winsor the truth. She was the only person he knew who truly wasn't afraid of hearing hard things; in fact, she thrived on the truth, no matter how ugly.

"S'okay," Haley told her. "I'm here now."

"Are you mad at me?"

He rubbed her cold hand between his. "No. I was never mad at you."

She gave a little nod. "That's good."

He surprised her when he hugged her, but he couldn't resist. He had loved her once, even though she hadn't loved him, and he had been afraid her soul would spend eternity in that canister.

I couldn't find you, he thought, remembering the empty feeling he'd had when he held her hand in the hospital. *But you're here now, too.*

She was smiling at him when he let her go, and as he stepped back, he saw something green flicker in the energy field around her heart, lively and quick. Then it morphed into an achy gray splotch. A moment later it flashed green again, and Haley realized that Winsor's physical injuries weren't the only reason her aura was so muddled and disorganized.

Someone broke her heart.

He would have looked more closely, but she pointed past him and said, "Who's that?"

Mirren was standing in the kitchen with her very confused family, watching Haley and Winsor. She was wearing her own smile, and Haley knew that she wasn't, not for an instant, jealous.

"That's my girlfriend, Mirren," he told Winsor.

"Oh," Winsor said, considering. "She's pretty."

"Yeah, she is."

Then somehow word of his return spread to the upper floors, and everyone was rushing down to see him. Haley felt shy and tried to sneak toward a chair in the corner of the living room, but people kept hugging him. They were all so excited and noisy that Kerstel had to take the baby upstairs, but not before she whispered, "You knew she was going to be a girl, didn't you?"

Haley just smiled, and Kerstel kissed him on the cheek.

"Thank you for not ruining the surprise."

If you think that's a surprise, he thought, *just wait a few years.*

Then Whim was grabbing him and hugging him so hard he lifted Haley right off the ground, and Deloise was crying and trying to show Haley her puppy, and Will was slapping him on the back. Alex was shaking his hand like it was the handle of a water pump, and even Saidy was smiling.

"Hi, guys," Haley said, laughing.

"Dude," Whim said. "*Dude.* Never do that to me again."

Haley smiled, until Whim added, "Not everybody's cut out to be a hero, you know?"

Whim hugged him again, so he didn't see the smile on Haley's face fade. But Will must have, because when his turn to hug Haley came, he said, "Don't listen to Whim. You're the bravest person I know—after Josh."

Distantly, Haley wondered how Josh would have reacted to seeing Ian again.

Almost as soon as he thought of her, she was there, hugging him so tightly it hurt, and this time he was the one picking her up off the ground. Such a brief separation, and he had already forgotten how little she was.

"I've been returning souls as fast as I can so we could get you back," she told him breathlessly. "I've already returned forty of them. A couple more weeks and we would have been able to get you, I swear."

"Josh," Haley said. He put her down on the floor so he could see her face. "I never doubted it."

That was *almost* true.

Josh teared up then, and Will put an arm around her, and there were too many shapes and colors in their auras for Haley to figure out everything between them, and then Deloise asked, "How did you get back?" and it didn't matter anyway.

Haley tried to think of an answer. "I died," he said finally.

"You . . . died?" Deloise asked, as a hush fell over the room.

He smiled at her. "Just the parts of me I didn't need anymore."

Mirren—who was the only one who had heard the whole story—put her arm around him. "He'll tell you all about it later," she said. "He's still getting used to being back."

"Well, it's only been what, two hours?" Whim said.

Neither Haley nor Mirren corrected him.

But Katia did. "No, he got back last night. They ran off this morning and had a picnic at the beach."

Protests sounded across the room.

"Last night!" Saidy cried.

"You couldn't have texted?" Whim demanded.

"Thanks, Katia," Mirren said.

"I don't care when you got back," Will told Haley. "All that matters is that you're here."

"Did you see Ian?" Josh asked, and the silence that followed was as loud as the protests had been.

At that moment, Haley happened to be holding Deloise's puppy, who was licking his thumb, and he used the puppy as an excuse to look down at his hands. If he'd been looking up, everyone would have known he was lying.

"No."

He couldn't tell them. He couldn't say the words. If he told them that Ian's soul was corrupted, Winsor would blame Josh. So would Josh. Deloise would be horrified that she couldn't do anything to help. Whim would try to lighten the mood and end up offending everyone.

Better just to lie.

Twenty-six

Josh was so happy to see Haley that she was reluctant to let him out of her sight. When he went to the bathroom, she had to stop herself from asking Whim to supervise, just to make sure Haley didn't go *poof!*

Even after everyone else had gone back to their lives, Josh couldn't bring herself to leave the guys' apartment. She watched TV with Whim and Mirren and Will while Haley took a shower and changed into clean clothes, and she convinced—or rather, made an offhand suggestion to—Whim to order pizza, just as an excuse to keep hanging around.

"You look like a huge weight has been lifted off your shoulders," Will told her.

"I feel like it," Josh admitted. "I didn't know how scared I was that we wouldn't get him back until I saw him."

"I feel the same way," Mirren said. "Like I didn't realize I was holding my breath for three months."

At that moment, Haley emerged from his bedroom in a pair of jeans, a worn T-shirt, and a red-and-purple cardigan. "Pizza!" he said happily.

"Eat up, man," Whim said. "I ordered mushroom and green olive just for you."

Haley sat down in the recliner next to Mirren and gave her temple a kiss before digging into his pizza.

"So, what did you eat while you were there?" Whim asked.

Haley swallowed. "I didn't. No eating, no drinking, none of that."

"You went three months without eating?" Whim's face was a mask of horror.

"I was afraid I wouldn't be able to come back if I did, like Persephone. But I didn't really get hungry or thirsty. And time moves differently there, so it only felt like five days."

"So you feel like you saw us last week," Will said.

"Yeah. It's kinda weird. When I left it was summer, and now it's fall. Kerstel had the baby. Everybody's hair is longer."

"I need to cut mine," Josh said.

"I like it long," Will told her, and she couldn't hold his eyes.

It would have been so easy to fall into his arms then. With Haley home, she felt like everything would be okay, like she could trust that Peregrine would turn up, and Feodor would go willingly back to Death, and she could take a chance on love and not get hurt.

Feeling brave, she scooted closer to Will. "Put your arm around me."

He smiled and did as she asked, and the pressure of his arm felt good, like the weight of a heavy, protective coat.

"That's what I like to see," Whim said. "See? Now that Haley's home, everything can go back to normal."

They hung out for a couple of hours, and then Whim got distracted and wandered off, taking the last of the pizza with him. Josh noticed Haley's eyes following him until the bedroom door closed.

"I need to tell you something, Josh," Haley said.

Ian, Josh thought. *It has to be about Ian.*

She didn't know how Haley could have entered Death and not seen him. Where else could Ian be?

She was caught completely off guard when Haley said, "I saw your grandmother."

Josh blinked. "Grandma?"

"Yeah."

"Is she—okay?"

He smiled. "Yeah. She's an angel now. And she sent you a message."

"Whoa," Will said.

Josh could hardly believe what she was hearing. For months after her grandmother's death, Josh had longed to speak to her, to apologize, to explain. She'd never thought to give her message to Haley.

"What did she say?"

"We didn't have much time. I asked her about you being the True Dream Walker. She said to tell you, 'You'll find the answers where the three universes overlap.'"

Somehow, Josh had expected the message to be *I forgive you.* Or at least *I love you.*

"I don't know what that means. That's all she said?"

Haley nodded.

"It sounds like she was talking about the Cradle," Mirren said.

Josh told Haley, briefly, about the vision of the Cradle she'd had. As she spoke, Haley began to nod, and as she continued, the nodding became faster and more emphatic. "Did you already know all this?" Josh asked.

"No," he said. "But it . . . explains a lot about you. About . . . the way I see you."

When Josh stared at him, he added, "You're all purple and silvery."

Well, that clears it up.

Aloud, she said, "But if Grandma meant for me to go to the Cradle, that's a problem, because I don't know how to get there, except to be almost dead," Josh said.

"Maybe you have to wait until the next time you almost die to figure out what she meant," Will suggested, and he didn't sound pleased.

"No," Haley said. "That doesn't . . . feel right. It has to be somewhere more . . . literal. A place Dustine could have gone when she was alive."

"The cabin?" Josh suggested. "I don't know how the three universes would overlap there, though."

Haley was shaking his head. "It feels like . . . less like a place than a thing."

A thing. Something Dustine had touched.

Dustine made that quilt . . . No, I'm sure she made it.

Josh's head snapped up. "The quilt!" she cried, and ran into Will's room. The others followed.

On the wall opposite Will's bed, in a large frame behind protective glass, hung the lap quilt Dustine had given Will. It displayed the three universes as overlapping circles full of spirits and nightmares and angels.

A single triangle of peacock-green fabric represented the place where the three universes overlapped.

"Help me get this down," Josh said, and she and Mirren lifted the framed quilt from Will's bedroom wall and set it facedown on his bed. Haley followed Josh's lead and helped her bend back the metal tabs that kept the frame in place so they could remove the quilt.

"Um, let's be careful with that, okay?" Will said nervously. "Because I really like it."

With the quilt facedown, Josh carefully pressed it with her fingertips. The fabric was old, the threads too supple and loose, and Josh was reluctant to ball it up in her fist. Looking at it now, she was more certain than ever that she was right. "I think we need to cut into it."

"Wait, wait, wait," Will said. "I'm not cool with that."

Mirren, who had never seen the quilt before, came closer to examine it. "If you're right, what we're looking for should be right behind this green patch. It's appliqued on, so if we're careful not to damage the fabric, it could be sewn back in place afterward. Katia's a wonder with a needle."

Josh was sold, but she left the final decision to Will. "It's your quilt, so it's your call."

"You're sure there's something there?" he asked, rubbing the back of his neck.

"I'm sure. But I could be wrong."

He let out a long breath. "Okay. But let's damage it as little as possible."

They borrowed a pair of Deloise's cuticle scissors that had small, very sharp blades. Haley held Will's desk lamp close to the quilt so that Mirren could painstakingly pick the golden threads out one by one. The process took nearly ten minutes, but when she was finished, the green fabric came away unharmed.

And revealed pages of onion paper hidden behind the quilt top.

Josh cursed. Mirren set the quilt down on the desk and very carefully slid the pages out. After unfolding them, she glanced at the top page and then held the packet out. "They're addressed to you, Josh."

The onion paper was yellow and semitranslucent. Dustine had folded the pages once lengthwise, making them just narrow enough to slide into the quilt.

Josh read the letter aloud.

Dear Joshlyn,

There's no way for me to anticipate the circumstances that might have led you to discover this letter. I left as many clues as I could, but it's impossible for me to know, so many years in advance, when or why you might need this information, or even what relationship you and I will have.

As I write this, you are only a year old, but already you are showing signs of exceptional ability. You can do forward and backward rolls, you can play catch with a soft ball, and yesterday you slid down the stairs on your belly. (Your father had a fit.) Though you don't talk much, your hearing is exceptional, and you always know who is in a room with you and where. I have never seen a child so alert, so aware of what is happening around her.

Your baby sister is nothing like you. She smiles and coos and giggles and makes complete strangers smile back at her, but at six months old she's still learning to sit up on her own. You took your first steps at her age.

But the most telling thing is how you will stand for hours at a time in front of the archway, watching nightmares as they pass. I have to keep one hand on the looking stone and use the other to hold the waist of your pants, because if I let go for one moment, I have no doubt you would rush right in. You get so excited, watching the nightmares. You stomp your feet and clap your hands, and point to things and shout. You never seem afraid.

By the time you read this, you might be fifteen or thirty or even fifty. If enough years have passed, I have no doubt that you will have started to wonder about your own uniqueness. This letter is my way of telling you.

It would take too long to explain everything, so I'll start by saying this: Your mother and I, and a good friend of mine whose name I will not write, came to a place in life where we began to fear for the future of the World. The Cold War is over, but its dangers are not. After WWII, humanity swore that we would never again allow genocide, but fifty years later we have already forgotten the lessons of the Holocaust. First Pol Pot in Cambodia, marching entire cities into concentration camps to starve. Then a million killed in Rwanda in three months, men slaughtering their neighbors with machetes in church. Now a year later—just one year— all the television shows is seven thousand Muslim boys lying in mass graves in Bosnia.

Do you understand, Josh? Will they still bother to teach history in schools when you are ready to learn? By then,

World War II may be just a footnote at the end of a
chapter relating far worse horrors.

We thought, after '45, that we had learned something.
That our collective memory of so many deaths—the Jews in
the camps, the Russians in the snow, the American boys on
French beaches—would be enough. We had finally had
enough of violence. But we hadn't. Five years after the war
ended, Truman sent boys to fight in Korea. Then the lunacy
of Vietnam, and whatever the hell we did in Kuwait. It just
goes on and on.

What I have learned is this: We cannot count on
humanity to save itself. We will all die waiting.

My breaking point was Peregrine's coup. (I almost wrote
"your grandfather." But by now you probably know the
truth. Count that among your blessings.) What he did to
the Rousellarios—and what he finally admitted to doing to
me for decades—ruined my last hope for this world. If his
obsession with staging destroys dream walking, he will upend
the balance of the three universes, and I cannot risk that.

I knew a man, some years ago, whose heart died in
Poland during the war. Maybe you will find his name, if
you search long enough through the records of the dream
walkers. He was so haunted by what he saw that he tried to
end the World, and although he has been gone for many
years, I find myself thinking of him more and more often,
and wondering if he was somehow right that we need help if
we want to become what we could be.

This is where you come in. Your mother has had a difficult
life, which is as much my fault as Peregrine's. I should have
taken her out of his house when she was still small, before he
could damage her the way he did. She understands what he is
capable of better than anyone. Except me, I suppose. Jona
and I, and a dear friend, began to wonder what we could do,
how we could lead the World toward peace and at the same

time create a countermeasure to Peregrine's evil. We came to a single idea; that idea was you.

On the pages enclosed, you will find a record of the things we did, before you were conceived, and after. Though they may seem cold, cruel even, keep in mind that we did them for love, and for the hope that you will make your World better than we made ours.

With Love,
Dustine

The rest of the pages were shaking so hard in Josh's hand she could barely read them. Awkwardly, she pressed them flat against the carpet and tried to make sense of the diagrams and formulae.

The first thing she saw were lines written in Dustine's practiced loops and a scrawl Josh recognized as her own mother's. A third hand she didn't recognize, but she didn't have to guess to whom it belonged; Dustine and Jona could only have gotten this information from Alice, and Alice could only have gotten it from Feodor's papers.

She really didn't burn them, Josh thought with despair.

She traced the formulae with one finger as she read them, tapped the diagrams as she parsed them out. The longer she read, the more hollow she felt.

They modified my aura. They differentiated my harmonics. They changed me.

"Is this all I am?" she asked. "Just another one of Feodor's science experiments? No wonder I can't control the Dream. I'm not the True Dream Walker—I'm not anything!"

Will set the note down and put his arm around Josh. "That's not what this means."

"It means I'm no different from Snitch and Gloves."

"Feodor told you that all those prophesies said something would bring about your arrival."

"Yeah," Josh said bitterly. "Mom and Grandma playing God. No wonder Alice looked at me like I was Frankenstein's monster."

Haley picked up the note again, and Josh watched him run his hands over the pages without reading them. "Nothing comes from nothing," he said softly. "We all came from somewhere. Your somewhere is just different from ours."

"My somewhere is literally a copper bathtub they bombarded with magnetic rays and ionized Veil dust."

"No," Haley said. "That's just the how, not the where."

"They didn't have the right to do this to me," Josh told him, but with less fire.

He smiled at her. When had his smile grown so serene?

"There's a lot I didn't tell you about Death," he said.

Josh didn't especially want to hear about Death right then, but she knew Haley was getting at something, so she shrugged and let him talk.

"When we die, we leave our bodies, but our souls carry who we were—our minds, our identities—with us to Death. We spend our time there letting go of who we were. I watched people release pain and anger, trauma and fear, release all the distractions of their lives. They came to understand the ways in which their experiences have brought their souls closer to perfection, and then they let go of those experiences. They only took the lessons and the joy with them."

"Where did they go?" Will asked.

"Back to the Dream. It's all possibility there. They picked up whatever they needed for their next life, whatever they were ready to learn next, and then they were reborn."

"They were reincarnated," Josh said.

"Of course. All the souls cycling through are trying to grow. They go around and around, and each time they cycle through, they vibrate a little higher, they find it a little easier."

"Easier to what?" Will asked.

"To remember. We remember and forget, and remember and forget that we are part of one another." He hesitated, then touched the back of Josh's hand. "Except you."

Maybe if Josh hadn't seen the cycle of reincarnation for herself while she was holding the Omphalos, she wouldn't have believed him. But she remembered the individual paths of light each soul had followed, and how her line had come from nowhere.

"I'm not part of the cycle," she said.

"This is your first incarnation," Haley agreed. "You came from *here*."

He held out the triangle of green fabric Mirren had cut from the quilt.

"What does that mean?" Will asked.

"Is that bad?" Josh asked.

"No," Haley said. "It's a miracle."

"That's what Mom and Grandma did? They, I don't know, *summoned* me from the Cradle?"

Haley thought, and Josh wished his thoughts showed more on his face. Will squeezed her shoulder as they waited, and she let herself lean against him.

"The three universes weren't always separate," Haley said finally. "We . . ." He frowned, the way he used to do all the time when he couldn't find the words. "We used to go through all the cycles in just one place. We were all one—all the energy, not just the people and the animals, but everything. And then . . ."

"The Big Bang?" Will asked.

Haley nodded again.

"But why?" Josh asked.

"We had . . . we had evolved as far as we could in that form. The same way we die when we've evolved as much as we can in this life, we had to die from that form. So the Big Bang separated the three universes, and we began to cycle. But one place was left the way it had been, and that's the Cradle. The Omphalos is . . . the last piece of what was before. And you're part of that."

"Why?" Josh asked again.

"Because Jona and Dustine prayed for something new. They said that they had given up hope for humanity, but really they were recognizing that we are stagnating. This form, like our form before the Big Bang, has taught us almost everything it can. What Dustine and Jona wanted was to move us to the next form, although they didn't realize it."

"And that new form is supposed to be me?" Josh asked.

"No. You're just the catalyst for the change."

Josh felt like a tiger, pacing in a cage. "But I don't know what I'm supposed to *do*."

"You don't have to."

"That doesn't make any sense! Am I just supposed to go about my life, hoping that someday I'll have a flash of—"

She had been going to say "intuition," but the word in her mouth was "wisdom."

You have to follow it.

In her mind, she saw the Omphalos, like a big white egg. It rested atop a black basalt pillar. Josh reached out for it, dipped her fingers in the cool water flowing out of the pillar, and—

"Josh?" Will asked.

Josh's attention snapped back. She had been staring at the bed; she turned back to Will and Haley.

"So, what," she said, "I'm supposed to merge the three universes so that they can form something new, some next incarnation for all of us? Am I the True Dream Walker or not?"

"Nothing's written in stone," Will said, but he glanced at Haley as he spoke.

"He's right," Haley said.

"Either I merge them or I don't."

"It's not that simple. The future isn't fixed."

Josh wanted it to be simple. She liked monster nightmares, ninja nightmares, zombie nightmares. She liked knowing her enemies and knowing how to beat them.

Haley reached toward her, and his hand hovered in the air a moment before resting on her knee. "When the time comes, you'll know what to do," he said.

That was not reassuring.

Twenty-seven

Haley was finally back in his apartment, his bedroom, his bed, and he couldn't sleep.

After making it very clear to her family that they had no right to dictate where she spent her nights—she was nearly twenty, after all—Mirren had fallen asleep in Haley's bed. Her sleeping aura was a pattern of scarlet red and deep orange, arranged in concentric circles, like ripples spreading out from her, spreading that peace, and Haley wished he could bring himself to lie down beside her and bask in her calm energy.

But he couldn't sleep.

He'd borrowed Dustine's letter. Josh hadn't wanted to ever see it again; she'd been upset and confused enough that she went down to the basement to dream walk, and had turned Will down when he offered to go with her.

Haley hadn't understood what the things he sensed about Josh had meant until he read Dustine's letter. Now he wondered if he had jumped the gun when he told Josh she was the True Dream Walker eight months before. He'd said it because it was written in her scroll and because he had no other explanation for the silver singularity that was her energy field.

Maybe Young Ben had run into the same problem when writing her scroll. Maybe there was no name for what Josh was, and they'd all assumed her uniqueness was part of something they'd heard of.

Will had told Haley about the prophesies, the True and False Dream Walkers, and Feodor's attempt to hide information from Josh. It had only confused Haley further. He knew what he saw when he looked at Josh, and what he felt when he touched her, and certain flashes of a possible future, but he didn't know how any of it fit together.

That had always been his problem.

He sat against the wall beneath his window and closed his eyes. He had his steno pad open on his leg and a Sharpie in his hand.

Show me something, he begged. *Let me help. Tell me what to do.*

His pen remained motionless, poised over the page, and he was still waiting when Mirren stirred. A flash of yellow anxiety burst from her third chakra at finding him missing from bed, and then a cooling rush of green when she saw him under the window.

Without speaking, she got out of bed and sat down beside him, slipping in between his arm and side. Her touch was comforting, her peaceful, sleepy aura a warm, red cloud around them. Haley waved his hand through the air where her scarlet aura and his violet aura overlapped, and smiled as little energetic sparks flew, both energy fields quickening.

"Are you playing games I can see?" Mirren asked, her tone lighthearted.

"Maybe."

"I almost think I can feel it. Like little waves."

Haley felt a stir of excitement. He'd always wanted to do this with someone, and Mirren was the first person he trusted. "Close your eyes."

Mirren closed her eyes and leaned against him, smiling faintly. "What are we doing?"

"Just tell me what you feel."

Haley wiggled his fingers in the air close to her elbow and watched as their auras began to spin, like stirred water. "What is that?" Mirren asked, but she was smiling.

"What do you feel?"

"It's like . . . you're kissing my elbow."

Haley swept his fingers up her arm, leaving a trail of twirling energy in his wake. Mirren inhaled sharply as the energy moved along her collarbone to the base of her throat, then up her neck and finally across her lips.

"Haley," she whispered, and her gray eyes, when they opened, were dark.

The energy kept moving when he kissed her, and through his

eyelids, Haley saw orange flares around them. He felt its heat almost as surely as he felt Mirren's hands on his chest, and he—

Suddenly he was watching her face on a computer screen, and she was speaking in a slow, deliberate manner. Yellow energy filled her aura, and it was pure and bright around her like a solar flare.

Haley pulled away, and the image vanished. He didn't know if he'd caught a peek at her thoughts or her future. If he warned her of what was to come, would she alter her actions? The dilemma was the same he'd been facing since he was a child, and whatever he had learned in Death or over the last three months meant nothing, because he still didn't know how to resolve it.

"What's wrong?" Mirren asked. Her parted lips were damp.

He didn't want to look at her. He knew his eyes were faulty and weak—too easy to read, like the rest of his face.

"You saw something," she said.

He nodded, picking up his Sharpie. He wanted to write Mirren a note, but what could he have safely said?

"I thought things would be different if I made it back," he admitted, forcing the words out through his mouth instead of his marker. "I thought *I'd* be different."

"You are different," Mirren told him. She brushed his hair out of his eyes. "I can see it."

You see it, Haley thought. *I'm not sure I do.*

"Do you want to know what I saw?" he asked.

Mirren's eyes widened. "Are you allowed to tell me?"

"I don't know. No one ever gave me any rules. Sometimes I told Ian things . . . but it always seemed to bring trouble."

"Then don't tell me."

Haley rubbed the palm of his free hand against his jeans. It hurt a little, and he liked that.

"Maybe I want to tell you. Maybe I'm tired of . . . being helpless. Always knowing what could happen and not being able to do anything about it."

"Why can't you do anything about it?"

He looked at her in the odd shadow beneath the window, startled.

"You told me before you went away that you were tired of being afraid," she said. "You said you regretted watching Ian fall apart and not trying to help him."

Haley thought of what he'd just seen, of Mirren on a computer screen. "I can't influence your decisions. I—I don't know how, but I know that's not what I'm supposed to do."

She nodded, as if she accepted his determination, but after a moment she said, "What about using your second sight to see something useful? Would that be wrong?"

"I tried. This is all I came up with."

He picked up the steno pad to show her the blank page, but the instant his fingers touched the paper, a memory woke in his mind. He was three years old, standing in the living room, and Josh was holding out a painted wooden nutcracker. It was her favorite toy, and she was going to let him play with it to be nice even though she didn't really like anyone else touching it. Haley had only known her for a few weeks, and he was still scared of her, the way her aura blazed purple and silver and was full of stars, but his curiosity had slowly overtaken his fear.

When he accepted the nutcracker, he let his fingers touch her soft, dirty hand, and for an instant, he was enveloped in that starry purple sky. He felt something his three-year-old brain couldn't comprehend, but his heart had understood: this girl was part of his destiny.

When he'd opened his eyes, he had been holding the toy out in front of him, and Josh had been frowning, and she'd taken the nutcracker back. "You make it bite the bad guy," she'd said, and demonstrated with a stuffed bear. *"Chomp!"*

"Is that a smile I see?" Mirren asked, and Haley was back in his room, sitting beside her, and yes, he was smiling.

"I think I can do it," he said. "But I'll need Josh's help."

Haley and Josh sat cross-legged on a training mat in the basement. He knew from the streakiness in her aura that she was feeling anxious, but she was trying really hard not to let it make her cranky. She looked different from the girl he had gone into Death with six days—no, *three months* before. She'd developed a dangerous, wiry look, one that suggested she could be trouble. And her eyes, those aventurine green eyes, had darkened. When Haley looked into her eyes, he saw Feodor's reflection instead of his own.

"I . . . I've never tried this before," he admitted.

Josh grinned. "Me neither. And what are we trying, exactly?"

It was easier to look at her with Mirren and Will standing out of eyeshot, easier to pretend they were alone while doing this oddly intimate ritual.

"We're . . . trying to direct my visions."

"All right. What am I supposed to do?"

"Hold my hands." He arranged their hands so that the lefts were on top and the rights were on the bottom. That felt important, somehow. "Now close your eyes."

Still trying to pretend they weren't being watched, Haley shut his own eyes.

I don't know what to do now, he thought. He'd never tried to use his abilities deliberately. *Show me Peregrine,* he thought. *Show me Feodor.*

Nothing happened.

He tried thinking of the future and waiting for an image to appear, but all he saw was how he must have looked to those watching.

Should I try calling on angels? he wondered. He had never really believed in angels until he visited Death. Mirren believed in gravity—that there was a predetermined course that led everyone to their destiny. Josh didn't believe in anything, as far as he knew.

But he heard Josh's voice then, and afterward he couldn't have said whether she had spoken aloud or only in his mind. *You have to follow it.*

Follow it? Haley wondered. *Follow what?*

Then he felt a tingle in their joined hands, as if a current were running between them, a purple line of electricity that expanded as he watched.

Follow it, follow it, you have to follow it.

Haley kept his mind trained on the energy as it grew into a beam of purple light, and then it wasn't just their hands that were a part of it, but their whole bodies, and the light just kept expanding into a tunnel cutting through the darkness of space, and Haley found himself standing in it, holding Josh's hand.

He blinked. He wasn't imagining this—he was really *there*. It felt as real as anything ever had.

"Where are we?" he asked. His heart was beating fast; that, too, felt utterly real.

Josh had a faraway look on her face. "You have to follow it," she said again, and then she walked toward the source of the light, and Haley followed, still holding her hand.

The light grew brighter and brighter until Haley had to close his eyes, and he stumbled along behind Josh until suddenly the light was gone.

He opened his eyes. They were standing in a room that turned to white nothingness, and in the center rose a pillar of black basalt with water pouring out of the top, and on the water rested a large, white egg.

"Where are we?" he asked again.

Josh just smiled at him and placed their joined hands on top of the egg.

It was not an egg, but a stone, Haley realized, and then not a stone, but a universe, and they were floating inside it, watching the souls come and go.

Each soul was a golden line, moving along its own course. Some had very short paths behind them, and others had traveled so far that Haley could barely see where they began. Deloise was one that seemed to stretch on forever, and as Haley watched her soul move faithfully along, he could see how she was growing from one incarnation to the next. Will, too, had many miles and many lives behind him.

Whim . . . not so many.

Mirren had been right—they did each have a destiny, an

inevitability. And at the center of it all was something good. Something beautiful and made entirely of love. They all came back to it in the end. They set out, individual souls, growing with each lifetime they lived, and when they had been made perfect, they returned to the whole, to make it even more beautiful. There was no hell, nowhere else a soul could end up. Except . . .

"Look," Josh said. "That's me."

Her soul's path was silver, and it was very short. Unlike all the others, it originated in the room behind them. And it had no set course before it.

Josh's sadness throbbed around them.

Suddenly all Haley's shyness was gone. It couldn't exist in this place, so close to that source of eternal love. "Don't be sad," he told Josh. "It's like I said before—you're something new."

"I'm young and stupid," she replied, but she smiled.

"We all were, once. But look here, at Feodor's path."

Feodor's soul had left a glowing, jagged trail, chaotic, crazed. But then it crossed Josh's path, and on the other side, it began to straighten out. The dramatic turns smoothed out, and the golden color intensified.

"See? You helped him." Haley pointed to his own life, like the line of a constellation drawn between stars. "You helped me."

But another line, one that had run parallel to his own for a brief time, had collapsed into knots and turmoil.

Ian.

Ian's life line wasn't leading back toward Haley's, it was—

"Why didn't you tell me—"

And the rest was screaming.

Twenty-eight

Josh didn't hear her own voice until she opened her eyes and saw the basement stretched out before her. Haley lay curled into a ball on the blue training mat, and Mirren was kneeling beside him and checking his pulse. Will was standing directly in front of Josh, his mouth moving silently.

Josh realized from the angle of the strange tableau that she had backed into the farthest corner of the basement. The reason she couldn't hear what Will was saying was that she was screaming, and the word echoing off the cement walls was, *"Forget!"*

Josh took in a deep breath to scream again, despite her raw throat, and Will put his hands on her shoulders and said quietly, "Josh, stop. You're okay."

She stared at him. She wasn't okay, but she couldn't remember why not, and as soon as she tried to remember, another scream rose up in her chest.

Forget, forget, forget!

"What the hell was that?" Whim asked, running down the stairs with Deloise at his heels.

"Whim, shut up," Will said. "Josh, you're safe. You don't need to scream."

The scream was a balloon filling with air, waiting to be released, and she wanted to let it out, but Will was giving her a reassuring smile and touching her cheek and saying, "Breathe with me. In . . . Out . . . In . . ."

Slowly, the balloon deflated. Josh didn't realize she was clenching her fists until she released them and felt the ache in her hands.

"Will," Mirren said tightly. "Something's wrong with Haley."

Will took one look at Haley's face and said, "We need to get him off the floor."

"What's wrong with him?" Deloise asked. "What happened?"

"I don't know," Will said.

In her head, Josh heard him finish the thought.

But it isn't good.

She watched, motionless, as Will and Mirren lifted Haley off the floor and set him gently on an old couch. Haley never moved; his body was as rigid as a cemetery angel. Curled up in the fetal position, he reminded Josh of one of those babies that turned to stone in the womb.

"His pupils are huge," Mirren said.

"I know," Will said. "He's in some sort of shock. Whim, get a sleeping bag."

Josh felt that she was watching them from a very great distance. She watched Deloise touch Haley's skin and look alarmed, watched Mirren tuck the sleeping bags in around Haley and speak softly to him, watched Whim call his mother at work.

Josh trained her eyes on the stained cement floor until two flats entered her field of vision. When she lifted her head, Deloise was standing in front of her.

So pretty, Josh thought, admiring her sister's brown eyes.

"Do you remember your name and everything?" Deloise asked.

"Yes. I'm Josh, you're Del."

"Do you remember coming down here?"

Josh nodded, and her neck popped painfully. "We were sitting on the mat."

"And then?"

And then the screaming.

Josh shrugged.

Deloise put an arm around her shoulder—*She's taller than me,* Josh recalled—and walked her back toward the couch.

"How's she doing?" Will asked.

"She's sort of stunned, but she seems all right."

"Good." Will smiled briefly. "I don't know what happened, but I think Haley's getting better. His pulse is slowing down and he's warming up. Maybe the best thing to do is just give him some time with Mirren to calm down."

"Mom says the same thing," Whim reported.

Will said, "Haley, we're going to leave you and Mirren here for a while. We hope you'll come upstairs when you feel better."

Deloise and Will dragged Whim and Josh up the stairs.

"That is *not* just Haley freaking out," Whim said as soon as the basement door shut.

"No," Will agreed. "It's Haley freaking out so badly that he went into some combination of shock and catatonia."

"Maybe some food would help," Deloise said.

"What would help is less stimulation," Will told her. "He needs to be quiet and warm and feel like he's safe, and then I think there's a good chance he'll come out of it. And then you can stuff him full of cookies or pot roast or whatever seems most appropriate."

"What happened?" Whim repeated. "We *just* got him back."

They kept talking, but Josh's mind drifted away. Something inside her head was different, and she kept being drawn back to it, the way her tongue was always drawn to the spot the dentist numbed.

But her mind was just that: numb.

She didn't come back until Will called her name, and then she realized they were alone in the hallway.

"Do you need to lie down?" Will was asking.

Josh shook her head. "I'm fine."

"You aren't fine," Will said firmly. "Josh, you just stared at a wall for ten minutes without speaking. That's not fine."

She felt bad that he was worried, and she could see that he was. But she felt no desire to argue, and somewhere inside she knew that wasn't normal for her.

"Saidy said you need to rest," Will said. "Can you go upstairs and lie down?"

Josh felt a deep fear at the idea of being alone. "Can I lie down in your room?"

"Sure."

The walk to the second floor took longer than usual, Josh thought. Or was time moving more slowly?

The guys' apartment looked strange to her. For the first time, she noticed that it had a sliding glass door to the second-floor wrap-around porch. *Was that always there?* she wondered.

Will tried to guide her toward his bedroom, but she felt compelled to go into Haley's room.

"Josh?" Will asked, following her in.

She walked past his unmade bed, Mirren's shoes set neatly against the wall, a dropped steno pad. There, in the catchall on the dresser, just where she'd remembered it, was a photograph.

Ian had hated the photo, thought the blue backdrop was cheesy and the lights made him look pale. Really, he had just hated the emotion in his eyes. But Josh had loved that photo, because she'd been standing behind the photographer when it was taken. Just before the camera had clicked, she'd mouthed, "I love you," and the photo had captured all the warmth and affection of Ian's resulting smile.

Josh stared at the photograph. She didn't know why she'd wanted to see it, and she didn't know if she should feel awkward about gazing at a photo of her ex in front of her current—?—boyfriend.

"What's that?" Will asked.

"Ian," she said without thinking, but as soon as his name left her lips, the photo changed. Ian's smile became a mocking smirk, and his green-hazel eyes turned wicked at the corners.

I'm going to kill you all, he whispered.

Josh slammed the picture, facedown, on the dresser. She was trembling again, and the numbness returned, like clouds cast before her eyes.

"Josh," Will said. "Tell me what's happening."

This time she was whispering, not screaming, but the message was the same.

"Forget, forget, forget."

"Josh," Will said, more loudly.

"Forget, forget—"

"Josh, you're okay. You're safe. There's nothing to remember or forget."

"For . . ."

She couldn't even remember what had upset her, or why. Will took her hand and led her into his own bedroom, and she was relieved to be away from whatever it was.

"Lie down," Will said, and gently pushed her back on the bed. He lay down beside her, and they shared her pillow.

"Don't leave if I fall asleep," she said.

"I'll stay."

"I don't want to be alone."

"What are you afraid of?"

She didn't know. And she didn't want to.

Twenty-nine

Will sat at his desk and watched Josh toss and turn in his bed. He'd hoped she would sleep, but she couldn't keep her eyes closed for more than a few minutes. Sometimes she mouthed the word *forget,* and Will was afraid she didn't know she was doing it.

Something very, very bad had happened in the basement.

Had they seen the future? Had they seen Josh merging the universes? Was that what was so terrifying? Or had it been something worse, something Will couldn't even fathom? Why had she gone to find that picture of Ian?

And why had Haley lied to them about seeing Ian?

Will had known from the moment Josh asked the question. Haley had retreated into silence for so many years that he had no idea how to lie, and he'd broadcast his lie in every way possible. He'd looked down, his voice had risen, and he'd even unconsciously nodded while saying "no."

Will hadn't pushed him, figuring Haley would talk about Ian when he was ready. Now, watching Josh doze and whisper and toss her head back and forth, he wondered if he had made the wrong choice.

Eventually, Josh sat up and refused to lie down again. The sun had almost set and the room was bathed in blue light, and the shadows seemed to swallow her up. Will sat beside her on the bed, their backs against the wall.

"How do you feel?" he asked.

"Hungover. I can't remember what happened."

"Maybe it's better if you don't try."

She leaned into him, and he put his arm around her shoulders. Touching her felt good, even better when she turned so she could snuggle into him and rest her head on his chest.

"I was thinking about what you said."

"When?" Will asked. He was relieved to hear that her voice had lost that frantic, shrieking sound it had had in the basement.

"In the car."

He smiled. "We have our best talks in automobiles."

"Yeah."

Will stroked her hair. He really did like how long it had gotten, how the locks framed her face. It made her look gentler.

"I was thinking about how you said you couldn't keep up with how fast I change. Sometimes . . . I can't either. And I keep thinking that we should wait until everything settles down to get back together, but nothing ever seems to settle down for long. There's always something else coming down the track."

Will knew all that, and only too well. He'd spent months thinking about it.

"So what do we do?" he asked.

"Well, I see three options."

Always the dream walker, he thought fondly, and he tried not to laugh.

"We can wait and hope for some kind of long-term quiet. We can give up. Or . . ." Josh glanced up at him, nervously, just for an instant. "We can throw caution to the wind and hope we don't get hurt again."

Will's heart throbbed, a spasming muscle. He was afraid to push; this possibility felt too delicate. "Which option would you like to take?"

Suddenly Josh was in motion, up on her knees and turning toward him, forcing his legs down so she could sit on his lap, their faces inches apart. She hesitated, though, before laying her hand on his chest.

"You've probably noticed," she said, "that I'm not a very cautious person."

"I might have picked up on that."

"Sometimes I act before I think; sometimes I make really bad choices."

"Only sometimes."

She smiled then, and all her insecurity seemed to melt away. "But I don't think I made a bad choice in you."

Will let his arms snake around her waist, felt his blood rise to his skin. She was so *close*. "I completely agree with that."

"So maybe we could try again—"

"Yes."

"—as long as you promise not to bail on me when the next storm rolls in."

"Josh, when the next storm rolls in, I want to be that calm in the center of it. I want to be your safe place."

She touched his face on either side, and despite the quick rise and fall of her chest, Will knew she was still deciding. He'd seen that expression on her face a hundred times in the Dream, just before she decided whether to abort or fight tooth and nail. And just like always, when she made her decision, she straightened her shoulders and nodded to herself.

And then she kissed him.

It was like it had always been with them: they started out so slowly, being so careful of one another, afraid of the trust that intimacy required, and then the instant they were sure of each other, they lost all control and Josh's shirt was on the floor and Will was on top of her, her fingernails biting into his shoulders, her neck arched up for his mouth, his hands lost in her hair, and he was telling her that he loved her because he simply couldn't hold the words in.

She cupped his face in her hands. "Say it again."

Will couldn't contain his smile, either. "I love you."

He said it again, and again, against her cheek, into her mouth, and then they were kissing hard enough to bruise their lips, and Will's arms were wrapped all the way around her torso, crushing her against him, and when Whim started shouting that they had to come watch the news, Will was just grateful he had locked his door.

Eventually, she said, "We have to stop. Sorry. I'm not ready."

Will nodded, swallowed, tried to convince his body that Josh was right. "You don't have to be sorry. It's okay. We shouldn't rush into anything."

"We went too fast before."

"I know. It was too much."

She was sitting in his lap again, facing him, and they were half-naked and covered in sweat.

"It's not that I don't love you," she said.

"What? I know that. I never thought that."

They were both breathing hard. After their first encounter with Feodor, they'd slept together the minute they were both healed enough to do so, in what Will now realized had been a frantic, desperate attempt to reassure themselves that they were still alive. It had ended up becoming another thing Josh didn't know how to talk about, and Will had a feeling that a second pass would yield similar results.

"We should wait," he told her. He grabbed her shirt off the floor and handed it to her.

"This is yours," she said, and she laughed and helped him put it on. She pulled her own on, but they remained sitting there on his bed, calmer but still unable to stop touching each other, and Will realized Josh had tears in her eyes.

"Hey," he said, brushing them away. "It's fine. There's no reason to rush."

"It's not that. It's . . . Sometimes I have a hard time believing I'm worth loving."

"Josh," he said softly. Her words hurt him. "You are so deserving of love."

"The only good thing about me is the dream walking. If whatever I do means that the World doesn't need dream walkers anymore, what use will I be? I don't even know who I am if I'm not dream walking."

How could he reassure her? Josh didn't realize how unfailingly loyal she was, how dedicated to her work, how competent she was at so many things, and Will sensed that if he tried to convince her, she would just dismiss him.

"Take away the dream walking, the whole True Dream Walker thing, the prodigy thing, the athlete thing, the science thing," he said, "and underneath all that, I still believe you're someone extraordinary."

It was the best he could do, and he knew it wasn't enough, but there were some things he couldn't make her believe. She had to choose to believe them for herself.

"Come here," he said, and he pulled back the blankets on his bed. Josh climbed beneath them, and they curled up together the way they had after so many of her nightmares.

"Do you still have nightmares?" he asked.

"Not the kind you mean. Not often."

He was glad to hear she could rest again, but some part of him missed waking up at three a.m. to find her crawling in beside him, all tears and supple warmth.

"Will," Josh whispered.

"Yeah?"

"Say it again."

He smiled.

Thirty

Josh and Will didn't get up until the next morning. Each time Josh woke, she just burrowed into Will's chest and went back to sleep. She didn't want to break the spell they'd cast around each other, and she didn't want to face her life.

She was so confused.

Finally, it was the worries that woke her. She worried that she and Will were setting themselves up to get hurt again, that she was meant to end the World, that she couldn't trust Feodor, that Peregrine was going to kill her, that Haley had been permanently damaged, that something terrible was coming to get them. She worried and worried, and after an hour she kissed Will's closed eyes and snuck into the living room.

Whim was parked on the couch, leaning toward the television with his elbows on his knees. Discarded food containers littered the coffee table.

He glanced at her and said, "I see you and Will got back together."

Josh felt herself blush. "Sorry if we . . . were loud."

"I was referring to the hickey on your neck."

"Oh, God, really?"

While Josh went into the bathroom to look at her neck, Whim called, "A third major tear opened up about six this morning."

Suddenly the hickey didn't seem so important. "A third?" Josh asked. "When were the first two?"

"I tried to tell you last night, but Will locked his door."

God bless him for that, Josh thought as she went back into the living room. She plopped down on the couch and reached for a bag of Cheetos. "Did you sleep at all last night?" she asked, taking in Whim's red-rimmed eyes and haggard look.

"Josh," he said, utterly humorless. "You aren't listening. The Veil is coming apart. *Look*."

Josh finally looked at the television, and the Cheetos in her hand slipped to the floor.

Over a city built close to a large body of water, dominated by a giant temple and an enormous bridge, a tear in the Veil stretched a quarter mile above the city and straight down into the ground. The camera cut to cell phone footage of a ghost man with red eyes and fangs tearing down a street on horseback. Another jerky piece of footage showed a purple wind howling around a corner, turning everyone it touched into flowers.

No, no, no, Josh thought.

"Where is this?" she asked, her mouth dry.

"Istanbul. The others are in Vidoño, which is in Venezuela, and Prague. They'll show them in a minute." Whim rubbed his eyes. "What's left of them."

Vidoño didn't appear to have been a large town before the tear, but it was hard to tell because part of it had sunk into the ocean.

"I don't understand," Josh said. "What's happening? There hasn't been a cluster of tears like this in seven, eight hundred years."

"Josh, there's *never* been an event like this. They're only show-ing the big tears on TV, but *The Daily Walker* and DWTV are re-porting hundreds of smaller tears. Everywhere. A cruise liner sailed right into one this morning and disappeared."

All Josh felt was panic. "What's the junta saying?"

"Nothing. They're doing what they can, but they aren't prepared for this. No one is. This is way beyond our ability to contain. There's footage all over YouTube of nightmares in Pittsburgh, vampire-angels attacking people on the streets, cars without drivers running people down. Some kind of plague is spreading in Cabo, and blood-snow is falling in Burlington, Vermont."

"Gimme your phone," Josh said, and Whim handed it over. She dialed Feodor, and she'd never been so relieved to hear him answer. Some part of her had been afraid he was somehow responsible for all this.

"Are you watching the news?"

"I am aware of the situation, yes. It's quite extraordinary."

"Meaning what?

"Meaning I have no explanation for it. Something would appear to have destabilized the Veil on a far larger scale than the phenomena we've previously observed."

"That's doesn't make sense, Feodor."

He sounded amused when he said, "I am not claiming that it does."

"Could this have been caused by Peregrine staging nightmares?"

"Only if the nightmares he staged caused enough turmoil to destabilize the Veil."

"I'm guessing that's what he did."

Which meant that Peregrine *had* managed to switch bodies with Snitch, and that he now had complete control over the Dream.

"I'm going to go in with the VHAG," Josh told Feodor. "I need you to start building duplicates of it. We don't have a choice about distributing them now."

"Yes, yes, I understand."

She woke Will up and told him what was happening, but he didn't really seem to understand until he saw the news footage. "How many?" he asked.

"Three huge ones, a hundred smaller ones," Whim said.

"But more will open," Josh warned. She ran a hand through her hair. "We're looking at a cascade effect. We could . . . it's possible we could lose the whole Veil."

And then the three universes will merge whether I want them to or not, she added silently.

Whim got off the couch, stood in front of her, and saluted.

"Tell me what to do," he said.

"What?"

She'd never seen Whim's face so serious. "If there's one person in the three universes who can fix this, I think it's you. And I can't sit here and watch it on TV any longer. So use me. Tell me what to do. I'm your soldier, Josh. Give me orders."

"I'm not . . ." she started to say.

"Yeah," Whim told her, "you are. You're the general. Deal with it."

She gave up arguing and hugged him, and he hugged her back with unusual strength. "I don't know if I'm worthy of that kind of faith."

"Maybe not," Whim admitted. "But you deserve that kind of loyalty. Besides, you and Feodor seem to be the only people with any idea of what's going on."

"Thanks." Josh let him go and felt herself slipping into action mode. "Is everybody here safe? How close is the nearest tear?"

"DWTV is tracking them. If their map is right, more than a hundred miles."

"Then I need you to call Feodor back and—"

Whim's phone rang. "It's your dad," he said, and answered it. "Hello? . . . Got it. I'll tell Josh and Will." He hung up. "Household meeting in the dining room in five minutes."

"Good," Josh said. "That's good."

Ten minutes later, the entire household had assembled in the dining room, the only room really big enough to hold them. Mirren, Katia, and Fel and Collena were there, too, and they'd dragged chairs in from the kitchen to cluster around the enormous harvest table. Josh wished she'd had time to go get Feodor—not because she considered him family, but because she wanted his input.

"Let's get started," Whim's mother, Saidy, said. "The junta is asking all fit dream walkers to form teams and go out and fight nightmares. Obviously, Winsor needs to stay here."

Winsor, Josh realized, wasn't with them. Had she not even been invited?

Doesn't she have a right to know what's going on? Josh thought. *She isn't made of paper.*

"As much as I'd like to help, I just had a baby," Kerstel said. "I probably need to stay here."

"That's good," Saidy said. "You can take care of Winsor and Keri."

"I want Grandpa Ben here, too," Deloise said. "He shouldn't be alone."

"Fine," Saidy said. "Haley, I assume you're staying, too. Josh—"

"Wait," Haley said, and then had to say it again, louder, before Saidy noticed he was speaking. "*Wait*. Why should I stay here?"

Saidy looked at him, momentarily speechless. "Didn't you have a catatonic panic attack yesterday?"

Haley shrank back, and Josh said, "It wasn't a panic attack, it was a psychic . . . episode, or attack, or something." Just the memory of the aftermath was making Josh anxious. "I went through it, too."

Every adult in the room was staring at Josh, and that's when she remembered that Kerstel was the only one who really understood Haley's abilities. Mirren's aunt, in particular, looked like she'd just walked in on a board meeting attended by chimps in business suits. Whim put a hand over his eyes.

"I mean," Josh stuttered, "Haley's a good dream walker."

Haley gave her a tiny, private smile across the table, one that was laughing at her just a little bit, and Josh smiled back. She was mostly relieved at seeing him conscious again, but she wasn't lying when she backed him up. Having seen him in Feodor's dimension and his courage when he remained in Death, she fully trusted his ability to handle an emergency.

"Yes, well," Saidy said, seeming irritated by the interruption. "Haley's eighteen, I guess he can make his own decisions. We should pack up today and set out by tomorrow. We'll need, what, three vehicles?"

"Wait a sec," Josh said. She knew she was interrupting—again—but she had to speak up. "You want the rest of us to form a single team? Doesn't it make more sense for us to split into multiple groups?"

"I don't want you girls going off by yourselves," her father told her.

"I agree," Alex added.

"Dad, that's crazy," Whim said. "Nobody walks nightmares in groups of twenty. And Josh can lead her own team."

Josh suddenly really liked having Whim as her soldier.

"I don't know," Lauren said, and Kerstel put a hand on his shoulder.

"Lauren, she's probably the finest dream walker on the planet. She's better qualified to do this than any of us. I know you want to keep her close, but she doesn't need us hovering over her shoulder."

Lauren frowned, but Josh decided to jump in anyway.

"And I want Haley, Del, Will, and Whim on my team," she said.

"I'm going with you," Mirren said.

Half the adults in the room broke into protests, and Josh held up a hand.

"Kerstel just made my point," she said. "I've done more dream walking than most of you put together. And the people I've done it with and trained with are my friends. I know what to expect from them, and I know what they are and aren't capable of. We can function together as a team."

"Mirren isn't going anywhere," Collena said. "Absolutely not. And Katia has never even been in the Dream."

Nobody mentioned taking Katia, Josh thought, at the same moment Katia said, "I want to go."

"Out of the question," Collena said, and for once, Josh agreed with her.

Releasing an angry breath, Mirren said to her aunt and uncle, "I trained with Josh, which makes me better prepared to help than either of you."

"Mirren—" Collena began.

"You haven't set foot in the Dream since we went into hiding twenty years ago. I passed a dream-walking trial less than four months ago."

"You don't have any right to risk yourself," Collena shot back. "You have a responsibility to stay alive."

"I have a responsibility to do what the dream walkers need me to do, and right now that's helping prevent nightmares from overrunning the earth."

While Josh appreciated Mirren's faith in her training, she was actually a little reluctant to take Mirren with her. Her training had been brief, and she'd nearly drowned during her dream-walking trial. Besides, her intelligence could serve a better purpose. "Actually, I could use you for something else. If you take over building and distributing the VHAGs, that leaves me free to deal with Veil tears."

"You've decided to distribute them?" Mirren asked.

"I don't see what choice we have now."

Mirren considered, then nodded. "I agree."

As always, Josh could trust her to be sensible.

To Mirren's aunt and uncle, Josh said, "Please don't take this the wrong way, but if you haven't been in the Dream in twenty years, today isn't the day to go back in. If you two and Katia help Mirren and Feodor, that will get a lot of VHAGs out there a lot faster."

"How many people do you need working on the VHAGs?" Lauren asked.

Josh thought. "Somebody needs to go fight nightmares on the streets. But that's only triage. I don't know how we can stop this cascade effect except by giving out as many VHAGs as possible, so anyone who isn't current on their dream-walking training should be working on the VHAGs."

"We'll never get them all back," Mirren warned.

"No," Josh agreed. "We won't. But I'm afraid we may already have passed the point where mere dream walking can stabilize the Veil."

"What are you saying?" Collena asked.

"I'm saying we might not come back from this."

The room fell silent.

"Well," Alex said. "VHAGs it is."

"You still need an adult to supervise your team," Saidy told Josh.

"An adult will slow us down," said Josh, who was getting sick of this argument. "We know what we're doing."

"You're *children*," Saidy said.

"Josh is right," Deloise cut in, much to everyone's surprise. "Saidy, I don't think I've *ever* dream walked with you. I have no idea what kind of leader you are, and if you tell me to do something I don't understand, I'm going to second-guess you. I won't second-guess Josh."

"That's not the point," Lauren said.

"It *is* the point," Will said. "Us kids have followed her through enough hell to know that what she says goes. But the rest of you aren't going to want to take orders from her."

The adults exchanged unsettled glances across the table, and Josh couldn't help smiling at Will, despite the seriousness of the occasion. Beneath the table, he put his hand on her knee and left it there.

Before anyone else could continue the argument, Josh added, "I think Alex should lead the other team."

"Alex!" Saidy cried, outraged. She and Alex had a fairly unhappy marriage, and part of that unhappiness was due to Saidy's belief that Alex was a hapless idiot.

"Alex dream walks more hours than any other adult here. Look at the schedule. He pulls four six-hour shifts a week, every week, most of them during peak nightmare hours. The only other adult who comes close to that is Kerstel, and she can't go."

"I'm a paramedic," Saidy began, and Josh interrupted her.

"Which means you need to hang back in case of injuries and treat as many field cases as possible. Dad, I don't think you've walked a single nightmare since Kerstel got pregnant. Alex is the logical choice."

"I want to go with him," Collena said.

Mirren cast her eyes at the ceiling.

The adults argued for another fifteen minutes, but Whim, who usually dream walked with Alex, stood up for his father, and eventually, Alex stood up for himself—quite literally. He rose from his chair, and said, "I want to lead the team. Thank you for the nomination, Josh. Saidy, if you don't feel like you can follow me, I'm sure a hospital could use your help."

Reluctantly, Saidy agreed, and the meeting broke up. Josh went up to her father afterward and hugged him.

"Thank you for trusting me," she said.

He held her by the shoulders. "You have three of my four children on your team. Don't come back with any less."

"I promise," Josh said. It didn't matter that it was a promise she couldn't make; he needed to hear the words.

Lauren nodded, but as he started to get out of his chair, he said, "What's that on your neck?"

Josh automatically clapped a hand over the hickey, which hurt. A few feet away, Will turned a dark shade of red.

"Training accident?" Josh suggested, which sounded ridiculous even to her.

Lauren rolled his eyes, but he smiled for the first time all day. "You two be careful," he told Josh and Will.

She didn't think he was only talking about fighting nightmares.

Thirty-one

Josh's team set out in Kerstel's van that afternoon. It would have been a fun road trip if they hadn't all been so afraid of getting killed.

Except Haley, Will reflected, *who seems to have lost all fear of Death.*

I should find that reassuring, but I'm too scared.

The drive to the nearest tear took less than two hours. The tear looked huge to Will—at least thirty feet across—but Josh reminded them that the size wouldn't matter once she had the VHAG going and was inside the Dream.

"Remember," she said. "This is what we trained for. You aren't going to see anything here that we haven't seen a hundred times in the Dream. It just seems strange because it's in the middle of a town."

"Um, Josh," Whim said, and pointed out the window.

In the center of the little town of Shepherd's Creek, a sixty-foot-high metal tripod was walking down the street.

"All right," Josh admitted. "Maybe you haven't seen *that* before. But we can do this. Go team!"

They tumbled out of the van and ran toward the tear. The tripod was moving away from them, which was lucky, but as they got closer, several dozen screaming pilgrims came running out of the Dream.

Josh pulled back, and they waited for the pilgrims to pass.

Nothing we haven't trained for, Will told himself. He wished he weren't wearing a gas mask; it limited his peripheral vision.

At Josh's signal, they ran forward. The tear was located on the next block, but to get to it, they had to run through a square that contained a large, rectangular fountain. Several people had been pulled underwater by pale purple octopus tentacles and were actively drowning.

"Haley, Whim, the fountain!"

Haley and Whim broke off while Will and Deloise kept running. Josh didn't hesitate before leaping through the Veil hanging in midair, but Will and Deloise glanced at each other before following. Will was carrying an ax, but he felt practically naked as the Veil dust soaked right through his clothing.

On the other side of the Veil was a grassy knoll that boasted a large tree, and hanging from one particularly sturdy branch were three witches. Their faces were bloated and blackened, but they weren't dead.

They were undead.

Josh sat down on the ground and turned on her VHAG. Will and Deloise were there for one reason—to protect Josh's body while her soul wasn't inside it. They even had a makeshift sling they could use to carry her—it?—around.

Will and Deloise stood facing opposite directions, Josh on the ground between them, and waited.

"Is this it?" Will asked, watching the angry witches trying to wriggle free of their nooses.

"Yeah, this is a lot easier than I was expecting," Deloise said, and her sentence was punctuated by the tear in the Veil blinking out of existence.

A second later, Josh was back on her feet. She threw an archway open and ran through it.

Will and Deloise shrugged at each other and followed her back into the World. They burst out into the square, where Whim and Haley had managed to drag the octopus—and its victims—out of the fountain and onto the pavement. Unfortunately, they had also been ensnared by tentacles and were thrashing around on the ground trying to get free.

"Del, get its head!" Josh said. "Will, chop the arms!"

Will ran to the tentacle wrapped around Haley and hacked it off. Haley, who had a machete in his hand, crawled to the nearest civilian and sawed at the tentacle holding her. Josh freed another townsperson, who had gone limp, and pulled off her gas mask to give him mouth-to-mouth.

By the time Deloise had reached the octopus's head and crushed its brains with her hammer, the man had vomited a half gallon of water and was sitting up against a storefront.

"I can't believe that worked," Josh told Will, putting her mask back on. "That almost never works. Back to the van, guys!"

"Wait," Whim said, "should we take down the tripod?"

"With what? It'll run out of Veil dust and vanish in a few hours. We need to focus on closing more tears."

They headed for the van. As they ran back through town, Will saw a woman attempting to fight off a ninja, but each time she tried to punch him, her arm slowed in midair, as if inexplicably losing strength. Will made a quick detour to hit the ninja twice in the face and break his knee with a swift kick.

"Oh, thank you," the woman said. "I don't know what's wrong with me!"

"Don't give up," Will told her, and started running again.

He was the last to jump into the van. Deloise distributed bottles of water and they all drank in silence for a moment. Then Josh said, "Where to next, Whim?"

"North," Whim said, checking DWTV's map on his phone. "The next tear is north."

They fell into a rhythm: consult the map, drive to the tear, close the tear, repeat. They slept on the road, often no longer than half an hour at a time, and slowly their initial enthusiasm and sense of purpose began to fade.

Because more tears just kept opening.

Every time Whim pulled up the map, new tears were marked upon it with red Xs. They began to remind Will of old cartoons where dead characters' eyes were Xed out, and in his mind, he gave up on the towns they represented. Their route began crossing back on itself as new tears opened in towns they'd passed through safely before, or worse—in towns they had already been to. No matter how many tears they closed, they couldn't seem to get more than a hundred miles from Tanith.

Will was the first one to get hurt. He got hit in the face—not even by a nightmare, but by a terrified man who saw his gas mask and panicked—and fell backward onto broken glass. The same hand he'd cut with a mirror months before took the brunt of the fall, and he spent the next drive picking shards of glass out of his flesh.

Then Deloise slipped in oil and twisted her knee. She iced it in between towns. Whim ran into a low-hanging sign while chasing an elf and busted his nose. A foo dog bit Haley's arm.

The longer they went on, the more they wore down, and the worse the injuries became. Josh fell off some scaffolding and probably cracked a rib; they weren't certain because she wouldn't go to a hospital, all of which were overrun anyway. Will narrowly avoided being stabbed, but he got cut badly enough that Deloise had to put nineteen stitches in his side while he bit down on Whim's belt. At the next town, a golf cart doing twenty miles an hour winged Haley.

They were all exhausted, weak, and cranky. But the breaking point came when Deloise's gas mask failed and she breathed in a lungful of Veil dust. Josh and Whim had to drag her, screaming, back to the van.

"We can still seal the tear," Josh said. "Will, you stay with Del."

Will, who was pretty sure he'd torn his stitches, bent over next to the van and pulled his mask off. Sweat dripped off the tip of his nose.

"No, no, no," Whim said. "You want just the three of us to go back there? Did you see the size of those lizards?"

"All right, we'll take Will too. Del will be fine alone for a few minutes."

"What?!" Whim shouted at Josh. "She's hallucinating out of her freaking mind!"

Deloise was inside the van, screaming about hotel soap—or soup? Will couldn't tell.

"Then I'll go by myself," Josh said.

Will looked up at her, at the hand she was holding against her cracked rib, at her bloodshot eyes, at the desperation that had brought her close to tears.

"Josh," he said. "No. We have to rest. Let's find a hotel, get some sleep, eat real food, and then see where we are."

Josh started to argue with him, but suddenly Haley leaned over and spit a bloody tooth onto the asphalt.

Will saw something go out of Josh then. She cast one last glance at the open tear and the lizards streaming out of it, and said, "All right."

They found a hotel, showered, bandaged their fresh wounds and rebandaged their old ones, and then fell asleep. Even Deloise's hallucinations couldn't keep her awake.

Will woke up in the middle of the night. Josh was sitting at the foot of the bed, legs pulled up against her chest, chin resting on her knees. A twenty-four-hour news station was playing on the television, showing one scene after another of Veil tears—seventy, ninety, some more than a hundred feet long.

"Estimates are that more than fifty of these major phenomena have now appeared, with thousands of smaller ones opening up all around the globe," a reporter said.

"Dear God," Will whispered.

Josh turned the television off and crawled over the covers to lie beside him.

"In the morning," she said, "we'll go home."

They had been gone four days.

Thirty-two

Josh arrived home defeated.

I failed.

Her house was still standing, but she passed a tear in downtown Tanith as they drove through. It was only a matter of time before the nightmares reached her family.

The reunions were less than joyful. Everyone felt guilty being happy, except the Bolognese puppy, Posey, who ran in circles for ten minutes when she saw Deloise.

Josh was just happy Deloise hadn't gone permanently insane from the Veil dust.

While they'd been gone, Josh's father had broken his arm, burst an eardrum, and burned off both eyebrows. He'd retreated to the house. Collena had also gone home after dislocating her hip on the first day out; all the hospitals were filled beyond capacity. Alex and Saidy, however, had gone to join Kerstel's brother's team in Savannah.

"I think they're actually getting along better," Lauren told Josh.

"Crisis," she said absently. "It cuts through all the bullshit."

Lauren lifted the part of his forehead where his eyebrows should have been. "I mean crap," Josh said hastily.

Josh wanted to drive straight to Feodor's, but Will wouldn't let her. She gave in without a fight; either she didn't have the energy to argue with him or she didn't really believe there was anything worth fighting for left, and she was too tired to know which. Mirren, however, came to the house as soon as she heard that Haley had returned.

Josh, Will, Whim, and Haley were sitting in the living room of the guys' apartment in complete silence when she arrived. Whim had handed Deloise off to her stepmother to watch over; she was still kind of loopy. Whim himself had flopped down in the bean-bag chair and hadn't moved in almost an hour. Haley was half-dead in the armchair, and Josh was curled up against Will on the couch. None of them even had the strength to shower.

"Oh my," Mirren said, surveying the room.

Josh opened her eyes and watched Haley drag himself off the chair to hug Mirren. "I got gored," he said, like a little child, and then he pulled up his shirt to show her where a baby unicorn had gored him.

Mirren gave his bandage a kiss, and they sat down together in the oversized armchair. "You all look . . . a little worse for wear," Mirren said.

"No shit," Josh said, and Whim began laughing.

Josh knew she should ask about the VHAGs, how many they'd made, how many people were using them, but she was afraid to know the answer. The specifics didn't matter, after all. Obviously, the number wasn't enough, just like she hadn't closed enough Veil tears.

"How's Feodor?" she asked instead.

"He seems to find it impossible to downplay how interesting he thinks all of this is."

"What about the VHAGs?" Whim asked.

"We've quit production," Mirren admitted. "The problem is distribution. We simply can't deliver them all around the world as quickly as we need to. Especially since all the package services have shut down. So . . ."

She hesitated, and Josh wondered why. Was she embarrassed? What did it matter that she'd failed? Hadn't they all?

"So I did something . . . I may have acted out of turn, but I didn't see any other way. I tried to call you a number of times, but the tears are affecting cell coverage. If I made a mistake—well, then I've changed the course of history in an unforgivable manner, but I truly didn't know what else to do."

"Just spit it out already," Whim told her.

"All right then. I made an instructional video explaining how to build and operate the VHAG. And then I put it on DWTV."

Josh sat straight up then, her fatigue, her aching side and split lip, all forgotten. DWTV was a super-encrypted television station made by dream walkers for dream walkers. Although it only aired in English-speaking countries, there were foreign equivalents all around the world.

Mirren seemed genuinely surprised when Josh said, "You're a goddamn genius."

"I would slow clap," Whim said, "but my hands hurt."

"Haley?" Mirren asked, and he smiled at her. "You knew I was going to do this, didn't you?"

"Not exactly," he said, playing with her hand. "But I knew you'd think of something."

Josh was still staring in awe when Mirren said, "I'm just afraid we don't have enough time. Dream walkers are translating the video into every language imaginable—the ones who aren't calling me an evil heretic for enabling staging on a massive scale, that is—but the devices take time to build. Maybe if I had thought of it sooner . . ."

We should go back out there, Josh thought. *Every tear that gets sealed buys us a little more time.*

Then, quite unexpectedly, Will said, "Is there anyone here who thinks Peregrine *isn't* behind this?"

Josh hadn't even been sure Will was awake, truthfully. He hadn't moved since he'd sat down.

"I don't know," Whim said, "but I'm going to blame him anyway."

"No," Will told him, "I'm serious. Assuming Peregrine has put his soul in Snitch's body and he can control the Dream, staging nightmares could have destabilized the Veil, right?"

"If he was creating emotional turmoil it could," Josh admitted, at the same time Mirren said, *"What?"*

Everyone looked at her. "Peregrine has switched bodies with Snitch?" she asked.

"Probably," Josh said. "Did we forget to tell you that?"

"Yes! He could be staging dreams on a tremendous scale!"

"Yeah," Whim said. "We know."

"No, you don't." Mirren got up and went to look out the sliding glass door to the porch. "I'm going to be all out of secrets by the time this is over," she muttered, and then sighed and turned around. "All right. I see no other choice. You asked me once, Will, why the monarchy outlawed staging."

"And you dodged answering."

"Well, today is your lucky day." In a low voice, as if she were still worried someone might overhear, she said, "The reason staging is so dangerous is that if enough people dream of the same thing, it will become real."

Josh felt less shocked than confused. "How?"

"Whatever they're dreaming of will literally form in the Dream, pass through the Veil, mixing with Veil dust and becoming real, and settle in the World."

"How can a nightmare pass through the Veil?" Will asked.

"The harmonic mass reaches a critical point and overwhelms the Veil. It's like . . . Have you ever stuck your finger through a soap bubble, and then pulled it out, and the bubble didn't pop? It's kind of like that."

The soap bubble explanation might have been enough for the guys, but it wasn't for Josh. "You're saying that the polarization of the barrier breaks down under migrant harmonics."

Mirren replied with an acquiescing nod. "That is what I'm saying."

"That will eventually erode the Veil," Josh pointed out.

"Theoretically. It's never been tested, as far as I know."

"I think we're seeing the test right now. You're talking about an alteration of the frequencies in the parabolic dimension. That's going to lead to nonregional destabilization sooner or later."

"Can we skip to the part where you explain it to the rest of us?" Whim interrupted.

"Sure," Josh told him. "If you can stage the same dream for enough people at once, that dream will become reality. And if you keep doing that, you'll screw up the Veil on a massive scale and cause a failure cascade, like what we're seeing now. If Peregrine did manage to swap bodies with Snitch, then he can probably stage enough dreams simultaneously to cause all that."

"But he'd know better, right?" Whim said.

"Of course not. He doesn't actually understand any of the science. He's working with Feodor's notes and Snitch's memories, and he might have been able to cobble together the information he needed to switch bodies, but he doesn't understand the ramifications of what he's doing."

"Okay," Will said. "Let's assume that Peregrine's staging is the root cause of what's happening. If we can stop him from staging, will that stabilize the Veil?"

"Not on its own," Josh said, and Mirren nodded her agreement. "We'd still need people to run around with VHAGs closing tears. But it would go a long way, and it might—*might*—buy us time until enough people have VHAGs."

"So?" Whim said. "This sounds like a plan. I'm already feeling slightly less suicidal. Let's get our stinky carcasses back in the van."

"There's a problem," Mirren said. "We still don't know where Peregrine is."

For a few minutes, Josh had felt a growing kernel of hope, but it was fading now. She flopped back against Will, who wrapped his arms around her.

"Haley?" Whim said hopefully.

He shrugged. "I don't know where he is. But . . . I think the bigger question is, what is he using staging to create?"

That is *the bigger question,* Josh thought.

"We need guidance," Whim said. "Let's do Trembuline's thing."

"What's Trembuline thing?" Josh asked.

"Who's Trembuline?" Mirren asked.

"He's this guy we met. He's a genius."

"Whim," Will said, "you realize he helped Peregrine screw up the Veil, right?"

"He's a slightly evil genius," Whim revised. "But he taught us this meditation thing, and it's awesome. It makes you feel like everything's going to work out. Let's try it."

"I feel like it's kind of close to what made Josh and Haley freak out," Will said. "I don't know if it's a good idea."

"Does it involve seeing the future?" Mirren asked.

"No," Whim said.

"Then I think it will be okay." She glanced at Haley, who nodded, a bit uncertainly.

Josh didn't know what they were talking about, and meditating bored the hell out of her, but she felt a curious desire to try "Trembuline's thing."

"I'm game," she said, and Will looked at her with surprise.

"Will, you lead it," Whim said.

"Why me?"

"Because you have that soothing therapist's voice."

Will shrugged. "All right."

Whim turned off the lights and drew the curtain over the sliding glass door. There was still more than enough light by which to see, but the living room felt smaller, cozier.

"So," Will said, "Trembuline taught me and Whim to do this, but I don't think he invented it. In fact, Haley probably already knows how to do it."

He instructed them to rub their hands together and then hold them close. Josh was surprised that she did actually feel as if something were between her hands, pushing them apart.

"I think Haley and I have played this game," Mirren said, and she and Haley exchanged a sweet glance.

"Now close your eyes," Will said, "and imagine something you love between your hands."

The first thing that came to Josh's mind was dream walking. She *loved* dream walking. She had since the first time her mother took her into the Dream. Nothing in her life was more satisfying than saving people from their nightmares.

"Open your eyes," Will said.

Haley released a little cry. "It's beautiful!"

Everyone's hands had moved farther apart—especially Josh's. There was almost a yard of space between them.

"Is this for real?" she asked Will, astonished.

"You tell me," he replied with a smile. "Now close your eyes again, and draw that big ball of love energy into your chest."

Josh obeyed. For a moment, she didn't feel anything, and then a tremendous sigh poured out of her. Her shoulders dropped an inch. She felt lighter and less exhausted.

"Now ask yourself a question," Will said. "Any question. Even the hardest question in your whole life, and wait for an answer."

Even though Josh knew her brain or her imagination or whatever she was feeling couldn't answer this question, she asked, *Where is Peregrine?*

You have to follow it, her heart said.

I should have anticipated that, Josh thought, despairingly. *Follow what?*

Your inner wisdom.

I don't have any wisdom.

No? You're listening to it right now.

Where is Peregrine?

You will find him if you are kind. Remember others.

I don't underst—

"That was lovely," Mirren said, and Josh opened her eyes. Everyone seemed to be finished already.

"Right?" Whim said. "It's amazing."

Will looked at Josh and raised his eyebrows. "It was . . . interesting," she said.

Her friends began to share their experiences, but Josh's mind kept coming back to what she had heard.

Remember others.

Is there someone I've forgotten? Josh wondered. *Someone I haven't been thinking of?*

Only one person came to mind.

Thirty-three

"Am I not going to PT today?" Winsor asked her brother the next day.

"Nope," Whim told her. "You get the day off."

"Good," Winsor said. "My head hurts."

Will wasn't entirely certain how much Winsor understood about what was happening, or how much her parents wanted her to know. As far as he knew, Saidy and Alex hadn't told her anything at all.

The day before, the question Will had asked during the meditation had been: *How can I help?*

The answer he'd gotten had been simple: *Be yourself.*

He didn't know what that meant—besides the obvious—yet, but he wondered if the meditation practice would have been beneficial to Winsor. Maybe Whim would teach her.

When Winsor asked about her physical therapy, she was sitting in the first-floor living room with Whim and Deloise and Will. Whim and Deloise were trying to narrow down the area where Peregrine could be and Whim—always the newsman—had come up with a not-completely-stupid idea. He figured that people would have noticed something unusual when the dreams Peregrine staged began turning real, and that one of those events might have made the newspaper, so he and Deloise were combing through online papers for peculiar stories.

"'Drug Dealer Eaten by Pet Tiger,'" Deloise read.

"That's actually pretty common," Whim said.

"How about 'Rain of Frogs in Asheville, North Carolina'?"

"No, that's a proven scientific phenomenon."

It is? Will wondered, but he didn't want to distract Whim.

"Okay, 'Officers Murdered by Redneck Cult'?"

"What? No. Peregrine didn't go join a cult."

"How's it going?" Josh asked, walking into the room with a manila file in her hands.

"Not well," Whim told her.

"I had an idea," Deloise said. "But I don't know if it will work."

"Try me," Josh said.

"You said Peregrine was in touch with this guy Trembuline through e-mail, right? What if you hacked into Trembuline's e-mail and found out where Peregrine's e-mailing him from? You could trace the IP address or something, couldn't you?"

Will didn't think it was such a bad plan, but Josh looked unconvinced. "Whim, can you do that?"

"Ah, no. My computer powers do not extend to hacking."

"But can't *you?*" Deloise asked Josh. "You have Feodor's memories now."

"Feodor was exiled in 1962. Steve Jobs hadn't even dropped out of college yet. Why do people think that anyone with any sort of scientific knowledge can hack computers?"

"Josh," Will said softly.

"I'm sorry," Deloise told her, and he saw Josh soften.

"Sorry. It's a good idea, we just don't have anybody who can pull it off."

Slumped in her wheelchair, Winsor said, "I know a guy."

Everyone looked at her.

"You know a guy?" Whim repeated. "What guy?"

"His name is . . . Phil."

Maybe because she seemed to have difficulty recalling the name, no one particularly believed her. Whim gave her an affectionate smile and went back to the map he was marking.

To Will's surprise, Josh sat down on the ottoman close to Winsor's wheelchair. "Tell me about Phil."

Winsor pushed her hair out of her eyes, as if she, too, were surprised by Josh's response. "You said you need someone who can hack."

"That's right."

"Why?"

Whim shot Josh a warning glance, but she said, "Remember Peregrine, the guy Del and I grew up believing was our grandfather?"

"Yeah."

"He's a crazy, terrible person. He's doing something to the Veil that's caused it to tear in hundreds of places—"

"Josh!" Whim said.

"Is that why everyone is so upset all the time?" Winsor asked.

"Yeah. They're all scared because the Veil is collapsing, and the Dream and the World might merge."

"Josh, enough," Whim said, rising.

"If the World's going to end, she has a right to know," Josh told him. "She's not a child."

"I'm not a child," Winsor agreed.

"I know," Whim said. "But you aren't well yet. You don't need to be worrying about things like this."

Will agreed with Winsor; she had enough mental capacity to understand what was happening, and she had a right to the truth. He was proud of Josh for standing up for her friend.

Winsor frowned. She removed her glasses and rubbed at her eyes. "What if I never get better? Are you just not going to tell me anything ever again?"

Will could see how much that question hurt Whim. He tried to hug Winsor, and she pushed him away.

"I'm not a child. I might be stupid, but I'm not a child."

"You aren't stupid," Whim told her.

"Yeah, I am," she said. She reached for Whim's tablet, lying on the coffee table, and Deloise handed it to her. "But I'm not a complete idiot."

Winsor struggled to type. Del offered to help, but Winsor declined. She was quite determined to do whatever she was doing by herself.

"There," she said, five minutes later. She offered the tablet to Josh. "Call Phil."

She'd navigated to a website for a business called the Mad White Hatter, owned by someone named Phil.

Josh glanced at Will, who shrugged. "Winsor, did this guy work on your computer at some point?"

"No," she said. "I met him."

"Where?" Will asked.

Winsor frowned. Her eyes weren't focusing, but she said in a low, rough voice, "In the canister."

All motion in the room stopped.

"*In* the canister?" Whim asked.

"Phil's my friend," Winsor told him.

While they were processing that, Will pulled out his phone and dialed the number on the website.

"Hello, Mad White Hatter," a man said.

"Hi, my name is Will Kansas. I think you might know a friend of mine, Winsor Avish . . ."

"Winsor? Of course! *Of course* I know Winsor."

"Oh," Will said, startled. "Um, we're having a little computer problem and she said you might be able to help."

"Absolutely. Come right over. Do you need the address?"

They took Whim's baby-blue Lincoln Town Car to Phil's house. Although Will hated the way Whim drove even more than he hated the way Josh drove, Winsor liked the comfy leather seats. She fell asleep as soon as they were out of the driveway.

Josh and Will sat in the backseat and held hands.

I'm so glad we made up before all of this started, Will thought. *If the World is going to end, I want to be by her side when it happens.*

Phil lived surprisingly close by. Or maybe not so surprisingly. Snitch and Gloves had burst out of the Dream through the archway in the Avish-Weaver house's basement and then made their way on foot toward Josh's mother's cabin, where there was an archway to let them back into Feodor's universe. Along the way, they'd gathered souls for Feodor. One of the souls they nabbed had been Winsor's.

Apparently another had been Phil's.

A smiling woman met them at the door of a cookie-cutter mini-mansion. The silver bangles around her wrists jangled as she reached for Winsor's hands.

"Winsor," she said, "I'm so glad to meet you. Phil has said nothing but wonderful things about you."

Winsor tugged her hands away, refusing to meet the woman's eyes. "Who are you?"

"I'm Phil's wife, Donisha. Please, come in."

Will wasn't sure why Winsor didn't know who Donisha was, but Donisha seemed unsurprised by Winsor's condition and uninsulted by her diminished manners. She led them through an intimidatingly clean formal living room into a more casual TV room, where a short, round, black man in flannel pajamas lay in a hospital bed.

"Winsor!" he said, looking up from a laptop. "I'm so happy you called! Come here, come here!"

Winsor grew shy, but she navigated her wheelchair over to the side of the bed.

"I'm gonna give you a really lousy hug," Phil said, "because I can't get out of this bed yet. But I'll try."

He rolled onto his side and hugged Winsor, and she seemed to relax then, and closed her eyes briefly.

"Hey, I know that smile," Phil said as he released her. "Are these your friends? Introduce me."

They ended up introducing themselves while Winsor sat silently beside Phil. He gestured to the television, which was showing a tear in the Veil that had just opened up over Minsk.

"Pretty wild, eh? It's like the world's coming to an end."

Will and Josh exchanged glances, but neither of them told Phil how right he was.

"Did Winsor tell you about me?" Phil asked. "You all look like you have no idea what's going on."

"We have no idea what's going on," Whim affirmed. "You guys met *in* the canister?"

"The canister? I don't know anything about a canister. We met while we were both in comas." Phil pushed his glasses up his nose. "I can't really explain it. If it hadn't happened to me, I wouldn't believe it. But somehow we were all part of the same dream."

"What kind of dream?" Whim asked, a little suspiciously.

Will couldn't fault Whim's big brother instincts, but he already liked Phil. And he liked that Winsor liked Phil.

"We were living on the same street," Phil said. "We were neighbors. It was summer, a long summer, and hot . . ."

He trailed off, but Winsor nodded.

"It really wasn't that exciting," Phil said. "We just lived on this street and had a lot of cookouts. When I woke up I thought I must have imagined it. Then Sam called me and said he'd had a dream with me in it, and I realized it had happened, somehow or other."

"Sam?" Whim asked. "That weirdo who keeps showing up at our house?"

Phil winced. "I told him that was a bad idea. Sam's a little desperate." He smiled at Winsor. "*Somebody* won't talk to him."

Whim shook his head explosively, like he couldn't believe what he was hearing. Before he could start bombarding his sister with questions, Will said, "We're glad you're okay, Phil."

"Yeah, me, too. I'm weak as a kitten, but my mind's mostly okay. Still can't remember my e-mail password, though." His gaze fell on Winsor again, and Will saw his lips tighten. Phil knew Winsor's brain hadn't come back okay.

"What's this you need my help with?" he asked her.

Winsor rubbed her temple. "I don't remember . . . Whim?"

"I've got it, Winny," Whim told her. "We need to find someone, but all we have is the name of someone he's been talking to. Winsor thought maybe you could hack into the other guy's e-mail account and find something that would help."

"The man we're looking for is my grandfather," Josh put in. "He's got Alzheimer's, and he's been missing for the last three months. We're just trying to find him. We . . . we miss him so much."

Josh was the worst actress who ever lived. Will cringed when she started pretending to cry by rubbing at her eyes and frowning.

Phil tried to keep a straight face and couldn't.

"Darling," he said, "I know I just got out of a coma, but I'm not quite stupid enough to fall for that."

"Don't tell lies, Josh," Whim scolded. "You aren't good at it."

"Who's this guy you're trying to find?" Phil asked, opening his laptop.

"His name's Peregrine Borgenicht," Will said. "And he *has* been missing for three months. We know he's been in contact with someone named Aurek Trembuline."

"Are you sure about those names? They sound made up," Phil muttered. "Have you reported him missing?"

"Yeah," Will said, before Josh could try to lie. "They have no leads."

Even as he typed, Phil said, "Does he really have Alzheimer's?"

"Uh, no," Josh admitted. "But he did recently lose his left hand."

"So for all you know, he's just taking a long vacation to get used to being a righty."

Whim laughed. "That's the best-case scenario."

His words didn't seem to convince Phil, who stopped typing. "Somebody clue me in," he said. "I don't just break into people's personal lives for fun, not even for my friends."

It was Winsor who answered, while Will and Josh silently debated how much to tell Phil. She simply pointed to the TV and said, "That's his fault."

"*That?*" Phil echoed. "Nobody even knows what *that* is."

"We do," Josh said. "And yes, we think that Peregrine caused . . . what's going on."

"What *is* going on?"

No one answered that, not even Whim.

"Winsor, I love you, kiddo, but you've got to realize that this looks a little far-fetched from my point of view."

Winsor pushed her hair out of her face. Her gaze was unfocused, and Will wasn't even certain she'd heard Phil until she said, "I didn't know you were married."

"I didn't know you had a brother," Phil admitted, the lines in his face relaxing.

"There's other stuff," Winsor said. "Stuff you don't know about me."

She looked up at him then, and her eyes were as clear as Will had seen them since she woke up.

Phil let out a long, slow breath. "Spell those names for me."

While he was working, the doorbell rang, and Will heard Donisha go to answer it. He also saw Phil's eyes flick toward the living room, not so much curiously as furtively.

A walker hit the foyer floor.

Will looked at Josh with alarm, but she didn't seem to have put the clues together yet. Only when Sam appeared in the living room and Winsor moaned did Josh realize something was wrong.

"Winsor," Sam said desperately. He looked even worse than he had when he came to the house, thin to the point of frailty, his knuckles knotty around the walker.

"No, no," Winsor whispered. She looked plaintively at Phil.

"I'm sorry," Phil said. "I had to. He's miserable."

Winsor began breathing rapidly, and Whim inserted himself between her and Sam. "That's close enough," Whim said, holding up a hand.

"Winsor," Sam said again. "Please, please just talk to me. Just for five minutes, and then if you never want to hear from me again you won't have to."

"No," Winsor whispered, and she tried to hide behind her dark hair by pulling clumps of it over her face.

"Please, sweetheart," Sam said, tears in his eyes, and suddenly Will understood everything.

"Let him talk to her, Whim."

Whim gave Will a look that said, *You're crazy.*

"He won't hurt her," Will insisted. "He's in love with her."

Whim did a double take. "What?"

"In the coma," Sam said, speaking to Whim for the first time. "We met in the coma."

"They fell in love while the three of them shared that dream," Will said.

"The four of us," Sam corrected. "But—Divya didn't wake up."

At the name, Winsor began sobbing. Phil put a comforting hand on her back, but Sam, unable to get past Whim, let go of his walker and fell to his knees. He crawled toward Winsor.

"Oh, God," Whim said, and he looked embarrassed and stepped to the side. "Come on, dude. You don't have to crawl on the floor."

But Sam had already made it to Winsor's wheelchair and was embracing her thin legs. "Please, please," he kept whispering.

"Don't look at me," Winsor said. "I'm—I'm not—"

"You're beautiful," Sam told her.

"I'm not like I was!" she cried. "I'm weak and . . . stupid. I get mad and I don't even know why. I can't—I used to be—I'm not what I was."

"I don't care," Sam said. "I'm not, either."

"But you're still . . ."

"You're still you," he said. "And I still love you."

He swept the hair out of her eyes with a tender hand and smiled when he could see her face again. Winsor kept crying, her jaw trembling, but she gave herself an awkward push forward and slid out of her wheelchair and into Sam's arms.

Josh leaned her head on Will's shoulder and hugged one of his arms. Phil wiped tears from his eyes.

"This is turning out to be the weirdest day of my life," Whim said, and threw himself onto the couch.

It took some maneuvering, but Will and Josh got both Winsor and Sam onto a sofa in the formal living room and left them to cry and kiss and whisper to each other in relative privacy. In the TV room, Whim was stretched out on the couch as if he'd just swooned, and Phil was typing away.

"That makes me happy," he told Josh and Will. "Seeing the two of them together again—that makes me very happy."

It made Will happy, too. He'd never seen Winsor happy before; maybe now he would.

If the World didn't end.

"Okay," Phil said, sometime later. "It looks like your friend Peregrine is using a computer in a town called Scleron."

"Scleron?" Will asked. "Where is that?"

"It's in the foothills of the Appalachian Mountains. Eight, ten hours from here. The Internet connection is registered to a trailer. Peregrine doesn't own it, but when I ran a property search on him, I found some land he owns about forty miles outside Scleron, way up in the mountains. Look."

He showed them a satellite image. All Will could see was treetops, but Phil pointed to a dark ring. "See this? That's some kind of building."

"So whatever he's doing, he's doing it there," Josh said, "and then renting a place in town."

"This image is from three weeks ago, though," Phil said. "The most recent images look like this." He clicked his mouse.

"Holy shit," Josh said, her voice breathy.

A small city appeared to have grown right out of the mountains.

"Now, I realize I've recently experienced a brain injury," Phil said, "but I'm still pretty sure that no construction company on earth can build something like that in three weeks."

"Oh my God," Josh whispered. "It's just like Haley said."

The city in the mountains hadn't been built.

It had been dreamt.

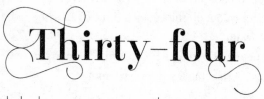

Thirty-four

Haley was with Mirren in her bedroom when she got the call. He couldn't make out the words, but he recognized Feodor's tenor.

Mirren held her hand over the phone's mic. "They found Peregrine."

Haley tried to smile, but all he felt was dread. He listened to Mirren talk, knowing that the minutes were counting down to when he'd have to leave her.

And he honestly didn't know if he'd see her again.

He went into the bathroom to wash his face. Cold water had always been his favorite method for washing off other people's energies, and there was a lot of that flying around these days.

But when he glanced at the mirror, it wasn't his face he saw.

It was Ian's.

ate the security system, the code to which Josh had given
fore leaving town.

this where you live?" Katia asked. "This place is awesome."

," Feodor said hastily.

ey sat on the edge of one of the tables and looked Feodor
is aura was no longer the crazed mishmash of zigzagging
it had been when they first met. It still swirled with dark
but all his chakras were back in their proper locations, and
rs were steadier, brighter.

look good," Haley told him.

or gave him a withering look. "Please take off your shoes
ks, Katia."

y?" she asked.

did not tell her?" Feodor asked Mirren.

your plan," Mirren said. "You convince her."

or sighed. "We're wasting time."

en didn't bat an eyelash.

well. Josh has already discovered where Peregrine is hid-
'll leave tomorrow to go after him, probably with her gaggle
ds. But she's already proven that she lacks the will to kill
e. Consequently, the task falls to me. I doubt she'll allow
company her, so I'll need to follow her to his location, then
ut I need a way to get close to Peregrine without him real-
a threat, and I need to strike before Josh realizes what
to do."

at that moment that Haley realized what Feodor was pro-
nd why Mirren had brought Katia with them.

aley thought. *No . . .*

eed an invisibility cloak," Katia said, obliviously friendly.

r nodded. "Exactly."

Haley was afraid to look away. He lowered his eyes slowly, too
slowly—he caught a glimpse of Ian's mouth spreading into a wide,
joyless grin.

Trembling, he backed out of the bathroom. As he closed the
door, he thought he heard Ian chuckle.

I'm going crazy, Haley thought. *I'm losing it. Forget, forget,
forget . . .*

Something had happened in the basement with Josh, something
he didn't understand. He couldn't remember anything from that
day, but since then, he hadn't caught a single glimpse of the future.
When he tried to look forward, he got panicky and—more
curiously—distracted. He couldn't focus.

During "Trembuline's thing," he had asked: *What happened in
the basement?*

But, although the love energy infusing his chest had filled him
with peace, his question had gone unanswered. His thoughts kept
slipping away—to how good Mirren's aura felt beside his, how
calming Will's voice was, how bad Whim's broken nose looked.

He'd never felt like this before. And he kept thinking he saw
Ian—just around the corner, in the shadows in his bedroom, duck-
ing through the back door the instant before Haley reached the
kitchen.

Why would I be seeing Ian?

He didn't know. In the eight months since Ian's spirit had died,
Haley had barely thought about him. Even when he was in the
Death universe, it had never occurred to him to look for Ian.

Haley wandered like a sleepwalker back into Mirren's bedroom,
a simple farmhouse bedroom with cotton curtains on the windows
and a patchwork quilt on the bed. She'd hung up the phone and
was making a list on a notepad. "We need to go over to Feodor's.
But we need to go shopping first."

"Okay," Haley said, and his bloodless tone must have alerted
Mirren that something was wrong, because she stood up from the
desk.

"Haley? You're shaking."

He opened his mouth to apologize, but the word that came out was, "Forget . . ."

"Haley?" Mirren said again, and she sounded frightened this time. "Come back to me, Haley. You're safe. You can come back here."

When his vision cleared, he said, "I have to go, and you have to stay here."

She knew exactly what he meant. He could see it in the subdued glow of her aura. With a gentle hand, she guided him to sit down on her bed.

"I have to stay here to oversee the VHAGs. That's what I heard yesterday, when we did Trembuline's thing."

"I don't know if I'll see you again," Haley told her.

She took a deep breath. "You don't know, or you don't want to tell me?"

"I don't know. Something is stopping me from seeing . . ."

Forget, forget, forget . . .

"What were we talking about?" he asked.

Mirren pushed his hair back so she could press her palm to his forehead. When she dropped her hand, it was almost with regret. "You haven't been right since you and Josh tried to see the future."

"I don't feel right."

"I would tell you not to go, but . . ." She tugged her earlobe, a mannerism that her aunt hated but Haley found adorable. "Haley, Feodor made a point just now with which I'm reluctantly forced to agree. Josh has already refused to kill Peregrine once. I stood by her and understood her reasoning, but I'm afraid that if she faces him again, she'll make the same decision. We can't indulge her pacifism a second time—not when thousands of people have already died." Mirren's aura was tinged with yellow and red determination, but an anxious pale blue suffused her third chakra. "Feodor has devised a . . . plan to kill Peregrine. I hate to go behind Josh's back, especially when she has been such a good friend to me, but I don't have a better idea. Peregrine must die, and maybe in the end Josh will be grateful she didn't have to be the one to make that call."

Mirren wrapped her hand around Hale[...] your help. And Katia's, unfortunately. I'll ne[...] her."

Haley didn't know what the strange p[...] meant, but of course he would keep an eye [...]

"I don't want to go," he admitted. "I just [...]

"And I just got you back. But duty calls."

Duty. It all came down to duty for Mirre[...] that made this easier for her. Haley didn't ha[...] that he couldn't explain and a sick fear in h[...]

She went to her jewelry box and remov[...] wrought star tetrahedron set in a circle of [...] "Do you remember this?"

He nodded again. Her family had sent i[...] was from them. It was part of the Rousella[...]

"Take it," Mirren said.

"I can't . . ."

"Take it," she repeated, and she closed h[...] don't get it back, I'll already have lost someth[...]

Haley drove Mirren and Katia to a big box [...] store, then a new age shop that he and M[...] before, on the way out to Iph National Fores[...] nets, tape, copper wire, a soldering iron, m[...] flatable kiddie pools, and petroleum jelly. [...] of worry formed in Haley's stomach. He kr[...] Feodor did with such items.

The expression on Feodor's face when he[...] worth everything, having spent five days in [...]

"Hi, Feodor," Haley said, like they saw e[...]

"How are you here?" Feodor asked, unab[...]

Haley shrugged. Feodor's confusion felt [...]

Mirren and Katia followed Haley into t[...] ing large shopping bags. Mirren set them [...]

Thirty-five

Josh planned to go after Peregrine the next day, but in the morning, before she had even started packing, she called the chair factory and got no answer.

Feodor always answers, she thought. She hung up and tried again, hoping she'd misdialed the number.

No answer.

Cursing, she grabbed Will and dragged him to the car.

"Maybe he's sleeping," Will said. "Like I was ten minutes ago."

"He always answers the phone. *Always.*"

Will yawned. "Can we stop for coffee?"

"After."

She drove at breakneck speed to the chair factory. No one noticed—there were stranger things on the streets these days than a twitchy driver.

"Feodor?" she called as she unlocked the door. "Feodor?"

"Hey, Feodor, wake up!" Will called.

No answer.

Josh felt short of breath as she typed her code into the security system. Afterward, she checked the small bathroom while Will ran up the stairs to the bedroom loft.

They had both walked right past the note Feodor had left in plain sight on the table nearest to the door, which Josh noticed when she ran out of the bathroom in a panic. On a sheet of white printer paper, in Feodor's elaborate scrawl, was a single word:

Apologies.

Beneath the word, in a small puddle of blood that had soaked into the paper and caused it to wrinkle, sat the microchip he'd dug out of his shoulder.

———

This isn't happening, Josh thought, as Will coaxed her into her car. *I thought I was being so careful. Now he's on the loose . . . He could be anywhere.*

Doing anything.

All they'd found was a blood-soaked washcloth in the bathroom and a freshly cleaned paring knife in the dish drainer.

Apologies, she thought. *What are your apologies worth, Feodor? Nothing. Just like your soul. I was so stupid not to realize you'd use all the chaos to slip away. I was stupid to think you'd want to help save the World.*

She felt embarrassed then, ashamed of having let him trick her, even more ashamed of having had such high hopes for his ability to change. She'd *wanted* to believe that he was redeemable.

"You talked to him yesterday, didn't you?" Will asked as he got behind the wheel. "How long ago could he have left? Should we drive around the block?"

Josh laughed grimly. She could just picture Feodor, walking down the street, the back of his shirt drenched in blood.

"I guess we can try," Will said.

"No," Josh told him. "He isn't stupid. He didn't go on foot."

"But he doesn't have a car. Does he even have money for a cab?"

He had all the money he needed and more.

It doesn't matter, Josh thought. *He's gone.*

She didn't have the time or the manpower to look for Feodor. Peregrine was still her first priority.

"How did he dig that chip out?" Will wondered aloud. "It was in the back of his shoulder. Did he have help? I mean, that's a hard place to reach. But I don't know who would have helped him."

"Will," Josh said. "Don't bother . . . It doesn't matter. He's gone."

Wherever Feodor had gone, he was the World's problem now.

———

Josh and Will were in the basement, packing weapons, when Haley brought Katia downstairs.

"She wants to come along," he said.

"That's not a good idea," Josh said.

"I'm coming," Katia told her, walking down the stairs. "I'm young and healthy. I can fight nightmares."

"That's not the criteria."

Katia stood awkwardly for a moment, thinking. Then she put up her fists. "Try to hit me," she told Will. "I'm fast."

"You don't know what you're getting into," Josh said. "It isn't about being fast or fit."

"Then what are—what's it about?"

Josh zipped up the backpack she'd been filling. "It's about being part of a team I can rely on, whose actions I can anticipate, who I don't have to worry about."

Katia thought some more. Josh wondered why Haley had brought her down here, if it was a favor he was doing for Mirren, and whether or not he'd promised her a particular outcome. If so, which outcome had he promised?

Katia said, "You're going to fight the man who held my family hostage, beat my mother, and shot me in the leg. I have every right to accompany you."

Josh sighed. She didn't have the energy to fight. "I feel for you, but you can't come."

Katia opened her mouth to argue, but stopped when she noticed that Haley was already walking back up the stairs. With a frustrated huff, she followed him.

Haley knew there was no point in arguing with Josh.

Thirty-six

They drove all night, keeping to country roads whenever possible. The hope was that they would encounter fewer nightmares in less populated areas, but the Veil had torn in so many places that avoidance was impossible. Will could tell that Josh was itching to get out of the van and go back to closing tears, but she got out only once—to stop an ogre from eating children.

About an hour later, as the sun was beginning to come up, Whim reached under his seat in the last row and began screaming.

"Pull over! Weapons out! Josh, kill it! Kill it!"

"It's only me," Katia said, sticking her head out from under the seat.

Deloise pulled over, and they extricated Katia from beneath the seat.

"How did you get under there?" Will asked, although truthfully, what he wanted to know was how Katia had managed to refrain from talking for eight hours and if she could be made to do so again.

"I snuck in while you guys were packing the van."

"The hell you did," Josh said. She was glaring at Haley. "I assume you did this as some sort of favor to Mirren."

Haley shrugged.

"Well, it's done now. But if Katia gets killed, you're the one who gets to explain it to her family."

Haley nodded and got back in the van. Whim took over the driving and they got back on the road, but Will's mind kept coming back to what Josh had said: *Some sort of favor to Mirren.*

Why would Mirren have wanted Katia to come along with them? Knowing that Katia had no nightmare fighting training to speak of, wouldn't she have wanted to keep Katia home?

Finally, they passed through the dumpy, backwoods town of Scleron. The trailer from which Peregrine had been e-mailing

Trembuline was abandoned, although it appeared that people had been camping out on the ground around it. On a piece of plywood nailed to a tree, someone had spray painted an arrow and the words TO PEREGRINEUM.

Josh went into the trailer and returned with a box of papers. "Feodor's?" Will asked, and she nodded.

"We should burn them before we go," she said, and they spent half an hour sitting around one of the fire pits dug into the ground, feeding Feodor's notes into the flames and eating sandwiches Whim had packed. Will wondered if it would be the last meal he ever ate; he didn't even like pastrami that much.

"All right, back to the van," Josh said.

The road ended at the trailer, but a trail had been blazed into the forest that grew over the mountain. It was wider than a single car, but Will saw no tire tracks, which made him think it had been created by the trampling of feet.

"He must have an army," Will told Josh.

She gave him a small, tight nod.

They followed the trail up into the mountains. More than once, all but Whim had to get out so they could get the van up a steep incline. Finally, though, they arrived at an impasse where Peregrine's people must have climbed over a rocky outcropping.

"We'll go on foot from here," Josh said.

"Let's turn the van around first," Whim said, "in case we need to make a fast getaway."

"I like your thinking," Josh told him.

Afterward, with the van parked toward Scleron and the parking brake supported by logs wedged under the tires, everyone pulled on their packs and began hiking. The packs had been Deloise's idea; they contained food, water, medical supplies, gas masks, and weapons.

They'd hiked approximately half a mile when they spotted a wall of Veil dust ahead. The forest was too thick to allow sunlight to reach the ground, but the tear illuminated the trees and plants with silver light.

"Masks on," Josh said, and this time Will didn't mind the smell of plastic.

"Is it a tear?" Whim asked.

"I think it's more than that," Josh said.

The closer they got, the more Will understood what she had meant. The wall seemed to have no end and no beginning—it stretched as far as Will could see in every direction. Although it was hard to tell through the canopy of trees, it looked like it was taller than the forest.

About ten feet from the wall of Veil dust, they stopped to debate, their voices muffled through the gas masks. "Should we go through?" Whim asked.

"Is it safe?" Deloise wanted to know. "Won't we end up inside the Dream?"

"I don't know," Josh said. Through the curtain of shimmering white-and-silver dust, Will saw what he thought were tree trunks.

"If Peregrine went through here," Whim said, "he has to be in the Dream now. We won't be able to find him there."

"I'll go through and look," Will offered.

Everyone seemed surprised, even Katia, who had been so freaked out she'd barely spoken the entire drive.

"I'll go," Josh said.

"No," Will told her. "They can't afford to lose you. Let me go."

He couldn't see the expression on her face, but she reached out to tighten the straps on his gas mask. "Be careful," she said.

He grabbed her hand and squeezed it before turning to the wall of Veil dust. As he took his first step into the wall, he felt the Veil dust slip through the weave of his clothing and twinkle all over his body—a cool, dry, dressed shower. He took another step, and another, until he was completely enclosed in the wall, and he held tight to the straps of his backpack.

His assumption that the wall was only a foot or two thick had been completely off. Without moving his feet and risking changing direction, he turned to look as far in each direction as he could.

His breaths began to echo in his mask, and the sound of his panic only made it worse.

He was surrounded on all sides by fairy dust.

Keep going straight, he told himself. He checked his feet to make certain he was following a perfect line and forced them forward, counting the steps.

One, two, three. I'm okay. I am safe in this moment. Four, five, six. In this moment, nothing is trying to hurt me. Seven, eight, nine. My gas mask is protecting me. Ten, eleven—

His face broke through the wall. He sprang forward and clear of the Veil dust, and found himself in a forest that looked very much like the one from which he had just come. He actually hugged the nearest tree.

It's just a wall of Veil dust, he thought. *All they have to do is walk through.*

He yanked off his pack, dug around, and pulled out a length of thin rope and a bottle of vitaminwater. After tying one end of the rope around the vitaminwater bottle, he lobbed the thing as hard as he could through the wall. He thought he heard someone shout. A moment later, the rope went taut. Will stood back a bit from the Veil dust and began to draw the rope toward him, trying not to go too quickly. In less than a minute, his friends had emerged from the wall.

All of them were covered in fairy dust. They looked like the survivors of a sparkle-apocalypse. "In the immortal words of Pete Venkman," Whim said, "'I feel so funky.'"

"Everybody okay?" Josh asked. After the affirmative replies came back, she put her hand on Will's shoulder. "That was smart, with the rope. If one of us had accidentally gone sideways, we could have been lost in there for a while."

"So are we in the Dream now?" Deloise asked.

"It looks like the same forest," Will told her. "Except . . ."

He pointed to an animal he had noticed while waiting for everyone to emerge from the wall. It was a boar, and it was sitting on its butt in the brush, staring at them.

"He's been here the whole time," Will said. "He just keeps watching me. And his eyes . . ."

"They move like human eyes," Katia said, as the boar's eyes flicked toward them. "He's waiting to see what we'll do."

"So we've entered a creepy Dream universe of animals with human intelligence?" Whim asked.

"I don't think so," Josh said. "I think we're in the part of the World that has completely merged with the Dream."

"Try the VHAG," Katia suggested, surprising Will with her practicality.

"Once we're farther away from the wall. I can't take my gas mask off here."

"Whatever this is," Will said, "it's expanding. If you watch the bottom of the wall long enough, you'll see that it's moving away from us."

"That makes sense," Josh said. "The place where the Dream and the World overlap is getting bigger as the Veil fails."

The trail they had been walking still existed on this side, so they began to follow it. The forest looked the same at first glance, but when Will looked closely, he saw unmistakable signs that he was in the Dream. Once a tree moaned when Deloise stepped on its root. A creek they crossed was flowing up the mountain instead of down. The boar continued to follow them at a distance, and Will thought he caught the creature smiling when Whim cracked a joke.

When they were a good quarter of a mile from the wall, they stopped to rest and let Josh try her VHAG. After less than a minute, she shut the machine down.

"I can't get out of my body," she said. "I should have realized before that it wouldn't work here. Usually my soul jumps out of my body so it can play in the Dream, but with the Dream and World merged, there's no reason for it to leave."

"Unfortunate," Katia said. She was frowning in a way that Will had never seen before, the corners of her mouth tucked in.

"You can fix this, can't you, Josh?" Deloise asked, and for once she sounded younger than her older sister.

Will turned to watch Josh answer.

He saw everything he'd ever seen in her eyes then. The awkward, uncertain girl he'd met on the night after her seventeenth birthday; the assertive, brilliant dream walker; the partner who had kissed him until he couldn't breathe. Even Feodor's shadow was there in her pale eyes.

"Do *you* think I can fix it?" she asked Deloise.

"It doesn't matter what I think."

"It matters to me."

Deloise smiled then. "I think you can do anything. But maybe all girls think that of their big sisters."

Josh smiled back at her, but Will could see the anxiety in her eyes.

They walked on, Josh pulling electrodes from her hair as they went. As they reached the top edge above a small valley, they met twenty olive-skinned men in short tunics, all of whom fell into formation with spears pointed at their guests.

"Who goes here?" demanded one wearing a helmet with a crest of short red horse hair.

The Lords of Death had asked Josh and Will the same thing, and Will felt the same trepidation about answering.

"Travelers," Josh said.

"Are you here to worship the emperor or challenge him?"

"Worship," Will said. "Definitely worship. Please take us to him."

"Then we bid you good welcome," the leader of the soldiers replied, and he performed something that looked alarmingly like a Nazi salute. "Come. The emperor is always glad to see new worshippers."

The soldiers righted their spears, turned in unison, and began marching along the path. With a shrug, Josh followed them, and everyone else fell in behind them.

"I'm wearing a vest covered in throwing knives," she said to Will in a low voice, "and they don't even care."

"There's something weird about these guys," Will told her.

"They're probably brainwashed," Whim said behind them, and Josh shushed him. They didn't need the soldiers getting offended.

They marched for an hour and then arrived at a flight of stone steps cut into the mountainside. The steps, Will noticed, appeared well-worn, the edges dangerously rounded in some places.

Either these weren't carved recently, or Peregrine imagined them old when he staged them.

Halfway up what turned out to be a very long trek, Will glanced over his shoulder to see how Katia was doing. The girl had been mostly quiet—astonishingly quiet, actually. Apparently fear was the one thing that could shut her up.

Katia met Will's eyes for a brief moment, her face a hard mask of determination, then focused on the steps again. He couldn't say why, but something in Katia's expression unnerved him. It was so serious . . .

They kept walking.

"Not long now," the lead soldier said twenty minutes later. "The hardest part is behind us."

"Josh," Will whispered, when the soldier had turned around and started up the stairs again. "The soldiers aren't sweating."

"Are you sure?"

He wiped sweat from his own brow. "I'm sure. They aren't even breathing hard."

Josh wasn't breathing hard, but she was sweating. Her group had begun to lag behind the soldiers, who climbed on indefatigably.

Finally, the stairs trailed off into a small grassy hill, and Will stopped short on the far side of the arch, stunned by the view.

In Phil's satellite photos, what Peregrine had created looked like dotted rooftops of sheds or perhaps cottages, but here, so close, it looked like what it was: a city built on a plateau, complete with homes, temples, marketplaces, and an arena. On the outskirts were orchards and fields of crops, and above the structures, running down the mountain at a slight angle, was an aqueduct.

"It did not look this big in the satellite photos," Whim said.

"Maybe it *wasn't* this big," Josh said. "Maybe he's been building onto it."

The lead soldier beckoned them forward. "Come, come."

"What's the name of this city?" Deloise asked him.

"Peregrineum, in honor of Emperor Peregrine."

"I knew Peregrine was an egomaniac," Will whispered to Josh, "but this is outrageous."

He fell back to walk beside Haley as they traveled down a well-paved road toward the city. "What do you make of the soldiers?"

"They don't have auras."

"That doesn't sound good. Did Peregrine suck their souls out?"

Haley shook his head. "I think they're part of this dream."

"What do you mean?" Josh asked.

"I think Peregrine staged them into being, just like everything else here."

Will didn't say it, but he grew increasingly worried as they entered the city. Peregrineum wasn't just a set or a sketch of a city; it contained hundreds, possibly thousands of people. They might not have auras, but Will was betting their spears were real enough.

No museum, no amusement park, no play had ever been so detailed. From the city dwellers haggling over prices in the market to the cats darting down the streets, everything was complete. The scent of lavender wafted from the bathhouse. A peasant fiddled for spare change.

There was some evidence, though, that not all of the people were figments of Peregrine's imagination. Will noticed a woman wearing a sports bra under her toga, and a messenger ran past in a pair of Nikes.

"Now that's irony," Whim whispered.

"What?" Deloise whispered back.

"A citizen of an ancient Roman city running by in a shoe from a brand named after a Greek goddess."

Will couldn't bring himself to laugh. They didn't have the manpower to take on an entire city.

"Some of these people are real," Haley said. He pointed out a few.

"What about that one?" Will whispered, gesturing with his chin toward a man in a blue toga who was partially hidden behind a garden gate.

His eyes were narrowed, and he was staring at Will out of the corner of his eye, as if he disliked Will on sight.

"Not real," Haley said.

The man turned to whisper to someone hidden behind the corner of a building. There was something sly about him.

"You're sure?" Will asked.

Haley nodded.

At the very center of the city stood the palace, looming over every other building. In front of it sat a fountain in which a marble visage of a chiseled man rode a dolphin among waves, a trident in his hand. The exterior of the palace was all columns and cornices; when they went inside, the interior was all frescoes and marble.

"It's beautiful!" Deloise said.

The walls were intricately painted, the ceilings were studded with gemstones. In the center of the palace was an open-air courtyard dominated by an enormous golden throne set on a block of marble the size of a golf cart.

The man sitting on the throne was Snitch.

Will barely recognized him without his raincoat and gas mask and empty black eyes. Now his eyes were blue, and his coloring had lost its unhealthy whiteness from years spent in a universe where it was always raining.

"It's Peregrine," Haley said. "I can tell by his aura."

Somehow that was harder to remember when Will was looking at Snitch's face.

"My lord," the soldier with the horse-hair helmet tried to say, but Peregrine saw them and sprang out of his throne screaming.

"*You!*" He pointed at Josh. "No! *No!* I already got rid of you once today! Who let you back in here?"

"Um," Josh said. She glanced at Will, who shrugged. "We actually just got here," she said. "The soldiers led us here."

"You can't fool me! I'm not stupid! It's Dustine, that bitch—she's plotting against me, but she won't get away with it. I'm the emperor! Bow down before me!"

Despite Snitch's face, the screaming left no doubt in Will's mind that they were talking to Peregrine. He paced back and forth on his marble block, spit flying from his mouth.

"You think you can turn my citizens against me? I know what you're plotting, you and the Praetorian Guard!"

"We aren't plotting anything!" Whim yelled. "We just got here!"

"What are *you* doing here?" Peregrine shouted at him. "I barely even know *you*!"

"We came to talk," Josh said. "What you're doing here is causing the Veil to collapse."

"Lies!" Peregrine screamed. "You can't defeat me, so you lie to me, to your god, your living god!"

"Um, Josh," Will said. "I don't think talking is going to work."

"Every day you come here seeking to undermine me, deceive me, confuse me, but I stay STRONG! No one can defeat the living god!"

"Yeah," Whim said. "He's off his rocker."

"He thinks we come here every day?" Deloise asked.

"He thinks Josh does," Will said. "Maybe he's been hallucinating her—"

"Back to the arena!" Peregrine screamed.

Will's vision blurred, then misted, and he felt a momentary vertigo. When his eyes cleared, he found himself standing on the floor of the Colosseum. Around a dirt oval thirty yards across rose tiers of stands, and they were all full of cheering, jeering spectators.

Will turned around, and his friends were behind him. Apparently Peregrine had teleported them all into the center of the arena.

"Did he just teleport us here?" Whim asked. "Nobody said anything about him being able to teleport."

"Peregrine can control the Dream because he's in Snitch's body," Josh said. "But if this part of the Dream and the World have merged—" She stopped, like she didn't want to say the words. "He might be able to control everything now."

"No," Deloise said softly. "That can't be what's happening."

"I don't have another explanation," Josh told her.

In his peripheral vision, Will noticed Katia watching Josh with an expression of . . . admiration? For a girl who'd been too terrified to speak all day, she certainly didn't look frightened now.

"But what did he mean about already sending you away today?" Deloise asked.

Josh shook her head. "I don't know. And I don't know what we're doing here."

Katia laughed a weird, wry chuckle. "Of course you do."

"What?" Will asked.

"Think about it," Katia said, and there was something oddly condescending in her voice. "Where are we? What did people do here?"

Katia's tone was all wrong. She didn't sound like herself, but someone older, and jaded. Whim, though, played along, saying, "We're in the Colosseum, we're . . . gladiators! Oh my God, we're gladiators!" He grabbed Josh by the shoulders. "I don't want to be a gladiator, Josh! I saw that movie—it didn't end well!"

"Calm down, Whim!" Deloise said. "We aren't gladiators."

"Then what are we doing here?" Whim cried, but the end of his question was drowned by a tsunami of cheers arising from the crowd.

A group of men in togas using four poles to hold up a sunshade entered the stands. Beneath the sunshade walked Snitch—no, Peregrine, waving to the crowd. A scantily clad, top-heavy woman cooled him with a fan of feathers. He was smiling a twisted, satisfied smile.

We are in very deep trouble, Will thought.

Peregrine sat down in a cloth-covered chair. Another buxom woman fed him a grape. He lifted his hand and the crowd quieted. "Let the games begin!"

Thirty-seven

"Oh, God," Whim was muttering. "Oh, God."

"Weapons out," Josh said. "Stay calm. Remember your training."

They dumped their backpacks on the ground and retrieved weapons. Josh pulled her machete out of its back holster. Will had a hatchet. Whim held a Taser in one hand and can of pepper spray in the other.

"What, are you walking home alone in the dark?" Will asked him.

"Shut up," Whim said tightly.

They gave Katia one of the spare weapons, a hammer, the claw end of which had been sharpened into vampire fangs. Haley held a hunting knife in either hand. And Deloise . . .

"Where the hell did that come from?" Whim asked.

Deloise swung the mace—a ten-pound spiked iron ball attached to a two-foot-long club. "I found it in the basement."

Josh wanted to ask if Deloise knew how to use that thing without killing herself, but she was more concerned about Katia who, as far as Josh knew, had never been in so much as a slap fight. Before she could inquire about either situation, the doors at each end of the arena floor opened. Out of the dark maw beyond, Josh saw a flicker of movement, a flash of light on fur. Something tall.

"Stay together," she ordered. "Watch your backs and each other's backs. Try not to panic."

Even as she spoke, she wondered if she was instructing the others or herself. *It's just another nightmare,* she thought, but in truth, she was as afraid as she'd been since she'd entered Feodor's universe. This wasn't just a nightmare, because a nightmare was a subconscious manifestation of fear. This was a creation specifically designed to kill them all.

"Everyone watch out for Katia, too," she added, but her sentence trailed off as kangaroos bounded into the arena.

Josh had never seen a kangaroo in person; still, she was pretty sure this wasn't what they normally looked like. Each stood eight, nine feet tall. Beneath their bloodred coats, thick knots of muscle rippled. Fangs, curved like the claws of sloths, hung over their chins, and when they jumped, Josh guessed they cleared fifteen feet.

And they were fast. They bounded toward their dinner at what must have been forty, fifty miles an hour.

Whim began cursing. "What are they?" Katia asked.

"You've never seen a kangaroo?" Josh asked, distracted by her own confusion.

"They're what?" Katia asked.

"They're blood-sucking, flesh-eating, steroid-popping kangaroos!" Whim shouted, his voice tinged with panic.

"Calm down, Whim," Deloise said. "Remember the time we fought the yeti? That was way worse than this."

"Yeah, but there was just one of those."

Josh holstered her machete and pulled three knives from her vest. Each was about seven inches long including the handles, the blades sharpened on either edge like swords. She had three kangaroos coming from each end of the arena, and as soon as they were in range, she began throwing.

The first knife missed entirely. Josh could hit a moving target, but she'd never hit a *bouncing* target. The second she got in the chest, right between the kangaroo's bodybuilder arms. It didn't miss a beat. The third knife slipped as it left her fingers, and it was only by luck that it caught one of the kangaroos in the shin, which slowed it down but didn't hobble it.

"Katia, Haley, Del, take those three. Whim, Will, with me. Don't let them surround us!"

As the kangaroos grew nearer, speeding up at the scent of their prey, Josh ran out to meet them.

As much as she wanted to look over her shoulder and make sure everyone was following her lead, she kept her eyes trained on the kangaroo closest to her. *I trust my people,* she told herself.

Except Katia, who shouldn't even be here.

Then the kangaroo was so close she could smell it, a strange odor like dung and curry. She ran straight into its arms, plunging her machete into its chest just below where her throwing knife had hit. The kangaroo embraced her with its iron arms and pulled her tightly against its chest, digging its claws into the backs of her shoulders. Josh lost her grip on the machete, and the handle caught her in the chest just below her breastbone. But as the kangaroo pulled her closer, the pressure on her sternum forced the machete deeper into the kangaroo's own body. Josh felt the rib she'd broken pop painfully, and she scrabbled at her vest to pull another knife free.

Then the kangaroo bit her. The pain struck in two places— a crushing sensation on top of her collarbone where its upper teeth landed, and a stabbing sensation four inches below where its lower teeth tore into her. Josh shouted, her face buried in the animal's chest. The machete handle was jammed so hard in her cartilage that she thought it would impale her if the kangaroo hugged her any tighter. She couldn't breathe.

Shit, she thought. *Shit. I have to—*

Despite the pain in her shoulder when she moved her arm, she managed to wrench a throwing knife free, cutting the vest as she did so. From far away, she heard an animal screaming and the crowd cheering hysterically. The chest against hers felt like stone with a layer of dirty fur stretched over it.

She stabbed the kangaroo's side as high as she could. The jaws around her shoulder tightened, and something inside her tore, but it only made her angry. She dragged the knife downward; it felt like trying to cut through leather with a paring knife. *Damage,* she thought. *I have to inflict maximum damage.*

She kept dragging, and the kangaroo released her shoulder to scream in a guttural, almost human voice. Josh took the opportunity to twist sideways, allowing the handle of the machete to slip out of the hollow beneath her breastbone, a blessed relief. She threw her weight behind the knife in her right hand and wiggled it up and down, forcing the blade in deeper. Getting stabbed was one thing, but the real damage came when the blade was removed. As long as a knife was in place, it acted as a temporary seal against the cuts it made, but once it was pulled out, the open wounds were free to bleed. With that in mind, Josh yanked at the machete handle, working it up and down like the end of a seesaw. Inside, beyond the pivot point of the animal's muscles, she knew it was cutting through internal organs.

The kangaroo vomited blood all over her.

I'm getting kangaroo blood in my shoulder wound, Josh thought, and that upset her more than the physical pain.

Suddenly the kangaroo jumped vertically. It couldn't keep its hold on Josh, but its claws tore up her shoulder blades as it lost its hold on her. Josh managed to keep her grip on the machete long enough for the blade to slice through eight inches of chest flesh, stopping when it reached the top of the kangaroo's pouch, and then she was fumbling to catch the knife by the handle as she fell to the ground on her back.

She landed so hard that the rushing in her ears stopped for an instant, leaving her in complete silence and darkness. Then she opened her eyes and the screaming of the crowd, the grunts and gasps of her friends, and the snarling of the kangaroos thundered back to her.

She clapped a hand over her shoulder wound and sat up, not as quickly as she wanted to but as fast as she could. As she rose, she grabbed the machete, which was now both bloody and sandy.

Two kangaroos were down already; one was missing most of its head, which Josh could only attribute to Deloise's mace. A third was pawing at its eyes, and two Taser electrodes were sticking out of its chest. Haley was fighting a fourth, both of his knives lost in its fur. He had his thumbs sunk deep in its eye sockets. Whim was holding the fifth down while Will hacked at its neck with his hatchet.

Deloise and Katia had the last one caught between them, and Deloise's mace was swinging in circles too fast to see. Katia was holding up her hammer, but she was bleeding from scratches all over her face, and the hand that didn't hold the hammer hung limply from her shoulder.

Josh turned and took all this in just in time to see the kangaroo she had maimed land in the middle of the chaos. She cursed and began running toward it, but her body was slow to respond. The left side of her shirt was soaked in blood from her shoulder wound.

"Del, behind you!" she shouted, as the kangaroo landed two feet behind Deloise in a spray of dust and blood. Deloise—*God, she's good with that thing,* Josh thought—didn't even start turning around before she was swinging the mace above and behind her head, and the spiked ball took a chunk the size of a hamburger out of the kangaroo's throat.

The kangaroo Deloise had been helping hold off jumped on Katia immediately.

"Will!" Josh shouted.

Will yanked his hatchet out of the brain of one of the kangaroos and looked around. He had a stripe of wet red blood down his leg, but he didn't seem to feel it as he launched himself at the kangaroo that had just knocked Katia to the ground.

Josh didn't have to tell Whim where to go—once the kangaroo he and Will had been fighting was down, he leapt to Haley's side. Haley was trying to break free of the kangaroo's hold, squirming like he was in a straightjacket. The kangaroo was holding him eighteen inches off the ground in an embrace that had turned his face the color of a tomato. Josh reached him at the same time Whim did, and she narrowly avoided being blinded by the arc of pepper spray that shot from the bottle in Whim's hand.

Haley had already gouged the creature's eyes out, but the pepper spray must still have hurt, because it made a sound like an angry dinosaur and snapped its jaw shut on Haley's left ear. Haley's mouth stretched wide over clenched teeth in an awful grimace, but he stayed silent.

Josh grabbed one of the hunting knives from the animal's side and yanked it out. She stabbed the kangaroo quickly, over and over, the blade only going in halfway. She was less concerned about damaging it than she was in getting it to release Haley, but the pepper spray must have worked, because it dropped Haley and clawed at its own face instead. Haley hit the ground with an *ooof,* his ear shredded.

Whim grabbed the other hunting knife and followed Josh's lead, and in the next ten seconds they inflicted more than two dozen cuts to the kangaroo's sides. Finally Josh's knife slipped between its ribs, and it reared back as she cut something vital. When she pulled her knife out, a torrent of blood followed it, pouring onto the dirt like the eruption of a spring. The beast collapsed beside Haley.

Deloise was standing over a jerking kangaroo, inflicting deep, bloody craters all over its torso. She had her face screwed up in a way that Josh suspected meant she felt guilty for hurting an animal, but she knew as well as the rest of them that the kangaroos weren't real, despite their excruciatingly human screams. Josh could tell from the sound of bones being crushed every time Deloise swung that the kangaroo didn't have much longer to live.

That left the one Katia and Will were fighting. Will had his arms wrapped around its neck from behind and was hanging on as the kangaroo tried to bounce him off. His grip must have been pretty tight, because the kangaroo's tongue was hanging out like a flattened snake.

For an instant, Josh was distracted by a memory. Will had done the same thing in the first nightmare they'd ever walked together—jumped on the back of a six-foot-tall albino koala puppet. Seeing him do it again made Josh smile fondly.

Until she realized that the kangaroo was also trying to stomp Katia to death. She was rolling back and forth beneath to escape its long, flat feet as it bounced above her. She'd lost her hammer.

Josh didn't know it if saw her approach or sensed it, but the kangaroo spun like a dancer and swung its thick, meaty tail across the ground. Josh jumped, but the tail caught Whim in the shins and knocked him over as he attempted to retrieve Katia's hammer.

"Haley!" Josh called, and she tossed him one of his hunting knives. He caught it perfectly, not even slowing his steps as he headed for the last kangaroo. Will had his hatchet back, and Deloise was approaching with her mace.

The four of them surrounded the last kangaroo and closed in like hyenas, and Josh felt a strange rush of pride. These were her people, her team, and they were good at what they did.

They struck like a team, too, a sudden storm of blades and moving metal, so fast that the kangaroo jumped from the ground breathing and landed dead, blood spurting from its wounds due to the force of it hitting the dust, its head nothing but a messy clot of blood.

It landed on Katia, unfortunately, and everyone helped drag it off of her, their hands moving in unison, like they were acting in a puppet show. Katia was winded, but had avoided any major injuries.

The sand around them was clumped with blood, and flies were already circling above the kangaroo corpses. Josh's team looked worse than worse-for-wear, half of them noticeably injured, all of them bloodstained. Deloise had brain matter smeared across what had been a pretty cute sweater.

"You're gonna have to teach me how to use that mace," Josh told her sister, and they were coming together for a high five when creatures burst out of the pouches of the dead kangaroos.

Joeys, Josh thought, watching in slow motion as the little animals sprang into the air, fangs bared. *They're called joeys.*

They looked like skinned rabbits—hairless, their pink skins stretched tight and dry over new muscle and thin cheeks. Their eyes weren't even open yet, but they had the teeth of velociraptors and the claws of wolverines. *And their legs must be fully developed,* Josh thought distractedly, *because that one's headed right for my face.*

The shock wore off in time for her to block with her left arm, but the joey was satisfied with sinking its fangs into her forearm.

Is that the crowd screaming, or is it Will? she wondered, tossing her machete into the air so she could catch it backhanded and stab the joey in the gut. Her blade went in the front and came out the back, barely bloodied. As she dropped to the ground, she thrust her arm beneath her so that she landed with her knees on the joey.

It let go of her arm, and its guts came out its mouth. Josh would have liked to take its head off, but from the corner of her eye she saw Will fall onto his back, a joey scratching at his face. The creatures were vicious, but they were light, and Josh caught it on her machete blade as she swiped, accidentally sending it flying across the arena.

One side of Will's face was a briar patch of scratches, but Whim's was worse. He actually had a hole in his cheek, and Josh gagged a little when she saw him stick his tongue through it.

"Oh my God," he said, holding a joey's corpse out in front of him. "I'm disfigured!"

Deloise had dispatched the nearest joey before it ever reached her, and she'd taken out Katia's, as well. It had managed to slice Katia down the face, breaking her eyebrow and almost taking out her eye, but once they wiped the blood away, she could see just fine.

The booing of the crowd subsided as Peregrine rose from his chair. "Citizens of Peregrineum, fear not! A worthy opponent deserves a worthy adversary! Release the peregrine!"

Will had grabbed a roll of bandages out of one of the packs and was wrapping it around a wound on Katia's hand. At Peregrine's words, he worked faster. Josh's eyes darted between the doors at either end of the arena, but neither opened. Will handed her what was left of the gauze and she bandaged the gouge in her arm, which was bleeding worse than she would have liked. She didn't know what to do about her shoulder.

"What about me?" Whim asked.

Will shrugged uneasily at the sight of the hole in his friend's cheek. "You want a Band-Aid?"

Whim poked at the hole with his tongue again. "You got a cork?"

"Folks," Josh said, "let's try to concentrate."

"Katia's bleeding pretty bad," Deloise warned. "So are you, Josh."

Josh looked down and saw a swath of blood down the right side of her shirt, stemming from where the kangaroo had bitten her. Her back hurt near her shoulder blades where the kangaroo had dug its claws into her muscles.

Above them, a hawk screamed.

"Great Jehoshaphat!" Whim cried, craning his head back.

A shadow fell over them, deep and dark enough that Josh felt a chill. She looked up and saw the white and yellow belly of a bird, a 747-sized bird, its stark yellow talons outstretched, each tipped with a black, sicklelike claw.

Peregrine laughed maniacally as the bird circled closer and lower.

"It's a hawk," Will said, and Katia corrected him.

"It's a peregrine falcon."

Of course it is, Josh thought.

"Falcons eat meat, right?" Whim said.

The bird folded its wings back and began to dive.

"Get down!" Josh cried, and they all dropped to the ground.

The bird dove so fast it made a whistling sound as it fell. The crowd cheered, and Josh had to force her eyes to stay open against the urge to hide. She was only a few feet away from Haley, who was very close to Deloise, who had not lain flat, but curled up in a ball with her hands over the back of her neck, like she would have during an earthquake.

"Del—" Josh began, but she was too late. The bird snatched her sister up with two yellow talons.

"No!" Whim screamed. He had grabbed Deloise's ankle and held on so hard that for a moment he was airborne.

Then Deloise slipped from the falcon's grasp, and she and Whim crashed back to earth. Josh was ten feet away, but she heard something crack when Deloise hit the ground.

"Oh," Deloise said weakly. "Oh, no."

"Move closer to Del!" Josh shouted. "Link arms and legs!"

They crowded together on the ground around Deloise, trying to remain flat, arms and legs spread like skydivers in formation.

"Del, what hurts?" Josh asked, linking her legs with Haley's on one side and Will's on the other.

"I don't know," Deloise said weakly. "My hips . . . maybe my pelvis?"

If Del broke her pelvis, we're screwed, Josh thought. *We'll never get her out of here.*

"Can you move your legs?"

The falcon was diving again, its shadow condensing and darkening.

"Maybe," Deloise said.

"I've got her, Josh," Whim said. "I'm connecting our pant loops with my belt."

That's love, Josh thought, and then she was squeezing her eyes shut as the falcon skimmed right over top of them, so close she could smell the dried blood of some unlucky creature on its claws, a scent like raw meat and mud.

Will pressed his forehead against hers, and Haley was close enough behind her that she could feel his breath on her neck. Deloise's head brushed the top of Josh's.

"Don't let go of me, Whim," Deloise begged.

"I'm not letting go."

"I mean it. Don't let go."

"Del, if you don't stop me, I'll hold on to you for the rest of my life."

Then they were kissing, and Josh didn't stop them even though the falcon was screaming toward them again. Katia released a little cry, but when the peregrine began flapping its wings, trying to gain height, its claws were empty.

"Everybody all right?"

"My shirt is torn," Katia said, "but I'm uninjured."

Uninjured? Josh thought.

"I'm amazing," Whim said.

"This is working," Josh said. "Stick together. Make yourselves as flat as possible and hang on to each other. It doesn't have the strength to carry all of us. Del, how are your hips?"

"I think they just popped. Whim saved me."

The falcon came around again, this time releasing a shrill scream as it dove. It managed to pick up Haley and Josh's entwined legs, but they all tightened their grip, like a sponge contracting, and Josh and Haley were only a foot off the ground when the falcon lost its grasp.

On the next pass, it tore out a clump of Will's hair. "*OWW,*" he cried, but he didn't let go.

The pass after that, it scratched up Whim's back. Then it managed to pull off one of Katia's shoes.

"I'm not hurt," she insisted afterward.

"How long until it gets tired?" Whim asked.

That was an interesting question.

"How long until Peregrine makes it more powerful?" Will asked.

That was an even more interesting question, and one for which Josh didn't have an answer.

"Can't he just imagine it more powerful?" Deloise asked, craning her head back so she could see Josh.

"I thought so," Josh admitted.

The falcon swept past again, screaming as it did so. This time it didn't even manage to grab a shoe. The crowd was booing and hissing in fury.

"Perhaps Peregrine doesn't know he can control things with his thoughts," Katia suggested.

"But he teleported us here deliberately," Will pointed out.

"Perhaps not," Katia began, just as the bird screamed past.

Perhaps not? Josh thought. *She sounds like—*

"Enough!" Peregrine hollered. "Only cowards lie on the ground when they face an enemy!"

"Nobody move," Josh said.

"No kidding," Whim added.

But the falcon flew away, beyond the arena to what Josh could only imagine was an enormous nest somewhere in the mountains.

"Get up!" Peregrine shouted, and suddenly they were all standing on two feet. Josh looked at Deloise, but she was dusting herself off and didn't appear to be in any pain.

"You are unworthy of an honorable death by combat," Peregrine declared. "I sentence you to death by cruelty."

Skippy, Josh thought.

She turned at the sound of one of the arena gates opening. A single man walked through, dressed in old-fashioned pants and a button-down shirt. His pants were wrinkled and filthy, his shoes scuffed and stained, a tattered newsboy hat on his head. He looked vaguely familiar, but Josh couldn't place him.

She searched the man for a visible weapon and found none. He looked like he had a kind of wiry strength, but he wasn't a muscular man. He appeared quite ordinary.

"Who are you?" she called when he was within range.

He grinned a mean grin. "Who the hell are you?"

"Friendly dude," Whim muttered.

"How did getting a hole in your cheek make you more talkative?" Will asked him.

"Shut up!" the stranger barked. "Stupid little shits!"

The stranger didn't so much appear angry as hateful, but it was an amused, happy sort of hate, a hate that obviously felt good to him.

"Line up!" he snapped. "Right now!"

Josh and her friends glanced at each other, perplexed.

"Make us," Whim said, an almost experimental tone in his voice.

The man got right up in Whim's face and lifted a threatening fist. "You want a piece of this, you little shit?"

Whim, who stood at least a foot taller than the man, began to laugh. "Sure, dude. Let's rumble."

"Whim—" Josh began.

"I will cut you apart!" the man told Whim. "I will smack that smart mouth right off your face and drown you in a puddle of your own piss!"

That made Whim laugh harder. Josh felt anxious, waiting for

the other shoe to drop. This man had to have a trick up his sleeve, some weapon they couldn't yet identify.

"Say good-bye to your cushy life, you little bastard! Fun time is over! From now on you belong to me!"

"Do you have a stand-up act?" Whim asked.

The man slapped Whim across the face, which prompted Josh to rush forward and grab his arm. He slapped Josh next, so hard it turned her head, and Deloise caught his other arm before he could hit anyone else.

He jerked, but Josh had correctly estimated his strength. It only took one kick to sweep his legs out from under him. "Can I get a zip tie?" Josh asked.

Haley retrieved one from a backpack and together, Josh and Deloise bound the man's hands and feet. Then they set him on the sand and listened to him rant.

"You want to eat? You want to sleep? You ask me!" The man was shouting, undeterred. "*I* decide when you piss, *I* decide when you shit, *I* decide what you put in your little mouths—"

"Am I missing something?" Whim asked. "Are we supposed to be scared of this guy?"

"I get it," Will said. "I know what this is!"

"What?" Josh asked.

Will put a hand on her uninjured shoulder. "He's Peregrine's father."

"Jaco?" Deloise asked, before Josh had even registered the statement.

"His father?" Whim repeated. "Why would he send his father to kill us?"

"Because he's the thing Peregrine is most afraid of, even now," Will said. "All of this is controlled by Peregrine's mind, see? He sent the thing he's most afraid of to kill us."

"But Jaco's just a man," Josh said.

"Not to Peregrine." Will smiled a satisfied smile. "To Peregrine, he's Satan."

Jaco was still shouting at them, and he'd progressed to some of the filthiest language Josh had ever heard. Racial slurs, sexual acts—nothing was off-limits.

"No wonder Peregrine has such a dirty mouth," Deloise said.

"So should we kill him?" Whim asked, retrieving the hatchet from the sand.

"No," Josh said. "We don't kill people for no reason."

"But he's annoying," Whim said, but he was grinning when he said it.

The crowd was booing, Jaco was cursing them, and Peregrine was sitting straight up in his chair, hands clenched around the armrests, the look on his face one of red hatred and . . . fear?

"Peregrine looks terrified. If he's afraid of Jaco, why not just make him disappear?" Josh asked.

"I don't think Peregrine's control over this place is completely conscious," Will told her. "And unconsciously, he might think his father is unkillable."

And we've defeated what he couldn't, Josh thought. She walked across the sand toward him, put her hands on her hips, and called out, "Is he all you've got?"

Peregrine's stare burned. From behind her, she heard Jaco say, "And *you,* my so-called son. *Daughter* is what they should have called you. Pathetic, whimpering little thing, always wanted to be held and kissed and told how good she was."

Somehow Jaco had managed to jump to his bound feet and was hopping toward Peregrine, sneering and spitting his words.

"'Daddy, look at me, play with me, *love* me.' What was I supposed to love? Huh? Tell me that! How am I supposed to love a weak-chinned little bitch crawling around on the floor with a snotty nose?"

Peregrine's whole body was shaking, his shoulders convulsing in a way that might have meant he was about to vomit.

"You were a weak little shit, and you grew up to be a weak *big* shit."

"No," Peregrine stammered. "I—I'm—"

"What? A simpering ass-kisser, that's what you turned out to be. If I could go back in time, I'd kill myself before I fathered you."

"I feel bad letting him go on like this," Deloise said.

Peregrine stood up from his chair, but he had to keep hold of the armrests to remain upright. "I'm—I'm the emperor!" he half-shouted, half-screamed.

"You're a little girl playing dress-up."

Peregrine began to shriek then. "I'll kill you! I'll *kill* you!"

He pointed his finger at Jaco, but nothing happened, and Jaco shook his head. "That finger—that's about the size of your—"

"*KILL YOU!*"

Any smugness Josh had felt had long since disappeared. Now she was afraid of the changing mood in the arena, the looks of disgust flickering across the faces of the crowd. Some satisfied, righteous smiles.

Peregrine was shrieking uncontrollably, his body seizing, and Jaco was laughing, louder and louder, louder than was humanly possible, so loud that the arena itself began to tremble, and then Josh could hear nothing but Jaco's laughter, reverberating in the air like a cannon shot that wouldn't end.

She saw Will's mouth move but she couldn't hear what he said. She stumbled across the moving ground toward him, and they grabbed each other the way they had when they were avoiding the falcon. Josh took Haley's arm, too, and the six of them hung on to each other, creating their own little island of stability within Peregrine's throbbing screams.

Deloise had her hands over her ears. A sound like thunder, but a thousand times louder, tore through the air, and when Josh looked up, she saw what looked like another Veil tear, but a tear so much brighter than the others, and golden instead of silver. It started right overhead and then tore down the sphere of the sky in all directions, flooding the arena with yellow light. The crowd began to scream as shapes formed in the light, lumpy and then more distinct, elongated, with rounded tops. Beings. People.

"What's happening?" Josh shouted. She couldn't even hear herself, and she couldn't hear Haley when he replied, but she recognized the word his mouth formed.

Death!

The Veil between the World and the Dream had collapsed. Now the Veil that held back Death was collapsing as well, and the dead were walking—*two by two,* Josh heard Dustine say—into what was left of the three universes.

Josh's head filled with a pain so sharp and raw it dropped her to her knees. She tried to open her eyes but the pain sliced through them, and it wasn't Peregrine's scream she heard then but Haley's—and her own—as the memory of what they'd seen in the Cradle tore through them.

Ian. It's Ian. Ian is coming back, and he's wrong inside.

She saw Haley's memories then, everything that had happened to him in Death, everything he had forgotten. He forced them from his mind into hers like a railroad spike. She saw how Ian had refused to let go of his life, how he had coveted Haley's body, tried to take it, even.

And worse, she saw what Ian would do next.

Somehow she was standing up, Haley beside her, and Ian was walking down through the air toward them, grinning as his feet finally touched the ground, breaking into a run, calling out, "J.D.! Haley!" and Peregrine was screaming, "*I am your god!*"

Then Josh was running, Haley's hand in hers, faster than she'd ever run. She forgot her pack, forgot her sister and her boyfriend and her friends, just ran and ran and ran, because she knew what Ian would do if he caught her, and it wasn't Peregrine's scream that followed her out of the arena, but her own.

Thirty–eight

Haley knew he shouldn't be crying, that it would only make Ian hate him more, but he couldn't stop himself. He ran down through a break in the stands and out of the Colosseum into the city at large, sobbing, Josh beside him, screaming, their hands clenched so tightly that he could no longer feel his fingers, just a pain where their bodies met. From behind them, Peregrine's laughter echoed.

"Haley!" Whim shouted. "Slow down!"

But Haley couldn't slow down. He tore down the street like an out-of-control bobsled, careening into walls, knocking people over, dragging Josh when she tripped, then Josh dragging him, and finally she pulled him through an arched doorway and into a building full of hot steam.

Hide, he thought, or maybe Josh was whispering it to him. Before the steam cleared they stumbled into a pool of hot, swirling water, and they began to swim, their hands still clamped together, swimming the butterfly in unison, and they didn't stop until they simultaneously cracked their foreheads on the pool's side and came up gasping and choking.

Then somehow they were holding each other, and Haley was still sobbing, and Josh was whispering, "Sorry, sorry, sorry."

Eventually Deloise found them.

"I forgot," Josh whispered when they were sitting against a wall, water running from their clothes. "I forgot, I want to forget."

Will was crouched in front of her, his hands on her knees, trying to calm her down. "You're okay," he kept saying. "You're safe."

But Josh caught Haley's eye, and they both knew they weren't safe.

"Was that Ian?" Whim demanded, and Haley hid behind his eyelids. "What the hell is going on?"

"The Veil that protects Death has collapsed," Katia told him, and Haley was glad he had his eyes closed so he could just hear her voice and not have to look at her traitorous aura.

"Is that even possible?" Deloise asked.

"Until today, I would have said no," Katia replied, and Haley knew she was about to blow her cover. He made himself open his eyes and glare at her, and she looked down at her crossed arms and fell silent.

"So it *was* Ian?" Whim asked. "Jesus."

"It wasn't Ian," Josh whispered. Haley felt her shudder beside him. "It's not him anymore."

"What does that mean?" Will asked. "Josh, you have to talk to us."

The bathhouse was full of lavender-scented steam, making the tiled mosaics on the floor slick as Haley stood up, preparing to run again. But Josh still had his hand, and she wouldn't budge from the floor, and after a moment of struggle he collapsed beside her.

"Sorry," she whispered.

"We have to go," he told her.

"Go where? There's nowhere left to go. All the Veils are gone. There's only one universe now."

"No," he whispered, urgently, hearing the panic in his own voice. *"There."*

"This will spread," Katia was saying, "until there are no Veils left."

There. The word echoed in Haley's head. *There.* The place with the silence and white light and the egg—the Cradle.

"I can't leave them," Josh told him, and Haley realized he had forgotten about his friends, about Mirren, about everyone else.

"What does that mean?" Whim asked again.

"It means we were wrong," Josh said. "I'm not the True Dream Walker—because *Peregrine is.*"

Silence except for the hiss of stream, the soft splash of old men moving through the water.

"No," Haley said. "That can't be right. The first time I touched you—I . . ."

"You what?" she asked. "You were scared of me—I remember. I was there. I was a weird little kid and you were scared of me."

"Because I—I felt something. You're special." Haley wanted to hand her the memory like he would have a photograph, to give her proof, to express to her something inexpressible, that he'd known from the moment she handed him that nutcracker that she was singularly special.

"Special," Josh said bitterly. "Yeah, I'm super special. Look at me, cowering on the floor of a Roman bathhouse. Running away from my ex-boyfriend. Letting my friends fight my battles for me. I'm really *special*."

"Josh," Will began, and she cut him off.

"The prophesies said that the True Dream Walker would re-merge the three universes. *I'm* not the one who did that, am I?"

No one could argue with her about that, not even Haley, not even when he felt so strongly in his heart that she was wrong, that they were missing something.

"Does that make you the False Dream Walker?" Deloise asked.

"I don't think it makes me anything," Josh said. "I think it means I just happen to be really good at dream walking, and that's it. The prophesies are wrong. Haley's wrong. My scroll's wrong. I'm nothing."

Haley shook his head but didn't speak. No one spoke, until . . .

"I don't care," Will said abruptly. "*I don't care.*"

They all looked at him.

"I don't care if you're the True Dream Walker or the False Dream Walker or a coward or just some random girl I go to school with," Will said. "I *love* you. Do you hear me? I love you."

He was trembling then. Josh touched his cheek with the backs of her fingers, gave him a sad smile.

Outside the bathhouse, people began screaming. Haley felt a chill go through him despite the heat of the steam, and he saw Josh shudder.

"What's happening?" Deloise asked.

"The dead are coming," Josh whispered.

"What do you mean?" Whim yelled at her. "Why would Ian kill us all?"

"He's not Ian anymore," Haley tried to say, but suddenly Josh was on her feet, screaming at Whim the way Peregrine had screamed at his father.

"Because he's ruined! His soul is ruined! He wouldn't move on and he wouldn't let go, and now he's nothing but the worst parts of himself, and he's going to make what's left of the universes far worse than Peregrine ever could!"

Whim cursed. He caught Josh before she could stumble back into the pool and handed her off to Will, who held her gently but firmly.

Whim sat down on a marble bench, and Deloise went to sit beside him. "So," she said calmly. "It looks like we need a new plan."

Whim laughed, then said to her, "You're amazing, Del, you know that?"

"I do," she said, but she gave him a smile Haley hadn't seen in a long time. "Let's start with what we know. Peregrine has destroyed the Veils—all of them—and merged the three universes. He has near-total control over everything now. And Ian is back from the dead and—not quite himself. Our original goal was to stop Peregrine and repair the Veils. Is that still possible?"

"No," Josh said.

"If you had the Omphalos . . ." Haley began, but the look of failure in Josh's eyes stopped him.

"What's an Omphalos?" Whim asked.

"It's an all-powerful egg-rock that Josh can use to control reality," Will told him.

Whim blinked. "Why don't I ever find stuff like that?"

"Anyone can use it," Josh mumbled. "There's nothing special about me."

"Where is this Omphalos?" Deloise asked.

Josh finally unburied her face from Will's shoulder. "It's in a place where the three universes overlap. It's called the Cradle."

"Can you get back there?" Whim asked.

"We reached it together," Haley told her. "Remember? We were there together when we saw . . ."

He couldn't finish. He'd meant, *When we saw what Ian's going to do,* but he couldn't say it. That would make it too real.

Josh nodded, but he knew she was afraid. "Ian will find the Omphalos before we do."

"How do you know?" Will asked.

"We saw it." Briefly, she explained what she and Haley had experienced a week before in the basement. "We saw the future. Haley and I were running toward the Omphalos, but Peregrine was running toward it, too, and so was Ian. And Ian got there first."

"Then what?" Deloise asked.

Josh met Haley's eyes, and he saw his own sadness reflected in her gaze.

"He's not Ian," Haley insisted. "He's . . . distorted."

"Then it isn't Peregrine we have to worry about," Josh said.

"But even if Ian is changed, or different, or whatever," Whim said, "he's not evil. He won't hurt people."

"You don't understand," Josh said. "He will destroy the evolution of souls—he's not who he used to be."

"He tried to steal my body," Haley said, and Whim blinked.

"He wants what everyone wants: control," Josh said. "And if he gets ahold of the Omphalos, he'll be able to control everything in existence. Good-bye, free will."

"Okay," Will said. "If the boundaries between the three universes have collapsed, has whatever boundary around the Cradle collapsed, too?"

"Not yet," Josh said. "But it won't be long. The Veil around the Cradle will be the last to fall."

Haley had a strange feeling then, that it was his job now to take the next step. He reached out for Josh's hands, surprised at how used to touching her he had grown, and he tried to stop shaking, to be strong for her.

"Remember what it felt like to hold the egg," he said. "Not the part where we saw Ian, the part before that."

Will kept his arms around Josh, encouraging her to lean back against him, and that was good. She was steadier when Will was touching her. Her hands were cold and small, but they were strong, too, strong enough that she could hang from a chin-up bar for fifteen minutes, and Haley wanted to remind her of that.

"We were looking at the map, remember? We could see all the souls' paths. Some were long, and some were short. Do you remember whose was whose?"

Josh's eyes had fallen shut, but her shoulders were sinking down as they relaxed. "Will's was long. And Del's was even longer. And yours"—here she opened her eyes again, and smiled unexpectedly—"yours was the longest."

Haley nodded. "And yours?"

"Mine was the shortest. Because I'm new."

"You're new. Maybe you aren't the True Dream Walker, I don't know. But you're here for a reason."

"Because Mom and Grandma—"

"No, Josh. Close your eyes. Quit telling yourself what to think. Just listen."

He used one fingertip to touch a spot just above and between her eyes—her third eye. He set the energy there to swirling. "Just listen."

The lines in her face softened; her jaw loosened. She let herself fall back against Will, and he held her weight; he was the rock he had always wanted to be for her. Her skin beneath Haley's fingertip warmed, and he prayed.

Haley had always believed in God. Not in a man with a beard or a paternal figure of judgement, not in a spirit that defied science or set down rules, but as something good. Something good and pure at the heart of the universe, something loving inherent to all life that connected all things. He had never doubted this belief.

He saw it in the auras around him, in the way Will stood behind Josh and carried her weight, the way Deloise put a hand on her sister's shoulder in silent support.

Haley had always considered himself lucky to be able to sense that source of love. So many people couldn't feel it. They were so caught up in the flotsam of their lives that they couldn't stop and listen, just feel. The older their souls were, the more times they had seen their lives rise up and then slip away, the easier it became for them to remember that the only thing that was eternal was this connection, but Josh was so young, so new . . . It was perhaps harder for her than for anyone else Haley had ever met.

Except Ian, now.

We remember and forget, remember and forget.

Josh needed to remember.

Will and Deloise had their eyes closed. Whim was pacing anxiously at the edge of the pool. Only Katia was watching him.

Haley winked at her, and Katia tilted her head. That momentary confusion was all the distraction Haley needed. He wrapped his free hand around the chef's knife in his pocket, pulled it free, and plunged it into Josh's chest.

Thirty-nine

Josh woke up with her hand on the egg.

I'm dead, she thought. *Haley killed me.*

She was confused about why until she realized where she was: back in the bright white light space, standing before the black basalt pillar with the egg on top and the water pouring down the sides.

Haley knew I needed to come back here, she thought. The peace and comfort that came with touching the egg surrounded her again, like the stone walls she had always imagined keeping her safe from the dreamers' fear.

I'm safe here.

The egg was warm beneath her palm. She picked it up, weighed it in her hand. Such a small thing, and yet so full of possibility.

What do I do now? she wondered, and she knew to wait for the answer.

You have to follow it.

The lifeline that appeared before her was Ian's. She felt an instant of panic, and her hand clenched around the egg, but what she saw was not the future, not the damaged, demented thing Ian had become. What she saw was the Ian she had known before, back in the basement, the night the cabin burned down and she'd believed he had died.

She was standing in the archway they had created, one hand holding Ian's in Feodor's dimension, the other holding tight to Winsor in the World. She was listening to Ian screaming, and all she could feel then was his hand and how tightly she was holding it, how she refused to let go, even when he was physically torn from her.

From above, she saw his soul then. As his body landed in Feodor's universe and his soul came back to the World with Josh, something happened to it. Something not right. A small change, a penknife slit in the fabric of his being, but it would grow, and grow, and grow. She had forced his soul off its path. That shouldn't have been possible, and it wouldn't have been, for anyone else. But Josh had no destiny, no path to follow, and so she was able to pull Ian off his path.

In all the universes, she was the only one who could really screw up.

I am special, she thought, and felt bitterly amused.

Josh saw that if she had let Ian go, his soul never would have chosen to haunt and possess Haley. It was, put bluntly, her fault.

But for once, Josh was incapable of feeling guilty. Guilt was a largely useless emotion, she realized, now that she was holding the egg and had perspective. Yes, she'd driven Ian off his soul's intended path. She had that power. But she could bring him back, couldn't she?

You can try, the egg told her.

That was the catch, she realized. Ian wanted control, Peregrine wanted control, even Will wanted control, but control was an illusion. It didn't exist, and what had misled them was the belief that it was attainable.

All we can do is try, she thought.

She saw again the future she had seen with Haley, back in the basement: that Ian's attempt to control everything would lead to the end of the cycle of reincarnation and the evolution of love. He would ruin the purpose of life and make them all spiritual slaves.

Somehow, in thinking of him, she brought him to where she was, and she could feel the desperate hunger within him, like a terrible wound in his gut, a pulsating pain in his heart. He saw the Omphalos and knew it for what it was, and Josh realized she had made a terrible mistake in bringing him here. She'd wanted to give him a choice, but he wasn't thinking clearly, all he could see was more power, he wasn't listening, he was leading instead of following, he was a ravenous wolf looking forward to eating eggs. And as the boundaries of the Cradle began to collapse, and as Josh and Ian were both sucked back into what was left of the universes, and as the Omphalos itself began to descend toward the palace at the heart of the breech, Josh saw Peregrine running toward them. Somehow he had been listening, and it was all power, all that power he had wanted; he was so frightened and so small and he just wanted to be safe, like every child, like every little boy, not realizing that it was his own mind that haunted him, his own mind that threatened him, not the World.

They were all running toward the Omphalos when Josh woke up.

Forty

Something sharp bit into Will's chest, right at the spot where Josh's back rested against him. Then he heard her gasp, and he opened his eyes and saw, over her shoulder, the wooden knife handle sticking out of her chest.

Katia shouted something unintelligible and threw herself onto Haley, the two of them skidding across the wet tiles. Josh suddenly fell limp, and Will caught her as she slid to the floor, fresh blood blossoming across the front of her already stained gray shirt.

This isn't happening, he thought.

"Josh!" he cried. "Josh, talk to me!"

Josh didn't say a word, just stared at him with her mouth open. Deloise and Whim were screaming at Haley, who had allowed Katia to pin him without a fight. He was trying to say something, but Katia had her forearm across his neck.

Josh lifted her hands, as if to touch the knife in her chest, but they just hovered uselessly in the air. "Lay her flat," Deloise was telling Will, and she helped him ease Josh onto the floor. The knife moved an inch out of her flesh, and Will realized that Haley had stabbed her straight through, and that the bite he'd felt had been the knife tip cutting his own chest.

"Don't remove the blade," Deloise said. "She'll bleed out."

She's already bleeding out, Will thought. He knew from Josh's many anatomy lessons that Haley had cut between her ribs and straight into her heart. It was a fatal wound.

Deloise was trying to apply pressure around the blade, but her efforts were useless. Will took one of Josh's confused, staggering hands and held it in both of his, caught between shock and panic. He desperately wanted her to say something; if this was the last time he was ever going to see her, he needed to hear her say something that he could hold onto. He wanted to know that, despite everything they'd been through, she still loved him, that she was dying without regretting being with him.

"Josh, Josh, say something," he begged.

Through her parted lips, Will could see that her mouth was full of blood. She made a choking sound, and the pool of blood got sucked down the back of her throat as she tried to draw a breath, and then she coughed and the blood exploded out of her—a hot, wet slap across Will's face. Josh shuddered, once, twice, and then went limp. Her head rolled to the side and more blood poured out of her mouth and onto the tiles, like a fountain that filled and emptied itself.

Deloise screamed. Will couldn't think; it had happened so *fast*, so utterly without warning. Katia punched Haley in the face, and Whim cried, "Is she dead? She's *dead*?"

Will's mind became strangely practical then. He wasn't surprised; his mind had retreated into denial before. *Without Josh, I don't think we have a chance of fixing this,* he thought, and he looked around the bathhouse that hadn't been there a few weeks before, at the people without souls who were watching the scene with confusion while continuing to bathe.

Finally, he looked at Haley, who was staring at Josh. His eyes were frightened, but there was also a strange excitement in them, as if he were hungry for the sight of her corpse.

"Why?" Will asked.

Haley glanced at him, surprised by the question. "She needed to go back."

Josh sat up and gasped.

Deloise screamed again. Whim screamed, too, and stepped backward into the pool. Even Will jumped back, although he kept hold of Josh's hand, which was suddenly vital, suddenly returning his tight squeeze.

Josh looked down at the knife in her chest. "Shit," she said, and pulled it out.

The wound didn't bleed. Josh dropped the knife onto the floor and coughed, blood spraying onto her palm. "That hurt," she said, and wiped her mouth on her sleeve.

"What the—what the—" Whim sputtered.

Haley was grinning from ear to ear. Katia, who was still sitting on Haley's chest, gaped at Josh.

"Are you okay?" Deloise asked her sister.

Josh nodded, coughed again. "Yeah. I'm—getting better."

She pulled up her shirt to reveal a two-inch horizontal gash beneath her left breast. Beyond the sliced flesh, though, the muscle appeared uninjured. Prodding the wound with a finger, she said, "It's going to hurt for a while, I think."

"What the hell is going on?" Whim shouted, pulling himself out of the pool.

Josh smiled then. "The three universes have merged. No one can die, because there's nowhere else to go afterward. We all just end up back here."

Whim bent and slapped Haley across the face. "You couldn't have just told us that?"

"No," Josh said. "He couldn't have."

Will touched the wound in her chest, quickly, like he was testing a hot iron. But he could see the edges closing together, the flesh beneath the skin knitting back up.

"It's like your pelvis, Del," Josh said. "You *did* break it when the bird dropped you. But whatever's happening with the merged universes, it's frozen us physically. That hole in your cheek is already gone, Whim."

Will hugged her. Too tightly—she coughed again, but he didn't care. Apparently there was no more danger in too tight. He just wanted to feel her against him, her physical, breathing form, the weight of her head on his shoulder.

I'm not ready to lose you, he thought.

"I know where the Cradle is," she said.

He pulled back to look her in the face, and the words that came out of his mouth were, "Do you think I care right now?"

Josh looked a little abashed.

"I'm all right," she assured him.

Will didn't know what to say, how to tell her that he needed more than that, he needed some guarantee that she was going to stay all right, needed to hear those last words she hadn't said, just in case . . .

"We have to get to the Omphalos before Ian does," she said. "Katia, let Haley up. He was just doing what he had to."

Reluctantly, Katia climbed off of Haley.

"And why couldn't he have just explained this?" Whim asked again.

"You wouldn't have let him risk killing me, and I needed to go back," Josh said. "Back to the Cradle, and that's where I go when I die."

She stood up, a little carefully, wincing but on steady legs.

"What did you see?" Haley asked her.

She held out a hand, and Will took it.

"I saw Ian. I'm the reason he's like this, the reason he can't let go. If I hadn't dragged his soul back to the World when we accidentally entered Feodor's universe, he wouldn't be confused. He wouldn't be so attached to his life."

"So what do we do?" Deloise asked, handing Josh a bottle of water from her pack.

"The boundaries around the Cradle are collapsing." Josh took a swig of water and used it to wash the blood out of her mouth. "We need to get to the Omphalos before Ian and Peregrine do. And we need to go *now*."

"I apologize for slapping you, buddy," Whim said, helping Haley up.

"S'okay," Haley said. "But don't do it again. Where should we go, Josh?"

"The palace," Josh said. "That's the very center of this tear, so that's where the Cradle will . . . empty itself."

Deloise hoisted her pack onto her shoulder. "I'm ready."

Josh looked at Will, whose heart was still pounding. "You all right?"

He shook his head. "I guess. If nobody can kill you, then I guess I'm okay."

"There are worse things than death," Josh warned, but she smiled at him.

They made their way to the door of the bathhouse. "Which way?" Deloise asked.

They had to stop a random citizen and ask. "Follow the street, turn left at the temple of Peregrine, and you can't miss it."

That we can't miss it, Will thought, *I don't doubt.*

They set out at a steady jog, which taxed Whim and Katia but felt good to Will. He wanted to be doing something. He wanted to be helping, even though he knew this was Josh's show.

Ultimately, it was all about her, wasn't it? This was her destiny—True Dream Walker or not.

He felt small then, and he wouldn't have minded being small in the grand scheme of things, except that he wasn't sure he was enough for her. Who was he except a homeless kid who'd showed up on her porch by accident because her sister ordered a pizza at the wrong moment? He wasn't magical, he wasn't powerful, he wasn't even a great dream walker. He just wanted to help her.

He remembered their first fight, in the high school lobby during the Valentine's Day dance. *I would do anything to help you,* he'd said to her, *if you'd just tell me what to do.*

Well, that he could do. He could listen to her, and do what she asked, and hold her up when she fell. He could be her safe place when the storms rolled in. And if he was only meant to be a footnote, then he'd be a footnote.

He was okay with that. He would be himself; hopefully that would be enough.

The entrance to the palace that they found was different than the one they'd used before, but Josh knocked the guard down with one sharp jab and ran past him. Inside, they sprinted down the frescoed hallways, the dozens of torches casting their light on the gems set into the walls, stopping only to ask directions to the throne courtyard.

"What are you—" a woman carrying a platter of small stuffed birds asked.

"No time!" Josh shouted at her. "The emperor must be warned!"

When they finally burst into the courtyard, Peregrine was already there, sitting in Snitch's body on his throne, wearing a crown of gold-dipped olive leaves. In the center of the courtyard, a beautiful young woman was dancing for him, weaving her arms sinuously above her head. She wore a toga of deep rose, and her blond hair tumbled to her hips.

Haley released a little cry and ran to embrace her. She smiled and held him close.

"Wait," Josh said. "Is she . . ."

"She's Dustine!" Haley said.

"She's mine!" Peregrine barked. "I destroyed Death, I got her back, and now she's mine!"

The smile on Dustine's face was so serene that Will doubted Peregrine owned her in any way.

"Grandma," Deloise said, and hugged Dustine.

"Get away from her!" Peregrine barked. "She's a slave! She's my concubine!"

"Del," Josh said, "do what he says."

Deloise reluctantly obeyed.

"What do you want?" Peregrine demanded. "This is my palace—get out!"

We need time, Will thought. *The Cradle hasn't opened yet.*

But Josh said this was where it would open, so they needed to stick around, and Will knew Peregrine was on the verge of teleporting them back to the arena, or to a dungeon, or to Tunisia.

This is something I can do, he thought. *I can help keep Peregrine calm.*

"We've come to apologize," he said, "and swear fealty to the emperor."

"What?" Whim asked, and Deloise stuck him with her elbow.

"This place you've created, Peregrineum, is astounding," Will said. "I can't even wrap my mind around its glory. Obviously, if you created this place, you *are* in fact, God, and we should bow down to you."

He took a few steps forward and got down on one knee, bowed his head. "Forgive me, my lord, for not seeing before that you are a living god. I beseech you—let me serve you. Let me be your instrument. Allow me to spend my days in service of your vision."

"Me, too," Deloise said. "This place is . . . so beautiful. I never knew such beauty existed. Please, make me your slave."

Will, still staring down at the flagstones, waited. He wished he could see Peregrine's face.

If he wants control, we'll give him control.

Finally, Peregrine laughed and said, "Now you see! Now the scales fall from your eyes and you see that I am the god of all things and all people! I am the alpha and the omega! I am legion! Bow, bow down before your god!"

Whim and Haley joined them, and finally Josh and Katia.

"Grovel, slaves!" Peregrine shouted, as he climbed down from his block of marble.

Will didn't actually know how to grovel. He did the best he could, lying face down on the flagstones and sort of wiggling, rubbing his face against the stones. Then he crawled to Peregrine and began to kiss the man's feet, which was less disgusting than he'd expected because the man was wearing shoes that Will was pretty sure were spun from pure gold.

"Oh, my lord," Will said, "I am overcome—"

"Call me *Father*," Peregrine said.

Will's stomach turned, but he managed to say, "Oh, Father, just kissing your shoes fills me with such . . . joy."

He nudged Whim, who chimed in about how he'd never heard the birds singing until today.

"And you!" Peregrine cried, kicking Josh in the side with his golden shoe. "Have you finally seen the blaze of my glory?"

"Oh—yeah," Josh said. "It's . . . really bright. Like, the brightest."

She's going to ruin this, Will thought.

"Like the sun," she added.

"And the moon combined," Deloise said, jumping in. "And all the stars—"

"What's this?" Peregrine asked, as Ian walked into the courtyard, wearing a twisted grin.

"Hey, ugly," he said. "Nice chair."

Josh's fake smile was gone, replaced with a fear that made Will anxious. He had barely known Ian when he was alive, but Will knew that there was something cruel in his eyes that hadn't been there before.

"Thought you could run off on me again, did you?" Ian asked Josh. As he spoke, Will felt the air shift above them, and a crack of light worked its way across the sky. "You're a false bitch, you know that?"

"Ian," Josh said weakly, shrinking into her shoulders, and for a moment, Will got a glimpse of what she must have been like back when she and Ian were dating. Her insecurity, her self-doubt—Ian knew how to exploit the weakest parts of her. "I never . . ."

"Yeah, yeah, yeah. You're even worse than this one."

He jacked a thumb toward Haley, who was suddenly trembling and pale.

The crack in the sky got wider, white light piercing the courtyard.

"Grovel!" Peregrine yelled at Ian.

"Fat chance," Ian told him. "In a couple of seconds here, you're going to be the one kissing my ass."

Peregrine launched himself at Ian, at the same instant that the crack in the sky turned into the burst of a white supernova, filling the courtyard with blinding light. Will threw an arm up against the light, and when he lowered it, the light was gone, and in the center of the courtyard sat a black basalt pillar with a white stone egg on top.

Ian was running toward it, and he didn't have far to run. Josh was running, too, springing into action the way she always did, but she was too late. Will could see she was too far and too late.

"Haley!" he shouted.

Then he saw another figure move, and he realized Katia was going for the Omphalos. She actually jumped over Will as she ran, and he was relieved that Katia was closer to the pillar than either Ian or Peregrine.

Haley slammed into Ian like a linebacker, their faces so similar and yet so different. Ian released an enraged scream, and he bit into Haley's neck, tearing out the flesh in a single terrible chomp.

Blood sprayed so far that Will felt it settle like a fine dust over his face. Horrified, Josh hesitated just a step, perhaps tempted to go to Haley, and that was all the time Katia needed to take the lead.

She snatched the Omphalos off its pillar.

Time stopped. Quite literally—for a moment, Will felt himself freeze just the way he had when Bash had found him in the Dream. His lungs stopped breathing, his heart stopped beating, every neurotransmitter in the brain stopped firing.

And then release.

Deloise tackled Peregrine. She didn't take him down, but he had to stop running to try to get her off his back. He scowled when he saw that Katia had the Omphalos.

Ian hit his unconscious brother in face, and Whim went to stop him.

Josh skidded to a stop a few feet from Katia. "Nice work," she said, panting.

Katia laughed at her.

All day, Will had sensed that something was off about Katia, but it wasn't until that moment that he realized what it was. Her quietness, her odd forms of speech, the strange expressions on her face—she wasn't Katia at all.

She gave a shake of her head, and her body changed as though she were shaking off a dress. From beneath emerged a pale man with white-blond hair wearing pleated slacks and a white button-down shirt. And he was holding the Omphalos.

"No," Josh whispered.

"*Tak,*" Feodor said, and he looked at her with what Will thought must be his true face, a hateful, jeering, ugly face.

Feodor laughed at them. He laughed when Peregrine shouted at him, and then Peregrine was standing in a glass cell, so sound-proof that not even the beating of his fists on the sides could be heard beyond it. Ian threw Whim off and tried to rush Feodor, and an instant later, he was stuck in a cell of his own.

A few feet away, Haley was bleeding to death just like Josh had, and it occurred to Will that he might not come back if Feodor didn't want him to.

"Feodor," Josh said. She was holding her hands up, plaintively, and she spoke softly.

"Be still," Feodor said. "I'm not your prisoner anymore."

"You were never my prisoner. We worked together, remember?"

"Of course. That's why you microchipped me like a dog. Because we're *colleagues.*"

"Feodor, please don't do this," Deloise said. "Remember all those times I took you to the grocery store? We were nice to each other. You were nice to me."

Feodor laughed. "Stupid American children. You worship freedom but what you really want is to tell everyone else how to live."

"I don't," Will said, getting up from the ground. He brushed his shirt off.

Feodor looked at him spitefully.

"I'm not going to pretend to be your friend, and I'm not going to bow down before you," Will said.

"I am not Peregrine," Feodor snapped. "I'm not so stupid and power-besotted that I would believe your pledges of loyalty."

"I'm not going to make one. I don't like you. I don't trust you. I don't like how much time you spend with my girlfriend, and I *hate* it when you talk to her in Polish."

Feodor laughed again. "Shall I applaud your honesty?"

"I don't expect you to applaud me at all. I actually don't need the illusion of your approval. I think you're a psycho, you think I'm an ant, and that's fine by me."

Feodor said nothing, but he tilted his head ever so slightly, and Will could tell he had confused the man.

"So, with the understanding that neither of us likes the other, let's just talk for a minute." Will leaned back against the block of marble that supported Peregrine's throne, deliberately moving away from Feodor.

"What do you think of this place?" Will asked. "This Peregrineum?"

Feodor again said nothing.

"I think it's fascinating. I mean, it tells you more about Peregrine than any psychological test I've ever heard of. A hundred hours of therapy wouldn't reveal this much about his mental state. Obviously, he's an egomaniac, and a phenomenal narcissist, but we knew that already, didn't we? The fact that his father was an abusive asshole is no surprise either. I could have guessed that much. I'm not even that surprised that he's incapable of controlling Jaco. Subconsciously, he believes he's unable to. But what I think is most interesting is the people who live here with him."

Every few seconds, Feodor glanced around to make sure no one was moving toward him. Will didn't worry about that. He didn't expect to distract Feodor, and the only person who moved was Dustine, who went to sit beside Haley's still form.

"I don't know if you overheard, but as we were walking into the city, Haley told me that most of the people here aren't real. He said they don't have any auras. They're the ones without anachronisms, the ones who aren't wearing watches or glasses or brightly colored boxers, like that guy." He pointed at one of the dozen guards assembled in each corner of the courtyard. This particular guard's orange boxers were visible through the white linen of his toga.

"See, that guy looks like a soldier, right? His chin is raised high—he's proud to serve the emperor. Aren't you, sir?"

The soldier said nothing until Feodor said, "You may speak."

"Serving Emperor Peregrine is the greatest honor of my life!" the guard shouted. "If I could move more than my lips, I would be tearing your throat out, traitor!"

"I think he means you," Will told Feodor.

"I gathered," Feodor said dryly. "Is there a point to this blathering?"

"See the guard next to him, the one who looks like a Roman soldier from head to toe? I saw another soldier pass him a note. Why don't you ask to read it?"

Feodor hesitated, then scowled and said, "Bring it here." The soldier delivered the note to him and then returned to his post.

"What's it say?" Will asked.

"'Tonight at dusk in the hallway outside the scriptorium.'"

Perfect, Will thought, and he let out a secret breath of relief.

Feodor frowned. "What is the meaning of this? Tell me the truth."

"Two other soldiers and I were planning to assassinate the emperor tonight at dusk," the soldier admitted.

"Why?" Whim said. "I thought you loved him."

"The emperor is a murderer and a tyrant. Thank you for imprisoning him."

Feodor ignored the compliment and looked back at Will, and for the first time, he appeared uncertain. "Why?" he asked simply.

Will shrugged. "You know Peregrine better than I do. Would you say he's a deeply paranoid personality who's always worrying that people are secretly plotting against him?" He let the question hang in the air for a moment, even though he didn't expect Feodor to answer. "I think he's incapable to creating a world where the things he believes are no longer true. I doubt he even consciously realizes what he's doing. But eventually, the people he created would have risen up and killed him, because that's what he expects."

Will dared to glance at Josh, who was trying not to smile. She couldn't help beaming at him, though.

Will looked back at Feodor before he broke into a smile. "And see, my concern here is that if you hang onto the Omphalos, whatever you create will turn out the same way. Not that you'll accidentally create a mutiny—no, I think it will probably be another world war. That's what you ended up doing the last time you had complete control over a universe, right? You could have created a nice little apartment for yourself, imagined Alice to come keep you company, spent your days reading and writing and doing your experiments. But instead, you recreated the Warsaw ghetto and lived there. For *sixty years*."

Feodor was staring at Will with an intensity that made them both tremble. Will forced himself to go on, knowing that he was playing with something far worse than fire.

"Haven't you ever wondered why you did that?" he asked. "Why you stayed there? Why you made it so hard for yourself? It's not your fault. It's something we all do, and we don't even realize we're doing it. We all think that if we only had control, everything would be fine, but there are parts of our minds we can't control. We create the same problems for ourselves over and over because we create what we expect. We walk into the same situations thinking that we'll be able to change the outcome, that this time will be different. You're probably telling yourself right now that you're not the same man you were when we met, that your mind is healthy, that you're in a different place now. I'm sure Peregrine thought the same thing when he created Peregrineum."

"You think you know me—" Feodor began, and Will interrupted.

"I *do* know you. I spent months researching you. But you don't have to trust me. Trust the one person who literally knows you as well as you know yourself."

He looked at Josh, and Feodor followed his gaze.

Her almost-smile was gone. Nor did she look hopeful, or smug, or even anxious. She looked like Will had just asked her to do something very, very hard.

"Sometimes," she said, "it's hard for me to tell your memories and mine apart. It's like there's a piece of me that's yours now, and I don't even realize it's not mine. I can't tell us apart. The worst part is, I know you too well to hate you. I know exactly why you became who you are and why you did what you did, and I can't hold any of it against you because I probably would have done the same thing in your position. When I look at it from your point of view, I don't know how we—I mean, you, could have done anything differently.

"And that's what worries me. With what you've gone through, I don't think you could have done it differently. And if you keep the Omphalos, that programming is going to drive you to do things the way you always have. I know you're thinking that I don't have any of your memories from your second life, and you're right. I don't. But I'm counting on that new, healthy part of you. Because the one thing I can say with complete certainty, knowing your old self so well, is that the Feodor who tortured me would never, ever, have handed over that egg. The old Feodor was incapable of trust. He didn't even trust Alice, and before you try to tell me I'm wrong, remember who you're talking to."

She ran a hand through her hair, a gesture so purely Josh that it made Will smile. "It's not the old Feodor I'm thinking about. It's the new one. It's the Feodor you are today. And I'm trusting you, right now, to know that you aren't the best person to make decisions for the entire universe."

"And you are?" Feodor asked, but his voice came out weaker than Will imagined he had intended.

Josh smiled. "Probably not. I'm a stupid American child, remember? I'm no one special, as it turns out. I'm not the True Dream Walker, I'm probably not even the False Dream Walker. I'm a very new, stupid soul. I'm awkward and I have no self-confidence and I'm thoughtless about other people. All I've got going for me is that, since I'm such a new soul, I've got a lot less karma than the rest of you. But if I were in your place, I wouldn't give the Omphalos to me." She inclined her head toward her sister. "I'd give it to Del."

Will could almost see the war being waged inside Feodor.

"I am as worthy as anyone to wield this," he said.

Josh walked toward him, slowly, but without trying to hide the motion. "Yeah, you are," she said. "It's just that this isn't about you. It's about all of us."

She stopped a few feet from him and waited. Feodor shook his head.

"I'm going to regret this tomorrow," Feodor warned Josh, who grinned.

"Add it to the list," she said. And then, somehow, they were both laughing.

Will had never seen Feodor laugh before.

"Come on," Josh said. "Prove you aren't who the history books say you are."

Deloise held out a nervous hand, and Feodor put the Omphalos in it.

"Happy?" he asked Josh, the bitterness back in his voice.

She hugged him.

And for once, Will wasn't jealous.

Forty-one

Deloise gave the Omphalos to Josh.

"No," Josh said, feeling like she'd somehow wandered back into the path of a bullet she'd just dodged. "You should be the one—"

"Josh," Deloise said. "I don't know what to do with this."

"And I do?"

Deloise smiled. "If you give it to me, I'll just fill the World with babies and rainbows. And I think we both know things aren't meant to be that simple."

"No," Josh said, but she was already using it, without even thinking, to heal Haley.

"I don't know what to do," she told Will desperately.

Haley sat up with a gasp and touched his healing throat. He

lifted one finger, asking Josh to wait until he could speak again, and once his vocal cords had grown back, he said, "Yes, you do."

"I can think of a couple of things," Whim said.

"No," Deloise told him sternly. "You can't."

The egg felt like an anvil in Josh's hands. Haley coughed as skin covered his throat again, and Will and Dustine helped him up.

"Please," Josh said, her heart beating too hard. "Please, help me. I don't know what to do."

Her friends gathered around her—except Feodor, who remained standing beside the black basalt pillar, looking cranky.

"Should I put everything back the way it was?" Josh asked. "Should I leave the universes merged? If—If I'm not the True Dream Walker, but the False one—"

"Josh," Will said, "forget about that."

"But the prophesies said—"

This time Feodor was the one who interrupted her. "I believe we are beyond the scope of prophesies," he said, his voice clipped.

"Haley?" Josh asked desperately.

He smiled at her, his beautiful, gentle, Haley smile. "Not everything can be predicted."

"So what do I do?" Josh asked.

"Do what you think is best," her sister told her.

The moment was growing more and more surreal. "Why are you guys letting me make this decision? I'm the worst possible person to do this. I have terrible judgment."

"No, you don't," Will said firmly. "It's no better or worse than any of ours."

The Omphalos weighed more and more, dragging her hands down.

"Will, please," she begged. "You're smarter than me. Can't you—"

"No," he said. "I can't."

He was using his grown-up voice again, his father's voice, the one he hardly ever used, and only when he really wanted her to hear him. But then his face softened and he touched her shoulder.

"Josh, I would love to tell you what to do now. Believe me, I've never wanted to tell somebody what to do more than I want to now. But . . . the thing is, it turns out I *do* trust you. I believe that, whatever else might have been written in a prophesy or a scroll or whatever, you are meant to make this decision. And I trust you to make it."

"But I'm just—I'm not anybody special."

He smiled then, and he leaned forward and kissed her. "You are to me."

Then he stepped back, away from her, leaving her with the egg. *He's abandoning me,* she thought. *He's leaving me.*

She wanted to feel angry, but he kept smiling at her, and his cornflower-blue eyes were as steady as they had ever been. *I love you,* he told her silently.

"I'm with Will," Deloise said, and she leaned forward and kissed Josh's cheek. "You can do it, sis."

Whim sighed. "Okay, look, I'm obviously going to side with Will and Del, I just want to *suggest* that *maybe* you take care of the puppy mill situation, okay?" He hugged Josh briefly, but as he was walking away couldn't help adding, "And maybe just think about—"

"*Whim,*" Deloise said.

"Yeah, yeah, I'm shutting up."

That left Haley and Feodor, and Feodor was unamused. "Haley," Josh said hopefully.

He put one of his hands over hers and thought, and she wondered what he saw when he touched her. "Maybe you aren't the True Dream Walker," he said. "Maybe I was wrong. I guess . . . I knew you were special, and maybe I assumed you were the True Dream Walker because that was the most special thing I could think of. But I wasn't wrong about the special thing. And I know you're the right person to have the egg. I *know* that."

"But can't you . . . at least give me a clue?"

Haley laughed. "But I don't know what you're supposed to do. I just know that you're the one who's supposed to do it."

He kissed her cheek then, and left her.

Feodor had a sour look on his face that made Josh want to apologize to him. But to her surprise, he said, "I will defer to the wisdom of your friends in this. Perhaps you and they are right and I'm not the one to make these decisions for the World." His shoulders slumped. "No, I suppose I know I'm not. What is the expression? *Old habits die hard?* So I will just tell you what you have told me so many times over the last few months."

He didn't kiss her, but leaned close to whisper in her ear. *"You have to follow it."*

And that was that. Haley and Whim went to the glass cube in which Ian was trapped, and Josh created holes in it so they could speak to him. Deloise went to talk to her grandmother. Feodor studied Peregrine. And Will just sat down at the foot of the throne and watched Josh with that kind, soft look in his eye, and waited.

They were all just going to wait while she figured out what to do.

Josh felt helpless and helplessly confused. Angry tears pricked her eyes. *I don't know what to do,* she thought. *I can't make decisions for everybody else. I don't want to be a dictator. I don't want to turn into Peregrine.*

A little voice in her head said, *So don't be a dictator.*

Finally, she went and sat down beside Will, the egg in her lap, and he held one of her hands and smiled at her.

"Trust yourself," he told her.

You have to follow it.

What if Feodor was right?

Josh closed her eyes. She leaned against Will, glad for his steadiness. And she shut up and listened.

The egg warmed beneath her hand, against the sides of her thighs and shins. She didn't go to the white, wall-less place, because it was all around her. Everything was all around her.

You have to follow it.

Strangely, what she imagined then were the stone walls that protected her from the dreamers' fear. She saw the little cork in them, and she pulled it out, but what got through wasn't smoke: it was light. Light that ate away at the stones and mortar, broke the walls down and surrounded her in warmth.

What should I do? she asked. *What's best? Not just for me, for everyone. What does everyone need?*

She saw herself then, lying on the cabin's basement floor in the Dream all those months ago, her skull broken, her elbow shattered, her blood slowly seeping onto the concrete floor. And Will beside her, using his last breath to tell her to believe in herself.

But I didn't believe in myself. I believed in the True Dream Walker, and I used that to bolster myself up. And that's why I've been so desperate all these months to believe, to be that. Because I thought I wasn't good enough.

But I got us here, didn't I?

Maybe I am *enough.*

The relief made her smile. She was young and stupid and rash and she'd done rotten things and hurt people and made bad choices. And she had done the best she could. And that was enough.

I am enough.

So what do I do?

Follow the wisdom.

Then somehow she was looking at the constellation of souls again. Every soul had a path—except hers.

She didn't have the right to control the rest of humanity. No one did. If she had tried, she would have failed, and she probably would have caused a Feodor- and/or Peregrine-sized disaster in the process. People weren't meant to control each other.

Control, after all, was an illusion.

Part of her felt disappointed. She would have liked to have ended war, eradicated disease, created an egalitarian utopia of peace. But doing so would have meant preventing everyone from evolving to that place in their own way. It would have meant pulling them off their souls' paths, the same way she had done with Ian. One way or another, it wouldn't have ended well.

No, people didn't need to be controlled. Their souls needed the choice to do better or worse. They needed guidance. *They* needed to follow it.

In all her searching for how to be the True Dream Walker, all

Josh had really learned was how to listen to that wisdom, that guidance, that flicker of goodness that connected everyone to everyone else. It was the insight Will had and the compassion Deloise showed and the connections Haley could see. Josh had followed it and it had brought her here, and she realized now that everyone could follow it, that everyone *wanted* to follow it, they were trying so hard.

Haley said we are evolving, that we've almost evolved as far as we can in this form. We're all trying to "follow it," but it's so hard. I know that better than anyone. But what if we could hear that inner guidance just a little easier?

She made it just a tiny bit easier for everyone to find their inner wisdom.

So little. A tenth of a tenth of a percent. That was all that was needed to start them all evolving again, each in their own way, each on their own path. Not by controlling each other, but by loving each other more readily.

That felt right.

And the three universes? she wondered. *Should I leave them merged?*

She knew it was an option, leaving them merged, letting everyone dream forever, but was afraid to do so, afraid of losing the dream walker part of herself, afraid of letting everyone go on living and dreaming forever.

She remembered what she'd told Feodor, and reminded herself, *This isn't about you.*

She looked back at the constellation of souls. Each path diverged now, one line showing what would happen if the universes remained one, the other showing what would happen if Josh separated them. The first path was longer and harder, the rewards slower to appear. The second path was easier, filled with more joy.

There's no benefit to suffering, Josh thought.

She separated the three universes again, put them in tidy order, neat parallels like the plates on a dessert tower. But she kept Peregrineum as it was, as a reminder of the chaos staging could cause, of what could happen when one person believed he had a right to make decisions for everyone. She kept it as a graveyard for the fantasy of control, even as she dismissed the soulless people with whom Peregrine had filled it.

That, too, felt right.

Eyes still closed, she went back to the night she had torn Ian's soul from his body. She remembered the feel of his hand in hers, the way she had squeezed until she felt the bones in his palm close together.

And she let go.

In her mind, she watched what would have happened if she hadn't pulled Ian off his path. Instead of becoming a perfect soldier for Feodor, he would have died while Feodor was experimenting on him. Most people did.

Josh knew what that death would have felt like, because she had almost died that way herself. Her heart broke at the thought of someone she loved dying so terribly. Luckily, she didn't have to change the actual past. She just had to correct the outcome.

If Ian had died, Snitch would have left Feodor's universe for the Dream, hunting alone for souls, but he would have been able to hurt fewer people without Ian's body to help him. He never would have gotten ahold of Josh's lighter, never would have left the Dream for the World, and would eventually have been caught by the Gendarmerie. After months of interrogation, the Gendarmerie would have put together enough pieces to realize he had come from Feodor's universe, and they would have stormed Warsaw, arrested Feodor, and released the souls he had collected.

Those souls whose bodies had died, Josh sent on to Death. That's where they were meant to be. Two still had living bodies waiting for them—one of them was Geoff Simbar—and Josh restored them. The souls Feodor would never have been able to collect without Ian's body—including Winsor's, Sam's, and Phil's—Josh put back into healed bodies or brought back from the dead—including Divya.

She didn't change anyone's memories, though. Her job was to repair what she had done, not to erase it.

That left Ian.

If she hadn't pulled his soul out of his body, he would have died in Feodor's universe. That meant Josh had to send him to Death, no matter how much she wanted to give him a second chance at this life.

Opening her eyes, she stood up and walked to his glass cell. He was shouting at Whim and Haley, telling them what useless friends they were and insulting their masculinity.

"Give it to me!" he began screaming at Josh as soon as he saw the Omphalos.

Josh pressed the Omphalos to her chest and it vanished inside her.

"You stupid, selfish bitch!"

Holding her breath, Josh stepped through the glass and into the cell. Ian tried to slap her and she caught his wrists. As he wrestled her, she said, "I'm sorry for what I did to you. I'm sorry I pulled you off your path."

He fought her, fought the knowledge, fought the change.

"I'm going to fix that now," she said.

She put her palms on either side of his face and healed him with a thought.

Ian calmed. He lifted his hands to cover hers, angry tears in his eyes.

"I wasn't ready to die," he said.

"I know. I'm sorry."

"I don't want to go. Please, J.D."

"Shh."

She kissed him then, because she loved him and she wanted to see him whole, and then she hugged him to make up for all the times she'd wished he was still with her.

"Please let me stay."

"Say good-bye to Haley."

Josh dismissed the glass cell, and Haley hugged his twin just as tightly as Josh had.

"I'm sorry I hurt you," Ian said. "I don't know what I was thinking."

"S'okay," Haley told him. "It's all forgiven."

"You can't talk her into letting me stay?"

Haley tried to smile and couldn't. "You're dead, Ian."

Ian ground his teeth, tears spilling out of his green-hazel eyes, and he said something Josh had never expected to hear.

"I'm scared."

"That's why she's here," Haley said, and he nodded toward Dustine.

Josh realized her grandmother was still with them. If Snitch and Gloves had never come out of the basement archway, they never would have frightened Dustine so badly that she had a heart attack. She should still be alive.

But she wasn't. *It was just a matter of time,* Josh realized. *She would have had the heart attack soon anyway.*

Dustine folded Josh in her arms. *I would have had it in response to hearing that Kerstel was pregnant,* she told Josh silently. *And that would have been a terrible way to announce Keri's appearance in the World.*

Probably, Josh agreed.

Dustine gave her a luminous smile and patted her on the cheek.

Deloise came over and hugged her, and then Haley, and finally Dustine held her hand out to Ian, and he forced himself to take it. "I love you guys," he said.

"We love you, too, Ian," Deloise said, and she hugged him. "Bye, Grandma."

"Miss you, buddy," Whim said.

Dustine took his hand, but it was Josh he looked at.

"I love you, J.D."

He'd never said it to her in front of anyone else. Not once. He'd been too insecure.

"I love you, too," Josh told him.

And he and Dustine vanished in a burst of golden light.

Whim hugged Haley, and the four of them who had loved Ian stood together and cried for a minute, and it hurt but it felt right. The old pain in Josh's chest, that Ian-wound that had haunted her for so many months, finally began to heal.

Feodor cleared his throat. "I suppose it is now my turn," he said stiffly. "I don't imagine I'll get quite such an escort."

Josh hugged him, too; she wanted to hug everyone. "No," she said, into his bony shoulder.

"No?" he asked, pulling away.

Josh squared her shoulders. "I'm giving you this life, Feodor, this second life. It's yours. You earned it, and . . . I trust you with it."

For a moment he trembled violently, and then he turned away. When he could speak, his voice was rough. "I will endeavor to be worthy of your trust."

Then he began to walk away.

"Wait," Deloise told him. "Wait. You can ride back with us."

He chuckled strangely, as if the idea were absurd, but he didn't go anywhere.

"Feodor," Josh said, and she quoted an old Polish proverb. *"Whom you befriend, you become."*

He smiled, still so stiff, still so formal. But then he said, "When the Lords of Death sent me back, they sent me back sane. You might afford Peregrine the same opportunity."

Josh looked at Peregrine, still raging in his glass cell. She had put him back in his own body when she restored Geoff to his. Now she regrew Peregrine's lost hand, and with a touch as soft as a kiss, she healed his mind—soothed his brain, reordered his neurotransmitters, cut the loops of obsession, and gentled the waves of hatred.

"What the hell are you doing to me?" he demanded.

"I'm giving you a second chance," Josh told him, and she dissolved the cell around him.

He glared at her. "I hate you," he said, but his voice lacked conviction. Looking confused, he wandered into the palace.

Finally, she turned to Will.

He was as misty-eyed as the rest of them, and at first Josh thought it must have been seeing Dustine as an angel that brought about his tears, but he opened his arms, and when she fell into them, he said, "You are so beautiful right now. I love you."

"I love you, too," she told him. "And Will—"

She swept her hand in a circle over her head, and the vision she had seen of the dance of souls appeared in the air before them. Deloise cried out in wonder, and Haley smiled.

"This is your soul," Josh said, pointing to a long, silver line. "And this is mine." She showed him her tiny line. "And see this little explosion?"

The moment their souls' paths crossed was marked by a twinkle of green energy, like a distant sparkler, a tiny explosion of goodness.

"I see it," Will said, grinning.

"That's where you became my apprentice," Josh said, and she kissed him.

 Epilogue

Haley McKarr married the newly elected prime minister of the dream walkers in a small sunset ceremony on the beach. Whim played the guitar—badly—and Deloise sang— beautifully. Katia threw flower petals and took photographs, and Winsor read a poem. Afterward, the happy couple and their families roasted hot dogs and drank Kerstel's sangria around a bonfire. Laurentius played alternately with his youngest daughter, Keri, and his middle daughter's dog, Poppy. Davita wore Mirren's family crest on a chain around her neck—and after twenty years of hiding it beneath her blouse, she wore it in full view. Haley's mother bonded with Mirren's aunt. Feodor rolled his eyes a lot, but he and Young Ben knocked back most of a bottle of fine vodka Feodor had brought.

Josh sat on the sand with Will's arm around her shoulders and felt happy.

When the stars came out, and the adults had all gone to bed in the newly rebuilt cabin, and the fire was burning the last of the logs they'd brought, and Haley and Mirren were still dancing but the music had stopped, and Sam had started hinting that it was time for bed, Josh pulled something out of a bag she'd brought.

"What's that?" Whim asked.

Josh held it up. "It's my scroll."

She tossed it in the fire, causing Deloise to gasp. But Will just smiled and kissed her cheek.

"To who we are," he said, and lifted his glass high.

They all drank.

Acknowledgments

First and foremost, to my agent, Rachel Orr, thank you for taking a chance on me, for holding my hand when I got anxious, and for riding the train to Queens to eat Romanian food with me. You're the absolute best.

To Terra Layton, who saw the promise in this series, and Sara Goodman and Alicia Adkins-Clancy, who took the reins and saw me through to the end, thank you for all of your hard work on these stories.

To my Polish translator, Maciej St. Ziêba, for your endlessly generous assistance with these novels, *serdecznie dziękuję*. All remaining errors are mine.

To my writing teachers, Joyce McDonald, Susan Campbell Bartoletti, Sena Jeter Naslund, Karen Mann, and all the faculty and students at Spalding University's MFA in writing program, thank you for making me a better writer, a better reader, and a better person.

To the teachers of the Young Writers Workshop, especially Pat Allison, Rae Cobb, and Liz Palmer, thank you for supporting my writing, each in your own way. To the amazing kids who turn out every year, thank you for the endless inspiration, the hilarity, and for making me feel young. Healer Baby lives!

To my writer friends, Hannah Strom-Martin, Sara Kasari, Kelly Creagh, Eileen Peterson, and Lillian Price, thank you for the laughs and the line edits. An especially huge thank-you to my editing partner, Megan Clayton, who spent more than a hundred hours with me at Panera Bread working on these three books. The next orange scone is on me.

To Meredith Young-Sowers, thank you for believing in me and teaching me to believe in myself. Your lessons are all over this story—I hope you don't mind.

To my parents, who helped carry this dream for so long, thank you for all your love and support, for giving me a childhood where my imagination could run wild, and for reading to me day and night.

To Gosha, thank you for being my rock. Thank you for your line edits, long plotting sessions, reassurance and validation, and for saying what every writer longs to hear from her partner: "Go write."

And to Sara Forward, my one and only sister, thank you for being my most devoted reader, my most honest critic, and the fan I still aim to please. If I hadn't had you to write for, we might never have gotten here.